HERITAGE LOST

S.M. WRIGHT

ISBN: 9781734155419 (E-book)

ISBN: 9781734155402 (Paperback)

This is a work of fiction. Names, characters, businesses, places, events, and incidents are either the products of the author's imagination or used in a fictitious manner. Any resemblance to actual persons, living or dead, or actual events is purely coincidental.

Cover illustration and design by Maria Freed, aka MissChibiArtist.

Interior formatting by S.M. Wright

Editing by Rachelle M. N. Shaw.

S.M. Wright/Far-Flung Press
smwright.wordpress.com

For my Mom,
Not a day goes by that I don't think of you
and miss you.

ACKNOWLEDGEMENTS

A lot of work goes into the creation of a book. I cannot thank my alpha and beta readers enough. Without them, *Heritage Lost* would not be what it is. Thank you, Amanda, Kylie and Rachelle, for going through it, warts and all, reassuring me it was a story worth pursuing. Thank you, Aubrey, Ann, Beth, Brian, Lauren D., and Lauren W., for stepping in as beta readers—your comments were invaluable and helped shape the story in ways I wouldn't have thought of before.

Amanda also stepped in as a final proofreader, catching silly little goofs. I swear sometimes my fingers don't know how to operate.

I'd also like to thank my cover artist and cover designer, Maria Freed, aka MissChibiArtist. She has done a marvelous job bringing two of my characters to life. She was also incredibly easy to work with.

I must also recognize my cat, Marinus, for all the little typos he's added throughout the process by lounging across my keyboard. What do they say about adversity? Something like *Ahfhjafjagargi zzkakkgaarikragrg* in cat.

Last but certainly not least, I must express my gratitude to my editor and friend, Rachelle M.N. Shaw, who makes sure everything is in order. She also provides copious amounts of support and pushes to carry on. I would be lost without her support! And, yes, she earned that exclamation mark.

TABLE OF CONTENTS

Without witnesses—Rein elsewhere inspecting *The Maelstrom* and Mina in the cockpit—Katya ground her fist into the metal until tingles shot up her arm. Her paranoia-fueled vigil throughout the ship had held merit after all. Gritting her teeth, she dropped her hand to her side.

"Of course it'd wait until we left the station."

She ran a finger between her own Res Publica de Magistratus uniform collar and her neck. Its Muma wool scratched her unprotected skin, and the sweat created by the thick dress uniform only made it worse.

Activating the small communications device nestled in her ear, she said, "Rein, meet me in the engine room."

A faint crackle followed before she received a gruff, "On my way."

With her hands folded behind her back, she resumed her patrol through the tight, narrow corridors—a claustrophobic nightmare—to the bowels of *The Maelstrom* and its engine room. Her footfalls echoed until the clacking and hums of the ship's mechanical elements smothered them.

At the engine room door, she keyed her code into a nearby panel, punching each pockmarked number harder than necessary. Silent relics. That's what it and its clones dispersed throughout the ship were. Holdovers from a time when such ships carried worthwhile cargo: currency, commodities, medicines, or materiel to whatever conflict called for it. The security had remained intact, out of a combination of laziness and austerity. Only Plasovern would target such a ship nowadays, and only if the terrorist organization wanted to send a message. Yet another reason to double-check their radiation levels.

The clattering increased the moment the double-blast door opened, disappearing into the wall. She wasted no time hopping between the consoles and getting a read on the systems, making minor adjustments.

CHAPTER ONE

Clack, clack-clat, clanck. A mechanical component of *The Maelstrom* heaved and protested, sending off-kilter vibrations through the corridor's metal wall to Katya's hand. No sweet or sulphuric aroma permeated the recirculated air. Promising, but some deaths were silent, odorless affairs — a morbid tidbit dropped by academy instructors. Vibrations always required care, especially while hurtling through space.

She balled her hand against the wall. It never failed. Troop transports frequently conjured up problems in the small Boita D-Class freighter — often helped by stray hands. Being thirty years in service, though, perhaps the old gal had earned the right to protest, if not all-out revolt. At least whatever plagued it this time wasn't emitting enough radiation to paint a target on their backs for opportunists, or worse.

Her brow knotted. The one lieutenant's smug face with its punchable, loose smile—the tyro fresh from some second-string academy—sprang to mind. He'd turned around as soon as he'd disembarked, that smirk. He'd probably burrowed some dumbass piece of code, the type an academy student would find clever, into the system. Small, so as not to be too dangerous, but enough to gunk up the Boita's mechanical works. Katya had initiated the diagnostic tool by the time the door reopened.

"You didn't touch anything, did you?" Rein asked, his voice grating.

"Last I checked, *Lieutenant*"—Katya squared herself as he approached—"she was still my ship."

"Sir." Rein hunched over a secondary console, setting to work. No salute, nothing else. They'd never stood on protocol, not since coming to the Fringe; however, it had bred . . . problems.

The lights changed with his touches. He shifted his weight when she moved in for a better view, blocking the screen.

A lopsided smile spread across her face when Rein reversed one of her adjustments. He'd never last on a larger ship, a more important one in the Mezzo, let alone in the hub of Magistrate space. Reznic had left its mark on him: a chip on his shoulder, paranoia, and a resistance to authority—at least her authority, even after five years. She often wondered why he'd volunteered to leave the planet, his homeworld, to serve under her. Likely, the allure of full Magistrate citizenship. Complete ten years of service, gain a tier; prove exceptional, gain the closest thing to being born on a core Magistrate world.

"I knew they were down here," Rein grumbled before changing to Reznic curses, something about Magistrate recruits and wishing their dicks—now that was cruel.

"Tyros," she muttered. "I'd wager on their lieutenant having been the mastermind."

He grunted.

Katya slid in next to him, noting the way his muscles tightened. Beyond that, he ignored her. His hands, however, scrambled to conceal the displays, even as she tracked each command. Rein's dingy brown hair clung to his face, leaving her to speculate how he could even see to work—not that she could talk. Her own golden-brown bangs hung low, always in her eyes, trapped in a tradition she had no memory or understanding of. Her father had always been like a lepidopterist, pinning her brothers and sisters to all their respective cultures and planets with fashion.

"Lieutenant," she said, "do you suggest we find a station?"

"Let me look at it. We may not have to do anything. It might be a loose bolt . . . maybe a line."

"Let the diagnostic scan finish. I'd place money on it being in the codes. Or the old gal's showing her age." Katya gestured to *The Maelstrom*'s patched innards with a sweep of her hand and then snorted. "Yet here we are still on Fringe runs. She should be making trips in the same sector, if not retired and scrapped."

"Scrapped? Most captains would rather be tortured than say that about their vessels, especially their first." A gleam of humor, so infrequent, flitted in his eyes before it vanished, though his gaze lingered on her.

"Why?" Her voice remained light and brisk. "Scrap's remade. I can't see anything wrong with that. Who knows, in her next life, she might be a C-Class destroyer, and I could be her captain again. It'd be a step up, that's for sure."

His jaw tightened, but he held his tongue.

She bristled at the unspoken: She'd be the first woman to ever command a C-Class destroyer.

Straightening the gold name tag on her uniform, she lifted her chin. "No" had never thwarted her before. Her primary and intermediary teachers had spoken of the Respecta Academy like a forbidden holy place. Yet she'd nabbed an opening through high standards, pure stubbornness, and the surname Cassius. And there, she supposed, lay the crux of the strife between her and Rein—a citizenship handed to her, through luck and the one man who'd welcomed her into his home.

A loud hiss emitted, followed by red lights flashing across the panels. A few feet away from them, the FTL released steam to cool itself. A string of Reznic vulgarities erupted from Rein, and he slammed his fists against the console, as if that'd stop the sequence. During his tirade, he kicked its metal frame, which only increased the level of insults.

"R-56 is in the next sector," Katya said. She placed distance between them while he bent over and rubbed his foot, his expletives now under his breath. "We should be able to reach it with the solar sails. I'll have Mina set the course."

As she closed the door, another string of curses flowed behind her. Always so quick to anger, only requiring a small spark to explode. She dusted off her uniform and trekked back to the ladder that connected to the ship's main floor. After surmounting that one, she climbed the next set, which led to the crew quarters and cockpit. She faltered in front of the hatch to her rooms, tempted to leave behind the uncompromising, overly starched dress uniform. With just Rein and her—the only magistrate officers onboard—there was no reason to wear it now.

Bowing her head and turning from the hatch, Katya thrust her hands into the outer jacket's pockets and strode down the narrow catwalk. Duty before comfort. It'd been drilled into her head enough.

Katya punched in her clearance code at the cockpit's security panel, nothing more on her mind than to check the radiation levels. The door swished open with the last number.

Mina, who sat in the pilot's chair, bobbed her head, her cropped hair—dyed red this time—sticking out at every odd angle. Katya envied its shortness, or would have if she didn't know the purpose behind it: to keep out Reznic's filth, plus its fleas and lice. The planet had definitely deserved its moniker, the Slums of the Magistrate. In fact, it had a special stench to it that she would detect even a year removed from Reznic.

But from a young age, the teenager had not only survived but thrived in the planet's decay. A smile tugged at her lips. While she admired the hair, she didn't covet Mina's neon pink top, which made her eyes want to bleed.

"Minding things, are we?"

Mina stiffened in the pilot's chair, and Katya barely caught the wires as the teen jerked her retro earbuds out and swung around, her feet dropping from the front console.

Before she could speak, Katya did. "Get the solar sails out." She folded her arms in front of her, hoping to convey seriousness despite the corners of her lips quivering. "The FTL's getting a rest until we get to R-56. Go easy on the old gal; she's limping as it is."

"As always!" A wicked, toothy smile spread across the teen's face, somewhat paler than its normally rich copper complexion—a side effect of ship life, with Katya probably resembling a spectral spirit—as she dislodged the lever to the sails. "I may have forgotten to check them on R-20, so . . ."

"If they don't work, we'll call for a tow."

A small portion of the viewscreen in front of them displayed the stars outside; the rest relayed data about the ship and external conditions. Radiation levels remained within normal ranges.

"What if R-56 doesn't have the parts we need?" Mina leaned forward, resting her elbows against the console; the light from the viewscreen reflected in her brown eyes.

Katya rested in the chair secured near the secondary consoles. "You tell me."

Mina shifted her dialect to what she undoubtedly deemed proper Magistrate. "Indubitably, we would set off posthaste to the subsequent way-station, where we'd presumptively find ourselves in another peccadillo."

"That word doesn't mean wha—"

Mina didn't stop, though her manner of speech shifted to its normal Reznic dialect. "It'll take us three times as long using solar sails. Meaning . . . it'd be more practical to wait at the station and contact Magistrate distributors." She ran her hands down her face, holding them on her checks. "We'll be stuck on a backwater cesspit for weeks."

Folding her hands in her lap, Katya snorted. "That's the life of a captain. Still want to—"

Blip! A band of red streamed across the viewscreen with a basic Magistrate warning.

"Mina, change course!"

"Eh—"

Katya swung around to the navigation console next to her, a second dot appearing on its grid-like map.

"Change direction to two o'clock!" she barked.

A sour taste filled her mouth. The dot's purple color meant the ship it represented belonged in Medzeci Empire space. The displayed information suggested a smaller vessel, probably Plasovern. Its ships used Medzeci signatures unless they'd misappropriated a Magistrate chip.

She clicked on her com. "Rein, cut the FTL. There's company in our front yard."

Over the intercom, he said, "If we cut it completely, we won't get it up fast enough to break away."

"With luck, they won't even see us." It was the only option, being in what amounted to a floating shoebox with pathetic armaments. Hardly a good one, but the lesser of several evils. "We can't afford to stress the FTL, and we can't fight them. That's an order, Lieutenant."

The viewscreen's data stream yielded the exact moment the FTL operations ceased. The unidentified ship, meanwhile, remained stationary, giving off a blip of radiation from its own FTL drive. The radiation emitted by their solar sails shouldn't even catch the other ship's notice.

"Keep it steady, Mina." She patted the teen's shoulder, eliciting a jolt. Mina's joints stiffened as she worked the controls. Her complexion had turned almost milky. "They'll assume we're just a natural occurrence as long as you keep it steady. We'll cut back toward the station and report the sighting to the proper officials once we're clear."

"Is it normal for the Medzeci to be in Magistrate space?"

"We're on the edge," Katya said, tone level. "More often it's Plasovern . . . Medzeci hasn't stepped in since the Fringe Campaigns. Not that they've had to. They've funded Plasovern well. But that's neither here nor there." The purple dot stayed put. "You're doing wel—"

"This is insane!" Rein barged into the cockpit. "We might as well paint a target on the hull." The muscles along his square jaw twitched.

"And running wouldn't be a shot into the brown?" Katya's lips formed a thin line after she'd thrown out that old gem learned on the firing range. The temptation to order him back to the engine room gnawed at her tongue. If things went sour . . .

He brushed up against her to get next to the console. "Plasovern, aye?" His frame shook against hers. "Idiots, the lot of them. And they're brazen enough to sit in Magistrate territory as if it were a day at the park."

"Even idiots can wreak havoc," Katya said. "A single cell took out an A-Class frigate while it was station-bound. The explosion crippled a quarter of the station, and there was barely anything left of the frigate."

"Can we not talk about stuff like that?" Mina whispered. "They're still stationary, right?"

"Haven't budged." Katya cleared her throat. "You're doing fine. Just keep us steady. Focus on what I've taught you."

"Can't you take the helm?" Rein pointed to the seat Mina occupied.

The girl's fingers shook over the controls, slight tremors passing through her arms. She sat the straightest Katya had ever seen her sit. Kindness would be to remove her from the situation. Katya tugged at her collar. Kindness could kill, as one of her instructors had fondly said. Maybe not now, but at some potential juncture in the future. So she remained rooted. Mina needed to meet this. No matter where she went, she would meet inescapable hardships.

"Keep us steady," Katya intoned again. "Rein, back to your post. If things get choppy, we'll need you down there. Mina's doing fine."

"Our lives—"

"Then you know how important the FTL drive is. Right, Lieutenant?"

"On it . . . Captain." Rein plodded out of the cockpit, his shoulders lowered.

"I can't do this," Mina sputtered as soon as the door closed. Tears collected in her eyelashes.

It brought a tightness to Katya's chest. She remembered all too well that little girl who had snuck onto a military base—so standoffish while peddling a bubbly exterior. She'd been terrified of the base yet clung to it, the one point that despite its rough, often crude, soldiers just happened to be safer than any other location on Reznic. The girl she'd promised to make a pilot.

Steeling herself, Katya said, "Then you can't be a pilot. What a shame . . . I had such high hopes when I pulled you off Reznic."

Mina remained silent; however, the tremor lessened.

"No matter what ship you pilot, Mina, it will have a Magistrate registration, marking you as a target." She tapped a finger against the sensor console. "Into the fire, my instructor would say. Our situation could be worse."

Mina pursed her lips and stared ahead as if expecting the enemy ship to materialize in front of them. Beads of sweat lined her brow, and they still had a ways to go. Katya cut the communications system. While often ill-equipped, there were no guarantees that this Plasovern vessel wouldn't have instruments capable of picking up frequencies from Magistrate communications consoles.

They crept on. The enemy vessel, meanwhile, remained an immobile fixture on the screen. Were they waiting for something?

Flipping communications back on, she rotated between frequencies.

Mina hissed a question, but it went ignored.

What were they after? A freighter? Cargo, maybe? Most frequencies were silent. This far out, not many ships would be sending out unencrypted calls; conversely, this far into Magistrate space, the Plasovern crew would likely be following strict silence. Frequency followed frequency.

"What are you doing?" Mina asked in a strident whisper, her attention wavering from her navigation console.

"Pay attention—"

A black command bar flashed across the communications console's screen. At its center, a white box waited for a passcode.

"Feeling naughty?" Valens's conspiratorial, rakish tone cut through the ether. She recalled the tattered paper being slid toward her, facedown. His smirk, the way his blue eyes gleamed. *"Type this in sometime . . . you'd be surprised where it gets you. Pays to have friends in the upper echelons, aye, Cassius?"*

The passcode might not be live anymore, much like its handl—she couldn't finish the thought; instead, she typed nine numbers and three letters into the passcode box.

PING! It engulfed the cockpit. Mina jerked at the sound, her face becoming more ashen. 969.021. Why hadn't she minded the frequency number? If Magistrate technicians ever found it on their communications system's records . . . Restricted was restricted, and only the most foolhardy would eavesdrop on private frequencies allotted to the Magistrate's elite military forces. More mechanical clicks followed, eerily echoing, as a code was ticked out. Long, short, shifts in tone —

"What's that?" Mina asked.

She shook her head, tuning out everything else. The code proved unrecognizable; it definitely wasn't taught at the academy. Then it stopped. A deep animalistic scream shattered the silence. Her hands collided with her ears to preserve her eardrums. It, whatever the creature was, shifted octaves, going higher, then lower, gruffer. A pause. The mechanical beeps and clicks returned, followed by a shrill bray. Katya flinched. It reverberated against the metal walls of the cockpit, chilling her. The beast stopped. The beeps resumed and lasted several minutes before the frequency went dormant.

"Can they trace us?"

Possibly. Class-A warships, run by Elites, had the tech to do so if they had reason to guard the transmission; first, they'd trace the passcode back to a dead man. That'd only leave them scratching their heads for a short time before pursuing it the rest of the way, to *The Maelstrom*.

The beeps picked up. The creature then rumbled a response. Silence. Katya shut off the communications console. *Blip.* The purple dot expanded, and then the spot it had inhabited on the sensor screen went blank.

She blinked. "They dumped waste and jumped."

"What's going on?" Mina squawked.

Nothing appeared on the sensor. So they'd jumped for good. Was a Magistrate ship on its way? Katya sank back into her chair. Her father might have recognized the clicks and squeals; he excelled with languages and would have been tickled pink to connect it to a species, a culture. She'd never had that gift, barely acquiring the two languages required at the academy.

"That was an Elite frequency. They're nearby." Mina opened her mouth, but Katya refused to be interrupted. "Keep going in the direction we were headed. We'll correct as needed."

"What if they traced us?"

Katya stretched their sensors' range but pulled in no other vessels. "We'll deal with that if we need to."

"They sounded like monsters."

Elites often were, but the girl didn't need that perception reinforced.

An orange-colored message darted across the viewscreen. "Mina, slow down."

The teen's hands flattened on the panel. "Now what?!"

"A Magistrate detour probe." The corner of her lips dipped further when accessing the probe's data via the sensor console brought nothing. "The path isn't clearly marked." The absence of additional probes was strange as well.

Reaching for a slate she had left at the workbench, Katya inserted the route number to access previous Magistrate work. The last had been more than a month ago: border security measures. No other ships were listed in the area, presently or in the near past. She left her seat and approached Mina and the main navigation console. Pressing two of her fingers against its smooth surface, she magnified the area. No alternative lanes stood out to her. Perhaps it'd been forgotten by the work detail.

"Go around," Katya said. "I'll monitor."

Mina did as instructed. As they went, Katya lost all sense of time, remaining focused on the navigation system and sensors, monitoring for space debris or any other signs of trouble. Tingles passed under the skin of her arms and legs, her muscles tight coils waiting to spring into action.

A faint reading pulsated on the screen. A blue aura barely stood out against the black background. It held no definite shape or text that marked its make or status, though the blue suggested it was Magistrate. In the pit of her stomach, a knot formed. She'd seen this type of aura before and associated it with dying ships. Katya pumped her fisted hands. It was blue, the only blue on the screen beside her own ship's signature. She clenched her eyelids shut. Duty beckoned.

"I'll take over."

Mina glanced over at her, uncomprehending until she noticed what loomed on the fringe of the navigation console's screen. "What's that?"

Katya slid into the pilot seat as Mina assumed her role at the other console.

"I'm not sure. But we're checking it out." And while Katya embraced hands-on learning, when it came to unknowns, she preferred control.

Mina gaped at her. "Why?"

"It's Magistrate, and it's having trouble. Rein and I wear the uniform. If we can help them before life support goes, we have to." Katya increased their speed, the Boita shuddering a complaint through the console's metal. "Whatever it is, it's not conveying credentials, which suggests it's on minimum power—that's when you stop with pleasantries and drop everything into life support and communications."

"Couldn't we com them?"

"Search the frequencies for distress calls, but don't break our silence. There's no telling where that Plasovern ship went. The Elites could be on their way, or they could be hunting that ship. All the same, we'll check things out and provide what aid we can."

Redirecting their course, Katya became absorbed with the chatter of the communications console. Absently, she ran her fingers along the lever controlling the solar sails. Ten minutes to return them, her mind chanted. A lot could happen in that time span. Plasovern loved setting traps, and they could be entering one right now.

As minutes rolled by, it would only be a matter of time before Rein got antsy and returned to the cockpit to voice his opposition.

"It's coming up in twenty minutes," Mina said.

Those minutes dragged. Katya counted in her head, her hand tightening on the solar sails' lever. She decreased *The Maelstrom*'s speed. Then one notch down, followed by two more until the sails collapsed. Ahead on the front viewscreen, a silhouette loomed, only distinguishable from space and the nebula behind it—the Nag's Head, according to the charts—by a faint metallic gleam. She retracted the sails into their metal compartments and activated the reverse thrusters, which brought them to a crawl.

Her breaths grew shallower.

An A-Class warship stretched a good distance before them, dwarfing their vessel. Flickers of electric sparks covered its entire starboard side. Katya swallowed against her tightening throat. Who was even capable of this? She lifted *The Maelstrom*'s nose and used the forward thrusters until they ran alongside the battered warship, its ravaged surface filling the viewscreen. With a few bursts of the reverse thrusters, Katya hovered over its serial number, visible though scarred.

"Mina, run the number in my slate. It'll give us the name and what we're dealing with, plus their frequency." She already knew it was an Elite ship—they didn't hand out A-Class warships to just anyone.

She piloted their vessel farther down its length. A large chunk had been blown off the upper levels. A flickering energy shield prevented catastrophe for those inside; however, Katya suspected some radiation had leaked in despite safety measures.

She flinched when the hatch behind her opened, and Rein entered.

His jaw went slack, creating a gap between his lips. "Wh-what is that?!"

Katya edged away from the crippled warship. "Mina?"

"Search is still running."

She reactivated the thrusters. The landing dock, at least one of them, wouldn't be far. Katya searched the exterior for an undamaged docking cluster.

Rein's hand landed on her shoulder. "What are you doing?"

"Finding a docking cluster."

His grip compressed, making Katya cringe and shift in her seat.

"It's our duty, Rein. We help our own."

"That's an Elite ship!"

"Their signal isn't working." She wrenched her shoulder away from him. "We're required to provide aid. The next time we stop for maintenance, our navigation system will show that we were here and did nothing."

Katya tempered their speed. Arriving at her mark, she popped the clamp and rooted them in place.

"We'll radio the location. No one would blame us for not entering an Elite ship. We can't do anything for them. Our ship is too small, and we only have enough supplies for ourselves. They'll overwhelm us, take what they want, and we can't stop them."

"G-guys." Mina cleared her throat, attempting to hide the quiver in her voice. "It's Oneiroi. The ship's called *Aletheia*. According to this, it's supposed to be en route to Meracus Domus on a delivery order. No cargo listed."

Could the cargo have been explosive?

Katya dismissed the notion. The damage had been caused from the outside. Standing, she said, "I'm surprised that much is listed. Mina, try to get them on the communications system."

Her charge followed her instruction but received no response beyond static. Katya ran her hands against her uniform front, hitting every gold button. More static. Her chest tightened. "Mina, keep a close eye on the sensors. If anything shows up, alert us immediately. Rein and I will make contact."

"Oh, oh no—we're not going on that ship!" he shouted as he chased her through the doorway like a Mramorian badger. Thankfully, he was more bark than a real one.

Beating a steady path along the catwalk before sliding down the ladder, Katya stayed in front of him, though he remained at her heels. His mouth never paused in its ravings. Then he caught her, forcing her to stop or lose all balance when he clasped her upper arm.

She spun on him, his nails digging into flesh, the top of his hand brushing against her breast.

"Don't ever," she snapped, pushing his hands from her. "Touch me. Again. Or I will make you bleed."

He blinked but relented, dropping his hands to his sides. This allowed Katya the opportunity to restore an appropriate distance between them. She straightened her uniform jacket, her glower never leaving him. They'd grown too lax in the time since Reznic. Far too lax.

"I am your CO. I am ordering you to aid our fellow soldiers. Is that clear?"

"Think for a moment." Rein ran his hands through his hair. "They may be on *our side*. But sometimes those on your side can't be trusted." His tone grew bitter as he scrunched up his mouth. "They're Oneiroi, capable of messing with our minds. We find a relay signal, and we report the location. That's the best we can do." After she continued down the ladder and toward the docking attachment, he shouted, "Listen to me!"

"I have. We will do our duty." Katya didn't pause in her even stride. "Suit up and prepare to go through the decontamination and pressure chamber."

In the prep room outside the chamber and docking attachment, Katya went on one side of the lockers, Rein to the other. With a split crew, she had rearranged it that way, allowing for privacy. The last thing she needed was Rein ogling her stripped-down form; it was bad enough that he did it when she was fully clothed.

Tugging her service pistol out of its holster, Katya set it on a bench. The Avitus MP-13, nicknamed The Preserver through a lengthy service, carried a full charge, ready for action. Yanking off her stiff uniform jacket, she tossed it aside. From one locker, she withdrew her spacesuit and tugged it on over her pants, regretting not having retrieved fatigues from her quarters. At least the suit, standard Magistrate-issued, didn't cut into her skin. Despite its three layers of tough material—designed to lessen radiation exposure for a time and prevent punctures from forming—it proved comfortable, and its interior climate control features kept the temperature bearable. Grabbing her helmet, she fastened it and slid her pistol into the suit's holster, which latched it in place.

Rein waited by the decontamination chamber's door, fully suited with a basic toolkit in hand. As she approached, he punched his code into the door's panel. "I hope you know what you're doing, Captain," Rein said, hitting the next number.

"Let's get this over with."

He entered the last digit, and the hatch flung open, fine mist seeping into the locker room. Without a word between them, they stepped into the sterile chamber.

CHAPTER TWO

Coldness. Its starkness struck Katya upon entering the Oneiroi vessel's decontamination chamber, which failed to release its disinfectants and other chemicals. Despite her suit's climate control, the chill bled through and sunk into her limbs. At her wrist, an environmental instrument beeped. Lifting it closer to her face, she took in the readings. Oxygen present, below normal readings but acceptable. Radiation, low, nonthreatening. Even so, her helmet remained in place. All it took was one second, one environmental shift—instant death. The wavering emergency lights didn't bode well.

"I imagine the survivors would have stayed together . . . probably on the bridge."

Rein glanced around, his helmet's light bouncing off the ebony-hued wall. "They'll swamp us." The bright beam landed on Katya before being redirect down the corridor. "The quest for continued life makes us all rats in the end, scurrying onto whatever refuse floats. Trust me. I know sentient nature. I've seen it at its *best*."

The way he emphasized best suggested a tale, perhaps several. "It won't come to that."

"Have you ever met an Oneiroi?"

"Have you?"

Through his tinted helmet, she made out his frown. All he had was the same hearsay and rumors that everyone had. Shadowy figures, cloaked by Magistrate bureaucracy, purveyors of phantasms. Brutal, effective. Katya brushed her hand against her service arm. How true those stories were remained to be seen.

"Mina," she said into her com. "Send over the specs for this class."

Mina voiced her affirmation, and Katya headed out of the decontamination chamber into a corridor with two doors: one to the lockers, another to the hangar bay. As she approached the latter, the lights vanished.

"She doesn't have long," Katya said. "We have to hurry."

"If we must."

The door refused to budge, even after the lights returned.

"We can still turn back," Rein offered.

She extended her hand to him. "Just hand me the torch."

After a slight delay, Rein yanked the instrument from the toolkit and pressed it into her palm.

With the mash of a button, a blue flame shot from the tube's end, and Katya used it to weaken the door, specifically a section loaded with wiring and clasps. The lights fluctuated throughout the process. The blowtorch, during their absences, cast a bluish hue on the pair and their surroundings. Paired with the chill, they became otherworldly, dredging up remembrances of the *mostellarias* that her brothers had loved with their cheap light effects and mechanical props that lurched at visitors in hopes of gathering screams.

Once the metal bubbled and turned orange, Katya deactivated the blowtorch.

"Let's get this open." She stepped back so Rein could place a small detonator, which had enough juice to pop open the door.

He applied it to the weakened metal and pressed the device's center. After receiving her nod, he yanked out the pin. A click was followed by another, and they both retreated, hunkering down behind a metal locker. Katya mentally counted, reaching ten before *pop!* The door had opened, marginally.

A beep echoed from her wrist device. Good job, Mina. Katya launched the newly received file. A projection of the vessel's schematics materialized into being, hovering inches above her wrist.

"Ahead is the main hangar bay. If this ship isn't a custom, we should proceed through the bay and reach this corridor" — she ran her finger along the route, a green trail chasing the movement, marking a path on the spec file — "and access this maintenance hatch. From there, we'll have to climb to the bridge. It won't be easy."

"That's an understatement. How many levels is that?"

"Ten. It'll be a race."

He gestured toward the door. "I know you don't want to hear it, but I'd feel better if I knew what our game plan is once we make contact. We only have two service pistols —"

"It won't come to that." Katya shouldered past him. "We'll behave like Magistrate officers, and so will they. Elites they may be, but they're humanoids and speak proper Magistrate. It's not like we're talking Jar'rasks."

"They may wear skin, look humanoid, but that doesn't make them any less a threat, or any more human. Mammals rip each other apart all the time."

An ominous sensation brewed in her chest. It prickled up her limbs, unearthing memories of delving into the Cassius family crypt to leave offerings during Parentalia. "Just help me with the door."

Straining, they pried it open and carried on to the hangar bay proper. All the way, Katya wished the lights would stop flickering. Her head ached at their constant shifts, dots clouding her vision, promising a migraine. What might as well have been an ice pick being driven through her head sent pain spiraling through her body. She clicked her tongue against her teeth and hunched over, pressing her palms against her upper legs. A hand rested on her back, causing her to stiffen.

"You all right?" Rein asked.

"Fine," she managed after the pain subsided. "The lights are bothering me. That's all." She straightened, forcing his hand from her back. A dull throbbing took residence behind her right eye. "I'm turning up my light's intensity."

As if on cue, the area surrounding them grew inky and undefined. Rein followed her example and upped the intensity of his helmet's light. With their two beams, more of the hangar bay revealed itself.

Several fighters were missing, their vacant spaces highlighted by glowing orange lights in the bay's floor. A few had been misplaced, drifting from their designated squares, possibly when the *Aletheia* had listed—as would be expected in an attack. Their positioning and the scattered bits of debris all spoke to that theory; however, the lack of damage on the displaced fighters didn't match. They would have toppled, crashed into each other. No, these were all too organized. That knowledge stuck to Katya like a burr. Then there were the missing fighters—including some from the suspended levels above—and the lack of wreckage upon their approach. Had the warship jumped and left them behind, or had it been the fighters that had left?

Katya walked around one of the fighters and froze, blood rushing from her face and lips. A large area had been cleared in the middle of the hangar bay. It . . . *Thud. Thud. Thud-thud.* Her heartbeat echoed in her helmet. A knot in her throat blocked the cycled air from her lungs. Corpses. Lines of corpses. Her eyes darted over them, trying not to linger on any one face. She lurched backward, nearly tripping.

Curses exited Rein's mouth while his suit rustled upon his stumbling away from the scene. Katya bowed, resting her hands on her thigh as tremors overtook her legs.

Inhale. Exhale.

She staggered forward.

Remain clinical. Look without really looking.

They all shared similarities: extremely pale with black, in most cases, wavy hair—all humanoid. Katya clenched her teeth together.

Inhale.

She shifted downward, nearly falling as she hunched over one of the corpses. Female.

Exhale.

She steadied herself. This was not the first corpse she had seen in her life, nor was it the worst she had seen to date. There'd been badly decomposed bodies on Reznic, some horribly mutilated, but she had never been confronted by so much death all at once. The vastness of the hangar bay—what else it might hold—towered over her.

Focus.

An exit wound glared at Katya from the corpse's forehead. Most, if not all, bore similar wounds. Blood smeared the metal floor, pooling, darkening, and congealing in spots. It coated her suit's feet, which conversely left imprints in it. If not for filtration, she would smell it. A blotchy blue tint had spread across the lower part of the woman's exposed neck; her blood had already begun to pool. Katya reached out and touched her arm. Stiff, almost inflexible.

"Let's . . . let's g-get out of here," Rein choked on the words. "Leave whatever devilry happened here."

Katya pressed her hands into her legs as she stood. She strode down the rows of dead, approximately one hundred in number: a good chunk of a crew. "Who could have done this? The Oneiroi . . . most would run rather than fight them or even speak with them. To be able to line them up and execute them one by one . . ."

They varied in age and sex. Some in uniform, others had probably been removed from private quarters as they wore partial uniforms, fatigues, or civvies. Not all displayed signs of rigor mortis yet, she determined after further examination. Katya, herself, had never met a member of the Oneiroi despite her long career with the Magistrate. It was always better to keep one's head down, and by following that adage, she'd minimized her brushes with Elites.

"We need to check the logs . . . their communications," she said, extracting herself from the rows. One part of her screamed: Leave the dead to the dead. Another feared they'd haunt her, their glassy, unseeing eyes never leaving her. Too many unanswered questions. Nausea spread through her body as she staggered back to Rein, who stared at her, mouth opening and closing.

Eventually, he found his tongue. "You've got to be crazy! Don't you see these bodies? We are next." He emphasized *are*, making it almost a bellow. "What if whoever—whatever—did this comes back? What if they're still on this ship? What if they come back, and we can't jump ship fast enough? We'll die here!"

Her chest tightened. So many what-ifs and variables. What if they were still on the ship? What if they were harvesting data from the ship? An Elite vessel would have data and tech that would mean lost lives when placed in the wrong hands.

Katya reexamined the ship's specs, following the highlighted path. This entire enterprise could really become a shot in the brown in a matter of seconds.

"Guard this area, Rein. Give me forty-five minutes tops."

"We need to leave." He waved his arms about. "Th-this doesn't concern us. It was a mistake to even come on board. If we keep digging, it'll be our own graves. We go back, forget ever seeing this."

But she would never forget. Not the glassy eyes, not the angry strokes of red. Katya swallowed hard. "We need to know what we've walked into. Upper Brass will want answers, especially if they took something or if Plasovern has found a way to nullify the Oneiroi. There"—she swallowed again—"might still be survivors. We need to at least make an effort."

He shook his head. Even through his specially coated visor, his face's deepened color bled through.

The lights died as if to challenge her sanity in lingering.

"We-I can't . . ." she started.

A mechanical knocking emitted from one of the panels when the lights returned. Probably the result of a system surge. She was out of her mind. Katya flinched, vision in her right eye blurring as a stabbing sensation permeated her head.

"Shii—" She doubled over.

"Are you all right?"

The room righted itself. "Yeah." Katya uncurled her body. "Fine, just fine."

"Something isn't fine. This ship . . ."

"It needs done." She flung a pointed finger toward the hangar bay. "Who could do this? I want an idea of what we're dealing with; the ramifications . . . could be dire for the Magistrate." She faced her intended route. "I'll be back soon."

Katya bolted, her feet pounding against the metal floor and blocking out Rein's voice. After several feet, a few scorch marks, powerful enough to dent the metal walls but not pierce them, served as silent testaments to a struggle.

Some of the marks were smaller, likely service pistols. There'd been heavy weapon fire as well.

A door to her side opened and closed repeatedly. She shuddered and withdrew from the room behind it. There'd been resistance, and those who had partaken in it had been dragged and deposited there. Likely, it wasn't the only room doubling as a mausoleum. She pushed forward, her jaw hurting.

At the sight of a crank wheel in the wall, Katya skidded to a stop, dropping to her knees in order to operate it. Several clicks later, the emergency passageway lay exposed. Her chest constricted: The shaft stretched endlessly in both directions. Forty-five minutes had been a stretch.

She activated her com, patching in both Rein and Mina. "I'll need a bit longer. Mina, boost power to the sensor array. I don't want us to be surprised."

"Boosting power now."

"How much longer?" Rein asked, probably biting his tongue.

Katya put one hand ahead of the other as she began her ascent. "A few more minutes. I'll keep you informed."

There was no answer, and she kept climbing. She had been overly generous. She wasn't an academy student anymore, though she hadn't slouched in her fitness regime in the intervening years. Gritting her teeth, she propelled herself upward.

Rein, you'd better not abandon me in this tomb.

Controlling her breaths, she buried the thought. One rung after another, she proceeded until the muscles in her arms and legs burned and pulled taut, threatening to snap. It conjured memories of academy life: the brutal martial arts training, obstacle courses, midnight runs, drills. She winced as the emergency lights failed once again, obscuring her field of vision beyond the path of her helmet's light.

"Dam—" She plummeted when her hand slipped off a rung. "Damn it!"

Her suit's magnetic safety components, sensing the sudden drop, activated and clapped her to the tunnel's metal walls, rattling her bones. Katya gulped for air, her limbs shaking. Experimentally, she pressed her tongue against her teeth, expecting to find at least one chipped.

Keep going. Keep going. Just keep . . . She rested her helmeted head against the rung above her. Deep breaths, steady breaths. When her heart settled, she deactivated the suit's magnets and swung upward.

"Got this," Katya said as she pressed on.

Her fingers trembled along with the rest of her body by the time she reached the bridge level's hatch. She wrapped one of her arms through a rung and worked the lever with her free hand, maneuvering it just right until it hissed open.

Katya fell through the hatch onto her stomach, huffing as her lungs struggled to satisfy her body's need for oxygen. She rested like that for a few minutes until her trembling muscles relaxed and her breathing grew more controlled. Only then did Katya stagger to her feet, using the wall as a brace. It'd be a long way back down. She shuddered, feeling clammy.

Her hand, as she stumbled on, brushed against a divot in the wall. A larger firefight had occurred on this level. Burns scored the walls in greater groups. Meters down, Katya came across more grime and bodies, left where they had fallen. All of them bore uniforms with higher ranking insignias. The elites of the Elites.

She stepped past a pool of congealing blood and other matter. Teetering to the side, she avoided stepping on a man whose head tilted up at an unnatural angle toward her, dried blood exiting the corners of his mouth. He and the rest had attempted a last stand here, to keep their attackers from the bridge.

Removing her weapon, she left him and dodged other bodies along her way. She tilted away from an open door, likely to private quarters, expecting more carnage. Her tongue clicked against her front teeth as another tinge of pain echoed from her right temple. The lights, while dimmed, remained a steady presence, the power proving more stable on this level. Katya lowered her hand. With her helmet on, it was pointless to try and massage the ache away. Still, it burrowed into her, spotting her vision.

Ahead, her destination's entrance beckoned, pried haphazardly open by force; the panel to it hissed and emitted sparks. The intruders had made it all the way, eroding any prospect of survivors. Finger on the trigger, Katya pressed on to the bridge, only to pivot out again, slamming her back against the nearest wall for cover from the burly figure at one console.

It was anything but Oneiroi.

Silence. No movement followed. Perhaps, she'd gone unnoticed? Use the lapse. Act now.

Charging in, Katya fired a blast into the back of the large, hirsute creature. It jerked, only not in the manner of something living.

Slinking forward—satisfied that the other three of its kind were equally as dead—she lugged the creature from the panel it had been draped over. She relinquished her grip, recoiling from the creature's pinched and pulled face filled with sharp teeth that poked out at odd angles. Fresh. The blood coming out around those teeth and down its flat, barely present nose was fresh. Her eyes darted to the deceased Oneiroi scattered across the bridge. Too fresh. The other three creatures exhibited the same type of damage. And they all bore Magistrate insignias. Had they been investigating, much like she was now?

She approached an Oneiroi crew member who bore a weapon's burn, large caliber, through her back and turned her stiff body over, revealing the woman's blotchy face, purpling in death. Her uniform bore the insignia of an admiral. A woman admiral. Katya blinked.

"Are you there yet?" Rein's voice boomed over their shared line.

Katya cursed in old Riautus, a phrase her father had been fond of using. "Yes. There are four others up here—they're not Oneiroi. Sharp teeth, angularly placed. Their faces are somewhat narrow with furrows around their jaws, flat noses. A large amount of body hair. Freshly killed—I'm not sure what did it; it's silent up here. They appear to be able to stand vertically, or largely vertically."

"You need to get out of there now. Those sound like Breks. They'll tear you limb from limb if there are more on broad."

She didn't doubt that. They harbored a massive amount of muscle. She'd never seen the species before but knew their reputations—particularly the one they'd garnered during the Re'alle Conflict. Conflict perhaps too polite a word to describe it.

"I'm going to get what I can from the system. It should take less time for me to climb down." Katya paused. "Mina, are we still clear?"

"Yes."

"Katya," Rein said with an edge to his tone.

"A few minutes more."

Katya freed the connector to her wrist device and plugged it into the console. No passcode screen popped up, allowing her to transfer what data could be salvaged. As she waited for it to finish, she noted that the other system consoles had been met with weapon's fire. Spying a bulky, high-tech device called a breaker, Katya realized the Breks had been in the process of clearing the ship's systems. Her skin prickled. Had it been their mission or their only recourse to finding the ship's inhabitants slaughtered?

A green light flickered, showing the rate of transfer. She scowled at the size of the download. Little remained, and it'd likely finish in a matter of minutes. She could take the breaker, but the thought of trying to lug it down the maintenance tubes curdled her stomach.

Her gaze landed on the woman, the admiral. Her eyes were open, staring into the ether. Above her left breast, an engraved metal tag remained in place: K. Sarris.

Her device beeped, signaling the end of the transfers. Disconnecting from the computer, she headed toward the exit, only to stop and approach the woman. Katya bent over her and, despite her gloved hands, closed the admiral's eyes. There'd be one less set to haunt her.

"Go in peace."

She implemented that saying, jogging from the bridge. Rendezvousing took priority—well, second priority. Her first remained not meeting whatever had done in the Breks. Fabric rustled. Katya swung around, leveling her AVI-13 as she did so. The service pistol, however, clattered to the floor.

A child. She'd almost shot a child. Her limbs shook.

The little boy, just a toddler, blinked at her, altogether unperturbed. Grasping the doorframe—the very one she'd passed over, expecting nothing but the dead—he stood on wobbly legs as if they couldn't support his weight. But his eyes . . . they stood out the most, a pale blue, with practically nonexistent pupils. Far too big for his small face. The rest resembled the dead in appearance, pale skin tone, black, wavy hair.

"Be grateful you've never run into them, Cassius. Given the order, they'd turn you into a comatose husk, shivering on the floor, just from looking them in the eye." Her previous commanding officer, Valens, had said that of the Oneiroi, for once all humor vacant from his face.

Katya backed into the wall, flinching as their eyes met. She knew nothing about the Oneiroi beyond secondhand stories . . . but he was only a child. She edged toward him, as not to frighten him or trigger any abilities he might have.

"I'm here to help." She stretched a hand out to him.

His legs gave when he tried to grab it.

"Whoa!" She caught him.

In her arms, he tilted his head at an odd angle, his eyes wide. She winced while pressing his head into her bosom, hiding the blood and bodies he'd already seen. Entering the stateroom he'd come from, Katya decided it had belonged to the admiral, given its proximity to the bridge. She freed one of her hands and grabbed a motion-photo from a nightstand. Sure enough, the woman from the bridge returned her gaze, this time with life. In the photo, she held the boy, who slept, while a man—the one in the hallway—stood to her left, his arm draped around her shoulders.

Setting the photo aside, Katya grabbed a bag that rested not far from a table. She opened it and shuffled items in: the motion-picture, a toy that had been left on the floor, wipes from the table, a couple of blankets, another toy, and a few other easily accessible items.

She rested the boy on the floor, patting his hands as he tried to cling to her. His chest moved up and down at an erratic pace. His breathing combined with his unsteady legs made her wonder if he'd been wounded during the chaos. No time to check now. She'd already wasted enough time. Pulling the bag across her front, she strapped the toddler into a nearby carrier and attached him to her back. As a finishing touch, she draped a blanket over him. He didn't need to see more.

Satisfied, Katya and her tagalong set off, arriving at the maintenance hatch within minutes. The added weight and awkward shape of the child created a challenge going down. Katya found herself panting after a few rungs. At least, he was still. Being familiar with the shaft, she skipped over rungs until her hands trembled again, forcing her to slow her pace.

The lights went out. She hitched her breath at the sudden plunge into blackness. Breathe. Calm yourself. Gritting her teeth, she pressed on, reading the door hatch numbers with her helmet's light.

Her com beeped. Draping her arm through a rung, Katya answered. "I'm not far. What's wrong?"

"Checking your whereabouts," Rein said. "The power's almost out. The energy shields here in the hangar bay won't last much longer."

"Damn it." Katya hissed when her shoulder reverberated with pain. "I'll be there. Don't do anything until then."

Have to hurry. She and Rein would be fine; they had suits. The boy, however . . .

She tilted her head down. The opened hatch from earlier waited not far below. It spurred Katya the rest of the way. Once she had extracted herself and her new companion from the maintenance shaft, she ran, ignoring that stabbing in her side.

The hangar bay corridor, however, was empty. Where was he?

"Rein!" Katya shouted, continuing toward the decontamination room. No answer. She flicked on the com. "Is Rein on board?"

"Yes," Mina answered. "He just came. He said you were on your way."

"I'll be there momentarily."

The line closed—then Mina shouted: "Hurry! Another ship's broken out of FTL. It's coming at a steady speed."

"Understood."

She darted through the warship and didn't stop until she was shielded by *The Maelstrom*'s decontamination door. The toddler stirred at the pressure change and the bursts of spray. It wouldn't harm him—at least she hoped it wouldn't. She knew too little about Oneiroi physiology, only that they were humanoid.

With the spray fully dispensed, the second hatch opened. Pulling back the blanket, she found a pair of eyes staring back at her, albeit sleepily. The blanket fell back into place as Katya ousted her helmet and flung it onto the locker room bench.

"Rein," Katya said over her com while rushing to the cockpit. "Fire up the FTL; we're going to need it."

"Already ahead of you."

She bashed her knee on the ladder in her haste to get on the catwalk. Mina wasn't ready to make a blind jump, even if luck played a greater role than skill and experience. Katya grimaced and pressed her free hand against her forehead. Her vision wavered, lines forming under the migraine's assault.

No time for this.

She stumbled along the catwalk, taking steps through the pain. The throbbing became manageable by the time she had reached the cockpit door.

Pounding her passcode into the panel, she swayed in through the door.

"You're back!" The teen's arms bubbled with energy as if she'd like to hug Katya.

Mina never did as Katya detached the child carrier and handed both it and the sleeping toddler to her before tossing the pack to the side. Launching herself at the helm, Katya unclamped *The Maelstrom* from the *Aletheia* and sent them into full reverse.

"How far off is the ship?"

Mina shot over to the navigation console, toddler still in hand. "Coming in fast. They've registered our presence."

"Rein, how long on the FTL drive?" she called over the com system.

"Give me a few more seconds!"

"Copy that. Putting distance between us in preparation for a jump. Everyone take your RMP pills." She flipped off the com system and nudged her head toward Mina. "Get me mine. We should have a liquid variety for the kid."

"What is he?" Mina shifted him and the carrier.

"Get the pills. I'll explain later."

Mina rested the boy in her seat and went to the cabinet, where she removed a pill container, a bottle of water, and a needleless syringe. She handed the water bottle and then one of the orange pills to Katya. Despite its awkward size, Katya swallowed it with a large gulp of water, shuddering as it went down and threatened to stick. She extended the water bottle back to Mina, who took her own pill.

Charging the thrusters, Katya raced toward open space, away from the Elite juggernaut bearing down on them. While doing so, she launched a program, which cycled through the necessary algorithms, preferably loading a destination fast enough to prevent the necessity of a blind jump. A nice short jump. That's what they needed. One with less chance of them becoming space debris.

"He's dosed up and strapped in." There was a pause. "The other ship . . . they're broadcasting their credentials and charging their FTL drive. They'll be on us—"

"You will stop," a mechanical voice cut through their com system, "and wait to be boarded."

Katya's stomach dropped when a Magistrate A-Class warship loomed above them.

"They're charging—they're charging their weapons." Mina swiveled from her station, eyes bulging in her face. "They're going to kill us! What the—"

We know too much.

Katya dug into the side of her mouth with her teeth as she careened away, throwing *The Maelstrom* into zigzags. Those Breks were Magistrate—all Breks were. What if the Oneiroi weren't dead when their fellow Elites arrived? What if the Breks had—but then what had killed the Breks? Katya prodded the bloody bump that'd formed in her mouth's lining.

"Rein," Katya called.

"Punch it!"

Purr kitten! She pushed the thrusters, rocketing the Boita above the warship.

"We're going to die!" Mina shouted.

The girl had her knees up to her face; her eyes were pressed into them.

"Mina, get your legs down!"

Katya caught the girl moving out of the corner of her eye before pressing the switch. Her stomach lurched at the increased acceleration. The back of her head plowed into her seat while *The Maelstrom* convulsed as if it were being torn asunder. The rattling stopped violently, sending Katya forward, her head striking the control console. She heaved before going limp.

CHAPTER THREE

There had been a brief moment of blinding light—or at least, the vague impression of one—before . . . nothing. Wincing, Katya struggled to piece together events but failed. The droning buzz in her head muddled everything. A gnawing voice kept talking, like a shrill bird, trying to overcome the pounding in her ears. She groaned and slipped while attempting to obtain an upright position, only she couldn't tell what was upright. Metal, seamed metal. She had to be on the floor. Stupid. How could she have forgotten to fasten—

She shook. No, someone had grabbed her shoulders and was wrenching her back and forth.

"Katya!"

She blanched, but the buzzing lessened, bringing pain to the forefront. Mina didn't let up, her high-pitch, frantic voice driving nails into Katya's battered head. Blinking, she swallowed blood; with her tongue, she prodded around her mouth and found a deep bite mark; meanwhile, memory flooded back.

All around her and Mina, red lights blinked erratically on almost all the consoles. Would the Boita explode? Swallowing, she climbed off the floor, using her seat for support. Blood traveled down her forehead into one eye.

"I'll get something—"

"D-don't worry about it." Katya grimaced and slumped in the chair. Something pulled in her back. She'd probably hit something or twisted it when she had fallen. "What is our situation?"

"We exited the FTL cycle. We took extensive damage."

"The Brek vessel?"

Mina swung back to the sensor display. "Still blank. They didn't follow. The array says we're not far from the Dynaris wormhole. We could take that and go to Gilga, patch ourselves up and regroup, figure out what we need to do."

The girl had learned well. Katya groaned as she pressed her hand against her forehead, coating it in blood. There was only one flaw in her strategy. "*The Maelstrom* can't be patched up, Mina. We'll sell her for scrap and go from there. Anything from Rein?"

"No. I think the entire com system's shorted."

"Of course." Katya stiffened and swept around, exhaling. The restraints still guarded the Oneiroi child. All tension evaporated from her body, leaving only fatigue and pain. "Is he all right?"

Mina nodded. "He slept through it."

"Good." Katya touched the console in front of her, dismissing several of the warning lights: FTL drive dead, propulsion system barely functional, communications fried, steering damaged . . . the list went on. "Mina, send over the course to the wormhole; it's the only way we're getting anywhere."

The course arrived, though slower than normal. Good. The wiring wasn't completely fried. Holding her breath, Katya activated the solar sails; they pulled, a grating sound emitting in the cockpit. Then the lever vibrated as it straightened the sails. She slumped over, releasing her bated breath. While a relief, the sails' functionality had taken a hit during and after the jump, according to the data before her. Despite all the red flashing at her, the old girl would get them through the wormhole and to Gilga.

She tested the autopilot feature, which, like most of the main console, proved functional and took the coordinates. Katya grimaced at the amount of radiation leaking from them.

"It's bad, isn't it?" Mina drummed against the dead communications console. She had her lower lip pinched between her teeth. "Are we going to blow?"

"No, but we're leaking radiation." Katya dismissed more warning lights. "We're a bright blue dot on everyone's screen." A Reznic slur exited her mouth. Privateers, Plasovern, and their ilk would be drawn to them like scavengers seeking easy prey. "With luck, no one will cross our path, good or bad."

Rubbing her eyes with both hands, she compiled a list. Her head ached. She willed her mind away from the rows of dead, the rooms of them . . . there was too much to do before they reached Gilga to dwell on them. She massaged her jaw. A wave of lightheadedness hit her as she pictured them joining the *Aletheia*'s crew.

"What—" The hatch's opening cut Mina off.

Rein stumbled in, limping. Blood trailed down his neck from a cut along the side of his face. "The FTL's junk, complete and utter junk."

"Luckily, the sails are operational, below par but operational. They should get us to Gilga. We've got a full docket before that. Are you up to it?"

Mina stared at her with her large brown eyes while Rein wiped blood from his face.

Katya smeared her own blood away from her eyes and then left stains on her suit's exterior. "We need to make *The Maelstrom* look like a civilian-bought decommission, converted into a cargo ship. Everything Magistrate — uniforms, layouts — it all needs to be changed or put out the hatch. On Gilga, we'll sell her as scrap and get a suitable replacement. We can't afford to keep her; she ties us to that ship."

"What the hell are you talking about?" Rein stopped rubbing his leg and stiffened. "We contact the Magistrate. We clear this all up. Nothing's changed."

Katya laughed, wincing with the action. "They were prepping to shoot us. We were on that ship, and they know it. We saw what they didn't want seen."

"We don't know that. They probably went on the offense with us because they thought we were looting a high-tech military vessel." Rein waved at the child. "Which we did. What were you thinking when you grabbed him? The Oneiroi belong to them." Rein widened his stance. "What are we going to do with it? We can't keep it—"

"He's a child. What would you have had me do? Leave him to die along with the rest of his family?" Katya rocked onto the balls of her feet. "Open your eyes, Rein. Plasovern doesn't have the armaments to do that amount of exterior damage on an A-Class warship—let alone board one, line up its inhabitants, and execute them. We are talking not just about Flites but Oneiroi. No entity, outside of the Medzeci Empire and the Magistrate, has that kind of power. If it was Medzeci, we would've seen one of its warships." She swept a strand of blood-soaked bangs from her one eye.

Rein scrunched his face, a vein protruding in his throat. "Not everything is a conspiracy!"

"That is rich coming for you. Who was it on Reznic saying they were using vaccines to sterilize people?" He balked, but Katya continued, "Then there were the Breks on the ship—"

"They could've been killed by anything. They could have been investigating, and then the Brek warship left pursuing something, possibly whatever murdered their compatriots."

Mina cleared her throat. "So this is an Oneiroi?" she poked the boy's cheek once before retracting her finger. He, meanwhile, remained still.

"Yes." After pushing Mina's hand down to her side, Katya unfastened the child from the seat and picked him up, resting his head on her shoulder. She faced Rein. "There are too many things off with this. We might be little more than collateral damage, if . . ." If she could bring herself to voice her suspicions.

"The Magistrate did it?" Rein finished. "Why would they attack their own ship? Why risk losing their interrogators? It makes no sense."

"You used to say Reznic's drug lords were being supplied by the Magistrate and were feeding money back into it via war profiteering." Katya flared her nostrils. "You're only shying away from this because it's ugly. You just want to keep your head down and carry on. Forget the bodies—"

"Damn straight I want to forget them!"

"I can't do that. Are you really willing to risk it? That we won't end up just like them? The heavy fire on the walls was on par with what the Breks carry."

He remained silent, hand pressed against his wound, eyes flicking around the cockpit like some caged animal.

"I might be able to learn something with the data I took from the ship, but the Breks deleted most of it."

Rein ground his teeth and placed more weight on his good leg. "So we rid ourselves of all the Magistrate trappings. Then what? Scrap won't buy us a suitable replacement."

"I've been saving up for a ship of my own."

Rein's eyebrow rose, causing the muscles in her arms to tighten.

"I'm thirty-four, and I'm practical. I know I'm facing the end of my career, not the beginning, so I've been saving money into a Novarti account."

"It'll be worthless. The Magistrate will freeze any account with our names on it; there's no way the Breks didn't ID us. Mina may be the only exception since she's not on the official roster."

"I'll think of something, but in the meantime, we've got a lot before us." She shifted the boy so most of his weight rested on her other hip. "I'll be along after I get him situated and checked out. He might've been hurt during the skirmish. Rein, go ahead and get to work on the changes. Bring *The Maelstrom*'s registration chip to the cockpit, and I'll hack into it . . . give us a new story."

He stood stock-still, his gaze condemning her. Oh, there'd be trouble down the line; she only hoped she'd have the higher cards when it reared its head. After grabbing the bag, she nudged past him, only halting when his hand went to grab her arm. At her dour expression, he dropped his hand.

"Watch yourself, Katya. He may be a kid, but he's still an Oneiroi, capable of putting you under his spell."

"I'll be careful."

Katya bypassed him and carried on to her quarters. Under his spell? Laughable. The boy so far had mostly slept. Even in the maintenance tunnel, he hadn't made a peep where most children would have been screaming their heads off. His lips moved in his slumber. So dangerous. Though, if he were older, she would be leerier. The Magistrate's dogs, interrogators most heinous. Those who entered their domain often didn't leave it sane or alive, and the Oneiroi kept their secrets to themselves and their uninhabitable, Magistrate black-zone planet.

That impenetrable veil now presented a challenge. Shifting him, his head lulled into the crook of her arm. Breath escaped him in rapid huffs, reminding her of a panting dog. He was burning up; however, there was only a minuscule amount of sweat. She guaranteed even an intensive search on the Net wouldn't turn up basic, cursory information on his species. She doubted its seedier avenues, known as *Intortus*, offered anything legit, beyond so-called facts that were bolstered with little more than hearsay and fanciful tales.

She thumbed in her passcode, and the door swished open. Items had fallen from their places during the jump and were strewn across the floor. A vase from Riau, which her father had given her several years ago, had shattered on impact; the water that had been in it created a pool while the flowers lay bruised. Eh, Papa, what would you say? Such a fine display of the Riauts' glassmaking lost. He would be devastated. The gift had been forced, and she had always assumed he'd forgotten her birthday again, despite having picked it, and grabbed the nearest item. With six children and a mind that flitted from place to place, it was understandable. He tried but could only do—remember—so much.

She laid the boy on her bed before stripping the spacesuit off, allowing the white cotton top underneath to breathe.

"Now"—she returned to bed—"let's see what's wrong with you."

His skin radiated heat like a mini furnace as she removed his shirt. No wounds evident on his body, except for minor scratches on his arms and several dully colored bruises, some a deeper shade of purple than others. Placing him on his stomach revealed more bruising on his back but no blood. She removed his pants and found him still in diapers. Katya frowned. He should be old enough to not need them, yet there they were as if taunting her for every time she'd passed niece and nephew to someone else. There'd be no passing the buck now, though it posed another problem. There were no diapers on board.

Scrunching her face, she sniffed, exhaling when met only by the scent of powder. Thank the celestial bodies.

She lifted his legs, finding more bruising. The boy lacked muscle mass throughout his body, much like a veal calf. No wonder he couldn't stand.

She furrowed her brow. "Were you abused?" She recalled the photo, the affection in which they had held him, held each other. A well-crafted lie? She dismissed the thought.

After redressing him in his clothing—somewhat dampened by sweat—Katya tucked him into her bed. They would get new clothes for him and diapers at Gilga, along with food an Oneiroi could eat, likely a matter of trial and error. She walked to the bag and dumped out its contents. She placed the stuffed toy she'd grabbed on the ship—a fuzzy, hoofed animal that she was unfamiliar with—under the covers next to the boy. She then set the family photo on her table with the bag's blankets.

Two children's books, presumably written in the Oneiroi's language, had also been in the bag, along with a hardback leather journal written in a small hand in the same language, ten diapers, a spare change of clothing, wipes, powder, and another toy. She lifted a dome thing, inspecting it from each angle before pushing a small button at its top. Little lights shot out creating celestial shapes on the wall, which danced around as music played. She pressed the button again, and the shapes disappeared, with only the music remaining. A third time and the lights returned with the music absent, while after the fourth hit, the device completely deactivated.

She added it to the table, her hand lingering on it. The boy slept fine without it; however, she could not deny something was wrong with him. So pallid, breath exiting his mouth in a manner she could only describe as unnatural. His black curls clung to his forehead. She clenched the device, then released it. She had no understanding of pediatrics, let alone the physiology of an Oneiroi child. Their medical supplies were limited and not geared toward one so young. Katya withdrew the duvet from the child, leaving only the lighter sheet.

"I'm sorry I can't do much else." Katya wiped the sweat away using the edge of her sheet. "I wish I could do more." But if she didn't change the registration, their gambit would fail, and then who knew where they'd all be. Maybe they would find a discreet doctor on Gilga.

Content he would be comfortable, Katya changed into less restrictive pants and joined Mina in the cockpit. The teenager, who sat in the pilot's seat, pointed to the small worktable not far from the hatch.

"Rein put the registration chip over there." Mina pulled her legs up to her face. "How's our little guest? You never said how you came by him."

"I've had a bit on my mind." Katya climbed onto the worktable's tall seat and reached for her tool tray. "I stumbled across him while leaving the bridge; that's all I know. He might have a fever."

"Do you think Rein is right? About him, that is."

"I doubt he's dangerous at this age." Katya reached up and adjusted the light over the station.

"Is there anything I need to do?"

"Keep watching the consoles. Beyond that, give me quiet. It's a tricky business rewriting a registration chip."

Katya gripped a small instrument from the tray and opened the chip with it, exposing the wiring and circuitry. Cut wires and burnt circuit boards would be red flags. She plunged the tip of the instrument under one of the clamps and nudged it up a fraction of an inch. Since registration chips were not built with ports, she would create her own.

"What's his name?"

Katya flinched, the tip of the instrument jostling, almost hitting the sensitive circuit board. "Pardon?"

"His name—the little boy's?"

"No idea." Katya placed the tool on the table and reached for connector wires, a roll of electrical tape, and a knife. "He didn't exactly come with a name tag. Now let me—eh—" She grunted, pressing her hand to her temple after a sharp prickling sensation dug in. The circuit wavered in front of her.

"Are you all right?"

"Just. Let. Me. Focus," Katya hissed between rubbing her head. She needed sleep. The headaches were because of that and accentuated by the stress that'd been dumped into her lap, or she potentially had a concussion. Forcing her hands down, she rolled her head from side to side. A slight ringing hovered in the background, and it wasn't coming from the consoles. She had definitely hit her head hard.

Mina cleared her throat as if to say something more, but she ultimately remained fixated by her console. Katya bowed her head and picked up one of the wires she had removed from the tray. Using the knife, she cleared away the plastic on both ends, exposing the wires beneath before using a set of pliers to connect them to the registration chip. Next, she produced her slate and unscrewed the bolts that held the back on. Once its circuit board was visible, she attached the wiring to the proper nub and turned on the power; the screen turned blue before the main menu appeared. She did a search, looking for connections and an encryption key box popped up.

She launched another program in the background; it was black market tech, but Katya had been able to justify it while stationed on Reznic. A seedy planet required such tactics to stay on top of the criminals; one needed to break through various types of encryptions to find and seize contraband, plus terminate the occasional species trafficking rings and other criminal activities. Symbols flashed across the encryption key box until all the slots were filled. Katya pressed the check mark and held her breath until the next screen came up, containing registration numbers, crew names, past history, and other data pertaining to *The Maelstrom*. She had a small window of time to make changes before the Magistrate software on the chip shut her out—the Magistrate had always been keen to prevent tampering, illegal thefts, and false reporting, rolling out sophisticated programming that, like the hackers themselves, continued to evolve.

She switched *The Maelstrom* to *Royal Justice*, a matching Boita that had been decommissioned and sold. It had been sold repeatedly, according to the rumor mill. So the odds were great that its whereabouts had been buried under piles of Magistrate paperwork, thus less likely to draw too much notice. More importantly, she remembered its registration number.

Next, she changed the crew list. She chose the name Clementia, an old primary school friend of hers, for herself and changed Rein's name to Ferrutius. All good Magistrate names. She picked equally bland, run-of-the-mill surnames. She added Mina to the roster as Hilaria—her absence now might catch notice. Designation changed to miscellaneous cargo.

Additional changes followed, such as previous destinations and cargos, until the system kicked her out. Without a registered Magistrate program, it would be too risky to repeat the break-in. Eventually, the chip would short circuit itself.

"Get used to the name Hilaria, Mina. You might be using it for a while."

"Why couldn't I pick my own? Hilaria." Mina stuck out her tongue.

Smiling, Katya removed the wires from her slate and the chip. "Not enough time for that. At the wormhole, we'll go over our story together and thoroughly." Katya resecured the back on her slate before closing up the chip. "When we get to Gilga, it'll be important not to talk too much." The girl rolled her eyes at that. "With the ship in the shape she's in, the fewer questions we have to answer, the better. Rein will do likewise."

Mina snorted. "Now that you don't outrank him, how are you going to keep him in line?"

"Let me worry about him. Continue your duties here. And keep an eye on the displays! If there are any changes in our systems or if our friends appear, report in immediately. I'll be helping clear out unwanted items. Eventually, we'll have to do some exterior work." Katya could have flinched at the last part: Exterior work had never been her favorite task.

"How long do you think the exterior work will take?"

Katya shrugged. "We'll do it while we're moving. With the clamps, we shouldn't have a problem. In all honesty, we can't afford to sit about and do it." She opened the door to the rest of the ship. "We don't want to dine with Elites. Stay vigilant, Mina. We're counting on you while we're working." A smile tugged at her face again. "No earphones."

Mina's face reddened, and she stuttered excuses. Katya, meanwhile, shook her head as she walked away. The door closed behind her with a *whoosh*. With the threat of Elites attacking, she welcomed any levity.

Before catching up with Rein, Katya revisited her quarters. Inside, the boy had pushed off the sheet. Grabbing a hand towel, she dampened it with cold water from her bathroom's small sink. The space bore only the necessities: a toilet, shower stall, and sink. Once thoroughly soaked, she squeezed out the excess water. As the water pinged against the metal sink, she realized he needed fluids. She grabbed a nearby cup, filling it before returning to her main room.

The bed sank under her weight as she wiped the towel across his face, both removing sweat and cooling him. Setting aside the towel, she propped him up and pressed the cup's edge to his mouth. As she tilted it and the water entered his mouth, he stirred, gulping down the liquid. Katya rubbed his back in a circular fashion while he drank—then he went limp.

"No, no, no . . ." Katya yanked the mug away, and water pooled from his mouth. She maneuvered him into a position where the rest hit the floor. Damn it, kid. His pulse still beat strongly, and her own heart resumed its normal pace.

Satisfied that he wasn't choking, she laid him onto the bed and draped the cloth across his forehead. To clean his mouth, she used the edge of one of her blankets, which she found herself clutching. Something was extremely off about the kid, and Katya had a sinking feeling no doctor on-world would be able to treat him.

Katya forced herself to her feet. She had other matters to address, ones that were within her realm of power to fix. She opened her footlocker.

Uniform tops and bottoms greeted her first. Katya smiled, remembering the joy of trading out academy brown for the polished blue. She traced the ribbons that marked her service and the pendants displaying rank. They were meaningless now, but she had fought hard for each and every one of them. Katya closed her eyes before she tossed them into a pile, along with her diploma and other documents regarding her service. Little remained in the footlocker now. She had never been one to buy civilian clothes; the ones she did purchase were worn under her uniforms and largely consisted of plain white tanks and T-shirts. Of course, there were the khaki mechanic pants and a few items her sister had insisted on sending her, often handmade.

She closed the lid and stood. Nothing else in the room connected her with the captain who had boarded the *Aletheia*—only the items given to her by her father, brothers, and sisters remained, but those were personal, not items others could tie to a Magistrate captain. She picked up an old framed photo and examined her much younger self in academy brown. The dreams she had held sprang to mind. So optimistic, overly naïve. She'd pictured a long career, moving through the Magistrate's ranks, eventually commanding a much larger vessel. Yet all she had been given were ground posts before ending up in command of *The Maelstrom*, the joke that it was.

She caught her lips between her teeth. *"Don't think of it as a gift from me. Think of it as a well-deserved turn, not fully what you deserve, but it'll at least get you away from here."* Perhaps not a joke, but still a far cry from what she'd envisioned. Better than Reznic, though, hence why Valens had pulled every string his own last name granted to ensure this one last gesture.

She removed the picture from the frame and placed it in the footlocker, sliding it between her white tanks. Another photo, more candid, followed it. Her and Valens. She only regretted that the effects of the illness had already begun to present themselves physically, ensuring that the image served as a constant reminder of an end. As she reclosed the trunk and straightened, she noted that the boy's face had smoothed, void of the crease lines, and he appeared to be in a much sounder sleep.

"I'll be back."

Katya picked up the pile she had created and left her quarters, heading toward the garbage chute. They were objects, created artificially, not important. Her hands tightened around her load. She reached the chute and thumbed it open, then stood, staring into the black abyss. This was happening too quickly. The bleakness of the garbage chute enveloped her. Beneath, a simple garbage disposal unit would incinerate everything, leaving behind only ash to be jettisoned.

Pressing her forehead against the metal above the opening, Katya steadied her uneven breaths, trying to push away thoughts of a future that resembled the chute: dark and obscure. What of those dreams? Gone. If they'd ever been more than pipe dreams to begin with. Her life might be over along with them. The Magistrate felt like a limitless territory. How could they hope to hide in it? Katya knocked her head against the metal. Why did she have to board that ship?

Her thoughts drifted to the boy, and she squeezed the pile before thrusting it into the chute; it plummeted out of her grasp, and there would be no retrieving it. Katya remained transfixed, left to hope that a set of high-power burners wasn't waiting for her. A chuckle escaped her throat, even as tears prickled at her eyes. Ironic how she had once placed ex-Magistrate pilots turned to cargo pilots or smugglers as little more than those who couldn't make the cut.

She shut the chute's door and turned to find Rein watching her, no doubt thinking her hysterical. She drew herself up and clenched her jaw as she dared him to say something, anything. The blood had already dried along his hairline, matting sections of it. His gaze remained a moment longer before he started to leave, saying, "We need to change the paintwork. Gear up."

She dusted her hands against her shirt and walked beside Rein. "What's been done?"

"I've been removing little things, stuff with *The Maelstrom*'s registration number on it. I've also cleared out what was in my room." Rein extended his hand. "Do you have the chip?"

Nodding her head, Katya placed it into his hand.

"I'll replace this real quick." He nudged his head toward the cockpit. "What are we going to do with the navigation system?"

"It will meet an unfortunate accident prior to our landing. With the shape the rest of the ship is in, it won't be unbelievable. The com system is already a lost cause. I switched *The Maelstrom* to the *Royal Justice* on the chip. It shouldn't catch unwanted attention."

"It bodes ill to change the name."

"We're already in bad straights. What more can be heaped on us? Besides, we won't be on *The Maelstrom* for much longer. The bad luck will be on someone else."

"Have you determined how we're going to unload this scrap heap?"

"Still working on it." He said nothing, but the area between his shoulders tensed. Katya continued as if she hadn't noticed. "Oh, by the way, your cover name is Ferrutius."

"Someone you knew?"

"There were a ton of Ferrutiuses in my primary days through to my academy days. I picked names that are common, forgettable. The only one that held any personal meaning to me is the one I choose for myself, Clementia. She was a good friend from primary and intermediary. We still keep in touch from time to time, less so now. Our paths diverged, I suppose you could say." Her path had diverged from a lot of her friends' own.

"What did she go on to do?" Rein asked.

"She married right after intermediary. She has two kids—a boy and a girl."

"Do you wish you had settled down?"

Katya bowed her head. The once. But they'd never been forced to cross that bridge, the disease rendering that decision null before it was needed to be made. From time to time, she'd reflect on it, debating whether she would have forsaken her career. It was only a matter of time before they'd been exposed. Given Rein's hardening expression and crossed arms, Katya assumed they had already been.

"I don't regret it at all." Her posture loosened. "It was never my calling." She passed him, heading toward the locker room.

He stood still, but she could feel his eyes on her. He made no comment.

In the locker room, Katya tugged on her secondary suit. As she slid her left leg in, her calf muscle tightened; her attempts to stretch it only made it worse. Her head bobbed as a wave of exhaustion washed over her, a certain chill greeting her lips. A few more minutes. Then she would sleep before they reached the wormhole. As she yawned, her eyes closed, and she almost gave into the fatigue that wrapped itself around her like a snake squeezing consciousness out of her body, beckoning her to curl up on the bench and join it. The headaches would be banished with just a few hours of sleep. She straightened when a door to a locker on the other side closed.

"Ready to go?" Rein called.

"Yes, just need to get my helmet on. Do we have paint that will do?"

"Yes. I also have the clamps and tethers ready to go."

The two moved to the decontamination chamber before spending the next two hours changing registration numbers and examining the full extent of the damage rendered by the semi-blind jump: namely, missing chunks of metal. None were in essential places, but it would severely cut down on the ship's value. Katya shuffled toward one of the few remaining identifiers, a set of bright red stripes that marked the ship as an active-duty military vessel, when her vision clouded. Her legs and arms shook against her will and grew clammy. Moments stretched while she seized. The paintbrush—she released it. Hands grabbed her and pulled her backward, her feet dragging against metal, where the clamps kept them. The back of her head roared, deafening everything. Light, a pure white as if her retinas were being torn asunder—then blackness.

Warmth seeped back into her lips, spreading to her limbs. As Katya lay on something hard, she realized her helmet was missing. Where had it . . . it had been important.

Blinking, her surroundings came into focus, and she made out Rein standing above her, panting. "Are you all right?"

Katya brushed her bangs from her face. Her muscles still tingled, tightening and relaxing. "I need to lie down." She tried to sit up, but Rein's hands held her in place.

"You are."

"In my quarters." She propped herself.

Rein steadied her, helping her stand. "Take it easy. I think you have a concussion . . . you need to get rest. Here, let me get you to your cabin."

Rein practically carried her there, putting her down in front of the security panel. At the panel, Katya hastily put in her code, obscuring it with her hand.

"Do you need help getting your suit off?"

Her face threatened to redden, but she shook her head. "I can handle it." She stepped into the room. "Give me a half hour of sleep, and then I'll come back to help."

Rein glanced at the Oneiroi child in her bed before accepting her words and leaving to finish the job. Katya sighed and shut the door. She yanked her suit down and then kicked it off, discarding it on a chair, rougher than necessary. Rein hadn't scaled an emergency tunnel up several levels, Katya brooded. She ignored the fact that they'd both smacked their heads.

She stripped off her sweaty clothes next and put on her sleepwear. The concussion theory seemed likely. She dragged herself to the bed, swinging over the child until she was between him and the metal wall. In her head, a list ran, items checked off, others not. After propping up her pillows, she rested her head on them. The world around her swayed. It'd be nice not to think for a while.

CHAPTER FOUR

Katya curled onto her side to silence the gnawing emptiness of her gut, only to stop when a weight anchored her in place. Groaning, she stretched under the object, her one hand reaching to push it away. Hair. The boy. She jerked her hand back. Realization dawned on her. Concussion. There'd definitely been one.

To prove that point, the room spun as she propped herself up using her pillows, setting the boy to the side. At some point during the night, besides crawling on top of her, he'd kicked the covers off, leaving her a small sliver. How hadn't the chill woken her?

The vertigo lifted once she'd been seated for a while, and when it did, she attempted to move. The last thing she needed was to blackout again. She kicked the rest of the covers off her feet and reached for the side console. After hitting the wrong button three times in a row, Katya found the right one: "It is 1000 hours MMT-Sector12." She groaned, brushing her bangs from her face. She'd overslept. Why hadn't Rein attempted to wake her up? Her stomach grumbled.

Katya stood from the bed and stretched. "Ow." She rubbed her back, seeking to soothe the taut muscles. She continued to work out the kinks as she entered her bathroom, where she threw on clothing. Bits of hair had loosened from the braids that looped down to her shoulders before joining the main body of her hair, so she redid them. Years spent doing this same routine had created deft fingers able to do the task rapidly. With the braids tucked back in place, she washed her face, gasping at the water's frigidness. Another failing system, or more likely Rein had shut down unnecessary ones to get the old girl to limp a little farther. Grabbing another cup of water and a damp cloth, she reentered the main room.

"We can't be calling you 'the boy' forever, I suppose." She scooped him up and dripped some water into his mouth. Nothing. He slept on.

Setting the cup aside, she undressed him, finding the clothes less damp than before. She lobbed them onto the floor. From the bag, she removed a spare diaper and the second set of clothes. They were heavier than the ones he'd been wearing, perfect for where they were going. Katya added the hand towel to the pile of dirty laundry.

"Such a sound sleeper." She brushed her finger against his cheek. "Hopefully, that jump didn't hurt you."

His black hair was a mess, tangled every which way like an ill-constructed bird's nest. She straightened it with her fingers as best as she could. If only they had something better able to accommodate bathing a toddler. They shouldn't be far from Gilga—two days out, if not less. She prepared to dress the boy but stopped. There was the diaper. Wrinkling her nose, she grabbed the spare from the bed. She struggled to loosen the one on him. One strap gave, followed by the last. Tears formed as the strong odor struck her. She hastily returned the diaper and retrieved her small trashcan. She would do it quickly—in and out.

Holding her breath, Katya yanked the diaper off and dropped it in the trashcan. As soon as the lid dropped, she scooted the bin away with her foot as far as her leg could stretch without losing balance. She cleaned him, finishing by pouring powder on him. Katya fastened the new diaper as best she could: lopsided and perhaps a bit too tight. Not bad for a first attempt. Besides, he gave no complaints, not even waking when she strung his appendages through their respective pant legs and sleeves.

With all in order, she strode to her small desk, only to find her slate absent.

"Cockpit. I left it in the cockpit." Katya rubbed her forehead. Her stomach growled again. She had wanted to handle their funds issue last night or early this morning, and there was the data gleaned from the *Aletheia*. But at this stage in the game, it wouldn't hurt to wait until she filled the growing hole in her gut.

"Let's see if we can find something for you, too, and get more fluids in you." Katya carried him to the mess area, which served as both a kitchen and a mess hall, located on the main section of the ship.

As she drew closer to the small rectangular room, the clatter of pots greeted her, leaving her to assume Mina was inside; after all, the sixteen-year-old, bound by habit, lounged about until around 1000 hours when she'd emerge from her quarters. Sure enough, the door moved to reveal Mina hunched over a pot on one of the burners, stirring something. Earbuds dangled from her ears as she focused on her task, unaware she was no longer alone. Katya adjusted the boy in her arms and came to stand next to Mina.

"So, what are we cooking?"

"Katya!" Mina jerked, almost dropping her spoon into the boiling substance. With her free hand, she draped the earbuds over her shoulder. "We were worried about you. Rein tried to page you but got no answer. How are you feeling?" Mina's gaze fell on the Oneiroi child. "He's still sleeping?"

Katya bumped her shoulder against the Oneiroi child's cheek; the jostling failed to elicit any response. "Hasn't woken since the jump. Unless he woke when I was out."

Katya peered into the steaming pot. Apparently, Mina was in a comfort food mood, desiring Reznic bok, which consisted of noodles and a special sauce. It could be prepared with or without meat, and Mina had chosen to add some ground meat. Her stomach bubbled. She could use the protein.

"Scoop me out some," Katya said while scouring through the cabinets. She reached for some powdered milk. It was nutritious and would hydrate him, even if it wasn't exactly filling. Could an Oneiroi stomach it, though? They were mammals so —

"I've been thinking," Mina said between dishing out the bok. "We can't just keep calling him, well, 'the boy.' So let's name him . . . How about Decimus?"

She smiled, similar to a snake having found a clutch of eggs, but managed to bite back any laughter that might have followed. "Decimus as in Lieutenant Decimus Livianus?" Mina's face resembled a beet in hue, and Katya couldn't resist. "He was pretty handsome. A bit young for my taste, but I'll acknowledge he had a remarkable butt."

The teen sputtered and ducked her head. "Th that's — how about Valens then, after the colonel —" Mina stumbled on her tongue while Bok landed on the countertop, missing the bowl. "I'm sor —"

"All in good fun." Katya set the powdered milk on the counter. A good man, a good name, but she couldn't hear it every day, not when the grief had just dulled. It'd been over a year now, or so she'd heard; the disease had sunk its teeth in and devoured its host rather rapidly. The cards had been poorly stacked, nothing more, as Valens had been fond of saying. One accepted that and continued on.

Mina blurted out, "What about Aquila? After candy bar guy."

Another good man who'd left existence far too young. She could still picture his smiling face. He'd had a good heart, far too kind for Reznic. He hadn't hesitated to step into that hail of fire, not when his body could shield the children behind him.

Swallowing, she said, "I think it's a good name. Aquila." She situated the toddler in an empty seat. "A strong name. Very Magistrate."

Keeping her back turned to Mina, Katya mixed the powdered milk and ignored the slight burning of her eyes. Once warmed, she removed the milk from the heat, poured it into a glass, and slid in a straw.

While positioning herself at the table, she asked, "What's our progress?"

"We made it to the wormhole. Rein said to go ahead through."

"Good." Katya lifted the newly dubbed Aquila, placing him on her lap. Tapping his cheek with her finger, she received no acknowledgment. Frowning, Katya navigated the straw into his mouth.

"Are you sure that's how you're supposed to feed him?"

She glared at Mina. "I've never cared for a child before, and, yes, you are probably right that this is the wrong—" Aquila coughed up the milk, sputtering to life. His tongue reached out, brushing against his lips before his mouth and face contorted. More milk oozed out.

"I don't think he likes it."

"I can see!" Katya held Aquila away from herself though her clothes were already wet. "Grab a towel!"

Mina raced to retrieve one from the counter. Katya took it and wiped the foamy mess from the toddler's face before resting the towel over her wet shoulder. "Well, you don't like powdered milk. You're a mammal so I'm assuming there's a variety you do like."

"Do you think he might be able to talk?"

"If he can, it won't be basic Magistrate. It'll be whatever language is in that journal." She poked the boy. "What are we goin' to do with you, little one?"

Mina pulled back one of the chairs with her foot while placing two bowls of bok on the table, pushing one of them toward Katya.

"We're about a day out," Mina said. "Maybe they'll have something edible for him there. Though . . ." Mina trailed off, absently spinning her utensil in the bok. "What's our plan? After Gilga."

Katya whistled. "That's the question, isn't it? And I'm not even sure how to answer it." She swallowed some of the bok, relishing its warmth and flavor, a mix of pepper and spice. "One thing's for sure: I won't be writing that recommendation for you." Katya smiled, though it lacked merriment.

Absently, she stirred her bok. Aquila's head rested against her shoulder, his small hands grabbing the fabric of her shirt. Where did they go from here?

Mina's fork clattered against her bowl. "You've done a lot for me, you know? Taught me to fly, operate the different consoles—I can make it as a private-sector pilot, so don't worry about that."

But she'd still worry. "Rein and I will have to keep moving. Once we've unloaded *The Maelstrom*, we should be able to hit up a bunch of small backwater planets until we get lost in Magistrate paperwork. Beyond that, we're going to be strapped for money, leading to 'a' we haul cargo, 'b' we work as smugglers, or 'c' we take on passengers."

"With the latter two being dangerous."

Katya chuckled. "With the situation we're in, they're all dangerous, but the third option would be insane." She took another bite of the bok, slurping the juice off the spoon. "Money will be the least of our worries. But for now, we just need to bury ourselves." After a few more helpings, Katya set down her spoon. "There'll be more options for you. You weren't on the roster, and the Magistrate troops we hosted didn't come into contact with you. You could disappear a lot easier than Rein or me. Or Aquila for that matter. When we get to Gilga, we could find you another transport."

"No." Mina dropped her utensil, which clattered against her bowl. Aquila swiveled his head toward the noise, more alert than he'd been since leaving the *Aletheia*, though a sheen of sweat still clung to him. "I only have one person in my corner in the entire galaxy, and that's you. And I'm *never*"—she placed so much heat on the word—"going back to Reznic."

"No. I wouldn't send you back there. I have numerous brothers and sisters across the galaxy. There's also my father, though he's getting on in years." Katya rested her hand on Mina's. "I'm sure you could find a much safer place with one of them. Take up whatever studies interest you, or continue your pursuit of becoming a—"

"I'm staying."

Katya pressed her lips together but accepted Mina's decision. She wrapped some of the noodles around a fork Mina had passed her way and brought it up to Aquila's mouth. He timidly stuck out his tongue, touching the noodles before retracting it and hiding his face into her shoulder, blocking his mouth.

She sighed. "We definitely need to find something for this kid to eat." Katya brought the fork up to her mouth and ate the noodles before reverting back to her spoon. Aquila tightened his grip on her while drool crept out the corner of his mouth. "We'll find something for you. I promise."

Mina shoveled food into her mouth, muttering something around it. Once her bowl was cleared, she rose and tore through their food supplies.

"Be careful!" Katya called after Mina almost dropped a glass of Dersory cosel, a thick dairy product from a type of buffalo that'd spread across the galaxy. "How's Rein?"

Mina furrowed her brow as she twisted off the glass jar's lid. "Broody. Been barking orders at me like no tomorrow. You'd think I was enlisted. I don't think he's fond of being on the Magistrate's bad side."

"None of us are."

"Though I think he's more upset about our little Elite guest. He keeps talking about him under his breath." She dipped her finger into the cosel and pressed it to Aquila's mouth. He clamped down on it. "He seems to like it, or at least tolerate it."

"It's hardly healthy," Katya muttered while Mina filled a bowl of the sweet gelatinous substance for Aquila. "We'll have to keep an eye on Rein's moods." She tapped the bottom of her bowl with her spoon, slicing a noodle in two. "He was so close to citizenship . . . but I think for now, his self-preservation instincts will overrule his desire to return to the fold." But for how long?

Silence fell between them, allowing Katya to finish her meal while Mina fed Aquila. Both women raised their heads when Rein entered the mess hall.

"You're up," he said, appraising her out of the corner of his eye.

"I'm up," Katya replied. "Sorry to worry you, but yesterday was more taxing than I originally thought. I'll be resting over the next few days and will be back in order soon enough."

Grunting, Rein tilted the pan of bok before grabbing a spoon and eating out of it. "I trust Mina updated you on our status?" he asked between bites.

"Yes. You guys did well while I was out." Aquila's head fell back against Katya as he used her breast for a pillow, his eyes already drifting shut. Again? Her touch, like before, failed to rouse him.

"What are we going to do with him?" Rein dipped into the pan, eating another large portion of the leftover bok. He chewed in a loud manner that made her cringe.

"He stays with us. He has no other place to go. His family's dead, and the Magistrate played some role in it. There's no guarantee how Aquila would be treated if we handed him over." She stood, ignoring the pointed look Rein gave her at the name.

"He has Demos Oneiroi, Katya." Rein set the pan down, clanking it against the stovetop. "I doubt his people would be too pleased knowing he's in the care of off-worlders who know nothing about his needs."

"So we deliver him to Demos Oneiroi, a planet with restricted entry?" Katya asked, her tone shifting into something harder. "Or perhaps you want us to leave him in a lurch on some planet for his people to find? They probably think he died with the rest. It'd be more likely someone far worse would find him. You know all too well what happens to unattended children in the galaxy." Her gut tightened when her thoughts turned to Reznic's trafficking rings.

"I'm just saying we need to consider placing him somewhere that's not with us."

"Enlighten me. How do you propose we do that?"

Rein nudged his head toward Mina. "We could have Mina make the delivery —"

Katya made a spitting noise. "As if they wouldn't question her! A non-Oneiroi with one of their children: It would set off a lot of questions, and it'd quickly lead them to the *Aletheia*, the only situation where an Oneiroi child could have been compromised." She walked to the door. "Rein, this is our best option for now. Should something viable appear, I'll pursue it. But for now, I'm going to put him to bed and then go to the cockpit and fix our current money problems."

"Katya!"

She faced him.

"Reconsider this," he said, face drawn, ashen. At some point, he'd addressed his wound. "We know nothing for sure. We're just speculating, jumping to conclusions. Maybe if we approach the Magistrate—explained ourselves—there would be no repercussions."

Katya licked her lips and shifted the boy. It was possible, but the Breks had so quickly charged their weapons. Breathing in, she calmed her mind. Her uncle had ties high up in the Magistrate government. How high? Even now, as an adult, she was unsure. He'd simply been a looming figure through her childhood with whom her father had had a fractious relationship. The thought of approaching him, the ever-stern man with a limp, stirred up a sinking sensation. She trusted her father's instincts when it came to his own brother.

"Speculation can be worse," Katya said. "They don't want what happened on that ship known—they won't take chances." She pressed her lips together. "We stumbled across a mass grave, Rein. This ship—not just the boy—ties us to it. It's possible the Magistrate might turn a blind eye and accept us back for silence, but I don't see that happening: I see us vanishing. If you want to take the chance, you're welcome to stay on Gilga and approach the Brass."

Rein clenched his fists before exhaling and relaxing them. He shook his head. Katya waited, but after getting no further comment, she left. Behind the door, she heard Mina clearing dishes for the wash. Unease passed through her, lingering and gnawing at her. Distrust for Rein. While normally she was not fond of him, these feelings had a foreignness to them. She glanced down at the boy before striding to her cabin. The sensation would pass once *The Maelstrom* was behind them.

Backstories, repeated use of cover names, and Katya moving funds from her not-yet-locked account to a family account, where her money would hopefully go unnoticed, took up the hours prior to their arrival. In between periods of mandated resting, Katya had also browsed the information she'd gathered from the *Aletheia*'s computers. The Breks had introduced a virus to the system, which jumbled the data it had been in the process of deleting. Documents and sequences that had been untainted by it proved mundane. In the end, Katya had deleted it all as a precaution and run her virus scanner. The last thing she needed was for the virus to destroy her slate.

The groundwork laid, Katya joined Mina in the cockpit about two hours out. Katya sat slumped in the pilot's seat, resting her head in her hands. Around her, the gravity in the ship shifted—almost unnoticeably—the closer they came to their destination to match the planet's own. At Gilga's checkpoint, Katya took over the helm from the autopilot, bringing them closer to the planet, a white, blue, and rusty marble. Mostly water, snow, ice, and desolate. Thoughts of impending discomfort from the cold vanished when a Gilga port official barreled by them in a small craft right as they entered the planet's atmosphere.

"Mina, start blinking the lights. They'll understand." Katya switched over to the ACPS system designed for atmospheric flight. "Be prepared for bumps."

Mina beat out a coded pattern, which traveled to the front lights, the meaning simple: communications down.

The port officials then sent their own message: Follow. Officials will board. Katya did as directed. Next to her, Mina leaned forward—her eyes glued to the viewscreen, which was enlarged to show the exterior. They skimmed over the city of Kazeeme. Its buildings were well tended and built to keep out the cold, while the actual spaceport, positioned south of the city proper, was dusty, rust-colored, and worn. Katya swore there was not an ounce of green in sight, just metal, dirt, and lines of spaceships, but given the temperature, a balmy twenty-five degrees as shared by the viewscreen, it wasn't surprising. Mina shifted in her seat after their guide blinked for them to land in an open space.

"Why do they have to board?" Mina asked.

"Don't fret." Katya set the ship down and launched the shutdown sequence for all the systems—wrecking the navigation system's data along the way—while also opening the back hatch. "They want the registration. They'll input it into the Magistrate relay, adding to the slew of paperwork the cogs in the system already have to weed through. As long as the registration checks out, we'll be good to carry on our way." Standing, she waved Mina along. "We have to meet our guests."

By the time they reached the main level, a group of officials had entered the ship and were speaking with Rein, which caused Katya to stiffen. Their greeters wore Gilga insignias and colors, not the Magistrate's. As the space between them dwindled, she heard Rein explaining that their systems had been damaged after a blind jump to escape pirates.

"We don't have any weapons on board, except for small arms, all decommissioned military," Rein said.

The officials turned toward Katya and Mina upon noticing their approach.

Katya extended her hand, shaking each of theirs while making sure to meet their eyes as she did so. "I'm the captain of this vessel. Clementia. I heard my partner apprising you of our run-in. I've uploaded the registration onto my slate, but you're welcome to get it from our ship's systems if you prefer."

One of the officials, whose insignia noted his higher rank, grabbed the slate from her hands and inserted a plug. "What colors did the pirates fly?"

"Red and gold. They were av'Koett."

"So you were near the wormhole?"

"Yes."

A beep drew the official's attention back to his slate. After sliding his finger across the screen for several seconds, he cleared his throat. "We'll still need to examine your system. Registration information on slates can be forged easily."

"Of course. This way." Katya led them toward the engine room.

As they walked, the sound of their footsteps resounded against the metal hall—it reminded Katya of a funeral dirge.

"And what are your intentions on Gilga? Do you plan on leaving the spaceport?" The head official asked in a clipped tone. He fingered through the menus on his device.

"We need a new ship," Katya said and opened the door to the engine room. "We have a potential lead for work on Horgi, so we need to find a replacement quickly, or we're going to miss that opportunity."

"Ships don't come cheap," the official said. Meanwhile, his subordinates busied themselves, checking the ship's equipment. "How are you going to pay?"

"This ship's been on its way out since we bought her at auction. It's been an expected expense."

The official gave no response; instead, he plugged his slate into one of the computer consoles and pored over the registry information. Next to Katya, Mina fidgeted. Stepping forward, Katya blocked her protégé from sight, elbowing her ever so slightly as she did so. A spark emitted from one of the FTL consoles after a Gilga port official entered a few commands. The man muttered under his breath that the console was fried, and Katya restrained herself from cursing the man, who could have sparked a fire or worse.

A beep emitted from the head official's slate. "Registration clears," he said before waving to his subordinates. "The systems?"

"Most appear to have been fried in a jump," the idiot said. "Extremely lucky the life support and gravity controls didn't go."

The senior officer bobbed his head, swiping his pointed finger toward the door. His subordinates filed through it, leaving their commanding officer with Katya and Mina. "You have a week's clearance to remain in port. If you decide you need to enter the city or another area on Gilga, fill out the proper forms at the MGCD office. There is a four-week waiting period, during which you can attempt to extend your clearance."

"We don't intend to stay that long."

The official's gaze narrowed on her, and Katya clenched her jaw. A moment passed before—"I didn't expect your type to." He brushed past her.

Forcing her fists to relax, Katya smothered the burning comment that longed to fly off her tongue. The unspoken retort burned all the more with the knowledge she would have made the same assumptions. How many times had she contemned certain captains and their questionable ships, dismissing them as second rate or smugglers?

"I wasn't sure they were going to let us go," Mina said under her breath.

"Good thing that idiot almost blew us all up, huh? I think that convinced them to mosey on." She squeezed Mina's arm before she left the engine room and caught up with the officials in time to see them disembark. As they exited down the ramp, which Rein shut behind them, Katya exhaled, her shoulders sagging.

"*Hilaria*, get some warm clothes on. It's going to be frigid," Katya said.

"How frigid is frigid?" Mina scrunched her lips together, resembling a fish.

"You don't want to know." Katya approached the ladder to the ship's upper level. "Just trust me: You'll want as many layers as possible."

Katya entered her own room to prepare herself as best as she could. Unfortunately, the majority of her warmer clothes had been Magistrate issued, so she'd hatched them all. Digging around her room, Katya scrounged up a purple knitted sweater her sister had sent from her own private label, claiming it would show off her figure; she'd never tested that—well, just the once. Frowning, she tugged on the garment and then a light jacket, which was better than nothing.

"Now you." She lifted Aquila, wrapped him in a blanket, and deposited him into the carrier. "Once again, I'm sorry I can't do better." His head drooped against her shoulder. "We'll get a ship and then find a doctor for you." The ship had to come first; it'd be their only shot at survival.

Aquila's weight against her back proved oddly reassuring as she returned to the main level of *The Maelstrom*. There Rein waited in a heavy sweater.

"Most of your gear Magistrate issued too?" she asked.

"Yes, but I'll be fine." He nudged his head toward the boy. "Do we have to bring him? It's going to be nothing but trouble."

"Nothing but trouble, eh? All he's done since he's come on board is sleep." They both glanced toward Mina, who was descending to the main level. "Besides, he needs clothes, and I'd rather make sure they fit."

The closer Mina came, the louder her mutterings grew, about the cold, about her added layers hindering her movements.

"Just be grateful you have those layers," Katya shouted over the grinding mechanisms that lowered the ramp upon Rein putting in the code.

A gust of cold air beat against Katya's face, causing her looped braids to flop about. It also cut straight through her jacket and sweater, eliciting a shudder.

"All right, everyone, keep your heads down and ears open." She led the way down into the spaceport. Her feet were met by frozen soil. "Ferrutius, start walking the eastern portion of the spaceport and inquire about spacecrafts for sale. Hilaria and I will do likewise on the western half." She raised her jacket's collar.

"Are you sure splitting up is a good idea?" Rein asked.

"We need something quick, and it's good to play the field." Katya scrunched her nose against the heavy smell of oil and exhaust. Around them, crowds moved through the narrow aisles created by spacecrafts. "We'll keep in touch via our coms."

"Are you sure you two will be fine?" Rein pressed. "This place is rough—there are all sorts."

"There were all sorts on Reznic. And I was just as much in the thick of it as you were. Besides . . ." Katya pulled back her jacket, revealing her service pistol. "We'll be fine."

Rein muttered under his breath, then more plainly, "Suit yourselves."

As Katya and Mina walked away, she made out his go-to: "confounded woman" in Reznic. Though, that was too polite of a translation. The hustle and bustle of the spaceport drowned out any remaining Reznic profanities. Shouts echoed while crews worked on their spacecrafts or blew off steam with various sports, one involving various-sized sticks and hover balls. Merchants also barked about their wares, trying to draw travelers to their booths, or in most cases, their ramps, which had been transformed into impromptu marketplaces. The smell of food tickled Katya's nose, some of it nauseating her stomach while other options aroused hunger.

The entire port, like most planetary spaceports, had been encapsulated by towering walls, separating the city from visitors. Keeping the riffraff out from the citizenry. Katya shoved her hands into her pockets. As a secondary purpose, it allowed for detailed collections of information on who went where and when.

Katya sidestepped a woman hawking a type of fish. Her scraggly gray hair flew every which way as she screeched and waved the fish in the air. "Five *bit vars*! Five *bit vars*!" Next to Katya, Mina flinched and stepped into her, seeking shelter. Even Aquila stirred. Pulling the blanket further over his head, Katya guaranteed his face was concealed, hopefully along with his talents. The last thing they needed was an overzealous fish huckster triggering them. He wiggled against her, struggling to free himself. After they were a safe distance, she allowed the blanket to drift away.

Katya reached back and carded his hair. Dry. The sweat that had hung to him was gone. The colder temperature. Perhaps, it had not been the failing life support systems that had caused the *Aletheia* to be so frigid. Oneiroi can't tolerate warm temperatures, huh? A massive flaw in one of the Magistrate's most-prized Elites. They'd hidden it well.

"There's a hotel." Mina tugged at Katya's sleeve, pointing at the establishment, which had been crafted from white brick. "They actually have hotels in a spaceport?"

"They're for merchants who are waiting for approval to enter the city or for travelers waiting for their next transport," she answered. She fell silent when a peace officer strode by wearing Magistrate colors rather than those of Gilga. He didn't give them a second glance. "Let's go this way." Katya grabbed the teen's mitten-covered hand to prevent her from walking into a ball-jointed automaton, which wouldn't have deviated from its intended path. "We'll speak with some of the captains and see if we can get any information about anyone looking to sell."

They meandered closer to the rows of starships yet remained out of the way of crews loading cargo and supplies. A few ships sat unattended, their crews no doubt enjoying time off. After several rows, the pair came across a group of men, all humanoid, who had set up a card game using a crate as a table. Their interest in the game didn't waver, not even when the two women approached. Now closer, her previous summation that they were humanoid proved wrong: Their skin was actually fine scales, smooth and nonexistent at a distance. But more importantly, their clothing didn't bear the slightest trappings of the Magistrate. One of them grumbled before slamming his cards face down on the crate. He stood, cursing—or so Katya assumed from its harshness. The others hurled a few words themselves, a couple of them waving him away, while another spat at him.

Katya undid the carrier and handed Aquila over to Mina; the boy squeaked as he changed hands. "I see you have an open seat." Katya stepped closer to the table. "What's the game?"

The remaining three men turned to each other before breaking out into that language, and then the one at the far end of the crate spoke. "For'geev a, ma'am. We aire not uz twa"—the man sighed and waved his hand through the air, making an almost 'S'—"yer ton-ed. Dradorian?"

Katya shook her head. "I don't speak Dradorian. But I doubt we need words to play." She smiled and took the absent seat. "This is troggen?"

A forked tongue poked out between the man's lips. "Eet iz."

Next to him, another Dradorian shuffled the deck and dealt the cards. As players received the cards, they tossed in *monetas*, Magistrate hard currency. The man to Katya's left threw in some more of the coins; the one who had spoken did likewise while also adding to the pot. Finally, the last man dropped his cards.

"Whass ma'am du?" the man—the only one capable of Magistrate tongue, or so it seemed—asked.

Katya removed the required coins from her pocket and settled them on the crate, adding three additional coins, certain her colors would carry the game. The remaining two in the game saw her addition with the talker adding even more coins. Katya saw his raise while the other man folded.

Her opponent laid down his cards before flipping them over one at a time, displaying Magistrate blues and a few blacks. She then laid out hers—all blues with patriarchs composing the majority.

The men around the table bristled, talking in their tongue—much like hornets who'd had their nest kicked—as Katya brought the chips toward her.

She paused. "I could share my wealth. I just need information: Is anyone here"—she gestured around to port—"selling their vessel?"

They glanced at each other and consulted. Finally, the one flicked out his tongue, brushing it against his upper lip before returning it to his mouth. "Ves ays, ze Vanderer rader. C-block, weny-feevs. Cap'vin Verrse-vo."

"Thank you," Katya said. She took some of the winnings—double what she'd put down—and left the rest. Returning to Mina, she reattached the carrier to her back before she pulled out her com and activated it. "Ferrutius, I have a prospect. Meet me at C-block, space twenty-five. I'm unsure on the name, but the ship is owned by a Captain Verrse-vo . . . the pronunciation might be off."

"On my way."

"What type of ship do you think it will be?" Mina asked.

"It could be anything." Katya glanced at Aquila, who had fallen back asleep, head lolling against her shoulder blade. The lower temperature, however, did have a positive effect on him. This marked the longest he'd been able to stay awake since they'd found him. A group of Magistrate workers headed in their direction, and Katya concealed the boy's face before grabbing Mina's arm. "We need to meet Ferrutius. Let's hurry."

Mina pressed her lips together, all the while following the path of the Magistrate workers with her eyes. She only faced forward when Katya tugged her arm. "They aren't after us yet, so act normal. Besides, we need to hurry and get our ticket out of here, don't you think?"

CHAPTER FIVE

The pair ran into Rein in D-Block. He rubbed his glove-encased hands together in an attempt to stay warm. As they approached, he removed a second pair, slimmer, more feminine. He thrust them into Katya's hands. "I thought you could use them." He averted his gaze. "Now, what are we looking at?"

Katya fingered the leather before she slipped them on, her fingers welcoming fuzzy interior and the protection from the cold. She ignored the smirk on Mina's face.

"Thank you. And it's hard to say at this point. My sources didn't exactly speak proper Magistrate."

He grunted in response.

"Don't worry." She motioned for him to follow her and Mina. "It doesn't hurt to peek. If it doesn't pan out, all we're out is time and a few extra steps."

They rounded the corner and entered C-Block, which was dominated by merchant ships and marked by blue pylons. Katya readjusted her jacket's collar. It boded well. A good freighter would do the trick.

Farther down, they came upon a small D-Class Garni freighter; ships of that make had earned the nickname "Badgers" for their ruggedness and surprising amount of firepower, though they couldn't compete with larger or more maneuverable vessels, nor would they win any races. Marked as *The Wandering Trader*, red lines ran down its sides until they formed a circle around an emblem—a stylized badger with bags on its back—and the ship's name. It appeared to be in good shape, but exteriors were often misleading, especially when dealing with a spacecraft's many systems and miles of wiring.

"Let's see if we can find the captain." Katya brought out her com. After shuffling through the frequencies, she arrived at one with the matching serial number in its description. "Captain Verrse-go?" She spoke into the microphone.

"It's Whereego." Static followed and then a crackled: "Who is this?"

"Clementia. I'm the captain of a ship called *Royal Justice*. I hear you want to leave the business. I have a proposition for you."

A moment's silence was followed by the boarding ramp lowering; a fur-covered humanoid male stood at the top, wearing baggy spacer garb with a series of pockets dotting his pants and vest. "What type of proposition are you suggesting?" His yellow eyes examined them with a mixture of amusement and curiosity upon their approach. His posture slackened.

"Rumor has it you want to move on to different enterprises," Katya said. "We require a new ship. Ours had an encounter with pirates recently—it's little more than scrap now. Given our situations, perhaps we can come to terms that are mutually beneficial."

"Come, come!" He swiveled on his feet, which were exposed, revealing six splayed toes, and reentered the vessel. "I'm getting far too old for this line of work," he continued as they followed. "It's funny. You start life striving to go far from home, but as you approach your end, you long for nothing but to return. Then again, all Michzes are overtaken by the longing . . . it also makes us ramble with strangers, it would seem." He chuckled into his hand, which had six long appendages. Various patterns dotted his coat, though his markings were not the bold red commonly associated with the species; no, his had dulled, taking on more of a rust-colored shade.

"You'll find her in good working order." Whereego pointed out several of the ship's features and made other small talk along the way while guiding them through the corridors—all clean and oddly vacant, no sign of cargo having been there for quite some time. "I purchased her four years ago," he said. "Never had a problem with her, just minor kinks that were easily sorted out."

"What about your crew?" Rein quirked an eyebrow. "None of them wanted to take over?"

Katya tilted her head to better see the captain. A common practice was for the crew to purchase ships and routes once a captain decided to give up the title; it was that or a family member would take over command.

"The last one left a year ago," Whereego said, a little wheeze evident as he did. "I had curtailed our cargo runs. In the end, he couldn't stand serving under a Michze with a homebound itch." He waved toward the end of the hall. "The mess hall is down here. We can discuss the details there after we complete the tour. Though, while we are by it, we'll just peek in. Of course, your mechanic can go over the ship. I have nothing to hide. I've lost my drive, my passion."

They entered the mess hall, which was bigger than the one on *The Maelstrom*, though not by much. It lacked the trappings of the Magistrate with its strict, uncomfortable floor plans. The designers at Garni had actually considered the living, breathing occupants of the vessel. Next to her, Mina's eyes grew to the size of saucers, no doubt imagining what the added counter space would do for her food prep. A small smile tugged at Katya's mouth; she had never expected the Reznic girl to be so taken with cooking, yet she had embraced it, molding it into her niche.

Whereego grinned. "The Badgers are known for decent mess halls. There's still plenty of space for cargo; however, the crew quarters are marginally smaller than some of the bigger classes. Now, if you'll follow me this way . . ."

The crew rooms weren't far from the mess hall—five total, three sharing a bathroom. Each room held a bed with storage compartments built in beneath, giving enough room to store clothes and other possessions. The captain's quarters were marginally larger and had a small sitting area. Its bathroom, however, proved as cramped as Katya's old one.

"It may be a challenge with the little one," the man said. He leaned forward, hoping to get a glimpse, but the blanket held firm.

"It's actually a step up from our old ship," she responded.

Their guide then took them to the cockpit, which appeared well kept with no signs of mess or tampered consoles. Rein and Katya spent a long span of time inspecting each station, opening the panels to check on chips, wiring, and other mechanical components—all appearing in good order. Next, they checked every inch of the engine room while Whereego and Mina, who had been regulated to Aquila duty, looked on.

"Does it meet your approval?" Whereego asked when they closed up panels.

"It seems to be in order." Rein stood after closing a low panel.

Katya nodded. "How much will you take for her?"

Whereego clasped his hands together. "320,500 *aurum*."

"I can give you 250,000 and the registration to the *Royal Justice*. I imagine the difference can be made up with its scrap. It is a decommissioned Boita D-Class."

Whereego tilted his head, undoubtedly calculating the value of said scrap. "Let's make it 280,000 *aurum* and the profits received from scrapping your ship."

Katya bit the inner corner of her mouth. It'd be tight. There would be no choice but to accept odd jobs to scrape by. Loosening her jaw, Katya extended her hand, which Whereego engulfed within his own. His fur warmed her through the gloves.

"She is yours then," he said while shaking her hand vigorously. "How long until we can do the trade?"

From her jacket's pocket, Katya removed her slate. "We can transfer the funds now and complete the registrations in a few hours. My crew needs to get supplies before we depart for Horgi."

"Good! It gives me time to book transport home."

Whereego brought out his own slate and connected it to Katya's. The transfer went without a hitch. With any luck, the Michze wouldn't meet any consequences from having dealt with them. Her throat constricted as she secured her slate back into her pocket and left *The Wandering Trader* with her crew.

On the outside, Rein returned to *The Maelstrom* to prep their gear to be moved while Katya, Aquila, and Mina went to procure supplies, which meant leaving the rows of tightly packed spaceships and entering the northern and pedestrian-only section of the port. The dirt path transitioned to brick. Shops lined it, packed so closely they resembled books on a shelf. Smaller stands had been set up in what openings they could find; their hucksters brayed about their wares. One woman sprayed perfume into Mina's and Katya's faces. They coughed and hacked as the odor overpowered their senses. Aquila jolted awake, pushing every which way against the sling to escape the lingering fumes.

"The nerve of some people," Mina said around coughs. They darted away from the woman, who had already selected her next targets to spread her "tropical oasis" to.

"Yep." Meanwhile, Aquila continued to sputter into her shoulder, his chin pressing into it as he did so. "Let's stay to the center of the path . . . we can use other travelers as shields."

"Ah!" Mina grabbed Katya's arm and dragged her toward a shop, rightly named the Pink Cloud Boutique. The color bled everywhere. Even the door was pink. Katya stuttered her complaints, but Mina turned, her lower lip sticking out, quivering even. "Please?"

Sighing, she dropped her head in defeat and allowed Mina to tow her into the establishment. Despite the pink storefront and displays, clothes of different colors actually existed, though they were in the minority. Mina tore through the racks, holding up a few articles, keeping some on the crook of her arm while returning others until satisfied with her clutch.

Then she turned on Katya, holding up tops to her before squinting and turning her head at odd angles. "Perfect! You needed new clothes anyway, so just let me" — she draped the olive top over Katya's shoulder and then went about finding others — "help."

When her arms began to buckle, Katya cleared her throat. "Mina, we don't have time to try all these! We need to get supplies more necessary to our survival than clothing."

Mina pouted. "You never treat yourself."

Katya chuckled. "People have very different ideas of treating themselves. Mine is not clothes —"

"Please!" Mina loomed on her tiptoes, her face now quite close to Katya's.

Dumping the jumbled mess of clothes into the dressing room, Katya swung off the carry, handing off Aquila to Mina. She shut the door and then threw on each piece of clothing, checking fit with barely a glance to the mirror. From the other side, Mina tossed over a teal, fitted long-sleeved shirt and a brown leather vest, stating something about the color going well with her gray eyes.

"I have enough, Mina!" Katya exited the dressing room, stopping Mina from tossing over more clothing. "These will do fine."

"Did you even look at them while they were on?"

"Yes." Katya bypassed Mina and deposited her pick of the original pile on the checkout counter.

Mina came alongside her with another pile. "I figured we should get him some clothes too."

Katya raised an eyebrow, impressed she'd found non-gaudy clothes for the boy. Her brow furrowed when the girl added, "And I picked a few for myself."

"I can see." Katya pried her slate from its pocket and paid. As they exited the shop, she muttered, "No more frivolous purchases. From now on, we stick to the list of necessary supplies."

Mina clicked her tongue against her teeth. "When we get a job, we should do this again. And who knows, maybe next time you'll actually enjoy it. You—"

A loud gong-like clang beckoned those in the area to a general information console. Katya frowned. A special Magistrate news report shot out and circulated above the pigmented holo-projector. The red banner gradually dispersed, with two women newscasters taking its place. Below them, bars containing the official five languages in Magistrate space rotated underneath them. The newscasters themselves spoke in the Magistrate dialect, or rather a watered-down variety only found in media.

"Plasovern has struck again," the woman with her hair in a bun said. Her tone was as unwavering as her facial expression. Katya smiled, one corner higher than the other. Most Magistrate newscasters, if not all, maintained the same guarded expression. "A Plasovern warship entered into the neutral zone, containing armaments previously believed to be beyond the terrorist organization's capabilities."

Next to her, her co-worker with clipped hair picked up where she had left off: "According to Magistrate peacekeeping ship *Bargerr*, these armaments appear to have been given to a rogue band of the terrorist group by the Medzeci System of Planets. The Medzeci System, also known as the Medzeci Empire, is a known sympathizer of these Magistrate traitors and has provided supplies and weapons in the past."

Katya ran a finger along the seam of one leather glove, watching the play unfold before her. Her eyes strayed from the projection to scan the crowd for any uniforms. She only found common people, but given the right incentive, they were more than capable of tearing anyone apart. Flash an image of Rein or her on the screen alongside the right amount of *aurum*, and pandemonium would ensue.

"This incursion into Magistrate space has already produced casualties," her counterpart resumed. "*Bargerr* has reported that the Oneiroi peacekeeping vessel *Aletheia* was attacked by the Plasovern. During the encounter, the vessel was completely destroyed."

Katya's chest tightened. The crowd around her was too close. An image of the Oneiroi vessel, whole and in its prime, flashed onto the screen.

"There are no reported survivors," she continued. "Magistrate officials believe the *Aletheia* was targeted for its extremely valuable cargo. Plasovern agents are suspected of boarding the ship and removing this cargo prior to destroying the peacekeeping vessel."

"Travelers should remain on high alert, particularly in the outer regions of Magistrate space known as the Fringe. All Magistrate citizens must remain vigilant and report any Plasovern vessels to the proper authorities," the short-haired one said.

"Do not try to reason with terrorists or confront them," the first speaker concluded. "Remember the *Aletheia*'s fate."

Katya tugged Mina away from the frenzied crowd. "I can't believe Plasovern could take out an Oneiroi vessel," one voice among many uttered as Katya and Mina slipped from the mass of people. A layer of panic hung in the air while they conversed among themselves. Gilga, after all, was a Fringe planet, closer to Medzeci than to the core Magistrate planets. Once they were farther down the promenade, Katya released Mina from her grip.

"Walk fast," she said. "We're finishing our shopping and leaving this world." Before any newscaster could divulge information on *The Maelstrom* or its crew.

"The newscast was wrong." Mina stopped.

"Keep walking and talk quietly." After they passed a few storefronts, Katya continued, "It shouldn't surprise you. Why not use the situation to fan the flames of patriotism? It reminds people to be afraid of Medzeci and Plasovern." Katya glanced over her shoulder. "There are still so many things I don't understand. Why was the *Aletheia* so far from its previous location and its intended destination? What cargo was it carrying?"

"Maybe we shouldn't ask those questions." Rustling followed as Mina moved her bags to the other hand. Aquila shifted in his carrier at the movement.

"We might as well. We've already been lugged into this mess. If the Breks had recorded some deterrent on that beacon . . . no, if I hadn't let my curiosity get the better of me, we wouldn't be in this mess."

Mina scrunched her lips. "Then what sort of mess would Aquila be in?"

Pride swelled in Katya's chest. Despite her world being turned upside down, Mina still considered the sole survivor of their ill-fated rescue mission—though the girl had always proven resilient and flexible in a way she envied. The boy slept, his face embedded against Mina's shoulder, unaware that he was now the topic of conversation. Likely he'd be dead; however, a quick death might have been better than what they had offered him so far.

"I imagine not a good one."

Several blocks from the crowd, they reached a broad service mercantile, which offered a variety of items from bulk food supplies to bedding products, even replacement sinks for a variety of spacecrafts.

"Let's try here," Katya said, opening the door and entering.

"Wow!" Mina swiveled about, her eyes darting between all the shelves and displays. "We didn't have stuff like this on Reznic."

"Trust me, Reznic had comparable shops . . . just not on the lower levels."

"Ah, those types of stores." Mina reached out to touch a shiny kettle. "The kind for the rich, huh?" She then held up the kettle. "Can I get this?"

Katya rolled her eyes and took a few steps away. "Why not? It can fit in with the clothing, category frivolous purchases."

Mina inspected several other items that caught her fancy, like a moth attracted to flame. Katya said no to the majority of them. They continued down the rows. As they reached the food aisle, she took Aquila from Mina. Now, how to do this without causing a scene? She nudged Aquila with her hand to attempt rousing him. He didn't exit his dreams if he even had them.

Next to her, Mina rattled a large canister of dried beans, drawing a scowl from Katya. "So, how are we going to find what he fancies without—well—looking like we kidnapped him and now have no idea how to feed him?"

"That's why"—she pointed to the empty spot where the beans had come from—"I was hoping to wake him and see what food he reacts positively to."

A smirk spreading across her face, Mina shook the jar beside Aquila's ear.

Nothing.

Sighing with the dramatic flair of a teenager, she returned the beans as directed. "I say we just grab a bunch of random stuff. One of them's bound to work. Besides, I'm not against trying to cook some of this"—she fingered a jar filled with a pinkish goo—"er, exotic cuisine. What you suppose this is?"

"It's Darr," a store clerk said, ambling down the aisle with a cart filled with boxes and jars containing food. "Bulk orders can be placed at the counter. There are options to order based on species and dietary needs."

"Thank you." Katya caught Mina's arm with her free hand and escorted her and the kettle to the front counter. More people had walked in, a few wearing Magistrate insignias. Mina stepped closer to her and adjusted the blanket to better cover Aquila's face.

"Can I help you?" the man behind the counter asked. "My store has everything you could want." He handed a clipboard to them. "Bulk orders are made through these forms and delivered as soon as they can be filled."

Katya leaned over Mina's shoulder, pointing to the options that she wanted checked. Mina still snuck on a few extra items to their order. Rolling her eyes, Katya wondered if the teen even knew what half of them were. Poisonous or not to humans, Mina would attempt to cook them all the same.

Katya passed the bags containing their clothing to Mina, leaving Aquila in his carrier on her back. With her arms free, she removed some check marks—garnering a pout from the teen—before signing off. Under miscellaneous requests, she added a toddler bed. "We'll also need a toddler bed delivered."

"That can be arranged—oh my, what interesting eyes."

Her face chilled when she saw Aquila. He was awake, with his large pale blue eyes—squinted against the light—darting over his surroundings before settling on the shopkeeper. The man stiffened. Katya willed her facial muscles not to flinch, though she knew she had paled, her lips far too cold. In the background, each and every Magistrate presence in the shop glared at her. They could descend on them in a second. All they needed was one word. A tremor shot up her legs when she met the shopkeeper's gaze. There was understanding there, an understanding that said he knew exactly what Katya had against her back.

"He takes after his father," Katya said after the silence lingered. "H-he's no longer with us."

The shopkeeper didn't blink, almost as if daring her to do so first. His attention only broke when Katya nudged the clipboard toward him. Lifting it, he scanned their order, taking his time, calculating the sum. When he finished, he smiled.

"That's a shame." The man lingered on the final word. He had rather sharp canines that might have been chiseled to points. "Will you be paying up-front?"

"On a time-hold basis," Katya said. "Supplies scanned at our ship. You'll receive your payment and a little extra . . . for your excellent service. Our location and ship are on the order form."

The shopkeeper licked his lips, letting the silence hang between them. A few more seconds passed before the man nodded his head. "Expect your order in a couple of hours."

"Good." She nudged Mina into step with her, taking her own bag of clothes from the teen. As they headed toward the door, her spare hand pressed Aquila's face against her shoulder.

Keep walking.

She fought her urge to peek around her shoulder.

Straight ahead, pick up your pace.

The door shut behind them. It did not reopen. Retracing their path to the ship, she gave in to paranoia and glanced behind. No uniforms. Her heart, however, didn't settle.

"What's going on?" Mina asked after a few blocks. "What's a time-hold basis?"

"It's to prevent him from getting two paychecks without having to lose one—in this case, our order." Katya ground her teeth together. "He's had some contact with the Oneiroi. He knew exactly what Aquila was." Mina skidded to a stop, but Katya caught her arm and whisked her onward. "There's no time to dawdle. Stay alert and listen. We're going to step up our movements, get things moved over, and then, when the supplies arrive, toss them aboard and leave."

"What if he has Magistrate forces waiting—"

"He won't. The Magistrate doesn't wait, not for a man to make a profit off traitors. He'll wait to report us until he has our funds. The bribe might get us a few extra minutes, but not much. We'll have to change our destination to buy time." Katya maneuvered her hand until she had a firm grip of her com. "Ferrutius? How's the transition progressing?"

"Everything's off the *Royal Justice*. Currently, working on loading everything into the cargo hold of our new vessel."

"We'll be there momentarily to help." Katya paused. "We *need* to hurry."

"What happened?" his voice cracked over the speaker.

"I'm afraid one of the merchants might know what I'm carrying."

Static. Katya imagined he was probably cursing and hitting—or stomping on—something. Then in a level voice, he said, "We'll be ready to leave in an hour, barring Magistrate bureaucracy and its red tape."

Within fifteen minutes, they arrived at *The Wandering Trader*; boxes were stacked in front of its ramp. The freighter that had been parked next to their new vessel had left; however, most of its other surroundings remained the same. Rein rushed down the ramp and gave *The Maelstrom's* registration chip to Katya. "You can hand this over to Whereego. He's already moved his personal belongings to a hotel."

Katya set her bag of clothes on a crate. "Mina, help Rein." She then surmounted the ramp.

She found Whereego outside of the captain's quarters, where he stood stonily peering into the room that had been his home for four years. He only turned when Katya stood next to him.

"I believe I have everything." He scratched his furry chin.

"Are you having regrets?" she asked.

"No. I'm going home."

Whereego reached into his pocket and removed a registration chip. Katya did likewise with *The Maelstrom's* doctored chip, handing it to him. Several screens popped up after he used a special scanner on his slate to read both of them. Whereego completed several questions about the transaction before he signed a digital document.

"Your turn." He handed the slate to Katya.

She signed with her assumed name. Her jaw tensed when the transfer went for certification. As minutes passed, her stomach clenched.

It's normal, she soothed. They'd need at least two reviews, probably more. Yet with each minute, their fraud could be uncovered. The Magistrate cog pushers, as they were fondly called, could dig too far, past what she'd been able to forge—

"These things take a while," Whereego said. "Transfers always take the most time. The Magistrate and its paperwork, eh? There's a form for everything."

A loud beeping brought their attention back to the slate and the chips. "The transfer has been confirmed. She's all yours." His teeth poked out around his lips as he offered her *The Wandering Trader's* registration chip. "Best of luck to you, your child, and crew. May she serve you as well as she has me."

"Thank you." Katya shook his hand one more time before Whereego tipped his head to her and left the vessel, one last bag in his hand.

Left alone, Katya entered her new quarters and set Aquila down on the bed. He rolled himself onto his belly, his eyes following her as she went to the door.

"I'll be back before you know it." He might not understand a single word coming out of her mouth, but Katya hoped the sound would be reassuring. Then his head lulled to the side, connecting with the mattress. Her lips parting, Katya crossed the room and placed the child on his back while her fingers sought a pulse. It beat steadily, and her own heart quieted slightly from its accelerated pace.

"Something's very wrong with you," Katya whispered. She draped her jacket over him before adjusting the room's temperature and making it cooler.

Katya lingered a little longer before leaving to help the others load their belongings. The task proved challenging with only the three of them; however, the equipment Rein had rented helped. The hovercart, in particular, was money well spent, easing what would have been backbreaking work. As the last boxes were secured in the hold for them to sort through later, Katya headed to the cockpit to acquaint herself with the controls while they waited for the supplies to come, if they ever did.

No codes were needed to enter the cockpit, a major plus. Its interior, though, presented another challenge, featuring new technology that would require practice to gain familiarity with. She powered on her slate, and for the next few minutes, she studied the Badger's schematics, which had been downloaded upon the registration transfer.

"Should be easy enough." Katya coordinated the features highlighted in the schematics with the ones in front of her. A half hour had passed, according to the time displayed on the slate. *What's taking them so long?*

"Such interesting eyes."

Katya clicked her tongue against her front teeth and flicked one of her looped braids back.

Hours dragged by, leaving her to reread the approval notice that allowed their departure and approved their submitted flight plan. They wouldn't go to Horgi—the risk was too great. They would be diverted to somewhere else, continue moving cargo, eventually fading into the Fringe like so many crews before them. The backwaters of Magistrate space would be their salvation.

She tapped the metal portion of the pilot's console. There was no ticking—it was hard to find a clock that did nowadays—but she could feel it, the steady progression of time; it ingrained itself in her head. The shopkeeper's words, his facial expression . . . they all—

"Katya!" Mina burst into the cockpit. "A Magistrate ship's landed next to us!"

"Its name?"

"*The Bogwharf.*"

Katya wrote the name into her slate, and the sight of a small peacekeeping vessel with no posted mission greeted her. The color drained from her face. Standing, she walked to the cargo hold and ramp.

"Got anything on it?" Rein asked in a hushed tone when she paused next to him on the ramp.

"Small peacekeeper." What they were doing in the port's trade section remained to be seen.

On the outside, the crew of *The Bogwharf* disembarked, several carrying duffle bags. They, largely officers by their insignias, sauntered toward the shopping district, or maybe to the city itself. The regular crew remained behind, unloading crates from the cargo hold. Their languid motions demonstrated no signs of haste.

"They seem harmless," she said. "Just docking at the next port." She straightened as a Neravah hover carrier, complete with an open bed, rambled toward them. "Ah! Here come our supplies. Not a moment too soon."

Katya and Rein stepped down the ramp and waited for the vehicle to stop. Once it did and its driver stepped out, Katya completed the transaction. The supplies were then quickly loaded. Mina joined in at one point, streamlining the process; however, they focused on loading, not storing their purchases. That'd wait until they were en route to whatever L Class planet—capable of sustaining oxygen breathers—their navigation console produced. As soon as they had finished, Katya locked up shop. Several clinks followed as the ramp's locking mechanisms fastened into place.

"Let's get off-world. Rein, give the engine room a watch and familiarize yourself with it."

He stiffened at the order, lines hardening on his face. He opened his mouth while Katya tensed. Nothing was said, and Rein left.

Katya remained rooted. "Mina, check on Aquila and make sure you give him some of the RMP; we'll make the jump once we clear the planet's atmosphere, so take care of yours as well."

"Sure."

While Katya went to the cockpit, the teen vanished into her quarters. She sat in the captain's chair, relishing the cushioning. Still enough fluff. She would be able to leave her own imprint, unlike the seat on *The Maelstrom*. Katya flipped several buttons on the control panel, and the ship breathed to life.

"This is *The Wandering Trader*," Katya spoke into the communications system attached to the pilot console, "requesting permission to leave."

"Permission granted."

Katya activated the thrusters after popping her own RMP pill. The ship shot upward, following the beacons that directed it past the atmosphere. The grayish sky of Gilga bled to black, with stars coming to surround them. Once clear of the planet's atmosphere, Katya brought the craft farther out.

"Prepare for jump in three . . . two . . . one . . ." Katya said over the ship's intercom. "Punching it now."

There were no calls for more time, so the jump continued. Her stomach churned before the effects of the sudden celerity lessened, the pill taking effect. "And off we go." She programmed in a course to a metro Fringe world and set the autopilot before leaving for her quarters.

It was a novelty to walk through a hallway rather than on a loud catwalk to get there. Civilians knew how to travel. She put in the code to the doorway and entered.

Inside, Mina sat hunched with a blanket wrapped around her body.

"How's our littlest traveler?" Katya asked.

She leaned over him. With the climate change, Aquila, while still pallid, no longer bore stress lines or a layer of sweat. "I'll have to keep this room chillier," she said. "Apparently, Oneiroi can't handle heat. I'll have to make do with warmer clothing and blankets."

Mina got her body under control and stood raggedly. "I'll be in my room with the heat cranked all the way up."

"Don't roast yourself." Katya slumped on the bed next to Aquila. "I'll worry about getting his bed together after a nap." She lifted her jacket off him and flung on a light blanket that Mina had pulled from one of the boxes that had made its way to her room. "Mina, get some rest. I have the ship on auto, and it's set to alert us to any problems."

"Good." Mina clenched her blanket tighter. "I'm going to nap like a pro."

She shuffled from the room, leaving Katya alone with the boy.

Humming, Katya tucked the blanket under his sides. Could he even feel cold? She carded his hair. He was a mammal, so likely there was a threshold. Trial and error. "Not how I like to do things," she told him. "I . . . prefer things to be more precise." A wave of fatigue and nausea cascaded over her.

Katya slumped over and waited for it to pass. Grabbing her head, she steadied her breaths, willing herself not to throw up. After several moments, the urge departed. It took longer to pry herself off the bed and to the collection of boxes that littered her floor. She opened them one by one until she found a pair of non-constricting pants and a loose shirt. She put them on before staggering back to the bed, which she crawled into. Twisting around, she found it lumpy with a dipping center.

"It's my turn next for a new bed . . ." Sheer tiredness struck again, and something resembling a needle penetrated her head. Groaning, she rolled onto her side, vertigo following the motion. The boy remained asleep, his head tilted toward her.

Grunting, Katya massaged her forehead as several more prickles formed behind her skull, like little ants burrowing in. It spread outward from the temples, proving all-encompassing. Her limbs grew lighter, almost foreign to her. She grimaced. Next to her, Aquila's eyelids moved rapidly. She reached out and brushed aside a stray lock of hair; some of the prickles lessened.

"I don't know much about your people, but I think whatever their ability is . . . you're using it." She opened her mouth to say something further, but instead, her head slumped against the pillow.

CHAPTER SIX

-Three years prior-

A breeze brushed against Akakios's cheek, rustling his short black hair. Gripping the balcony's heavy metal railing, he inhaled Demos Oneiroi's frigid air. Crisp, untainted. Not a single planet he'd been on could make such a claim. Below, snow rolled along the dips and craggy face of the mountains and valley floor as the wind pushed it. Warmth radiated throughout his body as he bathed in the moment. Oh, to finally be home.

Still, the planet's unforgiving environment would kill him given an extended length of exposure. Already, its chill cut through to his clothes and body, especially at this hour of the evening when what little sun they received was cloaked by Demos Oneiroi's ever-present umbra. After so many dry, hot, bright, or otherwise inclement planets, he relished the life-endangering cold and darkness. He'd been gone too long, and none of the planets he'd been forced to live on had come close to rivaling his homeworld.

Exhaling, he sought to allay the turning of his stomach with the steady cadence of his breath. His hands clenched the railing. Any other matter. Any other matter . . . he would have rather returned for anything but this. The wind gusted while overhead the skies darkened further, promising an impending snowstorm. His hands ached. Why did Sotiris have to be born with the defect? As the breeze shifted to a swift burst, Akakios knew he couldn't dally longer, not unless he wanted to freeze to death.

"Why are you out here?"

Akakios released the rail and faced his younger brother, Amyntas. "I missed this." His hand swept outward toward the scenery behind him. "We all haven't had a wife on maternity leave."

Amyntas pressed his lips together. "Are you upset for that reason?"

Little tendrils wormed into Akakios's mind. He chuckled and pushed back against his brother's intrusion. It reminded him of their childhood, the constant prying and overshare that came from their mental abilities, the primary means of communication until age eight when verbal language supplemented it.

<Nosy.> Akakios sent back through the channel, even though it took the form of a sensation rather than words. Then aloud, he said, "I'm fine without a wife, especially in my line of work. And if the Agoranomi and Etai don't see fit to arrange a marriage, I'll be fine with that."

His brother smiled, though there was tightness to it, and Akakios could still catch the tingle of him snooping.

"Are you done reacquainting yourself with the scenery?" Upon receiving a nod, Amyntas continued, "Then the ceremony can begin."

Akakios's throat clenched, and he dropped his gaze, prompting Amyntas to check the invisible link between them again, his mouth turning downward. His brother's shoulders slumped while melancholy etched itself onto his features. Akakios swallowed against the knot in his throat.

<Are you afraid of my son, big brother?> Amyntas's smile flitted back to life but lacked any mirth. "Imagine my brother, the big bad special ops officer, afraid of a four-month-old baby."

"Don't look at me like that." Akakios closed the distance between them, gripping his brother's upper arm and squeezing it. "I'm not afraid of him, per se. But the defect—"

A muscle in his brother's neck twitched. "Kallistrate has the defect under control. Sotiris isn't a danger to himself or others." He strode toward the door, not casting a glance back. "She thinks she can help him control it."

Akakios's lips chilled. There'd be no teaching him control. He buried the thought before it could be read. Turmoil, however, rippled across their familial bond, originating from Amyntas. It had been one of the reasons Akakios had not wanted to return home: the bittersweet nature of such a ceremony. They would be forming a connection with a child who, upon reaching the age of three, would be handed over to the Magistrate's care. Their technology. He'd be another key toward isolating the variance in their species' DNA and eliminating it.

"Please don't say it, not today," Amyntas said.

"I won't."

Together, they entered their family's home, nestled in one mountain. On the inside, the only light came from deposits of a special mineral, purple in hue, that glowed in the cavernous walls. Some rooms had additional lighting—brought to them by the Magistrate—but not much more. His people couldn't stand the abrasive lights that scorched their retinas.

This main artery in, like every other aspect of the home, had been molded by forces of nature. Only minor modifications had been chiseled into the rock face of the massive cavern network by his ancestors, and that had been to split it into different wings, introducing order and privacy to various lines of the family. Nowadays, their section sat largely empty, with much of its would-be inhabitants spread throughout the galaxy, serving the Magistrate in different capacities.

In many ways, they'd been scooped up from the back of the tech race and plopped to the very front. It showed in the most recent alterations: tech woven in. Not to the extent that the Magistrate had wanted, but Demos Oneiroi was an unforgiving planet not only for sentient beings but also for electric devices. Consoles and communication relays had been modified to survive, though they still had shortened life spans.

As they walked in the hallway's purplish light, Amyntas's lead increased, even though Akakios tried not to drag his feet. He only caught up when they entered their line's private wing.

It was smaller than others, but at this point, they required little space. Amyntas and Akakios's parents were long gone, killed in service to the Magistrate, along with uncles and aunts. Sotiris had been meant to breathe life back into their line. Kallistrate had come from a family with no notches, while their own line had only held one child born with the defect two generations ago. Despite efforts taken to make a good coupling, the defect had reared its head again. A numbness settled within Akakios. And now, their family's odds of future union contracts dwindled. They'd disappear like the others.

Amyntas opened a door, and they entered the communal living area where three fur-covered chairs had been positioned at its center facing each other. The space had been softened with tapestries and intricate designs chiseled into the rock—some centuries old. In the dimly lit room, Kallistrate sat in one of the chairs with Sotiris nestled in her lap. She played with the infant's little arms, occasionally jostling him by lifting her leg. The boy, for once, was awake and peering at the newcomers. He blinked his far-too-large eyes, a common Oneiroi feature in their young. Akakios restrained his first instinct to break off any eye contact. Sotiris, after all, didn't require it to pull him under.

Kallistrate's grin to Amyntas morphed into a smirk by the time it reached Akakios. "We thought you might've run away like the rest."

"Never. I was just enjoying the scenery. You wouldn't believe the places I've been." He refused to admit he'd tried to find excuses not to return, though he suspected that Amyntas had shared his less-than-exuberant response when invited to the bonding ceremony with his wife. He had tried hard to conceal it over the call, but he had paused too much in all the wrong places, trying to think of assignments that might prevent his return. Who knows what expression flitted onto his face. In the end, all it had taken was Amyntas's tone when he'd said: "It'd mean everything to Kallistrate and me."

Akakios sank into the chair to Kallistrate's left, leaving Amyntas the other, which befitted his position as husband and father. Absent from the affair were several cousins from their line and Kallistrate's, along with her parents and grandfather. The most glaring absence was that of an Oneiroi official. It loomed over their proceedings.

Kallistrate lifted Sotiris, kissing the crown of his head before handing him to Amyntas. After doing so, she squeezed Amyntas's hand, gaining a small smile from him.

Akakios's jaw clenched, knowledge boring into him. Together his brother and sister-in-law would weather the loss. He intoned this thought, wrapped himself in its solace, even if he understood it was too simplistic, too wrong. Still, he remained grateful his brother would have Kallistrate. Of all the potential contracts, she had and continued to be the best for his brother.

Amyntas peered into Sotiris's eyes, utilizing their evolutionary feature to cultivate a mental connection. A milestone. Once that connection was formed, eye contact would no longer be necessary, allowing typical Oneiroi children to communicate until oral language was acquired. For Sotiris, Kallistrate hoped these channels would cultivate control.

His sister-in-law nudged Akakios with her foot. "So how afraid are you really?" She cocked a smile. "On a scale of one to ten."

"I'm not afraid."

She crowed with laughter. "I'm sure. Just don't let your insecurities pass through to my son. He'll have enough to overcome without feeling his uncle's doubts and . . . fears." Her teeth poked out through her smile, giving her a predatory appearance.

She was enjoying this too much.

"Anything I might feel will remain with me."

Across the way, his brother remained too focused to comprehend their conversation. Amyntas's softened expression, sheer adoration ripped open a raw wound and constricted Akakios's chest. He dropped his gaze

"When will you two be returning to active duty?"

Kallistrate shifted in her chair. "I imagine in a few more months. I need to get back into shape first, especially if I'm to be an admiral. That little one did a number on my body."

"Admiral?"

"Yep, I'm getting a promotion and my own ship. The esteemed members of the *Agoranomi* and the Magistrate Brass themselves see me as invaluable. Of course, this is something we already knew."

"Quite the ego." Akakios exhaled and shifted in his chair. "But congratulations are in store. May your ship serve you well."

"I'm sure it will. It's called the *Aletheia*." She slanted her head toward Amyntas and Sotiris. "We should be quite content on her. After all, the Magistrate calls, and we answer . . . always answering."

Amyntas cleared his throat and extended the still-alert Sotiris to him. "It's your turn, big brother."

Akakios started but calmed himself and his expression. He buried his uncertainties, locking them behind mental barriers, before he gingerly accepted Sotiris. The boy was heavier than Akakios had expected, or perhaps his arms were weaker. His nephew's face harbored many similarities to his parents'; though presently, it was rounder and pinker. He wore a long-sleeved onesie, a never-ending line motif stitched into its cuff — the *meandros*. Unity . . . infinity. Yet, their line would come to an end.

"Don't take too long." Kallistrate prodded him with her foot again.

"Yeah, he might fall back asleep," Amyntas added. "Though, I think Sotiris is extremely excited to have other minds to touch. I've heard those born with the defect are particularly eager to reach out."

Of course, they are — Akakios blinked, burying the thought. His mind was no longer alone. Despite himself, a smile tugged at his face when little tendrils belonging to his nephew's mind reached out to his. Light, inquisitive, so bubbly, so innocent . . . "I would believe it."

Amyntas's grin deepened. "Then don't keep him waiting."

-Present-

Gone. All gone. Whimpers escaped his throat as the tremors returned. He couldn't shake them, not since he'd learned of the *Aletheia*'s fate two days ago. It'd taken place weeks before, yet he'd just been told. Rage uncoiled, his fist colliding with the synth glass. Service forbid they break off a pointless mission to give him word that his world had imploded.

Akakios fought the tremors, tried to kill them, but they wouldn't stop, much like the tears that coated his cheeks. He pressed the side of his face against the window—as if to support himself—before collapsing back to the floor where he'd been sprawled. He pounded his fist repeatedly against the window. Don't think, don't reach. But he couldn't help himself. His mind craved the connections, needed them—they needed to be alive. He pressed his trembling lips together. He would never see his brother again, never feel his presence, nor Kallistrate's, nor Sotiris's. There wouldn't even be bodies to lay to peace. He hiccupped. Nothing . . . there was nothing.

Akakios wailed, curling in on himself, knees pressing into his forehead. His teeth ground against each other while he struggled to regain composure. Inhale, exhale. Don't focus on the emptiness. Don't picture them dea—

Pushing against the floor, Akakios stood and stumbled to his bed, where he collapsed. Just a few months ago—he'd seen them a few months ago. They'd been well. Even Sotiris was growing at a rate comparable to other toddlers his age. He'd looked healthy for a child with the defect, only a couple of bruises from falls he'd taken after losing consciousness and control of his body. Kallistrate, through her strength and sheer willpower, kept the defect in check, for the most part. Then days, a few days before—his jaw tightened. He'd just spoken with Amyntas.

Gone. How could they be gone? Akakios bit down on his lip.

At a knock on his door, Akakios stifled his sobs. His team had left him to grieve, not attempting any form of communication beyond supplying food that often went untouched. He couldn't even think of eating; it seemed foreign, wrong.

"Akakios," a voice—one commonplace in his youth—called. "I need a word with you."

Kyros. An Agoranomi member, Kyros had been a longtime supporter of Akakios's family, particularly his specific line after serving the Magistrate alongside Akakios and Amyntas's father. Why would he be on Sergrey? He hadn't left Demos Oneiroi, to Akakios's knowledge, since completing his service. No sane Oneiroi would. Akakios grabbed his blanket and wiped his face before he opened the door to greet the council member.

"Kyros." He inclined his head out of respect . . . and the fact he couldn't bring himself to make eye contact with the man, even if etiquette prevented the elder from reading him. Though Akakios feared more that he'd break down in front of the Agoranomi member. "What are you doing here? I thought you detested traveling."

"I do." Kyros pushed past Akakios and proceeded farther into his room, making a loop while he examined every inch. His cane punctuated each step, clicking off the faux wood. "But I have business here. When's the last time you ate?" He waved toward an untouched plate one of his crew members had snuck in while he slept.

"I haven't felt like eating. It—the thought sickens me."

Kyros stroked his gray beard, one hand still clenching the cane. "I was distressed to hear of Amyntas and Kallistrate's fate. I'd watched him grow into such a fine man. And Kallistrate . . . she was a very special woman."

"I'm not ready to speak about them. Not yet."

"I understand and respect that. They've left a hole that cannot be filled. But with time, you'll be able to reflect on them more easily, and your memories will bring comfort, not further pain." Kyros sat in one of Akakios's chairs, resting his cane against its plush arm. "Life will never be the same, and some days will be worse than others, but you'll be able to remember them. Until then, I'm here to give you purpose."

"Purpose?" Akakios's mouth contorted at the word.

"The Res Publica de Magistratus Intelligence Bureau has shared with the Agoranomi certain information." He swallowed. "They believe Sotiris was taken by Plasovern prior to the *Aletheia*'s destruction."

"So-tir-is . . ." Air stuck in Akakios's throat. Alive. "H-how? How do they know that?"

Kyros leaned forward, deep lines taking root on his forehead and around his mouth. "The information provided to us is sketchy, and there are several holes that I want filled. But from what we've been told, the *Aletheia*'s destruction involved a Magistrate ship. That ship's crew then penetrated the ship and took Sotiris."

Akakios clenched his hands into fists. "That—that shouldn't have been possible. There was a full crew of our people. Kallistrate was on that ship! No other species would've been able to get on board, let alone get anywhere near to Sotiris."

"Arrogance doesn't serve anyone, Akakios." Kyros clapped his cane against the floor. "There are species that have evolved brains with immunity to our abilities. It's possible one of those species was used. Besides, there was a second Plasovern ship that undoubtedly added to the confusion. The first ship flew under the flag of the Magistrate, possibly carrying Magistrate goods, and they were allowed to board. Once they were in, the second Plasovern ship attacked. The agents on the inside used that distraction to get their target."

Pacing back and forth, Akakios shook his head. "Why Sotiris? He couldn't have been of much value—"

"They're after the defect."

"There were others on the ship. Why just Sotiris?"

Kyros sighed, leaving his cane resting on his leg. With his hands, he rubbed his brow. He reflected all of his sixty-some years in that moment—maybe more—grafted onto his body by a life of impossible decisions. "Whatever their intent was, it eludes me. I only know the defect in their hands isn't in our people's best interests."

The statesman rummaged in one of his coat's large pockets and withdrew a slate. After Kyros thumbed a few buttons, a holographic image popped into being: a woman wearing her hair in an odd fashion . . . and Sotiris.

Akakios's mouth contorted, and tears threatened to pour over his eyelids.

"All we know for certain is Plasovern has Sotiris."

Akakios reached out and touched the holograph, causing it to flicker and distort the image of his nephew. "Where and when was this taken?"

"Several weeks ago on Gilga in a mercantile shop. The owner recognized Sotiris as an Oneiroi and reported it a week later."

"Why did it take him so long? He should have reported it immediately."

"The Plasovern agents were paying good money, so he wanted to do business. Opportunists are spread all over the outskirts of Magistrate space—"

"But I guarantee they are no longer on Gilga."

"No, but thanks to the merchant's report and port officials, we have their trail. We also know the ship they're traveling in." Kyros shut off the slate, tearing a muted animalistic sound from Akakios. "It's yours, along with all the latest information. You and your squad have been assigned to secure Sotiris. You'll start with Ne'par. It's the last destination we've traced *The Wandering Trader* to. While they picked up cargo, their final destination was not readily available. You'll need to secure it from a Vanspere called Vlar.

"The Agoranomi and Magistrate Brass are hopeful your connection with Sotiris will hasten his return. At all costs, he's not to be taken into the Medzeci Empire."

Akakios's heart skipped. He fully met Kyros's unwavering gaze. At all costs . . .

"There are those who doubt sending you, Akakios. While the bond can aid in recovery, it can hinder the tougher decisions. The future of our people could depend on this. Do you understand?"

A tremor shot up his back. He recalled the weight he'd felt holding Sotiris that first time, the unspoken promise of the ceremony. His brother and sister-in-law, if there was a next life, would never want to see his face.

Kyros's lips curved downward.

There would be another team. They might take the easier route and not even bother with recovery. He nodded. "I do. I'll see this through. For our people."

In the silence that followed, Akakios flicked on the slate and skimmed the information. "They boarded the *Aletheia* on a Magistrate ship? Do we know which one or the identities of the agents?"

Kyros faced the windows, his expression deepening and displaying all his complexion's flaws: old scars, age marks, and discolorations. "Nothing. I feel—and these are my personal misgivings—that our Magistrate overseers are being less than forthcoming." Kyros stood and trudged over to the door. "Their answers fail to satisfy. But the rest of my fellow Agoranomi members have accepted the scant details. I'll do further digging; it is the least I can do for you and your family."

"I can't thank—"

"Then don't." Kyros touched the door panel but stopped short of opening it. "Pull yourself together. For the ethereal spirits, eat something! Neither Sotiris nor I will be best served by you flopping over dead."

"I'll find something."

Kyros fixed him in a hard stare. "You had better." His frown widened. "Also, begin to prepare yourself for the inevitable."

Akakios twisted his mouth as he suppressed delusions of rearing Sotiris, of keeping him. Warmth returned to his eyes, but he refused to acknowledge it beyond roughly rubbing the moisture away. "I understand."

"Do not think me harsh, Akakios. To lose him again after thinking him dead, along with his parents, is too much . . . but we must consider his best option. You've not fully witnessed the effects of the defect. Before you were even born, we were already reliant on the Magistrate. It . . . it's not a sight one wants to see, what can come from the defect."

"I know." An acidic flavor filled Akakios's mouth. "When the time comes"—he refused to acknowledge the worst-case scenario—"I'll be ready."

Nodding, Kyros opened the door. "I'll inform your team you intend to leave within the next hour. Take that time to compose yourself and pack. And one final word of advice: Keep your eyes and ears open." With that, he left, shutting the door behind him.

Akakios placed the slate in one of his uniform pockets before readying his bag. He never carried much, leaving sentimental items at home on Demos Oneiroi. They were only a burden when on the move. He reached for an overturned pigmented photovid and stuffed it into his pack, not bothering to turn it over. He couldn't afford another fit, not when Sotiris needed him. Akakios zipped the pack shut after adding his spare uniforms.

A small personal craft passed by the window of his suite. One of the pylons sent out a signal, jostling the craft away from the Magistrate base and back on track. Other drivers whizzed by, and more joined them from the many high-rise garages that dotted Sergrey's packed capital city. He watched the happenings for several minutes until a curtain of numbness settled around his mind. Only then did Akakios hoist his pack onto his shoulder and exit the room.

On the other side, the common room he'd shared with his officers stood almost empty. Just Chrysanthos, his mechanic, remained, putting away last-minute items into his and Ambrosios's packs. Ever the dutiful spouse. He stopped as he shoved in what appeared to be a bag of Sern hard candy, something Ambrosios had picked up for him during a layover on the planet, and saluted Akakios.

"Everyone's already headed to the ship." He lowered his hand after Akakios ordered him to be at ease and zipped one of the packs. "A few are overseeing the crates. Elpis had a new order of medical supplies come in. Since we're dealing with Plasovern, it's probably for the best."

"Plus, there's no telling what kind of shape Sotiris will be in by the time we find him," Akakios muttered. "Finish up here and help the others put the supplies away."

Akakios withdrew from the suite of rooms and entered the dimmed hallway. Several suites lined the corridor, all vacant. Elites were kept separate for good reason: They often hated other Elites—their biological differences placing them at odds—while the regulars were terrified of them and the roles they played in the Magistrate's mechanisms. Besides, the dimmed lights and lowered temperature would be considered uncomfortable by many species.

At the end of the hall, he flipped out custom-made sunglasses and put them on before entering the lift. Light streamed down on him, but it couldn't accost his eyes, and colors—unseen by unassisted Oneiroi eyes—emerged: reds and greens while others grew more vibrant and varied in hue. With the press of a button, he traveled to the hangar bay's top level.

Fumes, oil, and other odors that went hand in hand with mechanical work struck him the moment he left the lift. The bay itself was filled to the brim with military vessels and all manner of actions.

He proceeded down the walkway to the *Boreas*, a sleek B-Class Boita interceptor-class vessel tailored for speed rather than direct combat. Outside, three members of his team loaded hefty boxes into the main cargo hold. Elpis, black hair spun into a tight, uncompromising bun, guided fraternal twins Pelagius and Pelagia, both ensigns, as they loaded the medical supplies. Her sharp tongue berated them when the crate shifted at an odd angle. Easy-going Pelagius tried to salute Akakios upon his approach, eliciting further critique from the medic and Pelagia, the boss in their sibling relationship, a role her brother had never fought her for.

Akakios ignored the situation, proceeding to the bridge and crew quarters. He deposited his pack inside his own darkened room before entering his destination.

"Captain." Commander Charis Velis, his second, sprung to attention from where she'd been seated at the weapons station, completing a check on the system. Her hair, like Elpis's, had been placed in a bun; however, she'd decided to add two braids that dipped into it.

His first and second lieutenants, Ambrosios and Kyrillos, who'd respectively been sitting at the helm and communications stations, followed her lead. The two men stood in contrast, the former taller and the other stouter, more solidly built. Ambrosios had his hair closely clipped, while Kyrillos had shaved his head a month back. Word had it that his communications expert had made a bet with the wrong person. His gaze settled on his first lieutenant, wondering how long the wager had been for.

All three watched his every move in a vain attempt to establish his mood.

"I'm fine. And I'll be even better when we find my nephew." He swung into his seat at the bridge's center. "Have you reviewed the information provided by Magistrate Intelligence?"

"Yes." Charis tucked her hands behind the small of her back. "The course we'll take to Ne'par has been programmed in. It's a relatively poor world . . . really nothing more than a dustbowl."

Akakios snorted. Of course it'd be one of those. "Let's hope we find our Vanspere quickly. I'm sick of these dustbowl planets." He stood and handed his slate to Kyrillos. "Connect this to the relay. I want any hits related to our targets routed instantly to this ship."

"Understood." Kyrillos plugged in the slate as told and launched the connection. "Do we know what we're in for?"

From the helm, Ambrosios chuckled, a smirk present on his face. "Do we ever know what we're in for? For all we know, Hedda Strom could be in our future."

Kyrillos bristled, glowering at his superior. "What's that they say about summoning ghosts?"

"Ambrosios is right," Akakios said. "We only know of one agent, the one holding Sotiris. We should assume there are more, even the illustrious Strom. Likely we're dealing with the normal ten-person team that Plasovern favors. *Timiménos* Kyros" — he used the proper title of honor for an Agoranomi member — "has raised the possibility that the agents consist of a species immune to our abilities." Akakios shifted his gaze between the members on the bridge. "However, at this point, make no assumptions. It could be any faction within Plasovern, even if the brutality aligns with Strom's methods. Be prepared to take necessary actions, but none that endanger Sotiris."

At all costs . . .

His lips formed a stubborn line. They would not cross that threshold, even if it killed him.

"Don't worry, Captain." Ambrosios tapped his fingers against the smooth screen of his console. "The co-ords are in. We'll be on our way as soon as they're done loading the supplies. By the way, had our engineer left our rooms yet?" His pilot's smile turned fond.

"I do believe he was finishing your task of packing." Akakios sunk into his chair. "He should be right behind me."

Charis cleared her throat and addressed Akakios. "If it pleases you, sir, we have the bridge."

Akakios pressed his lips together, his jaw stiffening. Charis didn't balk, standing tall despite her deceptively slight frame. One did not tangle with her.

Already rotating back to her tasks, Charis added, "It's also my understanding the food supplies have been loaded. You might want to check them out, sir."

The corners of his mouth quivered, but instead of reproaching her, he activated communications to the cargo bay. "What's the ETA?"

There was a pause before Chrysanthos answered. "We'll be ready in thirty."

Ambrosios swiveled in his seat to face Akakios. "Better get that food and rest, sir. I wager we will be at Ne'par in less than twelve hours."

"Who am I to argue with my officers?" Akakios stood. "Charis, you have the bridge. If there are any delays or new information, alert me immediately."

Her eyes met his, and sincerity rippled to him over the link formed during the creation of a formidable team. "I'll do so," she said. <Sir, get some sleep.>

Sleep. A fickle beast if ever there was one. He walked out the door. There'd be none, at least not of the natural variety. Without drugs, he'd lie in bed until hollowness overtook him, followed by speculations about how his brother and sister-in-law had died—if there had been pain, fear. The answers would never come, but at least he could remove Sotiris from his nightmares. He entered his cabin and kicked his pack farther into the room. He then made his rounds, turning over frames and shutting off holopictures along his path to the bathroom. He clung to Kyros's words that one day they wouldn't hurt so much.

In his bathroom cabinet, he found sleep aids, normally reserved for individuals with trouble adjusting to space, and popped two into his mouth, chasing them with water.

He hoped, staring into his own bloodshot eyes via the mirror, he'd be dead to the world before their ship even left Sergrey's atmosphere. Mindless sleep, untainted by anything—without witnessing his brother's or Kallistrate's deaths or how he imagined them. Rubbing his eyes, he stumbled from the room. He welcomed the numbing sensation that engulfed his limbs, making them lighter, almost detached from his body. His thoughts shifted to Sotiris and potential justice—something unimagined before. He'd bring it to the culprits swiftly.

And at all costs, he'd bring his nephew home.

Dustbowl didn't quite describe Ne'par, Akakios decided now that he strolled its unpaved streets. Rubbish and a type of liquid waste, the kind that no one would care to imagine, filled them. The planet boiled, its red soil trapping the heat. The wind kicked up, and Akakios covered the lower portion of his face to prevent the foul planet's dirt from entering his mouth or nose. Charis and Ambrosios, who flanked him, mimicked the gesture. Oh no, dustbowl was too forgiving. Ne'par was a backwater dump far too close to its sun. With any luck, it'd slip from orbit—when he wasn't on-world—perishing in that very sun.

The life-forms who inhabited it, both by choice or through the misfortune of birth, had taken to the drink. It probably was a world pastime designed to forget the overbearing heat or the crushing poverty. They hung back as the three Oneiroi passed them, some disappearing into their shacks. The natives stood out with their airy clothes while spacers rolled up their sleeves and pant legs. The latter stood further out as they waved about money at Misbre's varied establishments, particularly the saloon.

Shacks comprised a chunk of the city's scenery and only made the large manors on the outskirts—guarded by soaring fences—stand out. They had been set far away from the slums and its seedy dealings; however, underneath— after digging deep enough—connections had to be present. Akakios spat off to the side, forcing dirt out. Like any of the other worlds he'd been on, the wealthy probably drew a great deal of their riches from illicit transactions that impacted the slums.

Among it all, large Magistrate buildings had been built, dedicated to planetary security, commerce inspections, medical care, and educational services, hauling the dustbowl into modernity and, with it, prosperity. The latter had yet to arrive.

Akakios tugged at the collar of his uniform. It had been custom-made for the Oneiroi to provide comfort on such repugnant worlds. Ne'par, however, tested its capabilities, and sweat slid down his neck. *Ah, Sotiris, what you must have thought of this place?* The world amounted to torture, at least in the mind of an Oneiroi.

"Our Vespar resides at this place . . . of business," Charis said, lifting an eyebrow.

"So the intel says." Akakios stepped past the patrons who drank outside at rickety round tables and into the actual building. Tepid air greeted his face, not cool enough to be considered comfortable, but enough not to be choking on the humidity and heat.

The conversation in the establishment ceased when patrons realized Magistrate Elites were present. In the back, two men darted out through a side door, leaving Akakios to assume they had active warrants.

"We need to speak with Vlar." Akakios's voice filled the room.

After hesitation, the Csek behind the bar waved two of her four blue arms toward a hallway, partially concealed by a rack of spirits. "You'll find him down there." Her hip jaunted to one side, and she quirked her thin lips. "You won't find anything illegal."

"We'll be the judges of that." Akakios crossed the now-cleared space to the hallway. The footsteps of Charis and Ambrosios trailed him.

The sultry twang of a string instrument coated their footfalls as it plaintively wailed from behind one of the closed curtains that separated several rooms from the hallway.

Akakios separated one of the segments of rust-colored fabric and froze, his mouth tightening. A topless Csek danced, her four arms moving in sharp poses while another humanoid species strummed a tall stringed instrument. Before them, on a large stuffed pillow, sat a Vespar, his reddish skin blending into the hazy room. His ember-hued eyes, on the other hand, glowed as they followed the dancer's every movement. His eyes left the dancer, connecting with Akakios before breaking away. Vlar downed a large gulp from the rummer he'd been holding, his long tongue extending after he swallowed to catch loose remnants of the drink.

"I feel honored to warrant attention from Magistrate officials, though I am shocked to receive Elites." Vlar lowered the partially full rummer onto a tray, the glass clattering against the metal as his hand shook. He then retracted both appendages into the large sleeves of his shirt. "Why do I deserve such an honor?"

"You're working with this woman." Akakios thumbed on his slate, the image of their target and Sotiris coming to life. "What cargo is she carrying, and where is it going?"

Vlar muttered something in his native tongue, and the music stopped. The dancer gathered her top from the floor and departed with the musician. Once they were gone, Vlar waved his hand in the air. "My shipping business is completely legal."

Akakios balled his fists. "I don't care about your shipping business." He encroached on Vlar's space, forcing him to shift backward on his pillow, almost falling from it. All the while, the man refused to lift his eyes. "You will tell me what your business is with this woman. And trust me: You'll not enjoy the alternative."

Ambrosios cocked his familiar, toothy grin as he slid in beside his commanding officer. "I do take a certain pleasure in my job." He crouched in front of the Vespar. "You'd be surprised what the mind holds. I wonder what plagues your nightmares, but we might be finding out soon enough, huh?" He winked at the man.

Vlar's dark lips, almost black in color, pressed together. "Th-that won't be necessary." He grasped his rummer, its contents spilling over the rim in his haste to bring it to his mouth. "She came a week ago, with a man. They called themselves Clementia and Ferrutius—they were looking to move cargo. I had grain that needed sent to Ereago."

"Certain sectors on Ereago have embargoes in place," Charis said. "I'm sure some of the less Magistrate-friendly cities and factions would pay handsomely for such goods. Plasovern also has an on-world presence."

"It was for Mertis! The war's exhausting their reserves, so it's perfectly legal—"

"For them to pay a pretty hefty fee for your generosity," Charis said, crossing her arms.

Vlar raised his hands. "War isn't cheap, and neither are my fuel costs to get a ship to Ereago, especially with vultures like Plasovern circling about! Do you know how many pilots are actually crazy enough to go there? Not many."

From his crouched position, Ambrosios pressed his hands into his thighs to maintain balance. "Did they have last names?" he asked. "Your hires."

"No." Vlar shook his head, his tongue flicking out to moisten his lips. "They didn't give any—but the woman, she spoke with a distinct Magistrate accent: a Core accent. Emmm . . . I would say inner Core by its fineness."

"She has a boy with her." Akakios brought the hologram closer to Vlar, who downed the rest of his wine. "Tell me about him."

"There was no boy—I saw no boy," the Vespar practically spewed the words. "It was only her and the man . . . and a girl—a teenager—at the ship. I saw no one else. She said she was just looking for work. Does this woman have a bounty on her?"

"Has she been paid? Will she be returning here?" Akakios pressed, the muscles in his jaw twitching.

"Half. I paid her half here. The rest will be paid by my associate on Ereago."

"His name."

Vlar fidgeted on his pillow, his mouth narrowing, a show of defiance even if his frame could not cease trembling. Ambrosios cleared his throat, and the Vespar straightened. "Her name is Usha. She's a Filitre and holds shop not far from the eastern spaceport in the capital of Mertis: Esh."

Charis rested her hand on Akakios's shoulder and squeezed. <Are we done here?>

Akakios nodded. "I can only hope this information you've given us is accurate . . . for your sake."

"I've nothing to hide! This woman—this Clementia— she's not a longtime member of my organization; she's just a freelancer. I've no reason to hide her." He flailed his hands in the air. "She had completed a run for an associate . . . a brief run, but she did well. If I'd known the Magistrate sought her, there would have been no business. I swear—"

"Then all should be fine, shouldn't it?" Ambrosios said from behind Akakios.

Akakios waited a few minutes—giving the Vespar time to amend his story—before exiting the small room, his officers in tow. Vlar never called after them, but Akakios hadn't expected him to. The man had spoken the truth. They vacated the saloon and embarked toward their more comfortable spaceship. Charis activated the com along the way and ordered Kyrillos to plot a course to Ereago's Esh, the capital of Mertis, a country where Magistrate dominance went undisputed.

"It doesn't make sense." Ambrosios fell into step beside Akakios.

"There's a lot that doesn't make sense," Akakios ground out. "You need to be more specific."

"Why are they moving cargo?" Ambrosios folded his arms across his chest. "According to each hit on the relay, all they've done is pick up cargo and transport it, each and every time."

"Maybe they're trying to get lost in the paperwork." Akakios wouldn't voice the thought already plaguing him: that Sotiris had been one of those cargo runs already dropped off.

Ambrosios snorted. "Captain, we know Plasovern. We've taken down cells; we've trailed agents. This doesn't feel right, especially when they have something as valuable as Sotiris in hand." He shifted his gaze behind them. "Given where the *Aletheia* was, why didn't they cut and run directly to Medzeci? They would've gotten away, and there, the Magistrate wouldn't have been able to stop them."

"*Bargerr* chased them into Magistrate space."

"Highly unlikely. You know that as well as I do. They could've easily made a blind jump into Medzeci space. But they didn't." Ambrosios stopped walking. "Instead, they jumped into Magistrate space and have chosen to linger here, performing courier missions from one backwater planet to the next . . . all the while having Sotiris, who Plasovern would undoubtedly want right away."

"This isn't the place, Ambrosios," Charis said as she shut off her communications device.

She was right. A group of curious locals had already crowded together outside a nearby grocery store to watch the interlopers like one would a visiting circus. They scattered into the store after the three Oneiroi faced them.

"We need to leave." Akakios resumed walking. <Need to play catch up.>

<They're in a freighter. We'll be fine.> Ambrosios sent.

They might be, but the crew—that he now suspected had been paid—had proven to be deft. Ambrosios had struck a nerve. These people weren't following known patterns. Plasovern didn't move cargo. They moved weapons and targeted weak points in the Magistrate, particularly on contested planets freshly inducted. Its agents displayed dedication to the point they would gladly die if it gave the Magistrate a black eye. Cargo loads meant too many relays tracking their movements, not to mention port inspections.

They boarded the *Boreas* in silence, acknowledging their team members' welcomes as they headed to the bridge. Once the door closed behind them and they returned to their stations, Charis broke the silence. "Do we continue to Ereago? It's possible Sotiris is no longer with our targets."

"It is." Akakios eased into his chair. "But if there is still a possibility, I'll follow it." His throat clenched. "Besides, they hold all the answers." They'd been on the *Aletheia*, were complicit in its fate.

Charis removed her sunglasses and lodged them in one of her uniform's pockets. "Your orders, sir?"

"Ambrosios, get us off this festering hole." Akakios leaned forward, resting his elbows on his legs as Ambrosios guided their craft upward, eventually leaving Ne'Par's atmosphere. The list of questions grew with each step. Kyros had been right: He needed to keep his eyes and ears open.

CHAPTER SEVEN

Katya clasped her headscarf—its seams snug against her cheek and neck—as she shuffled closer to Rein to avoid being trampled by a scruffy youth pushing a cart of foul-smelling melons. The whole city of Esh exhibited the same frantic pace, almost as if it were holding its breath, knowing that some great movement was coming—great, of course, being left to interpretation. The pockmarked buildings, sparse displays of goods, and ruined structures spoke volumes. Guerrillas from different sects in Mertis and the Vry Republiek had done a number on the "airtight" capital of Ereago, which is what the Magistrate had designated Esh, a decision not universally accepted on-world.

They scrambled to the side to avoid the numerous stained bricks that had been strewn across the western portion of the market district. Once stores, she decided. The blackened area brought a sour taste to her mouth.

"We need to get off this planet." Katya swallowed, the airy fabric of the headscarf—a feature shared with every woman walking the market—pressing into her skin. It at least had the benefit of protecting her head from the planet's oppressive sun. "It's a powder keg waiting for a spark."

Rein snorted. "To think, in two years, I would've been a citizen. Now I'm needing to worry about getting off another Fringe planet." A tightness formed around his eyes, which for a moment, lacked clarity. "Story of my life."

She frowned.

Ahead, a young girl grabbed a half loaf of bread and darted through the crowded street into a series of alleys. The merchant whose bread had been stolen stood shouting obscenities after her. The crowd continued, unmoved, rushing to satisfy their own needs. Reznic had held the same pace. Next to her, Rein watched the girl disappear in the throng of people.

She knew Mina's story, or most of it, and imagined Rein had a similar one.

"I'm sorry. I truly am."

A smile drifted onto his face. "I'd had it all planned out. Was going to settle on a Mezzo. I was thinking of Vergo."

She perked at the planet's name. "My family has a villa on Vergo."

"I know." His gaze grew distant. "I remember the way you described it: its rolling green hills, millions of lakes, oceans, mountains. You made it sound so gorgeous. I'd been researching the Bangnara Province, and it seemed the most ravishing. Could see myself getting lost on its lakes."

Katya almost stopped. Rein's face had taken on a wistful expression, so distant, and she wondered what exactly he was imagining. She'd only shared her stays on Vergo with Mina and maybe a smattering of her fellow officers, but she'd never gone into details, focusing on scenery. On Reznic, she wasn't about to rub a private villa in other people's faces. So she couldn't recall a single time she'd spoken with Rein about Vergo. A frigid sensation spread along her back. She'd shared details with Valens in more intimate settings, on more than one occasion . . . including that her family's villa was in the Bangnara Province. Her mouth went dry.

"Watch your step."

Rein tugged her from the path of a hover cart, his touch scorching her arm.

She stepped away, freeing herself. "Thanks." The moment she opened her mouth, strong spices assaulted her senses. They barely coated the smell of decay and rot that touched her tongue. She winced. A deep red stain, long dry, held silent testament next to remains of a store. Incense had been placed to burn near it. "The Gata don't appear to play fair."

"They're backed by Plasovern. It shows in their tactics." Rein lowered his hand, which had been covering his nose. "Give the Magistrate a few months, and Ereago will be back in order."

Back in order, huh? She couldn't see it. It'd take decades at least to repair all this . . . to smooth out the populaces' differences would take centuries. "Let's just reach our contact in one piece."

The rest of the way, they stuck to the side of the streets, out of the way, out of notice. Their contact, Usha, had operations in the southern corridor of the market. And it turned out to be a run-down sector: exterior facades crumbling, windows dirty—or, in some cases, smashed—and the clientele proved somewhat seedy, minding their own business and never making real eye contact as they dealt among themselves. Fewer scorch marks graced the buildings in this area, but rather than providing comfort, it made her stomach harden. Could Plasovern have contacts here? Or was it working with certain merchants here? There had to be a reason they'd leave this section intact.

"40A26." Rein gestured to one of the storefronts. A ragged sand-colored canopy provided minimum shade over its entryway. Under it, a set of four large Borvinian males sat on oversize stools, mugs in their bulky six-fingered hands. "It's our contact's address."

As the pair approached, the Borvinians stood, their large brown eyes inspecting them. Muscles rippled under their short brown hair, which covered their bodies. Her AVI-13, holstered to her hip, gave little comfort. They'd never stand a chance against these Borvinian bouncers. She resisted the urge to even brush her hand against her weapon.

"You two lost?" one of the Borvinians asked in a deep, rattling voice.

Katya placed her left hand on her hip. "I believe we've finally found our way. We have Ms. Usha's cargo."

The Borvinian inclined his head, his long snout pointing to the ground before he snapped his fingers and another of his kind opened the door. Katya bowed her head in gratitude and entered with Rein.

The windows to the establishment had been blacked out, and Katya narrowed her eyes at the shift in lighting from a natural yellow tone to a rusty red. It blanketed the interior, originating from the golden pendant fixtures that dangled in a sparse arrangement throughout the space. Overall, it created a murky, almost surreal image, with the red light capturing the smoke from the narghiles' progress to the ceiling.

She recognized what was in the instruments immediately. Heh'sha, a legal liquid cannabinoid, imbued the entire space, but it wasn't alone. Her nose wrinkled. Other fragrances—belonging to less legal narcotics—hid among the lesser evils. They stoked memories of Reznic, its dens, its burnouts. A wave of giddiness, closing in on euphoria, enveloped her mind from the excess in the room. All around her, a variety of species lounged on floor pillows while they were attended to by an assortment of males and females, largely Cseks, wearing silver clothing. Some of the patrons held long white pipes to their mouths. None of their choices appeared illegal, but narghiles could be tampered with to expand their offerings. Over it all, speakers played twangy Csek music.

Shaking her head, she fought against the fog that threatened to overtake her mind. The illegal wares must be in the back. Down the sparsely lit hallway.

"You're . . . the pilot," a slow voice said. "We've been expecting you." Tingles traveled down her spine as the speaker purposefully pronounced each syllable. Then the being, a Csek, a rare violet-hued one, stepped out from the shadows of the hallway. "Milady waits." Two of her four arms waved, the many bracelets on them clattering together almost musically.

Katya followed their guide into the hallway. It, like the previous room, only had red lights speckled along its length. They traveled several feet before the Csek palmed open a panel, which had blended into the wall.

"So, what exactly do you sell on paper?" Rein asked.

"On paper?" the Csek murmured. "We sell nothing but offer many of the finest services." She chuckled, flicking one of her fingers in Rein's direction. "Not of that variety. This is a day spa for those whose skin has special needs . . . or individuals who wish to explore alternative cures for very real ailments or the ills of the universe."

"The heh'sha," Katya said.

The Csek only nodded as she opened a second door. "Through here, please."

Katya entered first, followed by Rein. Their guide shut the door behind them from the other side. Smoke heightened the euphoria and fuzz, and Katya swayed. Ah, here were the illegals. She'd been hit by them before during Reznic raids. Familiarity, however, did not protect her from their haze. One in particular — purple lady — sprang to mind. The opiate had ruined plenty of lives on Reznic . . . it and resin, a dissociative drug.

"Eh. Definitely feeling it now." Rein coughed into his hand.

"Yep." Stupid . . . but her brain was working in fits and starts now. Licking her lips, she forced more effort. "In and out, and keep our wits."

The Csek smiled, revealing filed canines, which Katya's drug encrusted mind enlarged. No. That's not happening. As if hearing her thoughts, the Csek chuckled and opened the small antechamber's door.

They stepped fully into a room blanketed in silks. On pillows similar to those in the front, patrons lay taking drags from long pipes connected to narghiles — custom ones. She counted ten patrons, who no doubt had paid a high price for each drag if the market on Ereago resembled Reznic's in any way.

"Come in farther," a gravelly voice said. Under the red light, an extremely pale humanoid woman reclined on a large pillow, propped up above the rest on a marble podium, almost resembling a throne. In her hand, she held the same long pipe, though hers gleamed with jewels. It shined as much as the gold body necklace that cascaded down her torso, forming intricate patterns. The lighting made her skin pinkish in color. "You're the pilot that Vlar sent? You have the grain?"

Katya stepped forward. "All three tons of it. We'd . . . I want it off my ship." She swallowed hard. "Before this war breaks loose."

"It has been brewing for some time, ebbing and flowing. But when the Magistrate inserted itself, thinking it could settle centuries of hostilities . . ." She shrugged. "But it's inconsequential." Usha's lips wrapped themselves around the ivory pipe, taking another drag from the narghile. Once finished, she jerked her head toward a man standing beside her podium. He advanced, extending a case to Katya. "My men will be quick. They're already waiting at the port to remove it and to prevent complications."

"Complications?" Rein tightened his fists.

"Need is great in the city. There are some who would do anything to get ahold of such a valuable commodity."

"It seems you already have a commodity. Why grain?" Rein pressed. His lips were thin, and Katya resisted the urge to elbow him. They were in no position to be self-righteous.

Usha exhaled, sending smoke upwards from her mouth. "It doesn't pay to put all in any one commodity. Markets are volatile." A closed-mouth smile touched her heavily dyed lips, which were done up in a deep purple. "Times are changing." Snapping her fingers, a man with a case stepped forward. "As for your payment—"

"Not so fast." Rein sounded more drunk this time.

"What are—" Katya got no further as Rein staggered forward, his index finger leveled at Usha.

"We unknowingly flew into a war zone. You can do better."

Usha blinked and then broke out into throaty laughter. "All business comes with risks, known and unknown. You accept it the moment you agree."

"Yes, but if I've ever learned anything, markets fluctuate."

Katya held her breath as Usha pensively puffed at her pipe—all the while the corners of her lips turned upward, allowing plumes of smoke to exit. When she set the device aside, she broke the silence. "So they do."

The Filitre pointed to another attendant, who left and returned with a folded wad of hard Magistrate currency. It possibly amounted to an additional thousand or so *aurums*. The one with the case snapped it open, and the clip was added to its green and purple currency. Katya stepped forward and accepted the case.

"It's been a pleasure doing business," she said, bowing her head to Usha.

Their contact waved her hands outwards before pulling them back toward herself and finally to the side; by the end of the gesture, her palms faced the ceiling. "Business is always a pleasure. If you require future employment, be sure to return. An entrepreneur can do well here, relishing in the rewards of risks."

Passing the case to her other hand, Katya shook her head. "Your offer is appreciated. However, count me among the wise. We have other places to be."

"I'll com my men then. They will have the grain removed before you even return to your ship." Usha took to her pipe again. "Do be careful on your way back. As you have noted, Esh is a dangerous place."

Katya dipped her head in farewell, an action not imitated by Rein, and they swiveled to leave the way they'd come. The recreational users in the main room remained where they'd been and didn't even note the pair's passing or exit from the building. Once again in the market, Katya and Rein paused to clear their lungs and their minds. The drugs clung, sticking in like nettles, but the buzz lessened.

Rein leaned close, and she stiffened when he smelled her hair. "Better hope we don't hit any checkpoints going back into port."

Her shoulders sagged. "Heh. I suppose smelling like a drug den won't be smiled upon."

"Unlikely."

Inhaling until her chest couldn't expand further, she exhaled. "Good thing I think they have bigger concerns at the moment, and I say we leave before they become ours as well."

"Couldn't agree more."

Rein positioned himself closer to the center of the street while she stayed near the storefronts. She shifted the case so it was between them. Surrounded by desperate people, walking around with a case full of money was a new level of lunacy. Her free hand stationed itself near her service pistol.

"We used to bust places like that."

"So we did," she responded.

Rein's jaw clenched as his gaze shifted to a pair of men walking by. They were dressed like vagrants with patched and stained clothes. His body tensed, prepping for a fight, but the two men carried on past them.

"Hit them hard, ensnare them before they could fully clear the net," Rein muttered.

Katya tightened her grip on the case. "And change it up before they catch on to the pattern and adopt a new approach." She swallowed to drown the awkward laughter that bubbled up. "Here we are using their tricks."

He glanced at her. "It does burn, doesn't it?" He licked his upper lip. "I remember when you arrived on Reznic, so fresh, naïve. I'd bet on you succumbing to Reznic's mealing stone. Despite everything, though, you kept at it, even though—despite the never-ending fight. You'd look like an avenging specter."

Her skin crawled. "I had a job to do."

"She has Plasovern ties, you know." He nudged his head back toward Usha's business. "She'll be pouring funds from that grain into their efforts. You can't say it doesn't rankle you. I know you too well to think it'd do otherwise."

"It's survival." The words rushed out, even though he'd hit a mark. Her stomach clenched at the thought of the explosive materials the organization would be able to purchase with the price the grain would fetch—all thanks to the increased demand for such a commodity in a war zone, a war zone Plasovern had created.

"Survival doesn't mean we have to support Plasovern."

"When Vlar sent us here with the grain, neither of us were the wiser. And once here, we'd reached the point of no return. At least you managed to shake some more money out of them for our troubles."

She and Rein shifted closer together as they reentered the hub of the market, bumping their shoulders in an attempt to both guard their revenue and minimize their presence. Katya wished for a cord to tether the case to her wrist, something to slow a speedy pickpocket. Most of these people — if they had any clue to the case's contents — would descend upon them like rats fighting over the barest of scraps. And she couldn't blame them.

"I wouldn't have accepted this," she said, "if I had any idea of Ereago's situation or its ties to this bloodbath. But now here . . . we might have taken it elsewhere, but—"

"Survival," Rein finished. "We would've been out fuel, and anywhere else, we wouldn't have fetched a price to break even."

"Such are the times we live in." They were just fortunate to not have their names and faces broadcasted across the galaxy. She could only imagine the Magistrate Brass were determined to play their cards close to their chest . . . an all too familiar tactic they'd often deployed on Reznic. She didn't doubt for a moment that the merchant on Gilga had sold them out. "We'll be more careful with the next job."

The muscles in Rein's neck tightened. "All this for a small alien child."

Her own posture tensed, a reaction programmed into her body whenever Rein mentioned Aquila. "He reminds me of myself."

This raised Rein's eyebrows. He knew. Of course, he knew that Cassius had been a name given along with its citizenship. It was common knowledge, albeit one Katya spent her life ignoring and burying. Every so often, she opened the proverbial box and peeked in, only to shutter it, terrified that some demon might escape.

"Do you remember much of your homeworld?"

Her back ached with the tension that grew between her shoulder blades, made worse by the cramp brought on by the case's weight. "Not really."

He flexed his hands but ceased his probing.

They turned onto a side street to take a less crowded path to *The Wandering Trader*. Soon the messy grain would be gone—if Usha upheld her promise—and they'd be on their way, a little richer and able to change their identities again.

Meters away, the crunches of boots on pavement headed toward them. Her stomach clenched. Distant memories, amorphous in nature, scorched through her mind, and she nearly stopped. A sensation pelted against the mental walls she'd formed over the years—a sensation of cold and snow, reddened and blotched. She jerked her attention back to the path in front of her, hoping her trembling limbs had gone unseen.

"You should cut your hair or at least change the style," Rein said. "It's too distinguishing as it is now. We need to completely erase ourselves this time."

Warmth seeped back into her face, her hearing clearing. Yet, the thought of a haircut did little for her distressed stomach. Why? It'd always been her father's idea. As a child, she'd hated the time put into braiding and stringing each strand into place before fastening them with countless narrow pins—pins confining her to a culture, unknown and forgotten by her, that served as a barrier from the children surrounding her.

Clipped tones awakened her from her brooding, and she lurched to the side of the street behind Rein. A group of Magistrate soldiers bustled past them, an officer shouting while another spoke into his com, yelling, "Have civilians take shelter, either in place or at the designated locations!"

They're responding to something. A disturbance, maybe? Katya wiped her clammy palm against her pants before taking the case with it and doing likewise with her other hand. They needed to get off-world, and now.

She increased her stride, pulling ahead of Rein. More Magistrate peacekeepers poured by, headed in the same direction as the other group. Plasovern and the Gata were moving. Katya fumbled with her scarf and tilted her head away from the Magistrate troops.

Behind them, pops echoed, growing quieter by the time they'd traveled three blocks. They were almost nonexistent when they entered the spaceport. Security progressed throughout the port, a sizeable force stationing themselves at its entrance, where they scrutinized every inch of cargo and the documents of those spilling in, searching for safety. Katya and Rein passed through the security check quickly, carrying nothing but a slate and a case of Magistrate currency from what on paper seemed little more than a legal trade deal. Any lingering scent of narcotics went uncommented, perhaps because of Usha's establishment's name.

Once free of the security officer, Katya removed her headscarf, resting it along her shoulders. "We'll have to do the cosmetic work in space."

"I can take care of that. You focus on the chip."

The loading ramp still rested on Ereago's soil as if welcoming them back; the grain no longer crowded their hold. The only thing remaining was its dust, with their feet leaving imprints when they walked across the hold. It even clung to the metal interior, lightening its gray.

"Close up shop here, and I'll get us underway." She climbed the ladder and headed to the cockpit, intent to clear their departure and propel them as far from Ereago as possible—to escape the queasy sensation engulfing her.

In the cockpit, she found a bundled-up Mina with a somewhat alert Aquila resting his chin on her shoulder. The temperature had been lowered to appease the Oneiroi child. Mina plucked her earbud from its place, the other end following from where it had dangled near Aquila's ear.

"It's been silent." Mina set aside her device.

"I wish I could say the same." Katya slid into her seat and thumbed a request to leave port. As she did so, the headscarf fluttered from her shoulders to the ground. "The city's not nearly as secure as the Magistrate news sources would have you believe."

Mina's lips twitched. "What does that mean for us?"

No instant response from the Magistrate relay at the port was forthcoming. A lockdown? Rubbing her left temple, she said, "It could mean nothing."

"What's the worst-case scenario? You know, with how our luck has been going, we might want to go with that one first."

"I'll level with you, Mina." Katya swiveled toward the girl. "If the Magistrate has us pinged, if they've tracked our movements up to this point—"

"We aren't getting far."

Katya frowned at Mina's ashen complexion. She'd grown prone to staying with the ship at each stop, ever since Gilga. The girl who had been so eager to explore each new destination seemed gone now, all within a matter of weeks. Still, her reluctance to leave the ship provided Aquila with a caregiver. But Katya still needed to address it. Anything else wasn't fair to the girl.

She pressed her lips together. They'd all been different people weeks ago. She brushed her bangs to the side. And in a matter of what could be hours, they'd change again. Her hand touched one of her braids.

"Is something wrong?" Mina asked.

"It's nothing."

A loud beep emitted from the communications console, and Katya activated the system to receive the message. "Notice to all ships: All arrivals and departures have been suspended indefinitely. Those in need of refueling should divert your course to Ereago's sister planet . . ."

The mechanical message droned on, providing various scenarios and solutions. Their own solution: stay in place. Katya inhaled and applied more pressure to her temple. Another stab of pain blurred her vision. Trapped. Trapped on a ship that, if it wasn't already pinged by the Magistrate, soon would be. Only a matter of time. The trail connecting them to *The Maelstrom* hadn't been diluted enough; with a little digging, investigators would be able to follow the breadcrumbs. Elites would be involved in the hunt, bringing with them resources that far outclassed theirs.

She shifted her gaze to Aquila, who slept with his head resting on Mina's shoulder. What would be his fate if they caught up? Then there was Mina . . . her fate was more imaginable. There might be a time where Katya would pacify Rein's rumblings and leave Aquila and Mina, only not for the same reason he wanted them gone.

The intercom came alive. "What's the ETA?" Rein asked.

Katya throttled her initial response: when the war ends. "The port's on lockdown. There's no leaving."

A moment of silence followed, then he said, "We should start the work. Minor stuff on the inside."

"Get a start. I'm going to check out the port and see if I can dig up some information." Katya opened the case and removed some of the currency. She fanned it, counting out the amount prior to stuffing it in her breast pocket. It'd open possibilities; after all, hard currency offered many benefits: no traces and no worries about accounts being seized. "Mina, get him into bed."

"Is this wise?"

Katya stopped halfway through the door, reclaimed headscarf in hand, and faced Mina. "I want to know what's happening. It might even get us out of here. The last thing we can afford is to sit still." She fastened her headscarf into place. "If the port officials contact us, let me know immediately."

She then left the teenager, heading toward the cargo area, where Rein had already begun targeting identifiers and eliminating them.

He paused in the chore. "You shouldn't go out alone."

"I can handle myself." Her hand rested on her hip near her holster. "Mina is keeping an eye on the com traffic. Hopefully, the port will open; if not, there might be other means." Katya met Rein's glare with her own. "We can't be caught here. You know exactly what happens if we are."

He nudged a toolbox with his foot, bringing it closer to a serial number on the cargo hold's wall near the ramp. He reached down for the paint. "Good luck."

"I'll try to make some."

After leaving the ship, she strolled through the port. She kept her pace purposeful but slow enough to soak in the various conversations. Duty changes, trades, and random news from all over the galaxy—gossip in some cases—drove most conversations. A few talked about the port's current status, either spreading tidbits of the battle or venting about how the delay was impacting them. The port bustled with an assortment of travelers and crews, all stuck. Katya used her headscarf as a shield when a group of Magistrate soldiers marched by. A coldness seeped through her body with each step—boot-covered feet crunching in the snow. She shook her head, banishing the imagery.

Refocusing, she weaved her way to the row of merchant establishments, consisting of a couple small eateries and a bar called *Ber'sek*, a Varsaali slang word for a sex act. Quaint. Despite it, Katya entered, going between two bulky Borvinian bouncers who let her through. On the inside, she understood why: She was one of the few females in the joint, and the majority were dancing scantily clad on a centered stage against the back wall. A man near Katya caressed her butt. She slammed her hand into his wrist before bringing it back as a fist into his face. Blood squirted from the man's nose; even still, he managed to curse as he fell from his seat onto the floor.

Katya glowered at him. "Don't touch."

She then pressed farther into the dimly lit establishment, eventually arriving at the bar, where she favored a seat far from the entrance. Removing some of the currency, she laid it on the counter. "A stiff one," she muttered to the barkeep. He returned with a rocking glass of

Tecarian whiskey. She swallowed some of it. A decent vintage at that. Warmth spread through her face and chest.

The barkeep lingered while she drank more. Humanoid, vaguely handsome if he had not taken to the hard drugs; his face had begun to droop because of the usage.

"Does the port close frequently?" Katya asked.

"From time to time. Depends on the Gata." He departed from her, going down the length of the bar to a set of patrons waving money.

Katya swung on her stool until she faced the room. A fur-covered Faleean female danced on the stage, her body movements somewhat hypnotic, or maybe the drug cocktail she'd walked into now mixed with the whiskey made it so. Beyond the dancer, a crew of Garrs hunched over a corner table and talked. She took another sip from her glass and rose.

Quirking her lips, Katya approached them, taking her drink with her. Garrs were not exactly known for their loyalty to the Magistrate; after all, the majority of their planet had tried to retake control of their government, only to fail. Garrs numbered quite extensively among Plasovern—others, meanwhile, dipped their hands into less than legal trades. Of course there were crews that stayed on the legal end of business, but in their current situation, a bet might prove worth it.

"Got room for one more?" Katya rested her free hand on her hip and strengthened the smile on her face.

"The table is full, as you can see," said one of the men.

"You heard him, Magistrate *gercha!*" another Garr said before taking a big swig from his mug. "We have no need for Magistrate soldiers."

"I'm not a Magistrate—"

The Garr who had spoken snorted, spit rising up in his throat. "You talk like Magistrate. You walk like Magistrate scum soldier." He spat off to the side. "Take your stench with you."

"You misunderstand me." Katya set her drink on the table, the glass making a slight thud against the wood surface. "I'm not Magistrate—not anymore. I've reverted to my roots prior to being taken to Meracus Domus as a child."

"And what do I care?" He redirected his attention to his companions, pointed teeth revealing themselves as he chuckled—the sound raised the hair on the back of her neck. "Now, leave!"

Steeling herself, Katya brought her fist into the table; vibrations reverberated through her arm, along with trickles of pain. "You don't understand, my friend," Katya said through her clenched teeth. "I need to get my ship off this rock before hell breaks loose . . . without Magistrate trappings." She took another chance. "Usha suggested help could be found here."

The group of men straightened and glanced at each other, and one in the back corner cleared his throat. "Many suns are scattered across the galaxy."

Katya clenched her jaw. "I can't say what you want me to say." She shifted her gaze but found no unneeded attention centered on her and her new acquaintances. "I'm not Plasovern," she said, sotto voce by the time she reached the organization's name. "But I'm not Magistrate, not anymore. And without going into much detail, I possibly have Elites on my tail. You lot strike me as men of means— means to know every out."

"So the little gercha has found herself a *metmek* being chased by the ravenous *ketkerrs*," the rude one said. "Know what is like to not be a coreworlder." He took a drink from his mug. "Breathe easy. The ketkerrs don't know you are here. The Magistrate can't see what happens here, who comes, who goes." He smirked. "Not until they repair their precious relay."

She gaped, her limbs practically electric at the sudden boon they'd received. "That, however, doesn't stop troops and Elites from landing."

"The relay? No, that doesn't stop them coming, but other things maybe."

The marketplace with its blackened facades burned in her mind. "Things that might block others' departures."

"Unless they can pay the price." The one in the back corner spoke again.

"To whom is the price paid?"

The Garrs paused, trading knowing looks before the one in the corner stated, "A lieutenant of the port, Eligius. He will take bribes. If you pay the right price, he may let you out of lockdown. Now leave us, gercha."

Katya tilted her head and saluted them with two fingers. "Thank you." Whether she would genuinely feel gratitude, however, resided solely on whether Eligius was as bribable as they suggested or would instead throw her in jail.

She maneuvered toward the exit. The one man—now nursing his bloodied nose—slinked from her when she passed. This time there was no straying hand, though Katya swore he muttered a curse at her. She ignored it; after all, she was already good and cursed. Besides, further attention would be . . . imprudent.

Stepping into the street, Katya lifted a portion of her scarf to cover her lips before forcing herself to walk closer to a group of Magistrate officials, even meeting their gazes before checking their tags. None of them her man. With a hurried pace, they traveled past her, heading to the port's perimeter. As another Magistrate soldier walked by, Katya cleared her throat.

"I'm looking for Lieutenant Eligius."

"Now that's a familiar dialect." The soldier bowed his head to her. "Don't hear it much out this way. What brings you here?"

"Just another stop on the way home. My family made some bad investments, and I've taken on some extra work." Katya lowered her scarf and plastered a smile on her face.

"This was meant to be a brief stop before we headed back to the Mezzo and then home. But what we didn't know now has us stranded on this rock. Imagine people willing to blow themselves up!"

The soldier grabbed the metaphorical hook. "These people—Plasovern as a whole—are just dreadful." He leaned in closer to Katya and pointed toward an official Magistrate building. "Eligius is in the command post. He might be able to help a fellow citizen." The soldier winked and headed off, leaving Katya to approach the Magistrate port authority building alone.

The interior of the building had been mostly vacated, with a skeleton crew manning it. One of the few remaining officials greeted her. With the entire front of the building composed of synth glass panes, Katya had to shield her eyes against the glare of the sun, which made it hard to follow the man's movements.

"Please step to the side." The soldier motioned for her to drop the scarf. "No weapons or devices are allowed past this point."

Katya placed the scarf into the proffered bin. Her breath threatened to hitch as the soldier ran his hands over her body. He removed her slate, com, and AVI-13. The money, after inspection, remained in her pocket; the rest joined the scarf in the bin, leaving her feeling naked. The soldier lifted the slate from the bin and turned it on to determine identity. "What brings you to the port authority today?"

"I'm looking for Lieutenant Eligius," she said.

"What's your business with him?" the sergeant asked.

"That's between him and me." Katya quirked her lips while her hand trailed down her side to her hip. "Let's keep it at that, hmm?"

The man swallowed hard before he pointed to a set of stairs. "Take those; he's in the control room. Don't be surprised if your, er, plans have changed. And on the off chance you aren't one of Eligius's flings: Don't think you can try something stupid. We're on high alert and won't tolerate any actions that could be interpreted as subversive."

"You needn't worry." Katya bypassed the sergeant, fully aware of his gaze tracking her movements as she climbed the stairs. Beneath her feet, the ground floor loomed at her through the synth glass steps. Everything in synth glass. Would it fare any better than brick and mortar if a bomb went off? She had no desire to find out. As she cleared the top step, a device zoomed forward and scanned her for any weapons or devices that might have been missed at the door. The probe buzzed her face before retreating to its station.

Several consoles stood untouched, with only two people standing watch. One man paced back and forth as he talked in a clipped tone to someone over his com unit. "Don't give me that," he snapped. "You'll get that relay system back up. The damned Gata are moving, and the Brass are breathing down my neck! You will get your lazy asses to that relay—no, I don't care if you are taking fire. Get it done!"

He paced, freezing upon coming across Katya. His mouth tightened into a thin line, and he cut the feed. "Who are you? What do you want?"

The only other soldier in the room did not break her gaze from her station. A com device perched in her ears, suggesting she was listening to transmissions and unable to hear what was happening around her.

Katya stepped forward. "I hear you might be able to help a fellow citizen." She removed the wad of cash from her pocket. "I didn't stop at this world to get trapped here by a war."

"None of us want to be trapped here. These people have no understanding of gratitude." He swung his hand toward the window. "Bring them modern convenience— heck, cure their children of diseases wiped out centuries ago—and they attack us.

"No gratitude at all," Eligius concluded as he approached her, his hand brushing against her face.

Katya schooled herself not to move, allowing him to touch her as no man had done since he . . . since she'd left Reznic.

Eligius smiled, his eyes drinking her in. "We all want off this rock. But it does take some doing. Still . . . it's possible that Magistrate citizens might be given the opportunity. We do have certain privileges after all."

"We are blessed," Katya said. A smile crept onto her face when the lieutenant took the money from her hand. "It should help pay your way once you escape."

"Oh, I have no doubts." He unfurled the roll, skimming the paper currency. "It's a lot nicer than electronic transactions. More real—"

"Less traceable."

"Most definitely." He pocketed the money and glanced at his underling, who had yet to do anything beyond monitor her station. "Perhaps you could sweeten the pot even more."

"I'm afraid I have little time for that; I can't help but feel time is of the essence." Katya stepped closer to the almost seamless windows. "Do we have a deal?"

He followed her, caressing her face more. His fingers slipped down to trace her neck, the lining of her shirt's collar. As his hand traveled down her flesh, his mouth twisted into a smile. "I'm sure you can make time. After all, we have all the time—"

The room's other occupant spoke, her baritone voice displacing their bargaining and freeing Katya from Eligius's touch. "Sir, Elites coming in."

"About bloody time. Patch them into my headset."

"Their transmission isn't live, sir; they're sending generic instructions and requesting space to land . . . no mission listed beyond it being classified." She launched a diagram of the spaceport, waving through its sections. "It's a B-Class special ops vessel, sir; we'll need to clear space to accommodate it."

Eligius lifted his head, peering up at the sky—his hand blocking the sun—as if to spot the ship, which remained in orbit. "Sounds like brutes this time, sergeant. Alert our men to stay out of their way." Then to Katya, he said, "What block were you in?"

"B-4."

"Sergeant, clear section B-4. Effective immediately."

Katya saluted Eligius, making the motion loose, more fitting of her current persona. "I appreciate it, Lieutenant."

She paused at the top of the stairs when Eligius called, "What's your name?"

Katya replied, "Clementia." Waving, she descended the stairs at a steady pace, despite her heartbeat's frantic rate. Elites incoming. Breks? Had they finally traced them to *The Wandering Trader*? She approached the table with her belongings and returned them to their places.

"Didn't go as planned, huh?" the sergeant from earlier asked upon her return.

Katya shrugged as she wrapped the scarf around her head and neck, using its fabric to cover her mouth. "It wasn't the right time, but you already knew that."

Her possessions all in place, she waltzed out to Esh's spaceport. Her pace transformed into a jog once clear of the port authority building's immediate complex. B-4 already buzzed with activity by the time she arrived. Engines hummed as crews rushed to load supplies. Katya's stomach lurched when several ships lifted. Damn it! She ran now, clearing *The Wandering Trader*'s ramp in quick strides.

Rein, who had been going through boxes, jerked to attention.

"Rein, prep the FTL drive. We're leaving."

"I heard our block is being cleared—"

"Elites are incoming." Not waiting for a response, Katya hurdled up the ladder and into the cockpit.

There, she activated the engines. Mina, sitting at the communications station, gaped at her.

"We—"

"We've got to go," Katya finished. Via the viewscreen, she was alerted to another group of departing ships. She brought *The Wandering Trader* up, intent to stay clustered among them. "Keep an eye on the radar. Keep our signal a bland Magistrate one. And let me know if I get too close to anyone."

"Elites?"

"Yes. Most likely due to the conflict brewing on-world." Katya added the last part after Mina tensed.

Through the viewscreen, the sky bled to a deep blue, the stars coming into view, burning clearer as their speed built up. Katya held her breath as a few of the ships around her broke off, heading in different directions. She swung *The Wandering Trader* over until it hovered between a bulkier cargo ship and a pleasure yacht, matching their velocity. In the murkiness of space, light from Ereago's sun reflected off the metallic black Elite ship. As the sergeant had stated, it was a special ops vessel, a newer model at that—small, sleek, and beyond anything their ship could dish out in speed.

Katya kept her hands steady on the helm and begged the Elite vessel to maintain its course to the planet.

CHAPTER EIGHT

Those idiots. Akakios cracked his knuckles. Another group of vessels slipped from the planet of Ereago like fler rats scurrying to the escape pods. And like all the others rocketing through the atmosphere, they fled faster than the *Boreas*'s equipment could obtain proper identifications.

"Have the port authority send IDs on those ships," Akakios said to Charis.

His second leaned over Kyrillos's shoulder to oversee the request. Another pack of vessels raced toward them, a few already revving their FTL drives to make the jump before Charis said, "Their relay is down, sir. They have no IDs for the ships that were in that block."

Gritting his teeth, Akakios glowered when a few ships disappeared. Others—a large cargo vessel, a smaller one, and a pleasure craft—came alongside them. Another group of cargo vessels shadowed them. "Pull in as many as you can."

"Been doing that," Kyrillos said.

Akakios blinked, a sharp pang ruffling through his head, but as soon as it had come, it vanished, along with several ships that jumped away. He clenched his seat's armrest, his knuckles white. His heart banged against his ribcage. Fleeting, but there was no denying that presence. Exhaling, Akakios met Charis' gaze, but she quickly averted hers.

"The majority weren't displaying IDs beyond the generic Magistrate frequency," she said.

And there lay the problem with traffic in the Fringe regions: The majority had something to hide. The perfect place for Plasovern to go undetected, and it had allowed their prey to escape Ereago.

"Continue on course," Akakios said, forcing his posture to relax. "We'll speak with their contact."

As they entered Ereago's atmosphere, Akakios frowned at the amount of smoke, which billowed through the sky, coming from the outer edges of the capital. No army surrounded it, just miles of rail lines and an antiquated road system. So the struggle was based in the city itself. His muscles quivered. Their briefing had mentioned growing discontent among the planet's sects, one of which was suspected of having ties to Plasovern. But it hadn't revealed how far the situation had deteriorated. Another blotch of black smoke jetted upward much closer to the city's interior.

Ambrosios whistled. "That left a mark." He hit a few buttons, leveling out their descent with atmospheric thrusters. "And this contact . . . they wouldn't happen to be deep in the city, would they, Captain?"

"It's a good thing we're armed to the teeth, isn't it?" Akakios leaned forward. "Bring us in, but keep plenty of space between us and the skirmish."

Ambrosios's hands glided over the controls, inputting the commands to lower the landing equipment. Those on the bridge barely felt the transition from air to solid surface, just like they hadn't noticed the gradual shift in gravity.

"Sir," Kyrillos said. "The local officials are asking for aid against the insurgents. They seem to think that's why we came."

"Correct them on that assumption." Standing, Akakios stretched his arms to relieve a kink in his back before turning on his com device. "Advanced team will come with me to meet the contact. Come prepared: We're entering a war zone. Elpis, see to our welcoming committee. Keep them occupied. Try to determine what ships are still here and the names of any that left. Chrysanthos, keep the engines warm." He started to disconnect his device, only to receive an incoming call from Elpis.

"I'm a medic. Med-ic. It's not in my job description to track down ships or speak to foreign officials unless it's of a medical nature. My—"

"Your place is on the ship," Akakios finished. "But you are also a member of this special ops team, so don't forget your sunglasses. It's rather unsightly on the outside." He ended the call.

Charis smirked as she adjusted the sunglasses on her face. "With due respect, sir, you do know if something were to happen to you, Lieutenant Elpis would be the one holding the scalpel?"

"You know the captain," Ambrosios spoke before Akakios could. "He prefers living on the dangerous side. He wouldn't be in the job otherwise." His pilot then, with a flourish of his index finger, set the engines to idle. "Don't worry, sir, you're about to get a lot of that."

"I don't doubt it. I'll meet you outside in a few minutes."

Stopping in his quarters, Akakios added to his arsenal and grabbed his sunglasses. The interior of the ship grew darker when he placed them on his face, and in the oddest way, he was reminded of the caves his people called home. Months had stretched into a year since he had been there. His chest tightened. It would stretch even longer. He couldn't bear the thought of returning to those empty, silent caverns. There was nothing on Demos Oneiroi for him and no hope that there ever would be.

Akakios shoved his AVI-15 into its holster, both only months old. Thoughts of Demos Oneiroi returned to the deep crevices of his mind, replaced by thoughts of Esh and his nephew. He brushed his hand against the service pistol as he reached for his larger assault rifle, an AVI M-10, which he suspended over his shoulder. Going off the smoke, it'd come in handy. He disembarked fully armed.

Elpis, her hair perpetually stuck in a tight bun, already waited outside for the Magistrate port soldiers to arrive. After a jerky salute, she rounded on him. "I still think it would be better for me to stay with the ship rather than go digging through this port. What if you and the team need a hasty extraction?"

"We'll hold out until you can get back to the ship."

"I still think you'd be better suited to speak with the locals."

He chuckled, turning as the others made their way outside. "I doubt that, Lieutenant Commander. You're more of a people person than I am. It's more in my job description to be imposing and unapproachable. The elite of the Elites, they call us senior officers." Coming from the direction of the port authority's main building, a hovercraft barreled toward them. "But I'll tell you what, I'll stick around long enough to commandeer that craft and enlist their assistance for you."

The hovercraft stopped a few feet from them; its three port officials, clad in Magistrate blue rather than Ereago's tan uniforms, climbed out.

One called out, "We're honored by your arrival, the insurgents—"

"We have no interest in insurgents." Akakios took his slate in hand, thumbing it on and presenting to the man his Magistrate special detail emblem. "We're on a vital mission that involves a woman by the name of Usha. She operates a seedy business here in Esh, correct?"

"Usha?" The head official spat off to the side. "It's more than a seedy business, even if we can't prove it. She has her fingers in every aspect of Ereago, and I mean every aspect. Rumors say she dabbles with Plasovern." The man pointed to the smoke plumes. "Her lair's in the far side of the market, presently contested ground. So I'm afraid that unless you help us, you won't be speaking with her at all. That is if she hasn't already been killed."

When Akakios exposed his eyes over the frames of his glasses, the man stiffened and stepped back.

"If she's as clever as you paint her," Akakios said, "I doubt she'll be so easily killed. Now, we're borrowing your hovercraft, and sadly, I can make no promises that it'll be returned in pristine condition, but I'm sure you understand: war and all." Akakios clasped the man's shoulder, causing him to shrink under the weight. Upon releasing his grip, Akakios entered the hovercraft.

Charis, Ambrosios, Kyrillos, Pelagius, and Pelagia joined him. In the vehicle, Ambrosios took the helm, prepping their departure.

Akakios gave a shallow salute to the flustered port official who could only gape at this turn of events. "Our lieutenant commander, here, will be asking you a few questions; don't make her show you why others fear us." He resisted the urge to laugh when an image of Elpis trying to instill fear sprang to mind.

Feeling he'd cowed the man enough, he batted Ambrosios on the shoulder.

The hovercraft shot forward through the spaceport toward the walls that separated it from Esh—well, barely did that task. The large openings allowed people to come and go as they pleased. While guards monitored these gaps, the odds proved high that a Plasovern operative would breach the wall and enter the spaceport. One bomber—as they'd seen in the past—would be all it took.

"They have a map of the city loaded in the guidance system," Ambrosios said farther out from the port. "Barring a series of unfortunate events, we'll be there in ten to fifteen minutes."

Pelagia pointed upward while bracing herself with her other hand. "There's your unfortunate event!"

A massive dark object careened through the sky.

Ambrosios let loose a string of expletives and flung their hovercraft to the left. Its side scraped against a building, grating against the mortar—however, they avoided being buried under falling rubble. Akakios jerked his head up as another of Esh's taller buildings crumpled. With a whishing sound, a group of small planetary fighters soared overhead. He triggered his sunglasses' zoom feature, but the insignias on the fighters were foreign to him.

"They're not Plasovern," Charis said beside him.

"Probably the opposition." Akakios nudged Ambrosios's shoulder. "Take us farther east, away from the fighters. We can work our way back."

Ambrosios tightened his grip on the helm before giving a curt nod. "Understood. But we might have to abandon the hovercraft. At the rate they're going, the entire market and governmental areas are going to be leveled."

Akakios opened his mouth, but any words stopped after a boom shook their surroundings, distorting them. A cloud of dust swept past, enveloping them and filling Akakios's mouth. Sputtering, he hunched over to clear his passageways. More planetary fighters shot by. No doubt headed to the governmental sector, possibly the spaceport. His mind flickered to the *Boreas*. Chrysanthos should be able to react to the situation, but he wouldn't be able to prevent damage to the ship, which would be little more than a sitting target unless he gained enough altitude. Another hacking fit wracked his body.

One of the fighters sputtered as the anti-aircraft weapons spun to life, filling the air with bright orange tracers. They cut into the enemy's crafts, a few veering downward into the city, with black smoke trailing after them. New fighters bearing the Magistrate eagle entered the mix. Together with the smaller opposition crafts, they completed a deadly dance, which promised to end favorably for the better-equipped Magistrate crafts. As another opposition craft dropped, Akakios exhaled. They wouldn't be trapped here. The spaceport remained guarded.

Ambrosios cleared a corner and entered a main artery cluttered with people fleeing toward the safe point in the city: the spaceport. To avoid hitting any of the crowd, Ambrosios veered onto a secondary street with less traffic. Clumps of debris and building materials, however, required him to bob and weave. Their vehicle had not been created for such obstacles.

Akakios grunted and grabbed the hovercraft's sidebars, as did his crew members, before a clump of building bits lifted their craft well beyond its design. His teeth collided together, sending waves of pain, when the hovercraft skidded hard into the ground. Ambrosios muttered something and then used the vehicle's remaining momentum to veer to the side.

"Take—" Akakios bit his tongue and collided with the other side of the hovercraft, his forehead connecting with the guardrail.

"Bloody *farkus*, Ambrosios!" one of his men—Pelagius, who had a deeper voice—said.

A Magistrate fighter plane tore through a building a few klicks in front of them. Had Ambrosios's maneuver failed, they would have been buried.

"Forgive me, Captain." Ambrosios wiped blood from his lips, which he had bitten during his hasty gambit. "We'll have to proceed on foot. It's been fried." He pressed his sleeve against his mouth before lifting it and blinking at the blood. "What if Usha's abandoned her shop for safer ground?"

"We'll deal with that scenario if it arrives. Have your rifles at ready. Pelagius and Pelagia, take the lead. Ambrosios and Kyrillos, cover the rear. Charis, with me."

They maintained silence as they ran among the wreckage. Nearer to the marketplace, they had to climb over heaps of debris. Akakios stopped on one pile, noting a battered leg sticking at an odd angle out from under the concrete and brick.

"Sir, we need to clear this area now." Charis directed his attention to one of the wrecked buildings. An undetonated missile rested, partially concealed by the toppled building. A P-330 Razer capable of clearing the block. Medzeci's signature was written all over it.

"No." Akakios shimmied down the pile of rubble toward it. "We need to deactivate it and send in its location. There's no way we can clear its blast radius."

Ambrosios and Charis flanked him while he bent over to inspect the missile.

"So, Captain, how many of these have you disabled before?" Ambrosios drawled.

"I've seen the blueprints." Akakios dusted off its small hatch covering the wiring and circuit board. Once the fine seam could be discerned, he removed a small flathead screwdriver and pick from one of his pockets. Removing the screws, Akakios thrust the pick into the seam and jostled the inner clasp free.

"Sir," Pelagia shouted, running toward them. Apparently, she'd gone off with Pelagius to scope their surroundings. "We've got company!"

Akakios hissed. The pick almost slipped into the chip. "Keep them busy!"

Weapons fire rang around him. Akakios flinched when a bolt hit the building a few inches from his head, sending bits of debris pattering like rain on the ground and the missile. Surely, their opposition saw the missile sticking out of the building? Akakios wiped the sweat and dust from his face prior to ripping off his sunglasses, which were now coated. Useless. Flinching, he narrowed his eyes to block some of the light that assaulted his vision, burning his retinas. Another bolt shot high, bringing another stream of debris. Gritting his teeth, Akakios hustled on with his task.

Charis slid off the rubble pile to join the fight. Ambrosios had already left; he'd never been one to let a skirmish pass him by. Contorting his jaw, Akakios worked to remove the chip. Plasovern-favored Razers harbored a remote activation option, offering a nasty surprise. The chip came free, and nothing followed. Putting his tools back in his pocket, Akakios breathed while cleaning his sunglasses to the best of his ability. Returning them to his face, he stood and lifted his rifle.

Detonation with the right outside influence, such as a stray blast, remained a concern. He leveled his AVI M-10 and compressed the trigger. Across the way, an opposition fighter fell, the bolt hitting him in the head. He discharged a second round at another fighter.

The shot missed. Rather than try again, he abandoned the rubble pile while his crew persevered, dispatching their opponents one by one. By the end, ten opposition fighters lay on the ground.

Charis hooked one of them with her foot and flopped him onto his back, exposing his gray face. "Native Gata." She bent down and opened the man's jacket. No bombs. The others were checked as well. "They aren't as insane as Plasovern, sir. But it's almost certain given their tactics that Plasovern is on-world."

Akakios reapplied the safety to his AVI assault rifle. "That's not our problem. Just call in the Razer." He recommenced toward their destination as Kyrillos spoke with the locals via com. "Our port friends already seem aware of Plasovern's connection."

Likely they had reported it repeatedly to the Upper Brass. However, compared to the skirmishes on Varis, Aedelsten, or Skogarld, Ereago had been brushed aside, as the planet did not threaten the stability of the Magistrate—at least not like the former planets. Skogarld perhaps didn't warrant the number of boots on the ground it had received, but Akakios supposed it was personal. The planet had birthed Hedda Strom and thus Plasovern. With that tidbit of history, the Magistrate wouldn't so easily relinquish it.

"I'm surprised the Brass isn't giving more resources if they know Plasovern is here," Charis said, coming into step beside him. "They usually toss everything at them to prevent footholds from forming like they have on Varis and Aedelsten."

"We only serve. Let—"

A whining noise cut him off, followed by a large rumble shaking the area. Akakios braced himself against a nearby wall. A humanoid cry reverberated when silence fell; others joined it—some resembling angry shouts. In another area, rounds of shots being traded resonated. He waved his team forward.

They pressed on, finding the marketplace's streets abandoned except for a few citizens who struggled to free those trapped in the wreckage. A child's wail coated the area as a group of large men lifted what had been a wall. One of the men stepped back and triumphantly lifted a female child—bloodied, dust-covered, and stunned— shouting phrases in some native tongue.

"Usha's shop is a couple feet down that road." Ambrosios pointed in the direction. "In and out?"

"In and out," Akakios echoed, his hand grasping his service pistol.

They paused at a corner to check their surroundings— more damaged buildings, the perfect spot for Gata snipers, and a few loiterers. He made the hand signal to continue with caution. A few deserted storefronts down, Akakios halted and dipped into one building's recess. Two Borvinian males guarded the exterior of Usha's establishment, and given Usha's reputation, he doubted they'd be pleased to welcome Elites.

<On it, Captain.> Ambrosios clapped Pelagius on the shoulder, and the two swept forward.

The Borvinians reacted too late. The one in front of Ambrosios uttered a guttural wail and threw back his head before collapsing, as did the one targeted by Pelagius. The door flung open, and two more Borvinian bouncers ran out, roaring. They each swung a wooden rungu. Ambrosios, who had been off to the side of the door, jabbed his foot into the nearest bouncer, sending him to the ground and the rungu tumbling out of reach. The hairy creature tried to stand, but his attacker incapacitated him much like a cat would a mouse.

Pelagius—to which Akakios could only shake his head—tried to match the Borvinian in physical strength. Yes, he was built like an ox, but his opponent was out of his league in that respect. Blows met with blows of greater strength, knocking him back. Cursing, Pelagia fired her service pistol. The Borvinian wailed while gripping its bleeding knee. In that moment, Pelagius landed a solid punch to the creature's head; the bouncer toppled into a blacked-out window, shattering it.

"What did you do that for?" Pelagius rounded on his sister.

"We don't have time for your posturing." Pelagia returned her pistol to its holster and nudged her head toward Akakios. "Besides, you were embarrassing the captain. We have standards, you know?"

Pelagius shot heated words back at her, but Akakios didn't have time to play mom with the twins. Pistol in hand, he entered the store. On the interior, drugged patrons lounged on cushions, so out of it they hadn't reacted to the sudden broken window or the firestorm whirling outside.

No, they puffed their heh'sha, letting their city, their world, plummet into a civil war that would choke any prosperity. Akakios scowled at them and the foreignness of their choices—to let their world burn. His hand tightened on his pistol, tempted to shoot the machines and remove their fake pleasure.

"Who are you?" A violet Csek surged toward them. "I must ask—"

Akakios met the Csek's gaze; her frame stiffened as if doused with ice water, and a breathless gasp excited her mouth. Control of her limbs vanished, and she collapsed to her knees. Akakios released her mind, allowing the remnants of paranoia and fear to drift back to their hiding spots. Stepping over to her hunched frame, he dragged her up. Saliva dripped from her mouth, along with ragged breaths.

"Your mistress. Where is she?" he asked.

The Csek's head lulled to the side, slight tremors passing through her body. No response. Akakios tilted her face back, forcing her eyes to the same level as his. With the connection made, she shook. Images—distorted as with all non-Oneiroi—filtered like a corrupted film reel to his mind: a hallway, a door hidden within the paneling. Random images intermixed the connection—her running, falling, a man looming over her—Akakios used them to distract her, keep her pliant.

"This way." Akakios dropped the Csek and marched into the dim hallway, counting the panels until he arrived.

He touched the blended control panel. Nothing. Slamming his rifle's butt into it, Akakios cracked the glass screen, dispelling its hologram concealer and sending a few small sparks at his face. He rattled the weapon throughout the new opening, removing additional glass and exposing the wiring.

"Let me." Charis brushed his arm as she descended on the mechanism. After a few adjustments, she opened the door to a small antechamber.

Beyond it, they uncovered a larger room. Similar to the lobby and hallway, red light covered every inch. A good number of users lay drugged out on pillows, attached to their narghiles. The pendant light fixtures shuddered when another explosion hit on the outside.

"It's odd to find Oneiroi in my den," a gravelly voice enticed Akakios. A humanoid woman, sitting on a plush pillow elevated above the rest, flipped her long white hair over her shoulder. Taking in her pale, almost translucent skin that captured the red light, Akakios knew he'd found their Filitre. The woman, Usha, took a drag from her narghile. "What brings the Magistrate's dogs to me? My heh'sha? My purple lady? It is legal on this world, so weary with its trouble . . . at least, until the Magistrate's regulations fully phase it out in a couple of years."

"Ah, that's why you're supporting Plasovern and the rebels, then? To keep your little drug empire running," Pelagia said, earning a mental order from Akakios to shut her mouth.

"There are no such ties. You are grasping at straws, my little pup." More smoke emitted around the corners of her mouth. The Filitre curled her lips as if enjoying her own private joke.

"I don't care about your business dealings!" Even Akakios admitted he resembled a barking dog much like how Usha had painted all Oneiroi. Magistrate dogs. It'd been a popular insult hoisted at his people. "I only care about one of your business associates. A woman who came here piloting a ship called *The Wandering Trader*. And don't try to lie; I know she was here."

"I don't hand out details about my associates." Usha placed the pipe on a stout side table, which had a notched edge to receive it.

"You will, or else you'll meet the same fate as your employees out front."

Chuckling, Usha flowed upward to her feet from her large pillow. "You won't find me so easily vanquished." She clicked her tongue against her teeth, almost bordering on derisiveness. "But you should be wary of picking on the weak. Poor Hadjara. What phantoms did you conjure for her? What relics of the past did you uncover while on your *mission*? All for nothing." She met his gaze, winking at him. One corner of her mouth lifted. "The woman did come here, but I know nothing about her, only that she delivered my grain as promised. She didn't wish to conduct further business and departed to parts unknown. A shame, really. Such competent pilots are hard to find."

"Who was she with? Did she have a child, a toddler, with her?"

The lines on Usha's face smoothed, all signs of amusement erased. She got out a syllable — then the world upended. The light fixtures shattered to the ground, along with pieces of the ceiling. Akakios jerked his hands up to shield his head and neck. His vision blackened after something impacted with his back, sending him to the ground.

Coughing, Akakios met resistance when he moved. <Is . . . everyone alive?> Akakios sent out through the channels connecting him to his crew. He shifted to one side, displacing some of the pressure off his back. A crunching sound approached, and then more weight was lifted.

"Most of the building's down." Pelagius hefted more debris from Akakios, grunting at the exertion. "Charis took it worse . . . got a broken leg or something. Going to be a challenge getting her back to the spaceport."

"Poor dogs," Usha said. Akakios shifted to find her dusting herself off and lumbering to sit on a heap of her store. She squinted at the sun before blocking it with her hand. "Dig, dig, dig. You may free yourself here, but you'll remain collared, and you won't even see it—if you did: oops." The corners of her mouth tipped upwards.

A few of her patrons had survived the explosion, but others, a majority it would seem, had been too close to the eastern wall and had been buried, dead and alive alike.

"I don't know. I think I'd rather be collared than associated with people who have no qualms about seeing me, or my establishment, as collateral damage." Akakios groaned as Pelagius helped him to his feet. "The toddler—"

"There was no toddler. Just the woman, a man, and a teenager who never left the ship, per my men. Nothing more."

"Sir, we need to get back." Ambrosios staggered forward, sporting a gash across his face and holding his arm. <It's just a sprain.>

"Gather everyone. Pelagius, Pelagia, help Charis. Kyrillos, help me clear our path." Akakios faced Usha, flicking off more building crumbs and sending them in her direction. "Don't be surprised if the Magistrate completes a full investigation of your operations here."

"Oh, I have no doubts they will, but they won't find anything." She returned to her feet. "Good fortune on your hunt."

Akakios hesitated. She hid something, probably a great many things. Her people may be harder to affect, but they were not immune to the Oneiroi's gift, with the right amount of pressure . . . Yet, she had met his eyes in regard to the child, and in the end, that was the only question that mattered. Any ties to Plasovern mattered little at the moment, nor did her extensive drug empire. The investigators would find nothing once they left, not even Usha herself, but that wasn't his problem.

"Let's go!"

Together with Kyrillos, Akakios kicked through the panel door, which remained standing, along with the west wall. The blast might not have taken out the entire building, but as they entered the hallway, the creaks of stressed supports emphasized the need for haste. He waved Pelagius and Pelagia through with Charis.

The front room had been abandoned, minus a few of Usha's workers who busied themselves collecting various drugs from the narghiles. One worker, upon seeing them exiting, darted down the hallway the Oneiroi had exited, no doubt in search of her mistress. The others did not break from their tasks, and the Oneiroi did not impede them. The world outside Usha's shop featured new broken windows and more deeply scarred buildings. With no vehicles in sight, Akakios took off on foot, his crew following close behind.

"Keep your eyes open," Akakios called. Any way back to the port besides walking would be ideal. Surely, some mode of transportation had been left, something still in decent shape that would get them a few miles.

By now, the area had been vacated. Traveling several blocks, Akakios spotted an abandoned cruiser: a two-seater with a metal bar pierced through its engine block, in what had likely been the worst day of its owner's life. Akakios kept his team moving in search of other prospects.

The sounds of strife—now faint pops of weapons fire—remained a good distance behind them. Planetary fighters no longer swept through the sky, which was a shade of bright blue that would never be seen on Demos Oneiroi, or even by his unaided eyes.

"Captain?"

"Nothing." Akakios resumed his fast stride, not even remembering having stopped. He also hadn't realized he had taken a wrong turn in the maze that was Esh. He didn't know the city well enough, and the map's 3-D projection was worthless since so many buildings and roadways had been dismantled during the ruckus.

The road they were on led to a large green space in the city. A pavilion had been damaged, with its roof now sagging toward the south. The playground equipment sat untouched, the swings moving in the slight breeze. Beyond that, a few trees remained rooted, surrounded by swatches of grass and a few flowers and other plants. Clear skies. Aerial evacuation might be worth the risk.

Behind Akakios, Pelagia breathed heavily as she and her brother approached. Between the two of them, they kept Charis upright. His second grimaced with each step.

Any other way would take too much time, open them to a skirmish. Akakios clicked on his com. "Chrysanthos, trace this signal and pick us up. Tell Elpis to prepare for wounded."

"How bad?"

Despite the level, detached tone, Akakios caught the slight tension. "Not bad. Hurry before the opposition scrambles more fighters."

"Got your signal; we'll be there soon."

Pelagia and Pelagius moved Charis over to a round piece of playground equipment and sat her on it. Pelagia offered something from her pouch, a pain reliever, to Charis, who waved it away.

"Don't say I didn't offer it twice, Commander," Pelagia said under her breath before re-pocketing the syringe.

"So what now?" Ambrosios rubbed his arm, his face stuck in a grimace.

"We patch ourselves up and pray the trail doesn't go cold."

"They've changed their ship before, their identities; they're bound to do it again."

Sighing, Akakios ran his hand through his hair, dust lifting from it. "I'm well aware. We'll have to count on them making a mistake. I'd put my stakes on that rather than intelligence providing any useful information." A rattle of metal drew his attention to an empty swing. "But since we're rather beaten up, we'll go to the Mezzo, to the medical station orbiting Frete."

"Elpis will be pleased, her and plenty of eggheads."

"You two are too rough on her," Kyrillos cut in.

Ambrosios chuckled. "If she can't take the jesting, she's in the wrong career path. She could've been a doctor on Demos Oneiroi or on a station. I realize you're sweet on her but—"

Kyrillos's face scrunched as he lifted a finger to his superior and opened his mouth.

Akakios cleared his throat and pointed at a black shape approaching. "Our ride's on its way."

As their ship drew closer, a loud humming followed, deeper than the planetary fighters. Chrysanthos brought it to hover close enough for them to mount the ramp without requiring the ship to land. Elpis greeted them and rushed to Pelagius and Pelagia as they moved Charis up the ramp. Akakios followed, stopping Elpis before she could accompany Charis to the infirmary.

"Did you find anything?"

"The port officials were lax and failed to keep records. Between them and myself, we didn't find *The Wandering Trader* in port. It's possible they weren't even here." She shouldered past Akakios. "Now I have actual work to conduct. Be sure everyone else with injuries visits me. I won't condone actions that reflect poorly on my work ethic."

"Cuts and bruises," he said, referring to his own injuries, "will have to wait until we are out of orbit."

Akakios jogged toward the bridge, intent on getting them out of reach from any planetary fighters. With Ambrosios and Charis out of commission, he assumed the role of pilot, taking control back from Chrysanthos. The *Boreas* lurched upward. Outside the viewscreen, the blue sky blurred to a deeper shade before becoming a black that was littered with stars. From this distance, Ereago looked peaceful and undisturbed.

Reaching over the console, he solidified the coordinates for the medical facility. The world below continued to turn—a dead end that had left two of his crew members injured with nothing to gain, except for a brief presence in his mind. He hammered his fist into the console.

Patience. Drakon, the man who'd trained him, had drilled it into him many times. There would be leads. Akakios pinched his lower lip between his teeth after it threatened to twist. But ole Drakon had never lost everything.

The door to the bridge opened, and Kyrillos entered, dropping his hand from his bald head as he took his place at the communications station. The emotions fled with his entry, and Akakios initiated the jump.

CHAPTER NINE

After hours spent peeling away any remnant tying the ship to its original identity, Katya ensconced herself at the engine room's workbench. There, she cemented their new identities on the registration chip, a newer Magistrate version but one she'd worked with on Reznic. She quirked her lips. As much as she'd hated the planet, she could not deny her adversaries had taught her how to survive the life she now found herself living. Removing the wire that connected the chip to her slate, she closed both devices. The light remained green on the other side of the registration chip: her tampering undetected. Katya released her breath. They were now the *Minerva*, a ship with a cursory history that would cave if prodded too much.

"That'll get us by." She swiveled her seat around and handed the chip to Rein. "It's not as good as our previous one, but I have a limited knowledge of civilian vessel IDs. I suggest we stick to backwater planets for now. Limited Magistrate presence and no relays."

Rein examined the chip. "More carrier jobs, huh?"

"Just enough to put food in our bellies, refuel, and keep up on maintenance . . . add to our history and give them something to weed through so it doesn't look like we appeared out of nowhere."

"New identities?"

"How does Nereus sound?" Katya asked rhetorically since she wasn't hacking into the chip again.

"Any special meaning?" He leaned against her workstation. Too close.

"Just came to mind." Katya stood and distanced herself. "I didn't put much thought into it. We're bound to burn through identities. Hersilia is mine, and Mina's Aeliana. Aquila can keep his since he's never been listed on the ship registration chips before" — she raised her hands to stall his protest — "just like he isn't listed on this one."

Rein's mouth tightened.

"Get it in place," Katya said before she stretched, relieving kinks in her back. Her head pounded too much to get into an argument with her former lieutenant. It'd been like that for days now, ever present, no matter how many migraine pills she swallowed. "I'll check in with Mina."

She walked with a slant, the pain throwing off her balance. At least Rein hadn't noticed. She paused in the corridor outside the cockpit and leaned into its cool metal; it temporarily lifted the drilling in her head and eased her trembling frame. While she believed Rein still had her back, she feared showing too much weakness around him. Military order was no longer present to maintain balance.

Breathe. In. Out. She traced the seams of the wall with her left index finger. She reached almost normal and detached herself from the corridor.

More settled, Katya proceeded to the cockpit, where

Mina lounged with her legs resting on top of a console, though she returned them to the floor as soon as Katya entered.

"You really need to stop that." She shooed the teen from the pilot's seat. "One of these days, you're going to accidentally trigger something."

"I'm careful."

"I'm sure." Katya activated the planetary map system. While the isolation of space provided some comfort, they couldn't cling to it like a security blanket. "Any special requests, Aeliana?" Katya smirked. Mina had requested the name, drawn to it, no doubt, by a certain Magistrate singer.

"Somewhere temperate or tropical." The girl lifted her hand, her fingers splayed. "I've never been this pale in my life . . . it can't be healthy."

"It isn't." Katya needed to get Mina off the ship and under a sun. Ship lighting had been designed to infuse inhabitants with some vitamin D, but it didn't beat the real thing. "Temperate it is. I'm setting Cantno into the navigation computer. We'll enjoy some downtime there and pick up a job."

"How far?"

"A little over two weeks, but that'll give us time to get everything in order: our new stories and verify nothing survived the purge." With the coordinates in place, Katya rolled her head from side to side and stood. Brushing her tongue against her teeth, she fought the curse bubbling up her throat. More pain emitted from her right temple.

"Keep an eye on things, Mina. I need to take care of something else and check on Aquila. Let me know if there are any pings on the radar. I want to be here if we have to make contact with another vessel."

"Understood." Mina saluted her, the tip of her tongue peeking out between her lips. "You might also get some sleep." She lifted both hands. "I'm just saying. You've been up for twenty-six standard hours."

Ah . . . there was that. Hours spent repainting,

removing objects, and working on that chip. It likely accounted for her limbs feeling leaden. Biting down on her lip, she winced. Her mind might as well have been wrapped in cotton at this point.

Mina frowned at her.

"I hear you," Katya said, relaxing her face, even winking at her. Mina's expression grew less concerned. "I'll check in on you after my nap."

With a wave, Katya retired to her quarters.

She sucked in air when the cold struck her face. Grabbing one of the sweaters Mina had picked out for her, she bundled up, a necessity since the room was now kept at a balmy forty degrees. She approached the toddler bed, fastened in place by a series of bolts, and checked on the room's other occupant. He slept—always sleeping. But the sickly sheen of sweat had not returned. His weight had stabilized, though was nowhere near healthy. Between Mina and her, they'd been getting food down him at least. It remained a struggle, though. Trial and error, more often the latter. She touched his cool cheek; the gesture went unnoticed.

Stepping away, Katya dug through the storage unit near her bed, where she removed a small sewing kit her sister, Anaïs, had given her to mend her uniforms. A Tridetarian, Anaïs had always been talented with her hands in a way Katya could never hope to replicate, but that was all right as their papa had always told them: "The lot of you might be different, but you all have your own special talents and each other." They all hailed from different worlds and different species, were all disconnected from their places of origin. Instead, there had been world after world, following their papa from dig to dig, while he kept them tied to forgotten pasts with haircuts, clothing, books, and toys. Oh, he would tell them about their worlds, but it had likely been from the perspective of an outsider captivated by a culture.

The kit's scissors in hand, she entered her bathroom, where she froze in front of the mirror. Rein was right: The hairstyle was too remarkable, unique. Setting down the scissors, Katya freed her braids, allowing them to fall straight down her back, and set aside the pins. After untying their ends, she ran her fingers through, which resulted in two swatches of wavy hair. She freed the bun last. Her hair resembled a curly coated sheepdog.

Her shaking hands gripped the scissors and lifted them until the blade rubbed against her hair, severing a few strands. Grimacing, she dropped them; their metal clattered against the sink's basin.

"Tehh." Hunching over, Katya rested all of her weight on the small square countertop. Images of snow — stirred by Ereago and the soldiers' black boots — filtered from her deep subconscious. So clear. Snow, red stains, boots, screams — slamming her fist into the metal sink, Katya broke the images and forced herself up. Hair. Simple, regrowable hair. She groped for the scissors, her gray eyes avoiding them and the mirror, until her fingers wrapped around their plastic-coated handles.

Then, she clipped. One strand. Clip. Another clump. Others followed until hair coated the floor. The absence of something against her neck struck Katya for the first time in her life. For so long . . . Blinking, she found herself unrecognizable in the mirror. Her bangs remained long and boxy, but the rest had been unevenly cropped, looking like the work of a deranged lunatic. Mina could fix it. Katya shook her head, scattering more loose remnants before running her fingers through her hair and then air, so unused to its shortness.

Katya reentered her room and slumped onto the bed, where she rested her face in her hands. When she shifted, a pair of eyes blinked at her, still clouded with sleep.

"What do you think of me now, huh?" Katya hoisted the boy from the crib. He coughed, drawing a chuckle from her. "I've—we've managed to burn through so many identities." She brought him to the bed, the mattress sinking under her. "Though you still remain at two—but me, I'm on my fourth. I can't even remember my first. I was just a couple years older than you, I think." Katya yawned as she settled into her pillows. "I don't want it to be the same for you, but we'll make the best of whatever comes. I promise you that."

Aquila squawked. Katya's eyebrow rose with it, particularly when a second one followed. The boy had never been vocal before. "You can be talkative, huh?" The boy's lips moved as if mimicking her, only without noise—then another squeak. Katya's smile broke into a yawn. While the headache had lifted, her fatigue remained a constant.

"I know, I know." Katya rocked him. "You just woke, but I would prefer to sleep without you waking me." She relocated him so that his head rested against her shoulder. "Perhaps if I tell you a story, you'll let me have my nap."

Clearing her throat, Katya struggled to think of something. Her father had told several tales, many of which he had learned in his studies and time spent on various planets. Each had held a different core lesson, one important to the people who had crafted the story. Most of the stories had centered on individuals faced with challenges, ending with them surmounting them. Warriors, royalty, farmer boys, liars, and musicians—she'd spent too much time with her father.

She shook her head. "Dissecting components of children's stories . . . to make children's stories."

Her mind clouded, and she yawned again. She'd wing it. "There was a planet—you would love this planet—that was covered in snow nine months out of thirteen. A truly frigid planet, or perhaps only a portion of the planet—yes, just a part of it so we're both happy." Katya's head sank further into her pillows. "Mountains stretched in the north with streams and rivers bringing water down to the small villages and cities. The capital, just beautiful, resembled a gem shining between two mighty rivers. And it was in this empire that a . . ." Katya tried to blink the sleep away. "That a princess lived."

Katya smirked as Aquila's lips slowed in their efforts to replicate her own. "The princess was well loved, and she would ride her horse through some of the empire's villages. She would bring healing to the ill and alms for the poor."

Aquila yawned. "Heh, you need to be understanding," Katya said. "I'm not good at stringing together stories. But I think you're right, it needs conflict . . . but not a dragon, not—" Her hand shot to her head as pressure built. The last thing she remembered was Aquila's eyelids moving rapidly. The pain lessened when sleep swallowed her.

Cold. It cut through her, seeped into her bones. She shuddered, wrapping her arms around herself. A shroud covered her surroundings. Where was she? Katya—her name, yes—spun. Like a damaged, old-fashioned reel in a faulty projector, her surroundings refused to focus. Walking. Her feet carried her to a point in the distance as if on their own accord. Snow. It crunched under her feet. It was untarnished and reached past her ankles, slowing her pace, threatening to topple her. Sounds grew muffled under the loud beating of her heart.

Unaware of time, Katya continued to walk—her legs smaller and unable to move fast enough. Something dragged her along. Reaching up, Katya tried to wipe the film from her eyes. However, only one hand reached its destination; the other remained engulfed in a much larger hand. It pulled her along. She couldn't make out the garbled words, not over the blood pounding in her ears. Her free hand rubbed her eyes. The world cleared marginally, though a film blocked her peripheral vision. Moving beyond the hand, her eyes traveled up the arm. Tha-dump . . . tha-dump . . . tha-dump. A man. His strong back turned to her. Wavy dark brown hair, visible from beneath a thick winter hat, rustled in a stiff, chilly breeze.

Her chest constricted, and Katya tried to pull away. She wanted—needed—to go back; she couldn't go forward. Breaths morphed into wheezing gasps. She couldn't see. As her head turned back, like a puppet on a string, red blazed, littering the snow. Can't—she couldn't breathe. Tears streamed down her cheeks, her face twisting. She wanted to flee like a frightened rabbit. She didn't—she couldn't go forward. The invisible strings rooted her in this moment, the moment. She revolted against the threads, spinning and cursing. They threatened to uncover . . .

Ragged breaths shook her frame, and her back collided with a cavernous surface. The hand that had held hers gone. She clenched her pant legs and brought her knees nearer to her body, sinking her face into them as she sobbed.

Her ears buzzed. The world around her, while clearer for a time, broke apart. The rocky cavern walls wavered, turning to blackness before they returned. Mumbled voices reached her, muffled by something resembling gauze in her ears; even so, she would never have understood the foreign language.

At a burst of laughter, Katya scuttled to her feet. She ran toward the sound, but the world switched again to one of metal, not rock. She stiffened. This place . . . People walked by her, blurred as if traveling at a higher speed. But they were alive. They hadn't been. Yet here, they continued about routines on a doomed vessel, very much alive.

The image broke. Breks. In a flash, they vanished, replaced by panic and weapons fire ricocheting off the walls. The world clouded again. Grunting, Katya pressed her hands against her temples, struggling against the otherness in her head that, like a worm, weaved through her subconscious. It towed her under. Awareness faded—

Katya woke screaming; the sound, however, caught in her parched throat. Hands—her own—tore at her eyes, struggling to clear the tears. Voices. Rein and Mina. Someone touched her, held her. Mina. She had smaller hands. Aquila. Realization flared through the pain in her head.

"What—he—" Her throat, so raw, constricted.

"I told you!" Rein roared. He pumped his fists, his face a livid red. "I told you he was dangerous."

Was. Katya jumped from her bed and stumbled to where Aquila lay crumbled like a discarded doll on the floor. Her limbs trembled as if in the midst of an anemic fit, and by the pain in her stomach, she believed she might actually be in one. Pressing her fingers against the boy's neck, she found a pulse, but blood seeped from a decent-sized gash that snaked its way from his forehead to a couple centimeters into his hairline.

"What did you do?" Katya rounded on Rein, Aquila in her arms. The boy trembled in shock, low whimpers rumbling in his throat.

"I saved your life! That little demon spawn had you trapped."

"You were asleep for two days, Katya," Mina said, still seated on the bed. Her lips, now coated in a vibrant purple, quivered, and she started to bite her lower lip before almost instantly releasing it. "We tried everything to wake you. Shook you, shook Aquila, moved him away from you—but you wouldn't wake up." Mina lowered her gaze, unable to meet Katya's as she rambled about their methods. "We—"

"Physical force worked." Rein dusted the front of his buttoned shirt.

"He's a toddler!" Katya laid Aquila on the bed, blood specks marring her white sheets. "He wasn't trying to hurt me—he was . . ." She didn't know what he was doing, but at the moment, it didn't matter. "He needs medical attention."

"He just tried to kill you. He's probably the reason you've had so many blasted headaches. Are you even hearing yourself?" Rein threw up his hands. "I know you feel connected to him, responsible for him. But what if he drags us all into a deep sleep that we can't wake up from? Huh? What then? No one will be saving us. Mina and I did not sign up for that."

He stepped closer to her and the bed, hands in fists. Her chest constricted, pulse erratic. As she was now, deprived of food and water, she had no hope of besting him if it came to a physical fight. Like she'd feared, what balance military decorum had maintained between them had been shredded. There would be no orders to halt Rein, and she'd stored her service pistol too far away.

"We should airlock him and be done with it, for our sake and his," Rein boomed. "Look at him, Katya! He sleeps all day and barely wakes to eat. He's wasting away. Just look at his muscle mass. It's practically nonexistent, and eventually, his habits will create greater health problems. The merciful thing is to airlock him. End it quickly so he doesn't have to suffer."

"We aren't airlocking a child!" Katya spun toward Mina. The girl, who could be so sharp-tongued and bright, crumbled beneath the attention. "Do you feel the same way?"

"I don't want to hurt him." Mina wiped tears from her face. "But I don't want him to hurt us either."

Katya lifted Aquila and struggled with a pillowcase until the pillow fell out. Pressing the fabric against his wound, she distanced herself. "He wasn't trying to hurt me. If anything, he wanted to communicate." She opened the door. "Your concerns have been noted. But I'm taking us to the nearest medical clinic."

Rein flew after her until he was at her heels. She willed her limbs to loosen, to be prepared to grapple with the much larger male. Her training highlighted vulnerable body parts.

Incapacitate him. Run to the cockpit. What good did that do? He'd have all the access to the firearms. Never again. Never again would she be without her service pistol. Then he sprung, and much like a constrictor, he grabbed her shoulders, squeezing down as if to overpower not only her body but also her will.

"Reconsider this!"

She slapped his one wrist; the motion lacked real power, the type she'd normally put behind it. He did, however, drop that hand, though he left the other in place, his nails pressing in.

"He's a danger to us. And if we take him to a medical center, they're going to know he doesn't belong to us. The game will be up."

"I know what I'm doing." Katya bared her teeth in a primal show, wheeling away from him with her one hand pressing against the back of Aquila's head. "An isolated clinic won't have the same procedures as a Mezzo or Core med center. They don't ask questions. Now stand down, or I will show you what they teach Magistrate officers!"

"I gave up everything because you couldn't leave well enough alone, Captain." His jaw clenched. "I almost had citizenship! Not everyone has that handed to him by chance." The venom in his tone reflected on his face. "I worked—"

"And I haven't?" Katya roared, her throat bleeding with the effort, so dry—damn, she needed water. She surged onto her toes until she invaded his space, shouting into his face. "I fought hard and struggled to get where I was. You aren't the only one who lost it all, so stand down!"

Rein ran his hands through his hair, staring at her with bulging eyes. From behind him, Mina's breath hitched, clutching her hands in front of her. Her face was scrunched, eyes brimming with tears. Lowering her head, Mina bypassed him and chased after Katya as she sauntered to the cockpit. Farther away, Katya caught Rein's feet slamming against the metal floor in the opposite direction.

Katya's chest loosened once the cockpit door closed behind Mina and herself.

Between sniffs, Mina said, "I should've stopped him—I'm sorry, Katya . . . We didn't know what to do!"

"Shh." Katya laid Aquila on the empty bench attached to a small workstation, dropping the pillowcase off to the side. Despite her attempts to hush the girl, Mina sputtered apologies between harsh breaths. Katya, meanwhile, brought the first-aid kit to Aquila and attempted to stem the bleeding. Clenching her teeth, she applied pressure to a wad of gauze and the boy's wound. "Mina, calm—calm yourself. Come here."

Mina winced at her brusqueness.

Softer this time, she said, "I need your help."

She inched forward, and Katya took the teen's hands, putting them where hers had been on the gauze. "Keep applying pressure."

From the kit, she grabbed additional gauze, a wrap, a sanitizing agent, and *zerna*, a chemically engineered substance that promoted accelerated healing in humanoids and several other species.

"Lift the gauze." Katya knelt beside them. "Discard those and hold this." She pressed the new gauze into Mina's hand and then set out sanitizing the wound, which drew a low whine from her patient. Biting her lower lip, she broke open the zerna pouch. Please don't be allergic. With that, she smeared the gelatinous green salve onto the cut.

"The gauze." Katya directed Mina to place it on the wound. The girl's breathing had leveled out with only a few hitches. Mere hiccups really. Using the wrap, she secured the gauze in place. "There."

Mina lifted her head as Katya swayed to her feet. The room spun and bled before it righted itself. Waving the teen's helping hands away, Katya lumbered to her seat and sat. Mina blinked away tears.

Flinching, Katya reached out and squeezed the girl's shoulder. "You couldn't have stopped him even if you tried. He's stronger than you are. And you were rightfully scared." Her grip tightened. "You've been a help. I mean it. Never allow yourself to feel guilt over what you can't prevent; there's no use lingering on it. It'll only make you sick." It was one of life's hardest lessons, one she still struggled with herself. Releasing her grip, Katya gestured to the door. "Please fetch me something to drink and eat. Also, my service pistol's in my footlocker. Only grab it if you are comfortable doing so and Rein is not within sight."

Mina pressed her lips together and nodded. She slipped from the cockpit.

Katya rubbed her face, rocking in the chair. Her heart raced. If he wanted to stop them, he had access to the engine room. She forced her hands away. She could lock him out, but that didn't prevent him from mucking up the works.

First Aquila.

Katya hunted for a clinic; it would take a few minutes for the navigation console to pool possibilities. Katya tried to gather enough saliva to wet her mouth and throat. Two days. Except for the effects impacting her body, Katya would have sworn it had only been a few hours. Phantoms of nightmares, hysterics, and dementias . . . so said the tales spread by the lucky, those who left Oneiroi inquisitions with their minds intact.

Aquila lay still. The occasional moan was replaced by irregular breaths. He had shown her exactly why his people were feared, though there had been no real malice behind it. But there was danger even if she could not fully understand it. They needed to. Not doing so would open them to disaster. Rein, while extreme, was right. If they were all dragged under, they would likely die, but was that scenario even possible? What was the boy even capable of? Katya swallowed against the knot in her throat. Their survival depended on answers.

The cockpit door reopened after several minutes, and Mina handed her the service pistol first, which had been concealed in her hoodie, then a bottle of water, and a plate of Holgar summer rolls. Katya dove into the latter. Mina removed a second bottle from her hoodie but hesitated. Katya frowned around one of the rolls as Mina struggled to prop up the boy and force water down his throat. Guilt and fear mingled on the girl's face while her shoulders were pinched in quiet anxiety, ready for some response from the Oneiroi. Katya regretted the burden Mina bore now.

By the time she had eaten three of the rolls, her limbs had strengthened, growing less shaky. Her mind also cleared but still lay miles away from running on all thrusters as it were. Setting aside the empty plate, she imbibed more water and cleared her throat. "I want you to start carrying a weapon at all times."

"I can't." She shivered, well aware of what carrying a weapon meant.

"I'll show you." Katya waved the teen forward and gripped her hand. "I hope you never have to use it, but I want you to have that skill in case you do."

The computer beeped behind her with its measly selection of four clinics, but they couldn't wait a minute longer. Katya fretted that pressure might be building against the toddler's skull.

"We need to be prepared to leave Rein, sooner rather than later."

Mina swallowed, her hands diving into her hoodie's pocket. "I think that'd be best." She crossed the space to scan the results, changing the subject. "Not many selections."

"No, there aren't." Katya placed the water bottle by the plate and then selected a clinic on a station that orbited a gas planet. The station catered to miners and those passing through. Perfect. "S4-G3. That's the one. We'll have to backtrack some, but we should be able to keep a low profile."

"That's really on the edge of Magistrate space."

"Another plus." Katya entered the new coordinates and initiated the jump after making the call for RMPs. "We'll be there in a matter of hours."

Aquila remained unresponsive for the trip. While not out of the norm, it and his head wound put her on edge. Was there swelling? Would there be permanent damage? Katya held him close to her chest, humming to soothe him. She directed Mina to monitor the communications system.

After three hours passed, the FTL drive ceased the jump. In that span of time, Rein had done nothing to impede them or dissuade Katya from her course of action; however, she doubted he'd sat twiddling his thumbs.

Mina jumped to action on her console. "We're coming up on increased traffic. Looks like mining frigates leaving Derget."

"Keep an eye on them." Katya slowed their speed.

The station dispatched coordinates to an incoming lane, which Katya entered. Besides the outgoing frigates, very little traffic operated around the station. On her own screen, Katya noticed the majority of traffic was going to and from Derget.

"They're requesting to know our business on the station."

"Tell them we have a medical emergency and are in need of the station's doctor."

"We've been granted permission to proceed."

Katya kept their speed at impulse, following the mapped lane. The station sent over additional instructions that included their docking assignment, Port 3 on Cluster 4—the nearest availability to the on-station medical clinic. She activated their intercom. "Rein, we're approaching the station. I feel it'd be best if you stayed on board." Acid leaked through her voice on the last bit, hopefully serving as a deterrent against anything he had concocted, though she doubted it.

"You're going to leave him alone on the ship?" Mina whispered after Katya closed the connection. Then, "You're not leaving him alone with me on the ship, are you?"

"You're coming with me, and I'm locking the controls, including communications. He's not moving this ship or talking to anyone. I'd rather him be on a locked ship than out in the station doing whatever he has in his mind to do." Katya activated the thrusters while she lined their vessel up with their designated port. "We'll get your weapon on the station once Aquila's patched up."

Mina frowned, her lower lip sticking out more than normal. "And when he's fixed up, what are we going to do? What if he does it again? We . . . we don't know anything about him."

Katya pinched the interior of her mouth between her teeth. Their ignorance would prove catastrophic, and she could tell Mina nothing because she, too, had no idea what to say, what to do. Running her tongue against her teeth, Katya debated.

"There might be someone who can be of help." Katya attached the *Minerva* to the station. "He's not too far from here, and I wouldn't be surprised if he knew something about the Oneiroi. He's been contracted by the Magistrate for many projects." She activated the lock command on all the ship's systems, sealing it with a passcode that Rein shouldn't be able to break.

Mina stood as Katya did. "Who is he?"

"My father."

Katya allowed for no further discussion, scooping up Aquila and leaving the cockpit for the station proper. She only popped into her quarters to grab funds and her holster. She slid her service pistol into the latter before heading to the connector tube. Rein stood beside it, his arms dangling at his side. They were prone, at ease yet ready for action. She tightened her grip around the young Oneiroi child as she approached him, her left hand sliding within reach of her weapon.

"I'm not changing my mind, so save your breath." She reached for the control panel, but Rein seized the moment, his hand ensnaring her wrist.

"I hope you know what you're doing."

"I'm doing the right thing." She pressed forward, her fingers hitting the door panel despite Rein's grip. "Keep the ship in one piece while Mina and I are gone."

"You're taking the gir—"

"I'm coming!" Mina ran down the corridor toward them while zipping up a warmer jacket.

"I hope to be back sooner rather than later." Katya stepped into the connector tube, Mina close behind.

Once the door closed behind them and they entered the station's decontamination room, Mina whistled. "I didn't expect him to let us leave so easily."

Katya agreed, even if she didn't voice it. Rein did not cave. It was one of the reasons she'd accepted him onto the ship in the first place. That, and he'd shown calm under pressure, even disabling a bomb in less than ideal conditions. Shutting her eyes as the decontaminant sprayed over them, she almost relished the cooling mist that dissipated as quickly as it touched her exposed skin. In her arms, Aquila sneezed. They had arrived at an impasse, one Rein was as aware of as she was. Fates and lady luck, don't let him be proven right by this visit. The doors slid open with a harsh hiss. Mina exited first, in a hurry to leave the small room, but she jolted to a stop as soon as she crossed the threshold.

An older man, with a balding head and wearing a Magistrate uniform, waited for them. He'd probably staved off retirement by coming to the S4-G3 post. Despite his age and the fact Aquila's eyes remained veiled, Katya's adrenaline flowed.

The Magistrate soldier straightened as he turned to greet them. "What do we have here?" he asked in a craggy voice.

"My crew was forced to use creative maneuvers. My son, however, was in our quarters and fell into a bulkhead," Katya replied.

"Poor kid." The man leaned forward, and she mentally begged Aquila not to wake. He brushed his hand against the bandage on the boy's head. "How old is he?"

"Three." It was the closest she had been able to guess. "The medical clinic—where is it?"

The Magistrate official inclined his head and gestured to the narrow metal hallway. "Follow me. I'll get you there. No worries, mother."

The hallway had many offshoots, several of which curved to match the station's circular structure. Each was as narrow as the one they traveled down, which only allowed two regular-sized humanoids, or maybe three smaller life-forms, to walk down it. As a mining station, comfort took a backseat to efficiency. The merchant and cafeteria side of the station was likely less compact as priorities switched. Having worked on ships' inner workings, Katya had developed an immunity to cramped spaces.

"I didn't realize the Magistrate had much of a presence out here," Katya said, keeping her tone conversational.

"Not much of one, but the Delgat Mining Association of Parfor requested a small presence."

Katya resisted the urge to ask how small. But with such an old soldier on guard, it couldn't be massive. The Magistrate had decided against wasting manpower on the station, sending enough to appease the mining association. Sure, the gases harvested from the planet were a staple, but Helium-3 wasn't rare. Delgat also had a unique situation where the Parfor people had staked claim to a planet, receiving a high percentage of the profits from their mining venture. The Magistrate government saw little to gain, especially when they had gems like Vorspor and Tramor, which were farther from the Medzeci Empire.

Their guide turned down one of the curved hallways; it expanded as they went. Katya speculated they were a quarter of the way around the station before they entered a grand opening. It hosted a few odd shops, many offering mining equipment, plus a few odds and ends, while another shop offered weaponry. There were also a couple of eateries that had attracted people passing through, if not the Parfor miners.

"Doc Jia's this way. He's a legit doctor, unlike some you'll find out here practicing medicine," the Magistrate soldier said, giving special inflection to the last word. "Just through here." He waved them toward an open door but did not follow them in. "He'll take care of your boy." He dipped his head in what amounted to a shallow bow. "Don't fret, mother."

As the man left, another person cleared his throat. A man with silver hair leaned over a gurney, glasses hanging from the end of his nose. Despite his hair, Katya placed him at no more than middle-aged. Doctor Jia propped up his glasses prior to pushing away from the makeshift bed. "What do we have here?"

"A head injury . . . he hit a bulkhead. I sanitized the wound and applied zerna."

The doctor removed the bandage from Aquila's head. "No adverse effects to the zerna . . . good, good. Very good." He tilted Aquila's head at different angles. "It's already closing it. Was he climbing somewhere high?" His face remained a void, but something in his eyes put Katya on guard. There was a wrong answer to this question. He hopped over to a small wheeled cart filled with medical supplies, the most-stocked aspect of the clinic.

"He might have been," Katya said. "He was alone in our quarters at the time. I was at the helm."

"Hmm." He rummaged about, grabbing something before returning. Katya's breath snagged in her throat when the doctor gently lifted Aquila's eyelids to check his eyes with a small penlight. "The external wound's no longer a concern, but I'll need to run tests to check what's happening on the inside. In the meantime . . . I would recommend being honest with me." He unsnapped the bindings of Aquila's shirt and took one of the boy's flimsy arms into his hand. "This child undoubtedly experiences severe difficulty sustaining his own body weight with his legs, let alone being able to pull himself up using his arms. His body is in a complete state of muscular atrophy."

Jia's fingers skimmed Aquila's shoulder where a large purplish, black bruise had formed. He then examined another along his ribcage. Katya winced. Rein had thrown the boy hard, harder than his weak body could weather.

"One of my crew members threw him."

He bobbed his head. "The atrophy? Cruelty or disorder?" He laid Aquila out on a gurney near a large machine and then covered him with a shimmery blanket.

"Disorder."

"And it has progressively worsened?"

Mina took in a sharp intake of air, and Katya prodded the girl toward the door. "It has."

The doctor straightened his glasses as he flipped a switch; the machine hummed, coming online. After inputting a few commands, he wheeled the gurney into the machine's opening. "I can patch him up," Jia said, not even lifting his head, "but you would do well to see that detrimental forces are removed."

"I'm working on it."

"Good." Swiveling on the balls of his feet, he tinkered with the machine. "As for his other condition, the disorder . . . that, I can't even begin to treat." He paused. "I won't say what he is."

A tremor passed along Katya's jaw. He knew, and they were beholden to him. Aquila needed this man. Her mind raced but struggled to form any helpful option.

"No, that would make this too messy and draw unwanted attention to my little operation here. The last thing I need is for more like him to come digging." Jia shook his head and pressed more commands into the machine, printing out what appeared to be a report. "No, I don't care how you came by your 'son.'"

Katya cleared the distance between her and the doctor, her hand brushing against the service pistol fastened to her hip. "What do you want?" She pronounced each word with an edge. Jia still did not face her. "I won't ask you a second time."

"I'm a doctor." Jia pulled the gurney with Aquila from the machine. "I want to heal my patient. Beyond that motivation, I want nothing. As I said, I won't say what he is, making him no different than any other humanoid creature that walks, crawls, or is thrown through my door." He grabbed the printout from the machine.

He flapped the test results in front of her face. "The fall was perhaps worse for him compared to another humanoid child; then again, there appears to have been a lot of force behind it."

"He'd trapped me," Katya whispered. She inclined her head, thoughts of snow rising from the murky corners of her mind, along with a dead ship. A brief spike of pain reemerged, but she refused to lift her hands in a feeble attempt to relieve it.

"I can patch him up in a matter of a few hours. I might not have the supplies that medical stations and centers have, but I can easily repair a concussion and stem internal bleeding." He prepped the necessary instruments. "Then you should depart. You never know who has had run-ins with them."

She knew that all too well. Grabbing a wheeled office chair, she settled in it while the doctor worked on her youngest fosterling, attaching an IV unit to him as well. Fatigue hit her as the adrenaline rush from the past few hours vanished. She felt as if she hadn't slept in weeks. Wherever Aquila had taken her, it had been anything but restful.

"Katya!" Mina called from the doorway, forgetting her new name. "Please don't fall asleep again."

She chuckled. "That's a steep task to ask." Resting her head against the chair's headrest, she added, "I feel like I just took a physical fitness exam and had to run from the academy to Mount Albus."

Mina gave the mall outside the clinic one more glance before coming to stand next to her. "Maybe we could go ahead and get my"—she glanced at the doctor—"present. Then we can just leave after the doctor's done." Energy buzzed through the girl's frame as she kept leaning toward the door. Apparently, she'd had a change of heart on the matter.

Across the way, Jia injected a needle into Aquila before placing a neural device on the boy's forehead that was designed to lessen swelling around the brain and repair damage. To the boy's side, Jia had already fastened an IHBR pad to treat the injury there. All in all, it would take time to complete both processes. They could leave and be back in that time. But the Magistrate official could return, or the doctor could stab them in the back. The scenarios ran rampant in her head. Waiting for the procedures to conclude came with its own downside: They would have Aquila with them while they visited the store, and he could be recognized for what he was. She didn't want a repeat of Gilga, not when they had once again covered their tracks.

"Let's get it done."

Jia's concentration on his work did not break when Katya exited with Mina. As they walked across the large open space that separated the clinic from the merchant district, Katya tracked what occurred behind her.

"Aeliana," Katya said pointedly, causing Mina to blush, realizing her previous mistake, "when we enter the shop, keep your eyes open. If anyone enters the clinic or leaves it, we need to know."

The teenager gave a curt nod as Katya opened the door, causing a chime to sound. The weaponry store was empty minus one being, who sat in a tall chair, her small legs and feet propped on the counter while she smoked a large hor'roo. In all, the proprietress stood no more than four feet.

"Welcome to the Twisted Entry Wound." She withdrew her pipe from her mouth. "I have a wide variety of armaments perfect for surviving in the Fringe. All are perfectly legal, even the eviscerator and the assassin models. If you carry the right credentials, of course." She slid her feet off the smooth metal surface and instead rested her elbows on it as she leaned toward them. Her white teeth, with particularly pointed canines, gleamed against her ebony skin. "Let me guess, you're looking to purchase protection for the young lady." She pointed to Katya's weapon. "Ah! A Preserver, the weapon that holds together the Republic. A good, trustworthy, and sleek AVI design. Older, though. A MP-12 or -13? Ah, 13. I can tell by the notch. Military issue with the Magistrate stamp. It's not bad, but there are better. Perhaps a weapon for the young one and an upgrade for yourself?"

The proprietress jumped from her seat, vanishing behind the counter. She reappeared climbing a ladder, which she used to pluck an assortment of pistols from well-organized shelves. She hopped down, once again dropping from sight. A scraping noise followed as she dragged a stool over to the counter, where she piled the weapons. She gathered more, despite Katya's attempts to stop her until twelve lined the surface.

"For the girl, I recommend this." She pushed forward a small silver shock gun. "There's no way to mess up. Just point, shoot, and the bastard's rolling on the ground. Simple. Perfect for an untried beginner. Or I have—"

"Umm, Miss—"

"How incredibly rude of me! My name is Aylin. Now, this beauty is a Meynor design . . ." She provided a detailed description of each weapon—drowning Katya's interjections—and why they suited Mina and Katya despite only having known them for a few minutes. "Of course, I have more makers and models, though some are quite expensive."

"I think you were right," Katya said before the woman could resume her pitch. "The stun—" Her com chirped. "Aeliana, stay put."

Katya stepped out of the shop before activating the com. Rein's voice was on the other end. "How much longer? I want to get out of here."

"Everything should be taken care of in another hour or two." Katya brushed her angled bangs to the side; she remained unsold on the cut, but Mina gushed about how well it suited her.

Across the way, no action occurred at the clinic. Excellent.

"Leave him at the med clinic." Rein cut out and then, "What will you do if he does it again?"

Katya ended the connection and returned to the counter. "We'll take the shock gun, and while I appreciate your recommendations, I'm partial to my own weapon. It's served me well over the years."

"Ah yes, a trusty sidearm is not replaced easily." She began to pack the shock gun, but Katya stopped her. Not knowing Rein's mood, it'd be prudent for Mina to carry it. "Ah," Aylin said. "Young lady would like to carry it. No memory beats purchasing your first personal weapon. Mine was a Leshung knife. I gutted a Darion with that knife. Lost it on Perses's moon, and to this day, I miss it. Sliced through anything." She rested her hands on the weapon. "This beauty costs 500 *dinari*. Now how will you be paying?"

"The real deal." Katya removed the necessary currency, setting the bills in front of the proprietress on the counter.

"My favorite." She scanned them for counterfeits and, once satisfied, presented the shock gun to Mina, along with its holster. She explained some of the finer points of its use, including its safety features and what each button did.

"Conceal it," Katya said as Mina rotated the weapon in her hand. "It should never be seen until you have to use it."

Mina nodded and checked the safety before tucking it and its small holster into the inner pocket of her jacket. "Understood."

"Thank you," Katya said to the proprietress and then turned to part ways with the store.

"Always happy to help. One must be protected these days," Aylin called after them. "May all your enemies fall before you, and you be without a scratch!"

Katya waved at the woman as they continued their return to the clinic. The teen kept touching her pocket, checking that her newest purchase was still there. She almost told the teen to stop when a prickling sensation filled her head and silenced the merchant section of the station. Then, it passed. Aquila. Apparently, he felt better. The headache rebounded with his better health. What would they do? Her throat tightened.

"Do you think I can practice with my —"

"We'll get you used to it." Katya smiled. "But you heard the lady: Just point and shoot. You can't miss."

"I've fired weapons before." Mina puffed herself up.

Katya raised her eyebrow. "On the ship, you said you hadn't."

The girl shrugged, her face reddening, either because she'd been caught in a lie or an embarrassing memory had been dredged up.

Katya almost pressed her, but they'd arrived back at the clinic.

Doctor Jia sat in his chair, reading paperwork, which he laid on the table when they entered. "The procedure went smoothly," he said. "I want him on the machines and IV longer to 'put him on better footing,' one might say. I expect him to be good to go within the hour. There shouldn't be any long-term damage to his mental faculties, but without knowing his full physiology, I can't say for sure."

"Time will tell then." Katya exhaled and sat in the chair she had been using earlier. The list of unknowns was already long, so what was one more item added to it?

Leaning back into her seat, she closed her eyes, jerking awake when something pressed against her skin, the doctor's hand. In his other, he held a needle adaptor to an IV unit. "You looked like you could also use more fluids yourself."

"That's not necessary."

Jia whistled, his white hair jostling from the force. "Make things easier on yourself, rather than continue to run yourself thin."

Gritting her teeth, she caved. "Fine."

She allowed herself to be pricked by the needle, which was then attached with medical tape. With further prompting, she laid down on a gurney and let the IV drip needed hydration into her veins. Her eyes once again drifted shut. There was nothing else to be done as she waited. She stretched out her toes, tapping them against air. Next, Pestor. Her stomach knotted. Would she be dragging her father into this for nothing, or would he be able to help them? As she contemplated their next move, she dozed off.

"Hersilia!" Mina shook her.

Sputtering, Katya jolted into a seated position, the world spinning at the sudden change in elevation. "I'm awake—I'm fine!" Mina's hands clutched her shoulders. "I have to sleep eventually, and that was a natural catnap. A needed catnap."

"The procedure is complete," Jia said from where he removed his devices and the IV from Aquila. He then crossed the space between them to inspect her own, which was nearly empty. "I suppose that'll have to do. You've been here too long as it is." He detached it and applied gauze.

With Mina's help, she slipped from the gurney.

Lifting the sleeping boy, Jia brought him to Katya. "His brain activity is off the charts compared to when he was brought in, so I think it's safe to say he's on the mend."

"Thank you." Katya accepted Aquila into her arms.

Jia shrugged. "You might not be thanking me in the near future. The neural device seems to have stimulated his brain." He handed her the documents he'd been studying earlier. "His brain is truly amazing. I don't even know where to start." A new light, reminiscent of a mad scientist, glinted in his eyes.

"And that's not your job." It exited her mouth snappishly, but the man had already begun dissecting Aquila in his mind. She could see that. "Thank you for what help you've given. I'll gladly pay for your services."

"It's on the house."

She narrowed her eyes at the man, but he took no note as he reorganized his tools.

"Just like that?" she pressed.

"My doors are always open to the less fortunate—money is inconsequential, especially when my services are paid through the mining association."

"Very well then." Katya guided Mina to the door. "Thank you for your services."

They were almost through the door when Jia said, "Don't give up hope. I may not be able to help on the matter, but there are others who can."

The color drained from her face. "And who are these others?"

"That doesn't matter," Jia said. "They'll find you eventually."

"What have you done?" She gripped Aquila tighter to her body.

"Nothing." Jia closed a case. "I didn't have to. They already knew."

She stepped backward, her nails compressing against Mina's arm as she wrenched the girl from the clinic. The pair raced to the ship, Katya managing their pace to maintain some appearance of calm even as her heart fluttered in an off-sync cadence. Mina held her tongue the whole trip, blessedly. Before entering the decontamination chamber, Katya yanked her to the side.

"Not a word to Rein about anything we did. All he needs to know is we got Aquila patched up. Do you understand?"

"Who will find us?"

"I don't know." No one good crossed her mind, but she wouldn't voice that. "Be prepared. Never leave your room without the stun gun. Keep it on you at all times. Understand?"

Mina nodded, her hand resting against the spot that concealed the mentioned weapon.

They proceed into the chamber and found Rein waiting for them as they boarded the *Minerva*. He stood, arms crossed in front of his chest, brewing for a fight. Katya was well beyond that.

"He'll be fine, no thanks to you," she said as she shoved past him. "Prep to leave. We're heading for Pestor. I know someone on-world who might be able to help us with our unique problem."

"Who?"

"My father. He's familiar with a variety of races and planets, so it wouldn't be beyond reason that he'd have experience with the Oneiroi." Katya shifted Aquila in her arms, away from Rein. "He won't betray us, and Pestor is far enough removed from the Magistrate that we'll be able to come and go without drawing notice. It doesn't have a relay."

Katya marched to her quarters, where she tucked Aquila into his bed. She then sealed herself in the cockpit, where she got them underway to her father and his latest archaeological study.

CHAPTER TEN

After three weeks, during which Katya and Rein maintained an awkward dance of avoidance, they found themselves orbiting Pestor. Its surface, while largely shades of brown, harbored splashes of green around its coastal, river, and jungle regions. But of course, her father's latest archeological study had set its base camp in the savanna region of Pestor. From the information her slate presented, that area would at least be more comfortable than some of the planets they'd been on . . . well, for most of them. Yet Aquila had to come this time. Her father would be tickled to see her with a child. A fond smile rooted itself on her face.

She flipped on the communications and sought her father's signal; with it being mid-afternoon locally, he should be available. The screen blinked green once the signal had been found. Clearing her throat, she initiated the connection. A momentary pause, then: "This is Faustus Cassius."

"Papa, this is Katya . . . I need your help."

"I thought you were captaining *The Maelstrom*," her father said. If he was concerned, she couldn't tell over the speaker, one of the downsides of not having a visual image displaying facial expressions. But her father had long mastered the ability of retaining a monotone voice and guarded expression. Even when he'd received calls—no, especially when he'd received them—from Magistrate Central Police after her one older brother's drunken escapades, he displayed his masterful grasp of the art of disinterest.

"It's a long story."

"It's a good thing I enjoy a long story, no?" His line went silent until what resembled a sigh came through. "Land on the outskirts of the camp. I'll meet you there."

Katya closed the connection and orchestrated their descent into the atmosphere. With no Magistrate outposts on Pestor, there were no specific protocols to follow. Just land. As for the locals, they were primitives who lived in the coastal and river areas. A few sects of them traveled through the savanna, but her father in one correspondence had stated they gave a wide berth to the Magistrate archaeologists. Given the natives' lack of technology, the Magistrate had labeled the planet a preserve, allowing admittance only to scientists and scholars; of course, without an outpost or relay, policing unlawful incursions to the world proved impossible, so Pestor served as a halfway point for smugglers who hid in the jungles to the south.

"You're sure he won't turn us in?" Mina asked from behind her. The teen had been so quiet, Katya had forgotten she'd snuck into the cockpit.

Prepping the ACPS through the helm, Katya replied, "He took me in as a young child. I doubt he'd sell me out now after all that time and effort rearing me. He never did with Seneca, who's kind of a criminal—been in and out of prison. He struggles with substance abuse."

"What's he like?"

Katya pursed her lips. How best to describe her father? "He's extremely . . . passionate about his work. While we officially lived on Meracus Domus, he dragged us all over the galaxy with him. There was always something to be studied, to be dug up. And occasionally along the way, we would pick up brothers and sisters, though by the time I came into the fold, he was largely done picking up strays . . . just my youngest brother."

Mina leaned closer. "Do you two get along?"

"Oh yes." No hesitation came with the answer. "Of course, there's always some frustration there. He's incredibly intelligent, but he's extremely absentminded. As a teenager, and even now as an adult, that quirk drove me insane. He has a tendency to view people as a collection of their culture or as potential articles for academic journals rather than as individuals." Katya swallowed. "Despite those annoyances, we do care for each other, and I feel distance has helped."

"Sometimes distance is good." Mina placed her back to her, obscuring her face. She did not expound on her statement, but Katya assumed it had to do with her own parents. The girl never said anything about them beyond telling her that they were gone, which could mean a variety of things on Reznic. She'd never pried for more information, knowing all too well some traumas needed to be entombed.

They landed outside of camp as instructed, kicking up dirt and bits of grass in the process. In place, Katya launched the cool-down sequence and killed the engines before turning to the intercom: "Rein, we're here. Complete a routine check and conduct any repairs or maintenance work that needs done. We shouldn't run into trouble here, so be thorough."

"How long do you estimate our stay will be?"

"Knowing my father, half the day if not until tomorrow." Katya lurched to her feet. "I'll try to contain his propensity to ramble."

"Don't bother. I've noticed a variance in the FTL. It'll take a while to work out."

Rein killed the line. If only all their conversations were as productive. Once again, Katya locked the communications and navigation systems, only leaving open what Rein needed to work on the mechanical aspects of the ship.

"You can stay here if you want," Katya said to Mina. "I want time to speak with my father alone."

"I'll at least come to meet him." Mina leaped from her seat, a trace of excitement in her voice.

"He is quite the character." With that, Katya went to retrieve Aquila from her quarters.

She left her sweater draped over her chair, despite the cold temperature. Inside the bed, Aquila slept, blankets splayed around him. Crazy child. She carried him and the stuffed animal she'd taken from the *Aletheia*, which he held to his chest in a tight grip, over to the table. His hold on the animal never slackened, surprising her since he'd never interacted with the toy before unless either Mina or she had initiated it.

"Come now. We've got somewhere to be," she whispered.

She changed his diaper before putting him in lighter clothes, and once complete, they got underway: Aquila situated on her hip and a bag, containing the books from the *Aletheia*, dangling off her shoulder.

Mina waited at the ramp. No Rein. She stiffened, the corners of her lips dipping. Only a fool would believe he had let the issue go. He was biding his time.

As they disembarked, a person walking through the tall savanna grass greeted them, waving his hands. "Kat'ee!" the man called as he came closer. "Ah! My girl, it's been too—your hair! What has happened to it?" He rambled on even as he embraced her, giving her a good whiff of his strong cologne. The gesture proved short-lived when he met the lump attached to her side. "And who is this? You truly are starting to pick up my tendencies. Oh! And this young lady must be Mina." He engulfed Mina in his arms before releasing her. "My daughter has spoken very favorably of you."

"I try." Mina bore a deep blush on her face.

"She does well," Katya added before addressing her father's previous question. "And this is Aquila."

"Where is your ship? This is a cargo vessel, not a Boita or even Magistrate—"

"Let's speak somewhere more private." She shifted Aquila, distributing his weight to the other side.

"Ah." Her father rested his hands on his hips. "We can return to my tent; the rest are out at the site. We've found evidence of a more advanced civilization having inhabited this planet at least four centuries ago. We're trying to determine if they originated from this planet or if they were passing through and left after a few generations. They are completely unrelated to the current inhabitants. Isn't it—"

"Your tent will be fine." She gestured to Mina. "Mina will be heading back to the ship to give us time to talk in detail." Her father's gaze darkened at the last part. It'd become almost a family code for: "You're not going to like what I have to say."

Mina didn't protest, leaving Katya and her father to walk to the archeologists' base camp. He prattled on about the dig and the potential new culture they'd discovered. All the while as he talked, his hands punctuated his words.

"And if they did move on, it would be interesting to discover where their next home was," Faustus said. "We're already scouring the databases for similar uses of symbolism and design from the examples we've found. I imagine we'll find comparable cultures within a matter of weeks."

"I'm excited for you." Katya repositioned Aquila, who was making her one arm tingle. "I'm sorry to interrupt your work, especially—well, let's just say you might regret answering your com."

Faustus's face tightened, forming deep lines around his mouth and eyes. "No matter what situation you find yourself in, my Kat'ee, I doubt I will regret answering your coms to me." He lowered his head. "An interesting toy he has. He's obviously not yours, biologically, that is."

"It's a part of the long story." Katya exhaled. "Trust me, by the end of my tale, all will be clear, and you'll want me off-world faster than a Marion bird flies south at the first sight of snow."

Her father chuckled, resting his large hand on his rotund belly. "The more you keep building up this story of yours, the more interested I find myself to hear it."

They fell quiet while the grass surrounding them bowed to the slight breeze. Gradually, they arrived at the mini-tent city. She and her siblings had lived in plenty of such campsites in the past. She'd adapted to the setting and transient lifestyle quickly; it'd held familiarity. How? She could not remember. As a result of their moves, she'd seen more of the galaxy than most of her peers. The tents had been upgraded since their days of gallivanting. They now glistened as the sun hit them, thanks to the increased level of tech woven into them.

"Several Core universities are involved," Faustus said. "The world is seen as relatively safe and the dig is routine, so many signed on to provide their charges with real experience and perhaps gain the honor of hosting a few of the finds." He winked at the last part, a smile filling his face. "With luck, there'll be plenty to be hosted."

He paused in front of one tent, which rose above the others surrounding it, and pressed several buttons, creating an opening. From it bounded a large Vergian hound. "Pollux! Down, down!" Her father grabbed the beast's collar and yanked him into the tent before he could jump on Katya and, by default, Aquila.

Her dad had owned Pollux since the hound was a pup and they had been summering on Vergo. She had finished her officer exams and physical fitness requirements at that time. Katya smiled as the hound, on his hind legs, reached up and lapped her father's face with his enormous tongue. Time had turned that pup into a monster.

The smile grew wider. In contrast, her father had not changed. The interior of the tent screamed comfort. Luxurious seating options, climate controls set to cooler temps, and what she could only imagine was a fully stocked refrigeration unit. This was roughing it in her father's mind. And she supposed, compared to their family home, it was.

"Ah!" Her father slumped in one of his plush red chairs, a reproduction of their homeworld's Berretta era—he'd never bring the real ones to a dig. His fingers slid through Pollux's rust-colored fur. "Feels so good to be off my feet!"

Smirking, Katya sank into the sofa before laying Aquila beside her on it, his head resting in her lap. "Maybe you should stay on your feet more often. You're getting rounder."

"Baash." He batted his hand at her. "We're not going to talk about that. Let's talk about your little friend instead."

She smoothed Aquila's hair; he twitched. "I'm no longer a Magistrate officer."

"I figured as much with the new ship and your lack of proper uniform. Not to mention your beautiful hair hacked to pieces—" He took a deep intake. "An Oneiroi child."

He lurched from his chair, pushing Pollux aside, and cupped Aquila's face with his hands, further bewildering the boy by tilting his head in different angles to better examine him. Aquila scrunched his nose and eyelids, a familiar face he made every time she or Mina put something in his mouth he hated.

"How did you come by him?"

"We'd just finished dropping off a Magistrate crew with *The Maelstrom* and were on our way to R-56 for maintenance, but instead, I led us to a crippled ship. As you must suspect, it was an Oneiroi vessel."

"The *Aletheia*."

Katya nodded, her jaw tightening. "Aquila was the only survivor. We took him from the ship but ran into Breks and had to make a jump. We've been on the run ever since, though I'm not sure if they've connected us individually to the incident, not yet anyway."

Her father slid next to her on the sofa and stroked his goatee. "Why did you not approach the proper officials to sort out this misunderstanding? You've only made it more difficult for yourself by running, especially now with the amount of time that has passed. They'll be less likely to believe—"

"Oh, they'll believe us because they already know what happened on that ship, and it's not what they've been spreading over the news." Katya brought Aquila further onto her lap to give her father more room. "The Magistrate issued the orders for that ship to be destroyed, but only after most of the occupants had been executed. Why? I don't know, but it was obvious that we'd stumbled onto something we weren't meant to. I believe we know too much."

An expression she had never seen before lined her father's face, adding further age to it. Clearing his throat, he pushed Pollux away again and snapped his fingers toward a large dog bed.

"This is . . . troubling." Faustus stood and paced, his hands positioned behind his back. His strides quickened, then he stopped and faced her. "Very troubling. The Magistrate wouldn't turn on the Oneiroi unless something forced its hand. Of all the species the Magistrate has tethered to itself, the Oneiroi are one of its most valuable commodities; the magistrates—or the military, for that matter—wouldn't jeopardize that relationship."

Katya rested her head against the sofa, unable to support its weight with her neck at that moment. "It had to be something big." She moistened her chapped lips with her tongue. "But it would seem we've inadvertently sealed our fate: We're going to be snuffed out. Anything to prevent the Oneiroi from discovering the truth."

Hissing, Katya dropped her head into her hands. Her limbs shook, though her father held them, fingers pressing flesh into bone, grounding them, her. The tendrils—Aquila—tugged, beckoning her to leave consciousness behind. That's truly what it was: an insistent call for her attention. Between her fingers, she saw that Aquila had succumbed to sleep. Her father was speaking to her. She tried to focus on the words, not the tethers Aquila had set in her mind, which clawed at her, pulling, begging her to join him.

Katya woke sprawled on the sofa with the lights dimmed, her father's cologne calming her. Twisting, she sought the light source. Someone hummed. The melodic tune harkened up childhood memories: an unlit room, her father leaning over each of their beds, giving goodnight kisses, and that song. He would scold Katya sometimes for concealing a book under her pillow, but then he would always leave it where he'd found it. She wiped her eyes, regaining some control of her limbs, which might as well have turned to stone.

"Where's Aquila?" she asked.

Her father turned from his desk, where he had been examining a book. "I thought he'd be more comfortable in my bed."

He grabbed the bound book he'd been reading. Ah, the journal she'd removed from the *Aletheia*, recognizable by the particular black leather it'd been crafted from. Its texture was different than other leathers she'd handled, leaving her to assume it'd originated from an animal of their world.

"His original name was Sotiris," Faustus said, tapping on its unadorned cover. "But I admit, the name could belong to someone else. Given the number of times it occurs in this journal, and from my limited understanding of their language, I would say it's a safe bet that I'm not wrong."

He handed the journal to Katya after crossing the small space between them. Then he crouched and cupped her face between his hands. "Things are much more serious than I originally thought."

Katya let her head rest in his hands, relishing the warmth, the comfort, and remnants of childhood. "I was going to get around to telling you." Tears filled her eyes as her head pounded, particularly behind her eyes. She squinted in an attempt to lessen the pain. "There's something wrong with him . . . and it's affecting me."

"He was born with what the Oneiroi call 'the defect.'"

"'Defect'?"

Faustus dropped his gaze before returning it to Katya. Removing a kerchief from his pocket, he wiped the tears from her face. "Let me get something for the pain." He left her and opened a drawer on his desk, returning with a pill and a glass of water.

"The defect is hush-hush. The Magistrate and the Oneiroi are doing all within their means to hide it," he resumed after she swallowed the small round pill. "Perhaps the best way to describe it is as a mutation of the Oneiroi's abilities that has manifested to the utmost. As a people, the Oneiroi have taken extreme steps to lessen the number of children born with it due to its danger."

The corners of her father's lips dipped. "Those with the mutation pass from consciousness to sleep at alarming rates. Sometimes they remain asleep until they inevitably starve to death, because once they are so far into their minds, they can't be roused. There are, of course, other consequences. Given the excessive amount of time they spend in a sleep state—even if they don't fall into an endless slumber—it produces wear on their bodies. Muscle atrophy. Lungs weakening to the point of failure. Vitamin deficiencies. Congestive heart failure. Increased susceptibility to viral and bacterial infections. The list goes on."

Faustus poured himself a glass of something, something stronger than water by its amber coloring. "But that's not the only thing. They're a danger to others as well. Normally, an Oneiroi depends on vision to form a connection either for communication among themselves or to bring forth phantoms and terrors in those they interrogate. Those with the mutation don't have that limitation. No, when they are asleep, their abilities run rampant, and they can trap others with them, killing them as well if the poor soul isn't fortunate enough to outlast them."

"How do you know all this?" Katya eased into a seated position as the drugs dulled the pain. "Especially when you said both the Magistrate and the Oneiroi keep this mutation under wraps."

Her father took a deep gulp from his glass, coughing afterward. "I've been around for quite some time, as you know, and as a member of the Cassius family, I've lived a privileged life. I've worked closely with the government on many projects, enough to garner a reputation." Another sip from his glass, and then Faustus set it down, perhaps more roughly than he'd intended, but shaking hands were prone to do that. "Long before I adopted you or your brothers and sisters, I had an Oneiroi boy who had the genetic mutation in my care. The Magistrate housed him with me temporarily — for research purposes, of course."

Faustus rubbed his eyes. "He was taken from me after about a month to parts unknown. I've never been able to contact the child. It's my understanding that none of the Oneiroi parents have any contact with their children once they've handed them over to the Magistrate. It's all handled by their council, I hear."

"You never said anything," she said.

"It was classified, and it was a sad chapter in my life to see him go, to know he wouldn't have any semblances of a normal life." He swallowed hard. "It was perhaps one of the sparks for me to decide that the Magistrate government has no business raising children."

Seeing her glass was empty, her father reached for a crystal Vergian whiskey jar and uncorked the lid. "You're not supposed to mix them, but I won't tell if you don't." He partially filled her glass with the amber liquid. "Given the circumstances . . ." Even more of the liquor went into his glass. "I think it's deserved."

Katya shifted her gaze toward the ceiling, noting how little light penetrated the high-tech fabric. "What time is it?"

"Eh, don't worry. I've already contacted your friends and stated my intentions to keep you longer. They were quite accommodating, especially after I mentioned there'd be a home-cooked meal in the morning. Also, your mechanic's still having issues with a variance." He snorted. "You could have had that variance nipped in the bud by now, aye, Kat'ee?"

A genuine smile crossed her face. "But then I wouldn't be here talking with you."

She sipped from her glass, unused to taking Vergian whiskey straight. The liquid scalded her throat as it went down and numbed her tongue and lips, but it left a comforting burn in the pit of her chest. They drank in silence for several minutes before her father cleared his throat and abandoned his drink.

"You need to be careful, Katya." Faustus ran his hand through his thinning gray hair. "The defect brought the Oneiroi into the Magistrate's fold. After years of struggling with its increased frequency, they reached the point where there was nothing to lose by joining the Magistrate, not if it helped the children born with the defect and their people as a whole. They've willingly handed over their children born with the genetic mutation for further study and a hopeful treatment to counteract it."

"And has the Magistrate helped them?"

Her father shifted in his seat. "I've been told—and that is all—that the Magistrate has increased their life spans. More importantly, there've been no accidental deaths due to the Oneiroi's collective natures."

"So Aquila—Sotiris—is acting on that social need?"

"Yes." He tapped his fingers against his chair's arms. "In the month I had Euripides, I noted this characteristic. But maybe because I only had him for a month, or perhaps there was something else lacking, he never attempted to access my mind or pull me under, though he was about the same age as your little boy here, so he should've been as eager for the contact."

"Did you find anything that helped him?" Katya asked.

"I've composed a document on your slate with everything I'd learned. It's far too little."

She inhaled the whiskey, relishing its hints of vanilla. "And you've heard nothing else? About what the Magistrate's doing?"

"Top secret. Even my friends in office don't know . . . or they can't tell me. My own brother stonewalls me." He exhaled and stood. "If worse comes to worst, you'll need to attach an IV to him and force movement to prevent complete atrophy, but even so, he'll be susceptible to other medical conditions." He rested his hands on her shoulders. "And he'll continue to seek out mental connections; it's too ingrained in his nature for him not to. You've been very fortunate, my little girl. One of these days, you might not be so lucky. He might be a child, but in this case, it makes him more dangerous because he doesn't know better."

"What would you—what can I do?"

"Ah, Kat'ee, that's not a simple question, not a simple question at all. There really is no absolute answer. His people can't help him. They'd turn him over to the Magistrate." He nestled next to her, his shoulder brushing against hers. "You could give him directly to the Magistrate, where his outcome is unknown. Yes, he might live more comfortably and even have a longer life than what's natural for an Oneiroi with the mutation, or he might become a guinea pig for trial and error, no different than if he were with you."

"What would you do?" Katya struggled to keep her voice from breaking, utterly failing.

Her father chuckled, draping his arm across her shoulder. "I think you already know what I would do, no?" He squeezed her against the bulk of his body. "But this is your decision to make, Katya. Weigh each option as you are wont to do and pick the one that'll bring the least amount of regret. But in the meantime, I might be able to help you lessen his grip on your mind." He shook his head when Katya straightened. "No guarantees, little one. This is speculation on my part, but perhaps the Yolarian moving meditation stances will shore up your mental strength."

"Anything is worth a try at this point." Katya yawned, the medicine and alcohol setting in.

"Good, good. I'll add some videos detailing the rituals to the other things I'm sending with you."

"Oh please, Papa, no more vases or anything like that."

"No, just information. Though you'd do better to appreciate my gifts!" He nattered on about significant gifts he'd given her, and Katya really didn't have the heart to stop him or tell him of the one vase's destruction. "Ah, it's late. Finish your cup and head back to sleep, a natural one—er—more natural one."

He returned to his desk. Katya, meanwhile, stared at the flexible rods and fabric of the tent's ceiling, tired yet unable to close her mind to the waking world. Somewhere, an old-fashioned clock ticked. She hadn't noticed it before, not over the conversation and her pounding head. But now, her muddled state brought clarity to her surroundings. Biting her lips to stop the giggles from erupting, Katya fought the urge to ask her father for the rest of the bottle. It did seem to keep Aquila—no, Sotiris—at bay; but then again, she could be so out of it that she wouldn't notice his presence.

A few more ticks of the clock, and her father resumed humming. *"Down the road, I will go, down the road to where you wait. Never for a time will we be apart . . . though you may have gone, never will my legs fail to take me where you are. Down the road, I will go, down the road to where you wait, laid beneath the willow tree . . ."*

The words floated through her mind along with days spent in the nursery with her siblings. By the time she had been brought to the Cassius household, there had already been five. They would join their father, melodic in tone; even though, at the time, she couldn't understand the words, she'd known it was beautiful. It'd sparked something else, something that she'd later bury, like the faint, fleeting metallic scent she'd catch every so often. Or perhaps she'd simply forgotten the memory or inkling of one that surfaced periodically, over the steady march of time. And now, she couldn't even place her finger on the odd sensation that filled her gut.

"How—" Katya cleared her throat and tried again. "How did you . . . come by me?"

The humming ended, but her father did not speak. Katya could almost hear him thinking.

"There were a lot of Mramor orphans after its war. And they were offered to the Magistrate upper class in the Core sectors since Mramor had so few resources and its people couldn't take in extra mouths. Some, however, became wards of the state." Her father's chair squeaked when he shifted so he could see her. "As I said, I firmly believe the government has no business raising children that . . . and it was the right thing to do.

"You were a small string bean when I met you, and you wouldn't say a word. I couldn't tell if you were shy, confused by the language I was speaking, or had experienced trauma."

"I don't remember," Katya said.

"You were very young." Faustus moved something on his desk; it scraped across the wooden surface. "You shouldn't brood over that, nor should you regret any sudden interest in that forgotten past. It's actually more of a surprise that you haven't asked sooner." He adjusted the built-in lighting, which had been woven into the tent via special fibers, lowering it further. "His and yours are eerily similar situations; it's understandable that his plight would awaken memories and questions. Besides, it's only natural to want to know where you came from."

"My name—"

"I gave it to you. You didn't come with one, no background." The clock ticked a steady beat. "I only knew you were found in or near the capital of Moscanov Imperiya." He said something else, but she couldn't focus. ". . . A lot of the kids from Mramor were much the same way, though the older ones knew more about themselves." Katya barely heard this explanation as her eyelids grew heavier.

"Th-thank you . . . f'r e-every . . ." Katya tried to finish her ramble but only mumbled something incoherent, the whiskey lulling her to sleep.

Breakfast was a quiet affair, each helping themselves to the bread that had been prepared—along with olives and cheeses—by her father and dipping it in the wine, though Mina was only allowed milk. Katya ignored the bread and ate the fresh fruit and smoked saxum fish, a luxury one did not find on board spaceships outside of personal vessels or pleasure crafts. Katya plopped another piece of saxum fish into her mouth, relishing it and wishing she could drag a barrel of it onto their ship.

The main source of conversation came from Faustus, who kept topics light and neutral, choosing to share some of the finds he had made over his career. And among the innocuous factoids, he sprang personal questions to one of his breakfast guests.

"And what of you, young lady?" he asked Mina. "What do you plan to study?"

"Ship controls," Mina said around a piece of bread she had crammed into her mouth, along with a couple of grapes.

"Just that? No greater mental challenge, no schooling?"

"Papa, leave well enough alone."

"A monkey could oper—"

"Papa."

He muttered something about the importance of higher education before stating more clearly, "I'll load up a slate for Miss Mina as well. Speaking of slates, I've already loaded several videos and documents that might hold some solutions to your little problem."

"Am I going to need another slate, or is there still storage left in mine?"

"You know I'm not good at that type of thing!" Her father waved his hand about before diverting the conversation. "So, Rein, have you managed to correct the variance?"

"All's in order." The man didn't even lift his face from his now-empty plate.

Distrust blossomed in the pit of her stomach, a blend of her own and Aqu—Sotiris's. The toddler harbored such dislike for him, which had existed well before he'd been injured by him, only to be amplified by the abuse he'd received from the mechanic. That foreign sensation . . . he had been tapping into her mind since the moment she had found him. Had Aquila brushed against Rein's mind? And if he had, what had he seen or felt in it? What she'd give for that answer.

Katya finished her fish and stood. "Papa, we need to head back. We've probably stayed too long as it is."

"Don't worry; I have a story already worked up in case my colleagues ask questions."

"It's not your colleagues I'm worried about."

"I'll send along some of that smoked fish with you." Her father chuckled when Mina fed Aquila a piece of said entree. The boy gaped at first before chewing and swallowing it. "He seems to love it just as much as you do. I'll also send some of the bread and fruits with you too."

Katya tried to speak, but her father talked over her as he readied the unasked-for supplies, stating he would hear no complaints on the matter. By the time he had loaded them down with food and learning materials, nearly the entire camp had set off for the archaeological site. One person who remained called out to her father, asking when he intended to come, to which he replied, "Soon. Right now, I must see this delivery crew off."

The colleague didn't question why Faustus had bothered to supply a delivery crew with a heap of goods, allowing them to continue. Upon reaching the ship, Rein set to work warming the engines without a word. Mina hung back with Sotiris, only to be sent onto the ship by Faustus. After her departure, her father clasped Katya in a hug.

"I'll pursue a few avenues. Discreetly." He swallowed. "If I can find the right approach, I may tactically speak with your Uncle Pontius. But . . . I don't trust him to put family first. No, the Magistrate comes first."

"I always wondered what he did for the Magistrate."

Her father released her. "He's up there. Secret, secret. I do not doubt he could improve your circumstances. It's a matter of if he would bother to or not. He's a hard man. I once saw him nearly cane a man to death for insult."

Katya's eyes widened. No wonder her father had walled off his family from the man, preferring Vergo to the homeworld when not at excavation sites. He'd feared they'd become targets of his rage. His secretive position within the Magistrate had likely been a further stressor between the pair.

Her father embraced her again. "For now, stay strong, Kat'ee, and stick to the outskirts. Even if the Magistrate is on the lookout for you, you should be able to make a decent life. You're smart; you'll survive this." He held her at arm's length as if trying to capture every detail of her appearance. Moistness clouded his eyes. "Don't drop so far of the radar that you can't contact me. I don't care what might happen to me; I would — I would worry too much not hearing anything from you."

Feeling her own eyes dampen, Katya leaned in, embracing her father again; her head burrowed into his shoulder. "I'm sorry, Papa."

"Now, don't you start that; if you do, I'll join you." He squeezed her. "Take care, Katya. Not just of yourself, but that boy and girl. And be wary of that man. A man who feels his entire world slipping away can become dangerous."

"I'm watching him." Katya stepped away and wiped her eyes with her hand, eradicating all traces of tears. "It's been tough on all of us but particularly him . . . and he holds Sotiris at fault. If I can find a way to amicably part ways with him, I will. I plan to do it as soon as possible."

"Good, good."

There, they stood in silence, neither wanting to say what had to come next. Gradually, Katya took that first step onto the *Minerva*'s ramp before hesitating. "I'll be in touch."

"I don't doubt it."

He waved her toward the ship. By the time she had reached the top of the ramp, he'd already started the trek back to the camp and his research. Katya pressed her lips together while her whole chest ached. Then, bowing her head, she strode inside and initiated the hatch closing sequence. As it shut, a mantra ran through her head: Stick to the backwoods, stay alive. The hatch latched, and she turned on the balls of her feet. There was no time to waste on a past no longer feasible.

CHAPTER ELEVEN

With sinuous motions, Katya traveled through the stages of what amounted to a Gorgian dance. She visualized herself moving in sync with the holographic images. As she completed the next steps, the musky scent of fermented tea seeped into her. Follow through, turn—her knee connected with a tea crate.

"*Krezk!*" Grunting and rubbing her knee, Katya hobbled over to another tea crate and sat. Already bruising. Terrific. She massaged the damaged tissue.

When had she gotten so close to them? Ah, she'd miscounted. She'd been so lost in the movement of the dance that she'd failed to account for the eighty-some crates that the *Minerva*'s cargo hold now contained; each crate emitted a smell akin to fungus and mold. Their employer had assured her that the tea was a delicacy, but after spending weeks with it stinking up her ship, she harbored little interest in trying it. Yet it couldn't be worse than the *hesricht* juice her father had forced her siblings and her to drink: Now that had tasted like swill.

Katya brushed outs her sweat-lined hair with her fingers. It had gotten longer in the two months between Pestor and their latest shipment. A month spent training Mina with her weapon and treading carefully around Rein, but things had settled once more, threatening to breed complacency. Her story to Sotiris had continued, recounting harmless adventures for the princess and her steed, which had begun to resemble Pollux more than a horse.

Reaching for her towel, she massaged her scalp, removing some of the excess sweat. Mina would undoubtedly want to cut it again. Going off the teen's late nights prowling the Net, she'd gathered quite the list of new styles to try out on Katya. It was tedious to be a lab rat. But without a clear idea of what she wanted, she didn't mind delegating the task to the teen. She only drew the line at having portions of her head shaved despite how fierce Mina proclaimed she'd look.

Standing, Katya retrieved her water bottle and guzzled its cold contents. The exercise had some effect, though part of her believed Sotiris's lack of mental activity came more from boredom with her focus on the same repetitive motions, never straying from them. This hypothesis had shaped the stories she told him, keeping them bland, away from whatever portion of her brain they were triggering. The other hypothesis—her expression clouded—was that the sudden interruption and head trauma had resulted in long-lasting damage. Or maybe, as her father had gauged, Sotiris remained a waiting disaster.

She draped the towel along her shoulders and climbed the ladder to the next level. She stepped off into the main hallway.

"Is it working?"

Katya turned to find Rein, who'd just exited his room, behind her. His gaze drifted down her frame, lingering on her sweaty tank that clung to her figure. She met it, jaw tightening. At least the towel concealed the girls. She ensured that was the case.

His posture was looser than it had been in months. Their routine of shepherding lawful deliveries throughout the Fringe agreed with him. And now he even dared to broach the topic of Sotiris for the first time since Pestor.

"It's hard to say," she said, choosing an honest answer. "He hasn't been as active. Whether it's because of my new routines or not . . . that remains to be seen." Katya took another sip from her water bottle, wiping excess liquid from her mouth. "Is she still running fine?"

"She's a whole different beast than *The Maelstrom*." A genuine smile graced his face. "I find I've more time without a tool in my hands. We'll have no problem reaching Dandis VII by tomorrow. We've even been able to pull in the station's programming."

"Anything interesting?"

"I've been pulling in Magistrate news. There's been more activity with Plasovern attacking shipping routes in the Fringe. We'll have to be careful if we pick up more cargo on Dandis VII and choose to stick to the outskirts." Rein cleared his throat before he stepped closer to her. "There's been no mention of the *Aletheia*, *The Maelstrom*, or any of us. I even did some searches using the Net. They don't seem to be looking for us."

"Appearances can be deceiving. You know that as well as I do." Katya faced the cockpit's door. "We've got to stay low."

"Maybe we change our approach. Plasovern took our ship, held us hostage, stole the boy, and we managed to escape with him from Medzeci space."

One of her eyebrows rose. "Maybe you can escape from Medzeci space. As for Mina and me, we aren't taking the chance they don't buy it."

"It has to be all of us. If they capture you after I've already made contact, they'll know I lied."

Sweat flipped from her hair as Katya shook her head. "I'm not going to the Magistrate. I'm not taking that chance with Mina's and Sotiris's lives. They're my responsibilities. I took Mina with me, and I don't take that responsibility lightly." The once-prized Oneiroi crew plagued her, their eyes open, shot through by executioners. If they couldn't receive a trial, what hope did a replaceable freighter crew have?

"And where does that leave us?" His voice fluctuated. "Just moving cargo from one planet or station to the next?" He stepped closer, fingers twitching. "I know you can't be happy about this type of life. But you seem so willing to drop everything—everything you've ever worked for. What do we have to look forward to when we're constantly looking over our shoulders? Without a goal?"

"Opportunities will present themselves," she said. "But for now, we're free and seeing new, exciting locales."

He snorted. "That's one way to describe them."

"Something will come along; we just have to wait for it."

"Do you really believe that?"

Katya kept her expression neutral, despite the pressure in her chest cavity. "I have to. I'm the captain."

He digested her words, hand absently scratching his jaw's stubble.

Turning away, Katya wiped the towel against her face.

"You are a remarkable woman."

She straightened and was certain the blood had drained from her face. *I don't think you fully appreciate what you're bringing on board with him.* Valens's words—so easily dismissed as they'd huddled off to the side of *The Maelstrom* during their final goodbye—reemerged. She opened her mouth but couldn't find words.

"I do car—"

"Thank you for your kind words." She stepped closer to the cockpit. "Keep an eye on the engines. Let me know if anything's off."

She retreated, leaving him alone in the hallway. She inhaled as she stepped into the cockpit, only releasing that breath when the doors closed behind her. Why else had he volunteered for a dinky, rust-bucket freighter crew? She pulled the towel tight around her shoulders and sighed. Clutter had been spewed around the cockpit: toys, slates, jackets, and plates—some still having bits of food on them. Her right eye twitched.

"The cockpit is not an extension of your quarters." Katya tossed one of the jackets, which had been obscuring the communications console, hitting Mina in the head with it.

Mina grunted. She screwed her face—puckering her lips until she resembled a fish—as she balled up the jacket and placed it in her lap. The teen then resumed playing with Sotiris's legs, ignoring Katya as she sorted through the mess. The Oneiroi child tried to free his legs from Mina, who remained blissfully unaware of the practically non-attempts. He squeaked when Mina tugged one of his feet again. Even though he hated it, the forced daily exercise sparked a positive change beyond staving muscle deterioration: He exhibited more signs of wanting to interact with them while awake as if a gear in his biology had been flipped the other way. Katya kicked aside an empty can. Another bonus—she smiled as more squawks followed—was the fear hanging over Mina's interactions with Sotiris had dwindled until forgotten. Though that was only true when he was awake and nothing more than a normal toddler.

"I'm here practically all the time," Mina said, releasing her captive. "It only makes sense that a few things would make their way here."

Katya tossed a few more articles of clothing at the girl. A shirt's sleeve caught Sotiris's face as it sailed toward Mina. "And they can make their way back to where they belong." She stacked the plates. "We may not be a Magistrate vessel anymore, but I will have order in here. Imagine this"—she waved a plate in front of Mina's face—"hitting you in the head in the event of a blind jump or during some evasive maneuvers. It wouldn't be pleasant. But then again, you might not even feel it because you'd be dead." She deposited the plates in Mina's arms. "No plates in here. Take these back to the mess and get them washed. Once done, you can come get the rest of these things. I'm taking over in here."

Mina grumbled, but she carted the plates away all the same. Katya, meanwhile, jumped between stations while continuing to dry off. More traffic dotted the screen of the navigation console, all registering as Magistrate. It was the closest to the hub of the Magistrate they'd come in a long time. Still located in the Fringe but with regular traffic. Almost Mezzo. Katya draped the towel over the pilot's chair and commandeered one of Mina's oversized sweatshirts. She sat as she maneuvered her arms through its sleeves.

Unable to help herself, Katya reached over to the co-pilot's seat and tugged at Sotiris's foot. He rewarded her with something resembling a hiss. He also yanked his foot away, knocking his knee into the side of the toddler seat. His mouth kept moving with little sounds exiting it. He tried so hard to form words, but all that came out amounted to gibberish and odd sounds. Not surprising. Her father's research had stated that verbal skills developed much later for Oneiroi. He didn't pinpoint the exact age, however, leaving her to wonder if Sotiris was ahead or behind development-wise.

Remembering Rein's words, Katya flipped on the extended com system and was greeted by blaring music. Mina, she groused, lowering the volume to a level where words could be made out—something about the female singer missing her love who had gone to work on a transport. She stuck her tongue out at Sotiris, who chortled. In the background, the singer crooned on, up until she switched the station.

"Hey, everyone out here in the Belt," a deep voice rang over the cockpit's speakers. "We've got the latest in from the Core, plus some homebred talent, lined up. But first, Jace the Snore's goin' to get you caught up on the latest news."

Katya snorted. "Jace the Snore. What podunk part of the galaxy have we found ourselves in?"

"The magistrates have met in regards"—a new voice, a lethargic and monotone one, took over—"to the annexation of Verdra. After drought and civil unrest, the planet's ruling class has asked for Magistrate assistance. Meanwhile, in other sections of the galaxy, Plasovern is setting up strongholds, including on Ereago, where intense fighting has resulted in high casualties. Opposition factions threaten the capital city of Esh and have staged executions of Magistrate soldiers and regular citizenry alike. Brek forces are being brought in to quell the opposition—"

"You heard that right, folks, no more Breks in the Dandis VII sector," the previous voice crowed. There was a loud splooshing sound, followed by a sputtering noise. "Sorry, out of time as always, Jace. For those new to our show or those who don't have the visual feed running, Jace has just had a tub of Horgi gluck dumped on him because he's a Jorgian and talks too slow." Then, over the sputters and coughs, the disc jockey continued, "Avoid lanes two and four if you know what I mean; they're crawlin' with bluebacks, and the waits are—" A farting sound effect took the place of words. "Now, how about the tunes you're cravin'!"

Katya decreased the volume further as the wails of a stringed instrument blared through the cockpit, followed by the screams of someone who probably called themselves a singer. Sotiris jerked at the being's screeching. Unable to stand it herself, Katya scanned through the various stations attached to Dandis VII, along the way discovering several ship-operated stations that touched on a variety of topics from the innocuous—air time for smaller bands, probably their own, and the ramblings of Captain Jip—to the iniquitous and illegal—gambling, Magistrate troop positions, coded trafficking similar to what she'd seen on Reznic . . . The list went on. Dandis VII was proving to be a cauldron of interesting beings. Sure, every city, station, or planet had its underside; some were just festered more than others.

"Are you listening to where Magistrate officials are stationed?" Mina asked upon reentering the cockpit.

"Yes, I thought it might come in handy, but then again, one of the main stations already tipped me off that we don't visit lanes two or four."

"Can they trace the station?" She then narrowed her eyes. "Is that my shirt?"

"It was in the cockpit. It became a community shirt." Katya nudged another one of the sweatshirts toward the girl with her foot, but Mina failed to pick up the hint—or perhaps she chose to ignore it—and instead, she slumped into the chair by the communications console.

"To answer your question, they can't trace where the signals are going," Katya said. "They can only trace the source; however, the signal's probably routed via many mirrors, making it hard to retrace it to its origin." She wormed her foot under the sweatshirt before catapulting it over to Mina. The girl caught it. "Dandis VII seems to have a light Magistrate presence, especially since its Breks were called to Ereago." She changed the frequency to one with music.

Mina narrowed her lips. "Breks . . . wasn't that the species that was going to fry us?"

"So far, we're having tons of good luck."

"But if they'd been here, while we were—"

"But they aren't."

Mina toyed with the sleeve of the sweatshirt. "What about . . . well, what the doctor said."

Katya shook her head. "If *they*, whoever they are, find us, we'll deal with it. Have you been doing as I asked?"

Dropping the sleeve, Mina rested at her hand against her chest, where her stun gun had been concealed under her clothes, and nodded.

The male vocalist filled the cockpit as he sang in a rich baritone voice about leaving his homeworld. A full band backed him up. He'd launched into the third verse by the time Mina cleared her throat and asked, "Are you afraid of anything?"

A lot of things. Instead, Katya wet her lips and said, "That we'll be caught . . . that your future will forever be shaped by my decision, that—" Katya glanced at Sotiris, who slumbered. She reversed course, unable to voice that particular fear. "But I can't focus on those. I can't even begin to imagine the future five minutes from now, which is frightening enough."

"You don't show it." Mina shoved her hands into her bulky sleeves. "Everything just happens, and it's like it doesn't impact you." The girl pinched her lips with her teeth.

In the background, a bubbly singer gushed about her alien lover.

"Magistrate officers undergo specialized training," Katya said, "to control ourselves. It wouldn't do for a captain to show their fears and uncertainties to their crew; we have to be above that." Robotic. It's what her eldest sister had said of her behavior afterward, though Zhihao had always been standoffish toward her.

Mina leaned forward, a question burning behind her pensive face, but she never asked it.

The singer continued her sickeningly sweet song. When the song changed to a synth dance beat, Katya stood, draped her soiled towel over her shoulders, and picked up Sotiris. Small beads of sweat covered his brow, signs he'd been in the warmer environment of the cockpit too long.

"I haven't forgotten about the clothes and mess in here." Katya paused by the door. "I expect to see them gone before we reach port tomorrow."

Mina bobbed her head; however, it matched the beat of the song, leaving Katya to sigh as she exited the cockpit. Once in her quarters, Katya shivered against the frigid tundra it'd become. She deposited Sotiris into his crib before stripping off her sweaty clothes for fresh ones after a quick shower. She then settled in her chair and busied herself on her slate, taking advantage of Dandis VII's network.

She lost track of time while she trolled newsfeeds for Magistrate movements that pertained to them, but nothing struck her as out of the norm. If they were being sought, it was being done off the record. The *Aletheia*'s destruction remained pinned on Plasovern, but the press divulged hardly any information on how it'd been destroyed . . . and life went on.

Achoo! Katya set the slate aside as Sotiris stirred and sniffled. He squawked when she lifted him back into her arms, and his large sleep-encrusted eyes fixed to her face. A yawn escaped him.

"Lucky for you, I think you've had enough physical therapy for the moment."

She paced with him, making cooing noises while rocking him.

"Ah, our princess had just returned from the witch's den." She settled in her chair, resting Sotiris's head against her shoulder. "Now what? Hmm . . ."

She strained for further adventures. A dragon loomed in her mind, a symbol that'd spanned cultures, planets, according to her father. It took on various meanings and served as both antagonist and guide.

"Ah, yes, she'd bartered with the witch for the potion to save her brother, but almost home, she found her path blocked by a dragon, its scales pitch black." She brushed a finger against his cheek. "It had *three* heads, each with a different attack! One decimated the soil with just one great fireball, scattering it high in the air. The second sent out numerous little balls that tore trees to splinters. And the third, well, you'd hear it whizzing and then BANG! There'd be no time to even duck. The dragon's breath alone blackened the sky in a way the princess had never seen before.

"Her horse, frightened, bolted into the pines." The words flowed, pouring out of her mouth. Perhaps her father's storytelling skills hadn't been lost on her after all. "Fire followed her, scorching the trees and snow. The creature burned it all . . ."

She swallowed and adjusted herself in her seat, shifting Sotiris so his head rested in the dip of her arm. His eyes popped open at the motion but closed as her voice resumed the story. "She escaped riding fast; her steed, after all, was no ordinary horse. No other one could match him in speed. When she burst through her city's gates, she rushed to the palace, giving her mother the potion." The heat had made it worthless, or perhaps more worthless than it'd already been. She flinched. "And then she warned her father of the scourge. He prepared his armies, sure it would descend on them." Lines of men in long, thick jackets—khaki, almost green . . . brown straps, shining metal.

"There were factions on her planet. Some believed the dragon was a lie, accusing her father of using it to increase his military might, or worse, that he controlled it. It happened so fast, the princess setting aside her dresses and days spent roaming for troop inspections. Then, the dragon struck, and it was as if they'd all lost"—their minds—"their wills to the dragon."

Her voice faltered. "There were causalities, steep ones. She'd visit—" A hunched man in a khaki uniform, he wouldn't face her. A bottle cast off to the side, its amber liquid largely drained. A young lady, military dress, yet wearing pearls . . . she'd grabbed her hands. Katya flexed hers against the soft cotton of Sotiris's PJs. "She'd visit them, the wounded and those serving." The words cascaded from somewhere within her. "She'd wanted . . ."

Black boots collided with the snow and her breath caught as she swiped tears away. Sotiris didn't budge, even when she bent over him.

She knew how the story ended: blood in the snow, a ruling family eradicated, and a world left in upheaval, smothered in smoke and ash. She'd read enough about Mramor to know. During it, that hand . . . it'd disappeared. She covered her mouth, breathing into her left hand in an attempt to ground herself against the tremors shaking her frame. A hand. She could almost see it now, long forgotten, dredged up by Sotiris. It stretched out toward her. She followed up its coated arm. Wool—dyed in a khaki, almost green—made up the uniform. A smile, lopsided, not unlike her own. The acrid metallic scent of antiquated gunpowder clung to him, permeated his clothing. Her mind failed. It couldn't fill in the blanks beyond the mouth and that smell long confined to reenactments.

Katya blanched at a sharp pain in her head. Sotiris's tendrils filtered their way in, drawn to the activity, eager to piece it together. She shot to her feet, clearing all her thoughts. She deposited the toddler into his bed and tucked him in. Then after grabbing her slate, she fled the memories, her nosy ward, and that hand. She only stopped when she reached the cargo hold, where she fell into the first steps of the Gorgian dance to douse any remaining interest Sotiris might have.

Dandis VII made a decent-sized speck in the foreground of a swirling, rusty-cream gas giant, Areos. Katya navigated the *Minerva* through the cluster of traffic that whizzed around the enormous station, similar to bees around a hive. Mina whistled as they drew closer and forgot her duty to get approval to dock at Section 25, Port 34, where their contact and the other half of their payment waited.

Katya cleared her throat.

"Ah yes!" Mina swung over to the console and broadcasted their purpose and destination. "This sure beats the other ones we've visited. What makes this place so special?"

"Some stations take off, and others just don't." Katya's brow furrowed in deep concentration after approval flashed across her screen, and she brought them in. "The gas giant likely brought Dandis VII a lot of wealth, and by the looks of it, they just kept adding on. Soon word spread. Naturally, people jump when they hear about a place of opportunity. Then when people realized the Magistrate placed few restrictions out here, even more came, only not the right sort."

Mina quirked an eyebrow. "Why's the galaxy filled with delinquents?"

"Sentient nature." Katya smiled, one corner of her mouth higher than the other. "But in all seriousness, riffraff tend to group together, especially when you have a strong government like the Magistrate. They go where there's less oversight."

Gritting her teeth, Katya weaved through traffic, a swarm of freighters and personal crafts. Her screen highlighted their course to their destination. It, however, did not account for crazy pilots cutting into her path en route to their own destinations.

"Krezk." The Riautus curse word was barely audible as she pressed her fingers against the control panel to clear a sleek personal craft that zigzagged into their path before leaving it. The guiding light on her console turned an angry shade of red when it blinked at her. "I'm correcting!"

"At least they don't give it a voice."

"Yeah, I imagine she'd be screaming at me right now." Katya put their ship back on course and into Port 34.

A variety of ships already resided there, with Katya resting the *Minerva* next to one of the personal crafts in a spot highlighted by yellow and orange blinking lights. Rolling her head from side to side, Katya stretched the aching muscles in her neck while initiating the cool-down sequence. Outside, a group of people approached their ship with wheeled carts.

"Our welcome party desperately wants their tea," she said.

"Will we then have time to explore the station?"

"Why not." Katya stood, her back cracking as she stretched upward. "It's not terra firma, but a station's just as good when it comes to stretching the legs. We'll stock up."

"More hair dye?" Mina lift strands of her much longer hair, which had returned to its normal burnt umber. The girl had compensated with a bright yellow shirt, gold eye shadow, and ruby lipstick. The makeup stash remained bountiful at least.

"If you use your own pay."

Her red lips peeled back as she flashed her white teeth at Katya. "Good thing I've saved up." She flipped her hair from her face. "I don't feel like me right now."

"What color?"

"Purple and black. I found a tutorial." Mina winked at her. "If I have extra—"

She shook her head. "No, thank you."

With unnecessary systems shutting down and the com systems and controls locked, Katya exited the cockpit along with Mina. As they were about to pass Katya's quarters, the teen almost entered them.

"Leave him here," Katya said, already at the ladder. "He's in one of his deep sleeps, and I don't want to risk it. We won't waste too much time exploring."

"How much time are you allotting to exploring the station?"

Katya laughed as she swung her legs over the edge and placed her feet on the rungs. The slight edge in Mina's voice—worried her shopping spree wouldn't happen—hung in the air, all too palpable.

When Katya reached the cargo bay floor, she called up, "Just enough."

She didn't hear the girl's response over the noise of the hatch being opened by Rein. Katya clapped him on the shoulder so he'd hear over the gears and clamps. "Our buyers are outside and waiting."

He nodded in confirmation.

The hatch open, she greeted the buyers as they climbed up the ramp. An official-looking man—humanoid in appearance and wearing expensive silks—led the group. His spectacles rested on the end of his nose, which pointed down to his gold-plated slate. The large veins in their contact's neck stood out, a deep blue, barely concealed by the thin skin that separated them from the environment.

"I am Vel Da'Tarr." He lowered the slate.

"It's a pleasure to meet you." She extended her hand, which the man took. "And a pleasure to do business."

"Yes, yes." Vel's head jerked a few millimeters before straightening again. It then jerked again. "The tea is in good order, so I will pay you now."

Not one for small talk, huh? Katya freed her own slate from her pocket. They synced the two devices, and Vel routed the rest of their payment to the account she had created about a month ago; it was the type that would not be easily traceable, in case they did need to dabble in the illegal.

"Transaction is complete." Vel's head jerked while he continued his odd cadence. "We have no further needs for a freighter at this time. We will contact you in the event such a need comes. Your contractor might have further uses."

"We'll check back with him, thank you." Katya bowed her head to him. "We'll leave your men to move the cargo."

"We will have it out within the half hour."

Their contact then, with his head jolting ever so slightly as he went, traveled down the ramp, nose once more buried in his slate.

"A real talker, huh?"

"They're better that way," Rein said.

She stepped aside while Vel's men unloaded the tea crates. "It does make it easier."

Together, she and Rein approached the engine room's door, pausing outside of it.

"I'm taking Mina and getting a few supplies. Maybe even catch a lead for a new job." Katya shifted her weight between her feet. "Will you stick around until they are through?"

He seemed to mull over it, and Katya half feared he'd circle round to their unfinished conversation.

"Yeah, no problem." Rein faced the men as they filled their carts. "Afterward, I'm going to lock up shop and get a drink. I won't stay long, though. You two shouldn't stay out too long either."

Katya gestured to Mina, who remained on the small railed observation deck above, beckoning her to come. "Wasn't planning on it."

Rein grunted, then cleared his throat. "You're not taking the boy, right?"

"He's staying put," Katya said as Mina drew closer, chomping to explore. "He'll be fine while we're out. Just leave him be." Katya didn't inform him that her door remained locked, the passcode having been changed, something she had begun to do on a weekly basis. "We'll be back within an hour."

Beside her, Mina moaned and muttered something under her breath. Rein merely inclined his head, though his gaze lingered on Katya, her skin crawling as it remained.

Grabbing the teenager's arm, they disembarked. She'd deal with the man another day.

Along the way, Mina peppered her with a one-sided conversation, voicing her dismay that they'd have so little time. Katya let her talk, all the while scanning the bustling bay. Maintenance crews sent sparks flying as they worked on the bay itself. Plus, there were crews set in constant movement, working on a variety of tasks. A few simply lounged, having imbibed too much. The pair walked past all the commotion and entered a large corridor connecting their hangar bay with a cluster of others. Upon entering it, a sickly sweet odor struck Katya. Smooth sticks, a stimulant. They were innocuous enough but often led to harder drugs and the start of a lifelong addiction.

The door to the station proper swooshed open in front of them, and a set of guards wearing station garb, not a Magistrate mark on them, stormed by, en route to the burners. She shepherded Mina to the side, noting the graffiti along the wall, one in particular. It was small, but that did not make it any less inflammatory. The Magistrate eagle pierced through its heart with its own lance. A Plasovern calling card.

She nudged Mina through the door to fresh, heavily circulated air. A spacious promenade with lush green plants and seating options greeted them. Travelers mingled in the area, some waiting to board their next ride while others soaked up the artificial rays and socialized. Next to her, Mina whistled and touched a dinner-plate-size leaf that belonged to one of the plants.

"Stick close."

"I haven't seen anything this green in a long time," Mina said, pressing her fingernails into the leaf as if to verify it was real.

Shaking her head, Katya edged her way to a 3-D map. The station consisted of a hodgepodge mess of sections, which lacked any rhythm or reason. They stood in one of the newer sections, which had been added solely to attract travelers passing through. Other sections catered to other needs, from living quarters and Magistrate offices to different markets. A few sections flashed red and warned of travel restrictions and the potential for violence. She settled on a market area two decks above their current location.

"Come along," she said, grabbing Mina's arm.

A group of Xanta, an insectoid species, clicked at them as they bypassed them. Their sleek bluish, black shells gleamed in the artificial sunlight. They wore masks over their face, ensuring they could breathe in the oxygen-rich station. A few of them bypassed the two women on their way to the elevator, clicking piercingly as they accessed the panel to call for the lift.

"They're in a hurry," Mina mumbled, her mouth slanting at an odd angle.

"They have a herd mentality. If one goes, they all go." Katya smiled, only it vanished when a small security drone whirled by. "We'll catch the next one."

While they waited, two more drones hovered by, less hurried than the previous one. Katya followed their progress until they left the area around a distant corner, and even then, she could only tell by the sudden absence of the glint caused by the overhead lights hitting the drone's metal bodies. The doors to a lift swooshed open.

"Step lively now."

They entered it before more of the Xanta could dart in. Inside, she hit the door mechanism, closing them off.

"Remember, we're just having a quick look and getting a few basics."

Mina bobbed her head; however, the vacant expression told her the girl was already lost in her own thoughts. She should mention the large presence of monitoring drones, but the less paranoid they looked, the less attention they'd garner. Mina had yet to develop the skill of being nondescript, untroubled, even when under stress.

The lift launched upward, Mina having pressed an option while Katya had been distracted. They hurtled past several levels.

"Where are we going?" Katya asked.

"Level 20." Mina lifted one of her eyebrows. "It's one of the main marketplaces on this side of the station."

The lift sped from level to level, making Katya's stomach sink. She almost stopped the lift and returned it to the smaller market she'd originally intended to visit. But she hesitated too long. The lift slowed and halted, its door opening.

On the other side, a variety of sentient beings waited to board: their pace hurried, their whispers barely audible, their gazes dropped, shifting. Katya draped her arm around Mina as they sidestepped the group, which pressed into the lift. Another drone moved through the still-crowded market; shoppers, meanwhile, clung to the sides of the open paths, none leaving the shelter of the awnings set up by many temporary shops.

"Stick close to me," Katya whispered in Mina's ear.

Mina's expression grew somber, but she said nothing.

They joined the crowds along the storefronts of the temporary establishments, made of tents and fabric tarps. Surrounding them and embedded in the station's structure were the permanent stores, including one specializing in parts. Katya made a mental note to visit it. Some parts it paid to have spares in. Mina darted between booths, leaving Katya to race after her. They had to stay close, but her warning had been all but forgotten with the addition of shiny objects and clothing.

They almost made it to the end of the first row of temporary stores, with Mina already having spent a good portion of her share on overpriced wireless headphones—but oh, the sound quality was so much better than her retro set—a rainbow of hair dyes, and some new shoes. Katya hadn't bought anything, despite Mina's goading. Rather, she tracked and counted the security drones. As Mina disappeared under the trap of another store, Darnaah's Rare Finds, a herd of shoppers scuttled by Katya, fleeing from something. She frowned and ducked under the tarp. Inside, Mina browsed odd-shaped sculptures with open mouths that stretched almost to the bottom of their bodies. They had no eyes and seemed withered in pain.

Katya edged along tables on the other side of the dimmed space, working her way to the proprietress. Once in front of her, she picked up a large stone that glowed and turned it about in her hand; the woman, an extremely pale Filitre, jumped at the chance to start a conversation.

"It is Gammorah salt, very healthy to have on long journeys. It helps cut back on space sickness and improves air quality in whatever room it's placed." The woman, presumably Darnaah, laughed. "Except the engine room. Nothing can purify that!"

Katya tilted the salt lamp and eyed the compartment that held the bulb and electronics. "How long is the battery life?"

"It uses soolarian crystals—also good for purification. It'll outlast you!"

Darnaah stepped closer and pointed out more features, in addition to mentioning the price and what a good bargain it was. While she did this, more foot traffic plodded by outside.

Katya reached into her pocket and removed actual hard currency. As she unfolded it, she commented, "The market has quite a bit of activity today, huh?"

Darnaah made a hacking sound as if to spit. "Unwelcomed company. Keep your heads down." She took the money proffered to her and opened her register to place it within. "Magistrate Elites are never welcomed. They have a bad effect on business."

"Understandably," she said while Darnaah wrapped the lamp. "No one enjoys shopping in fear." She cleared her throat and glanced around at the other items in a casual manner. "These Elites must be something to effectively shut down this market."

"They're some of the worse." Darnaah handed her a bag with the lamp that Katya didn't even want. "Watch yourself and your girl."

"Thanks for the tip." Katya walked over to Mina with her purchase. "Come on, you've shopped enough. We'll get our parts and head out. We have another shipment to pick up."

Mina complied by falling into step beside Katya, the mention of a nonexistent shipment registering in her mind, eroding the distraction of all the shops. As they headed to the parts shop, Katya grabbed Mina's arm and yanked her under an awning.

The store, though lit, was void of any customers, save for two men dressed in Magistrate uniforms, special ops markings displayed on their arms. They had shades over their eyes. Black hair, covered eyes, pale skin, a homogeneous species . . . Katya realized she was staring at what Sotiris would grow to resemble. The connection brought a prickly sensation, a ghost remembrance of the boy's touch. Could they do that? No, her father had said Sotiris's ability was abnormal. Even so, Katya wouldn't test her father's theory.

A woman, similar in appearance and wearing the same uniform, paced in the store's doorway, her arms crossed. Saliva caught in Katya's throat, but the woman briefly faced them. She then turned back to the men and said something in the Oneiroi language.

"Slowly," Katya whispered through her teeth as she directed Mina toward the lifts. Any lift. Next to her, Mina shook, her head craning toward the Elite soldiers. Katya squeezed her arm. "Don't look back. Walk normally, not too fast. We're shoppers with nothing to fear."

"But—"

"No." She kept the girl in step with her.

A crowd of shoppers had already gathered near the lift by the time they arrived.

"We're going to fit into this one no matter what," she told Mina.

She weaseled her way through the crowd with Mina, earning them curses, but they managed to squeeze their way into the lift. Her face set, Katya selected their ship's level before the others also put in their intended destinations. She hated the number of lit lights, which trapped them, slowed them, and caged them like animals. Her fight-or-flight reflex raged. Varying routes back to the ship flashed through her mind. All the while, she willed Mina to be prepared to move fast, all while not saying a word. Rather she expressed it through her tense body language. They could very well find themselves against a wall, quite possibly with a blindfold on.

CHAPTER TWELVE

Akakios leaned over a series of computer panels. The operators, who had occupied the space, hung back while their chief fumbled to describe their operations to the Oneiroi—an unexpected and, by their tense posture, unwanted intrusion to their day. Drones. His attention returned to the chief as the man mentioned their surveillance drones being connected to their systems. With a hand gesture, Akakios ceased the man's shudders and ramblings and launched Charis into action.

"Is this your input pathway?" Charis asked as she removed a facial recognition device, which would sync with the drones, from its padded carrier. It was gathering use in the core Magistrate planets, but out in the Mezzo and Fringe, few, except for Elites, had seen it. Akakios and his crew had only received the device themselves three weeks ago as their search had lost traction. Magistrate command had decided it might speed up their task, or at least make it achievable.

"Y-yes—"

"Good." Akakios cut off further incomplete sentences. "We'll take care of the rest."

Charis plugged in the device and waited for it to boot. The security personnel moved farther away from their stations, giving them space, though a few allowed their interest in the device to get the better of them and inched closer.

"It'll be a few minutes, Captain." She ran her fingers over several buttons and screens on both the facial recognition device and the consoles directly next to it. "Their system has a few components of older software that's slowing down the process."

"Understood." Akakios reached for his com. "Where is your current location?"

A minute passed before Ambrosios responded. "We're in a parts store. Our grease monkey—"

There was a brief hissing sound, and then Chrysanthos spoke, "We're leaking, sir. I'm getting a new trap and new lines to correct the problem."

Akakios frowned. "Chrysanthos, you're not with the ship?"

"No, sir. I wanted the correct parts the first time around. I should be able to fix the problem while we're station-bound before it becomes a health hazard."

"Can it wait?"

"Yes. But, with all due respect, sir, we shouldn't hold off too long. It's better to do it now while it's an easy fix than wait until we have a bigger problem on our hands. We don't want any of the coolant getting into our life-support systems. And I'm not going to be the ship's canary. I . . ."

More followed, but it never fully registered with Akakios. The numerous screens in front of him crackled, and then multiple life-forms appeared, scuttling about their days. Was Sotiris among them? The station marked a small chunk of an expansive galaxy; Dandis VII was a major hub on the Fringe, and he couldn't shake the thought that maybe they'd passed through. The images broke again and returned. One screen stayed blank longer until the facial scanner commandeered it, lines of red sweeping over beings' faces.

Over his team's coms, Akakios broke the silence that had fallen after Chrysanthos's explanation: "Stay alert. The facial scanner is live. If they're here, be prepared to move fast."

"If there is . . ." The security chief trailed off when Akakios faced him.

"You" — Akakios smirked — "can prepare your security teams to scramble if our targets are here."

"And who are your targets?" The man withered beneath Akakios's attention and tried to retract his question.

"Plasovern sympathizers." Akakios crossed his arms. "Are the drones also controlled in this room?"

"Th-they're programmed to follow designated lines," the security chief squeaked. "We keep them monitoring on those lines, with more drones in certain areas, areas prone for incidents."

"Incidents?" Charis prodded while she hovered over the facial scanner.

"With any station, there are bound to be situations of unrest," the man said, bordering on disrespect with his hardened tone when his professional pride stirred. "Whenever you cram hundreds of beings in what amounts to a bucket of metal plates, bolts, and wiring, they're bound to lose it. Of course, with the miners, you have their working conditions playing a role. Yes, we have brawls, drug problems . . . cases of vandalism —"

"Any cases of Plasovern making appearances?" Akakios cut in.

"Plasovern? Never." He stood as straight as a board by this point. "They may pass through, the ones whose faces aren't widely circulated, but they don't mess with the station. The drones are a major deterrent for that type. They value anonymity so they can continue to troll through Magistrate space. Can't very well do that if their faces are caught while they're setting off bombs, can they?"

"So no graffiti linked to Plasovern?"

"There've been kids—stupid kids—who've gotten their hands on spray paint, but their 'art' wasn't solely Plasovern inspired. They were just trying to get a rise out of people, stuff juveniles do."

Akakios stepped closer to the man. "I'm sure." Then glancing at the many screens, he asked, "Can the drones be piloted remotely?"

"Yes. My men are trained to manually pilot them."

"Do you maintain surveillance records?" Akakios pressed.

"Only a month's worth. Special cases involving arrests, felonies, and other offensives are kept longer."

"We'll review those—" A loud, frantic beeping emitted from the scanner, and Akakios's heart skidded. "What do we have?"

"One moment, sir."

Charis entered a few commands, and screens went blank before being filled with the feed that had triggered the facial scanner. The grid scanned a woman's face before turning green with several small blimps. Data ran next to her on the screen, verifying within 98 percent accuracy that she was a match for the woman who'd taken Sotiris. Her hair may have changed styles since Gilga, but she could not change her face.

"Zoom out." He pointed to the adolescent humanoid beside the woman. "Pull that girl's face and run them both through the banks. What level are they on?" Akakios fought the encroachment of bitterness that Sotiris's absence triggered. Ambrosios's voice ran through his head, questioning their targets' actions, particularly as he watched them stroll calmly—though the girl's movements were stiff—through the passageways, shopping purchases in hand.

Behind him, the security chief said, "Level 12 B. It's one of the main docking sectors."

"Take control of the drones, Chief, and get any of your men in that area to apprehend them." Akakios grabbed the man by the collar and yanked him close so his eyes were visible through his dark sunglasses. "They're not to leave this station, but do not kill them. It is imperative that they be taken in alive."

He released the man, who inhaled and raced to a communications station, where he issued orders to security officers on the level, which included telling them to hook into the drone feed. The security command center rumbled with noise. Some of it came from Charis inputting commands into both the scanner and the station's security consoles; the rest of it was from the security force leaping into action and taking control of the drones.

"Don't crowd them," Akakios said. "We don't want them to know they've been discovered."

Walking to a quiet corner, Akakios opened his own com, setting it to the wideband before addressing his entire crew in their native tongue. "On station. Security forces rendezvousing to pick them up. Once secured, we'll take them into our custody. Sotiris does not appear to be with them."

Echoes of affirmation crossed over the line before Akakios disconnected it and returned to Charis's side. "Any hit on the man?"

"I'm getting the hang of the system," she said. "There are hardly any drones in the actual docking bays; however, I've patched into the security cameras there." She frowned. "They're older and might be erratic with the facial scanner or not even compatible."

"Do what you can." Akakios shifted his weight, tempted to pace. The energy building in his limbs needed to be released as it coiled, demanding action.

"Sir." Charis pointed to a nearby door. "I can handle things here." Seeing his hesitation, she jerked her head toward the doorway. <Go.>

<Thank you.> Akakios strode out the door; his pace accelerated as he entered the nearest lift. Inside, he jabbed a signal blocker into the lift's panel so he wouldn't be stopped by anyone, not until he reached his destination.

Katya undid the locks on their ship remotely before clicking on her com. "Rein, where are you?"

"Still at the ship."

"Prep the engines; send out a request to leave." She handed Mina her bag before wiping her sweaty palm against the front of her outfit. A drone went by.

"Katya, what's going on? Departures are being declined."

"Pick up your speed," Katya said to Mina. She returned her arm to the girl's shoulder, forcing her to keep up. Behind her, the drone never strayed far. She clicked the button on her com. "We could be in trouble." Rein cursed over the line, but she talked over him: "Be prepared to make some interesting maneuvers. We'll be back in a few minutes. Don't draw attention to the ship."

Katya and Mina passed a group of travelers, who'd been milling by one of the station's general information consoles, in time to see a group of security officers come around a corner. Pulling Mina, she forced the girl through the crowd and toward the station walls. They were almost at a full run now. The pounding in her ears drowned out the curses and noises from the crowd as she and Mina rocketed past them, or maybe as the security officials did. Katya gripped her service pistol.

Additional security officers exited a corridor in front of them, the corridor they needed. The ones behind them were closer.

Swallowing, Katya tightened her grip on Mina's shoulder. "Stay down but keep moving to the ship. Don't look back."

With that, she yanked her AVI-13 from its holster with her left hand and fired.

Screams echoed throughout the area as bursts of weapons fire beat out a chorus of chaos. Mina followed orders, darting for the corridor while Katya laid out a suppressive fire. As she did so, she weaved between and around the decorative structures and planters to avoid being hit. Blasts ricocheted around her. Gritting her teeth, she ducked, a blast missing her head by an inch. An entire career with the Magistrate — she fired — but this was the most she'd ever been shot at, and she'd been shot at a lot. A man closed in on Mina. Bringing up her pistol, Katya compressed the trigger. The blast struck the man high in the shoulder, and he tumbled to the floor.

Need to move — Katya thrust up from her hiding spot and ran. Her firearm burned her skin. Would it overheat or run out of charge first? She shot a bolt at a security officer who was in her immediate path, catching his leg. Turning back, she fired a few shots at the ones behind her, trying not to hit bystanders. *Bam!* A shot hit the wall not far from where her body had been — but she was getting closer to the corridor. Just a little farther. Mina had long disappeared in it. Hopefully, she'd make it back to the ship unhindered.

"Stop her!" one of the security officers shouted.

"Stop!" Another — one too close — screamed.

Katya spun and discharged her pistol. It connected with his shoulder but didn't stop his return volley. Katya hissed when the shot grazed her arm.

Can't stop now. She fired again, disarming him. Closer to the corridor. She had to get closer. She was a foot away when, across from her on the other side of the promenade, a lift door opened. The blood and all its warmth drained from her face.

A mess greeted Akakios. Several security officers lay scattered on the ground while others chased after the woman's retreating form, which forced its way to a corridor. Smoke clung to the area. In one case, a stray shot had struck a console panel, sparking an electrical fire. A couple of the officers doused it with a special foam before it could spread.

"Captain," Charis's voice said over his com. "The girl's entered the section with the older cameras; I'm working on getting her movements ascertained."

"Get on it." Akakios removed his AVI-15 and ran into the fray. "Don't kill her!" he shouted.

If he got close enough, he could end this, prevent further bloodshed, and keep the idiots from killing one of the few people who knew where his nephew was. A shot barely missed his head. Another security officer fell. And then, his target's firearm lost charge or overheated. In the grand scheme, it didn't matter. Akakios reached outward with his mind, prepping the contact. Look up, look up! He charged close—only a meter away—but now she was in a full bolt.

She vanished into the corridor, with Akakios in pursuit. Leveling his AVI-15, Akakios fired a warning shot. She twisted her head toward him enough. Akakios took full advantage. Their eyes met, and Akakios reached—air rushed from his lungs. He toppled to the ground face-first. A familiar presence grappled at his mind, overeager and spewing images that blurred together and proved discordant. He hissed and drew in breath while trying to protect his mind from the overpowering connection.

"Cap-tain—" Charis . . . but her contralto was a trickle over the gushing torrent of emotions, images, garbled words, phrases that made no sense . . . then the connection broke. Akakios wiped his mouth, which had pooled with drool. His mind reeled in pain. They still had him.

Katya burst through the secondary corridor. So close to being in the clear. She heard the Oneiroi captain fall to the ground but did not attempt to get visual confirmation. No, she charged on while her brain burned. Sotiris. Apparently, he'd grown bored. Still, her mind also strayed back to the fully grown Oneiroi. Had he managed to do something?

"Out of the way!" she screamed as she passed a crew of Cseks. She brandished her firearm, now worthless, for good effect. They scattered. With a clear path, Katya tore up the *Minerva*'s ramp. The light tremors coursing through the metal beneath her feet told her the engines were primed and ready. Hitting the closing mechanism, she barreled toward the cockpit.

"Rein," she all but shouted into the com, "bring the engines all the way up. We're busting out."

Mina waited for her in the upper hallway, sliding up against the metal wall as Katya rushed into the cockpit. "Serve as my point. My head's been affected. If I get dragged under. . ." She paused when Sotiris's tendrils, or at least that was best she could think to describe his mental fingers as, brushed against her mind. "Take over and get us out. I have absolute faith in you."

With no time to do a preflight check, Katya pressed the necessary controls to bring the *Minerva* up. Screens sprang to life, showing information that went ignored for now. She reached over and activated the planetary entry shields.

"What are you doing?" Mina asked from the communications station.

"They're our ticket out of here." Her mind had already turned to the barrier that separated the station interior from space. She modified the planetary shielding further to null the barrier without breaking it—she couldn't bring death upon those in the bay. Even as she finished the adjustments, Katya lifted her vessel from the bay floor.

"*Minerva*, cease your actions and prepare to be boarded," a masculine voice came over their communications system. "Turn off your engines immediately."

Outside, a growing number of station security officers swarmed around them, all bearing heavy-duty plasma weapons designed to leave pockmarks and immobilize ships. Katya kept the *Minerva* hovering. A warning shot went off at a powered-down level, jostling them but leaving no damage. Once the last of the modifications was finalized, she punched it. A hovercart that'd been left in the open flew clear across the bay, as did other materials. Katya increased their speed further. Three meters separated them in what could be a jarring breach.

"Plasovern agents," a low female voice came across the communications system, "there is no escape. Power down and prepare to be boarded. We want what belongs to us."

One meter. She braced herself for the coming impact, as did Mina. Then they hit. All speed ceased, jerking her and Mina forward. Katya winced, her hand moving to apply more power. The *Minerva* whined, its engines at the brink of overload when the force holding them disappeared. Beside her, Mina screamed.

"On it!" Katya sent their ship into a spin.

She kept it tight, preventing a crash with a freighter. A ship whizzed by their out-of-control vessel. What are they . . . Shit! She righted the *Minerva* in time to avoid another collision.

Wiping sweat from her face, Katya piloted them away from the shipping lanes. Too congested. It'd be foolish to even consider using them to ditch the security ships. The open exposed them; however, they couldn't make a jump in these confined lanes. No matter what, staying near the station for an extended time period was suicidal.

A plasma burst shot from one of the security ships forced her to bank and spin. They were targeting the engines. Grunting, Katya made their moves erratic, weaving, darting, dipping — anything to minimize the target they presented.

"Mina, what's on the radar?"

"It's blank. I've never seen it blank —"

"They're jamming it." Or they'd uploaded a virus. Katya focused on the viewscreen in front of her. It wasn't ideal, especially if it too became infected. This took the prize for the most strenuous flying experience of her life. She gnawed at her lip as if it'd provide more focus, skill. Today had become a day of unwanted firsts. "Mina, take your RMP and get the juice in Sotiris."

"What about yours?"

"Just do as told!"

Sending the *Minerva* into a dive, Katya sought empty space to make a jump. The security forces, smaller, more agile, maintained pursuit much like wolves stalking a meal and fired with little discrimination

Just let us get clear.

She raced around a freighter and went underneath another. Another plasma blast. More security ships joined the hunt, shifting the odds further out of their favor, and they seemed to be losing interest in not destroying the Badger.

"What's the plan?" Rein asked over the intercom.

"Continue to hold tight." Her breath gusted out. "I —" The *Minerva* was tossed about like a buoy at sea after a plasma bolt exploded near its undercarriage. "Damn —"

Maneuverability all but disappeared, yet they shot forward into more traffic. Her hand drifted to the weapons control panel. Biting her lip, she removed her hand from it, not willing to chance catching others in the crossfire.

"Stabilizers and shielding are partially down," Rein's voice stated over the intercom. "If you're going to do anything, do it now!"

Activating the planetary bursts, Katya managed to give them enough of a push to avoid becoming space debris. Still close to several civilian ships . . . but the security vessels were breathing down their necks. Bowing her head, she made the call: "Blind jump in three . . . two . . . one!"

"Captain!"

"Ch-Charis." Akakios lifted his head, which swam, still sifting through the vast array of information Sotiris had shoved into it.

"Sir, they've blown the bay. The Dandis VII security force is in pursuit and is trying to disable the ship."

Coughing, Akakios cleared his throat and tried to right his mind. "How? I mean, what are the security ships using?"

"They're using plasma cannons and targeting vital systems." There was a pause. "I've emphasized moderation, but they've almost taken out the Plasovern agents' ship several times now, sir."

"Sotiris is on that ship." Akakios pushed himself into a seated position with his back against the corridor wall.

He was on that ship. Akakios rubbed his hands against his face, meeting a fine coat of sweat. If the ship escaped, if they did make a run to Medzeci space . . . Kyros's words flitted through his mind. At all costs. Clenching his fists, he swallowed, his vision narrowing again. At all costs.

"Sir?"

Swallowing, Akakios decided he'd be damned. "Under no circumstances are they to destroy that vessel. Do you understand? Order them to withdraw immediately!"

"I have—"

"Knock it into them," Akakios squeezed out through his gritted teeth. "If you do not, I will when I return to the security center."

Pushing against the wall, he stood on shaky legs and staggered forward, swaying with each step. One of the security officers approached him, only to slink back upon catching his dour expression. He had no time to deal with the morons who'd let one Plasovern agent make a mockery of them. The officer instead resumed helping his fallen comrades, all still breathing.

As they moved, not really worse for the skirmish, Akakios frowned.

Ambrosios had been right. Something was off. He reentered the lift and headed to the security center. Still—a nonsensical, gaping smile formed—Sotiris was alive and seemingly healthy. His touch at least had not been distressed; however, all of Kallistrate's efforts to teach him control had evaporated. Akakios's chest constricted. He'd progressively destabilized like all the other children before him.

"Captain," Ambrosios's voice said over his communicator, "is there a rendezvous?"

"Negative." Akakios stepped out of the lift. "Agents, I suspect, have escaped with Sotiris. But they won't be able to hide long with their cover blown. Regroup at the *Boreas*; more information will be available then."

He disconnected the conversation and entered the security headquarters. "Charis," he said.

Her features were pinched, and she ducked her head, avoiding eye contact. "They made a blind jump . . . with their navigation system jammed and regular stabilizers damaged." The station's chief security officer shrank when Charis finished. "They were pressed."

Akakios inhaled and crossed the room in seconds, taking the security chief by the collar. "If that ship did not survive the jump . . ." He bared his teeth at the man. "Let me give you a taste of what awaits."

He pried the phantasms harbored in the man's mind to the forefront, holding him up after his legs buckled and his body began to spasm. Akakios allowed the abuse to continue for several minutes before he dropped the chief. The man huddled on the ground, his muscles convulsing.

"I hope for your sake that we don't have to meet again." Akakios gave a sharp gesture toward the door. "Charis."

"I need to pack up shop. I'll gather relevant information as well; if that is fine with you, sir."

"Make it quick." Akakios tightened his jaw, though pain gradually forced him to relax. <We need to keep moving.>

Akakios then left for their ship, which was located in a bay reserved for smaller Magistrate military vessels, not far from the connecting veins that allowed larger Magistrate vessels to dock at the station. Ambrosios waited for him there, inside the cargo hold.

"So what happened down there?"

"Our allies failed to put up a show." Akakios passed Ambrosios, on course to the bridge. His third officer fell in behind him.

"What were they up against?"

"A woman."

They proceeded past Pelagius and Pelagia, who moved closer to the wall to make room for them. Out of the corner of his eye, Akakios saw Ambrosios wave them away. They did as told and scuttled on their way, undoubtedly to warn the others to give the bridge a wide berth. Akakios ran his tongue against the back of his teeth as his frustration swelled. He punched the controls to the bridge far harder than necessary. When the door opened, Kyrillos—a thin layer of black hair emerging from his scalp, the bet having ended—swiveled in his chair to face them. He rose and, without a word, left, no doubt at Ambrosios's signal. Akakios let it be. He neither needed nor wanted an audience, nor did he desire sympathy. He sat. No, all he wanted was to work uninterrupted.

"A humanoid woman?"

Akakios glared at Ambrosios and his smirk. "A well-trained humanoid woman. She has to have a military background." He launched the DRTD program and inserted a request for transportation records pertaining to the Badger named *Minerva*. It would take hours for information to be delivered to them. He cleared his throat. "You're right."

"I often am." Ambrosios lowered himself into his seat. "But what am I right about this time?"

"Something is completely amiss."

Ambrosios leaned toward him, his smile vanishing. "So, what's the next step?"

"Trace where they've been and send another request for possible IDs from the Magistrate's bowels of data. We have all their faces, yet we're being slowed by officials even though our search has high priority." Akakios slammed his fist into his console. "I had found him—felt him, his excitement. He might be dead all over again."

"Might, but most likely isn't." Ambrosios shrugged. "Let's call it a gut feeling. This prey's proven to be cagey. I wouldn't put it past them to survive."

Akakios leaned into his seat. "He wasn't afraid." A mirthless chuckle escaped his throat. "He might as well have been on a grand adventure. And he wanted to share all of it with me, all at once." Akakios winced. "It hurts to know that Kallistrate's efforts have been wiped away. That he was able to knock me down . . . He's dangerous, and I don't think his holders fully appreciate that."

"It might be a boon to us."

"If we can get to him before he starves or their vessel crosses into an asteroid belt."

"So, how are we going to get to him?"

The DRTD program blinked before loading the confirmation page. "We wait for that ship's past from the DRTD, and we let Chrysanthos install the new part." Akakios rose from his seat and prepared to go to his quarters. "There's no point in running around the universe searching for what amounts to a tiny pinprick. Tell Charis to continue her digging within reason. I need to clear my mind."

241

CHAPTER THIRTEEN

Endless space dominated the viewscreen even though only a small portion displayed it—the ship's inner workings, navigation charts, calculations of potential jump locations, and various data streams took up the bulk. However, the faint pricks of light and vast black seized Akakios's attention, not the information. Limitless. He clenched his fists. They could run all the calculations available, and even then, their quarry could be anywhere. It would take more than a lifetime to comb through an inch of it.

Rubbing his eyelids, Akakios blocked out the screen and his spiraling thoughts as he rested against his chair. The present required his focus, though it felt like wadding through the thick-syrupy concoction Magistrate citizens called molasses.

Presently, his senior officers strove to ferret out new avenues while completing routine tasks. They worked as if the slightest noise would break the perceived levee keeping him hinged. He grinned. The debacle at Dandis VII burned, but it'd been salved by having felt Sotiris's presence, something more tangible than a hologram. It spurred him on.

Their targets were on the move; he didn't doubt that. They, meanwhile, had been shackled by the CDTR, which, like most bureaucratic wheels in the Magistrate machine, crept at a snail's pace. In their own time, they had forwarded the routes the *Minerva* had taken, tracked by the Magistrate's DRTD program. Despite having the routes in hand, the only concrete data they offered were the times the ship had landed on a planet or station. The catch was those locations had to have a Magistrate relay. The last such location had been a station orbiting Derget, called S4-G3, and that had been three months ago. They'd visited it with a medical emergency. It now served as their destination. With no clear avenue, they would retrace and learn more along the way. The stop at the station so far had been the sole anomaly in their targets' actions, with all their other destinations involving the moving of cargo.

None, except potentially the delivery to Ereago, held any ties to Plasovern. Then there was the highly prized Sotiris: He had remained with them at each and every stop, a goldmine unspent. His value to Plasovern and countless other independent buyers far outstripped any of the cargo they had hauled.

"Sir," Kyrillos said, "we've received a transmission from Central. They've denied our request for additional access into its case databanks. Just like with our requests to get *The Maelstrom*'s crew roster."

Central had been firm that *The Maelstrom*'s crew had been disposed of and replaced by Plasovern agents; they'd also been quick to bury *The Maelstrom*'s existence. Why wouldn't they budge from that assumption, a fatally flawed one? Akakios rubbed his forehead. It failed to explore all angles. In the crew roster's place, they'd received notification that not all family members had been informed. A cursory probe on Charis's part had revealed that the data had been sealed behind several layers of encryption. Attempts at bypassing it, in her words, would be as easy as setting off a bomb in the center of Magistrate Command: foolhardy and ending without setting foot in the complex itself.

"Thank them," Akakios said.

Kyrillos did as instructed, only to address Akakios again. "They've requested our destination."

Akakios frowned. Not content with blocking invaluable information, they now tracked their movements. "Tell them." He added along their mental link, <But keep the details sparse.>

Kyrillos did so before removing the small headset attached to his left ear and forehead. "We appear to be in the endgame. So far, the Plasovern agents have been able to change the registry on their ship and do cosmetic changes. Command now has a triple-hold on the registry; if they attempt to modify it again, they'll be setting off a red beacon."

"Unless they jump or limp into Medzeci space." Charis stood from her console.

"They haven't tried to do that yet," Ambrosios opinioned.

"So they haven't." The charts before him noted their ETA, an hour away. Akakios tapped his fingers against his armrests. "I hope this journey might be more illuminating about these people."

Akakios straightened his sunglasses and exited his quarters. They'd arrived at the station on schedule and had already connected to it with the retractable shaft. Miners and people passing through made up the bulk of its traffic, ideal for their targets. Medical emergency. What had it been?

"Sir." Charis saluted him, her rosy lips pursed. "The station's security is waiting for us."

His eyebrows lifted. "Central?"

She nodded, her arms locking behind her back. "They have the same information as us. They were able to conclude our intent once they knew we were headed to S4-G3. They've taken the station's doctor—Jia's his name—into custody."

"Is he still on-station?"

"For now, they'll be transporting him into the Core."

His mouth narrowed. Why the Core? Surely, he'd be shipped off to the nearest Magistrate court in the Fringe or Mezzo. What had the man done to warrant being shipped into the Core?

"The doctor seems to have dug himself quite the hole," Charis said as if reading his thoughts. "Apparently, he tried to flee."

"And that opens a number of questions. How the hell did he know we were coming?"

"No idea, sir." Charis paused as the door to Ambrosios and Chrysanthos's quarters opened. A fully readied Ambrosios stepped out, saluting both of them as they passed, and then fell into step behind them.

Charis tucked her bangs behind her ears as they approached the connector tube. "I suspect the doctor has certain ties."

"Plasovern?" Ambrosios whistled. "What a fine mess we find ourselves in."

Oh, what a mess indeed, Akakios thought upon crossing over with his officers and Pelagius. After they completed the station's decontamination sequence, they entered the station proper to find two security guards with Magistrate colors waiting.

"Sirs," the one in front addressed them. "We have Doctor Jia in custody. We're in the process of reviewing security measures; he shouldn't have known Elites were coming."

"Sounds like a guilty conscience is involved, doesn't it?" Akakios said, following the security officers. "I imagine you've pulled the good doctor's records."

"We tried to, but he destroyed them before his attempt to leave the station." The man's hands, which rested behind his back, clenched. "His compatriots escaped after realizing the eventual outcome, doing some damage to our lower docking clusters. We've been unable to pin them to any possible organizations, but I have my suspicions."

"Plasovern," Akakios pressed.

"Out here, it's a high probability, Captain."

Little conversation followed as they arrived at the prison block; there, a guard escorted them to a small room. Akakios signaled, with a short hand gesture, for Pelagius to remain outside while he and the rest entered a dingy room. Once the door shut behind them, Akakios removed his sunglasses and slid them into one of his outer pockets. He stepped closer to a metal table and the man behind it. The doctor, quite pale, did not so much as flinch when Akakios stood over him.

"Didn't get far, did you, Doctor?" Akakios rested his hand on the man's shoulder. "Not very smart to run. It suggests you know something or you have illegal connections who tipped you off. If you'd carried on about your business, our visit might've been a mere blip in your life. We only knew our targets came here on a medical emergency. It could've been that you didn't know who came in your door searching for help. Being the good doctor that you presumably are, you helped them out." Akakios cleared his throat; the action carried in the tight metal room.

"But no, you tried to run after destroying your patients' data, which damns you even more. Because that one action all but says you knew who you were treating; it also suggests you've been treating other individuals you shouldn't have been for quite—"

Jia spat at the table. "Or maybe I was concerned for my patients' rights to privacy."

"I doubt you had the same reasoning as most doctors." Akakios tightened his grip on the man's shoulder. "No, you had to protect your patients because of their 'special' activities."

Charis stepped forward with a projector in her hand, which she activated. The hologram that had launched their mission sprang into the air before being replaced by the week-old photos of the woman and the teenager. Charis circled between the three images while keeping the device level with the doctor's face, its light illuminating the creases forming in his skin.

"Pay close attention," Akakios said into the doctor's ear. "These people came to you. It might have been this woman, the girl, the boy, or a man—or any given number of combinations. I want to know which ones and why they came to you."

"We all want things," Jia retorted, his voice low. "I would like to be off this station without Oneiroi breathing down my neck, but that isn't going to happen. No, I'm going to be—"

Ambrosios surged forward, hoisting the doctor from his seat by his collar and slamming him into the room's metal wall. Two solid thuds followed—one, the chair colliding with the floor, and the second, the doctor's head bouncing off the wall. The man's legs twitched as gurgling emitted from his mouth. Akakios squeezed his second lieutenant's shoulder, and he ceased the use of his abilities, though he kept the doctor pressed into the wall.

"You don't want him to do that too many times," Akakios said to Jia. "While our abilities are nothing to others of our kind, to most other species, the effects are quite adverse."

"Optic nerves . . ." The doctor coughed. "Thicker than most, tied to the brain, larger than most, with an unnamed part that is undoubtedly unique to the species. The wiring is fascinating."

Akakios gripped the man by the throat. "What did you do to him?"

"Stemmed bleeding in the cerebral cortex. Reduced swelling. Applied IV fluids. Addressed additional internal bleeding." The corner of the doctor's mouth twitched. "Scanned him for further damage and to see what makes him and his kind so interesting."

"Tell me more. Tell me everything."

Jia chuckled. "A mother and her 'son,' only they couldn't have been that, but I'd already known. She was worried, even though he'd dragged her under . . . needed fixed up; she didn't approve of my interest in his anatomy."

"How did the injury occur?" Akakios applied pressure to Jia's throat.

"A fall . . . a throw," Jia choked out as air became scarcer for him. "A comrade . . . got overzealous . . . breaking the kid's spell. Jealous type from the force."

Akakios released his grip, and Jia collapsed to the ground. Both Akakios and Ambrosios towered over him. Steadying his breathing, Akakios strode to the door. His jaw ached, and a strong urge to punch something—that man—was overwhelming. Charis touched his arm, bringing him to reality.

<He knows more.> Charis's presence echoed through his mind.

Ambrosios came to stand by them, his hands folded behind his back. <I can get more out of him.>

From the floor, Jia interrupted their conversation. "I'm nothing but an open book, Magistrate dogs."

Akakios took a step toward the man but stopped when Jia spoke again.

"Muscle mass is deteriorating. Try as she might, she can't combat the disorder like the mother."

The blood drained from Akakios's face while a tremor traveled up his back. "How do you know that?" He kicked Jia over so the doctor's face was in plain sight. "How do you know about Kallistrate? Answer me!"

Jia smiled at Akakios—no, at the ceiling. "Kalli-strate. I know nothing of her, or not by that name. But I do know the people who came to me weren't Plasovern, just hapless suckers who got in way over their heads. But don't worry, help is coming to them." He chuckled, almost delirious in nature. "A *storm* of change."

"Storm?" Akakios blinked, his mind scrambling through known criminal codes. Then he hissed. "Strom." He yanked Jia up so their faces were inches away. "Where are they?"

"That, I don't even know. I'm a mere doctor. I patch people up. I don't keep track of them afterward. Nor am I asked to." Jia cleared his throat. "Captain Sarris, you aren't going to beat the storm: It's well on its way."

Akakios's jaw tightened, some bit of it popping. The dam broke. Jia uttered a muted wail when Akakios dug into his mind, ransacking it for additional information, past care for an insect that'd sought to dissect his nephew like some science project. The doctor launched into a shrieking fit, his mind recoiling from the assault as if it were being bludgeoned, though Akakios supposed the effect of his abilities resembled such an action to the humanoid. Despite it, information refused to come easy, instead taking the form of brief blips and flashes.

<Captain.>

Akakios broke the contact with Jia at Ambrosios's prompting—his hand on Akakios's shoulder almost a shock in its odd role reversal. Breathing heavy, he dropped the doctor to the floor, straightening and distancing himself, a feeble attempt to hide his lapse.

<Feeling better?>

Akakios dusted off the front of his suit before yanking out his sunglasses and placing them firmly onto his face, anything to avoid looking at either of his officers.

Composed, he said to Charis and Ambrosios, "We need to be on our way." Across the connections that bound them, he added, <Say nothing until we reach the ship.>

Behind them, Jia laid on his back, eyes open but unfocused. He would come around, probably finding himself on a Magistrate vessel, and from there, he'd be swept under the rug. Straightening his collar, Akakios exited the room and came face-to-face with the security officer from before. The man flinched and gave the Oneiroi a wide berth.

"I was coming to see if you need any help, Captain."

"We're satisfied." Akakios waved two fingers for Pelagius to follow them as they walked back to the *Boreas*. Over his shoulder, he added, "I apologize for the shape of your prisoner. But he should be fine for trial . . . given time."

The security officer trailed after them, stating that he should escort them back to their ship. He didn't say anything during the trip through the narrow station corridors, and neither did they. The officer was watching them. Why? Station security — given the opportunity — made it a point to distance themselves from Elite business. Yet here, this one inserted himself when unnecessary. Fear radiated off him, too, visible in his stiff posture and the slight tremor he tried to conceal in his right hand. So, he had been forced into a job he disliked: to watch them. Akakios toyed with the idea of flaunting his rank and dismissing the man if only to see what he would do: capitulate or resist?

Ahead of them, the empty corridor grew narrower, much like their search. They weren't Plasovern agents. That information was . . . disquieting, but not unexpected. Their actions were anything but Plasovern in nature. However, it brought forth unpleasant possibilities. What if *The Maelstrom* had remained a Magistrate vessel? If that was the case, why would the Magistrate effectively burn its crew? Or had it? After all, the crew members' identities had been concealed. A knot tightened in his throat.

They arrived at the docking section. But their guide did not depart until they prepared to enter the decontamination chamber. Charis activated the door for them; however, Akakios hung back.

He saluted the security officer. "Thank you for your escort."

"No problem, Captain. Safe journeys on your journey to . . ."

"Sergrey," Akakios said. "Unfortunately, the good doctor didn't have any suggestions for a possible destination. We'll regroup and try again."

"That's unfortunate."

They saluted once more before Akakios followed his team to the chamber and then onto the *Boreas*. Once on the bridge, Akakios had Ambrosios initiate the undocking procedures.

"Ambrosios," Akakios said from his seat. "Submit a route to Sergrey." Then privately, he added, <But keep our speed at a creep. We have digging to do.>

Ambrosios did as told, and Akakios addressed Charis. "I want to know where Hedda Strom's been seen recently. That'll give us an area to concentrate on, rather than jumping around hoping to get lucky." He leaned toward her. <Don't use official channels.>

"Strom?" Kyrillos perked at his station, eyes widening at the name.

"The very same." Akakios activated his slate. "Let me know what pertinent information you find." He messed with its security settings. "We can't let her intercept Sotiris."

"Would they really send Strom into Magistrate space?" Charis's hands hovered over her console's screen.

"To get a hold of the defect, I wouldn't doubt it," he replied. "If Jia wasn't lying about these people, they've been backed into a corner, and Plasovern's overtures are going to start looking better than their current predicament. If approached, I don't see them rejecting anything. Strom's persuasive . . . she's swayed plenty to her cause.

"And she's known for passing through Magistrate space and has a reputation of being a chameleon of sorts." Akakios thumbed through his slate's menus. "Intel has suggested she's dabbled in repeated cosmetic surgery. Then again, other sources say Hedda Strom is actually a collection of agents who have taken up her mantel; that theory, of course, hinges on her having been killed during the uprising on Skogarld."

"The first way," Ambrosios commented, "we'll be able to get a pinpoint; however, if there are multiple Stroms, we're still without a direction to follow."

"Charis."

"I'm on it, Captain." Her shoulders tightened as she launched into action, her hands skidding along the flat console. "It'll take a while."

"Understood."

All his officers fulfilled their roles, the quiet hums of the machines filling the void. Akakios opened a file on his slate, a photo of Amyntas and Kallistrate. They stood side by side, his brother a few inches taller than his wife, both garbed in the fur garments traditionally worn by their people. It'd been taken some time after the fulfillment of the pair's contract. They both looked so young. Akakios ran his finger across their faces. His mouth contorted, and he closed the photo. In its place, he reopened the files that pertained to the destruction of the *Aletheia*, this time with new eyes and a creeping sensation tinged with dread. He wanted to crush the feeling and bury it where it'd never be found; though, it'd likely reemerge. His gut clenched.

The report read clinically, containing location and assumptions of the role played by *The Maelstrom* and an unknown, assumed-Plasovern, vessel. His chest tightened at the photos of debris, which consisted of torn metal plates. A few blackened, battered metal plates were all that remained of it, a huge A-Class warship. Plasovern lacked the capability. If they had that kind of firepower, the whole galaxy would combust as they went about liberating planets. That left only the Magistrate and Medzeci—no independent system or planet would dare such a move. The reported location put the destruction well within Magistrate space but still slightly off course from the *Aletheia*'s intended destination to deliver Sotiris.

A thought, insidious as it was, stirred and rooted itself further in the forefront of his mind. Could they have been farther off course? Had that part of the report been changed? He closed the documents and went back to the photo of Kallistrate and Amyntas. As if examining their captured faces would impart some answer, tell their secrets. Would they have . . .

"Sir," Charis said. "I've been looking at various streams, and I think I might have an area for us to target."

"Relay the coordinates to Ambrosios. Do not report our redirection or our hypothesis on Strom." His officers stiffened and shifted toward him for answers. "I want to apprehend them before any other Magistrate officials do. It's the only way I'll ever get the truth of what happened."

"You're not suggesting—" Kyrillos said before Akakios cut him off.

"You're right: I'm not suggesting anything at this point." Akakios approached his communications officer. "However, what I do know is that our mission's been purposely complicated from the beginning. Why is the Brass withholding information from us?" He rested his hand on Kyrillos's shoulder. "For now, I want to interrogate these people." Before they disappeared under Magistrate red tape.

Ambrosios scratched his chin. "But you're starting to suspect something."

It—that unspoken question, more an answer now—clawed at him: They were traitors. Unwanted, painful but defiant, it refused to be inhumed any longer.

"Nothing for sure." He slipped back into his seat.

"Increase our speed." He picked up his slate, which now displayed the information Charis had sent to it, all about their destination. "Get us underway."

Katya bounced Sotiris on her knee in the galley as he did something he hadn't done before: a full-out wail. No matter how she held him, he repudiated any attempt at being placated. And between his fits and tending to their ailing ship and her own wound, she threatened to buckle. Mina winced upon walking in on them, forgetting her own search for food. The girl had spent hours in the cockpit, monitoring the situation there; of course, she would be hungry now. And if she were honest about it, Katya would have to admit she was hungry too.

"What's wrong with him?" Mina asked before shoving a ration bar into her mouth.

"I don't know. He's been fussing since he woke up." She pointed to the pan of food she'd been warming for the boy. "Can you check and see if that's done?" Overhead, the lights flickered, and the burner under the pot ceased before resuming. "Damn it." Standing, she handed Sotiris to Mina, who still had the ration bar in her mouth.

"Hey!" she mumbled around it.

"I can't stay with him right now. That" — she pointed to the lights above them — "is a sign I've been out of the engine room for too long. Rein needs help. It isn't a one person job to keep this ship in one piece."

Mina swallowed. "Are you sure he's all right?" She poked Sotiris's cheek.

"Physically, yes. His crib kept him safe during the jump." Katya opened the galley door to exit. "And the gravitational dampeners kept us all from having our insides turned to mush and our bones crushed. Get him to eat. Tell him a story or something . . . I've been telling him a story about a princess and a horse-dog."

Mina quirked an eyebrow. "Horse-dog?"

"A horse that acts like a dog," she supplied. "Once you finish up, get back to the cockpit. Someone needs to stay there."

With the girl's affirmative grunt, Katya trekked down the dimmed corridors to the engine room. The lights blinked on and off, a sign that another system was buckling. She kicked the corridor wall beside her and screamed. Frustration poured out even as pain traveled up her leg. Everything was falling apart, and they were out of options, limping through space completely reliant on momentum resultant of the jump. Just waiting for systems to fail.

Rein had been right.

She sank to the floor, pressing her back against the wall. As her face contorted, she buried it in her knees. Sotiris's original death had returned, and this time they'd share it with him. All their efforts . . . moot, wasted. Really, they'd been no better than mice caught in a cage trap, foolish enough to not see it for what it was. The cards had been fully stacked against them. She sobbed, the sound coming out pinched. Tremors followed despite her best efforts to stifle them. The invisible noose tightened. Rubbing her eyes, she fought to calm herself, but her mind plunged her down all manner of bleak, unyielding routes.

Papa, I'm so sorry.

Muted sobs wracked her frame, and tears flowed more readily. In front of her through her obscured vision, the railing to the overlook morphed into bars. There was no way around it. And she morbidly couldn't decide which was better: the firing squad or the bars. Her jaw and fists tightened as the lights vanished. *"Is this how I raised you?"* she could practically hear her father say in that tone he'd used when school assignments had been haphazardly thrown together and received unacceptable marks; it hadn't been often, but those few times lingered. She'd hated the disappointment that resonated from every inch of him.

Katya pushed herself to her feet. She would burn this deck of cards. Her legs carried her to the ladder as she used her hand on the railing to guide her in the darkness. Valens's gaunt face—hollowed by illness, which also marred his color—joined her father's look of disappointment and crossed arms. She couldn't bear them following her. If she stopped, gave up—Valens had fought his damnedest until a good death had been his only option . . . She'd made a promise not just to her father but to Mina and Sotiris the moment she'd brought them under her wings. Feeling with her feet, she cleared each rung of the ladder before proceeding, hands outstretched, to the engine room.

She wasn't going to die here. None of them were.

Tracing her way using her hands and memory, she reached the engine room. There, she found Rein cussing up a storm while he tried to keep them afloat among the growing list of repairs. The room itself was black as tar, excluding the light fastened to Rein's head.

"Do you have another one available?"

He grunted, and the light bounced as he retrieved a second pair, which he handed to her. "About time you got back down here."

"I had things to take care of topside." Katya turned on the light and attached it to her head. "The navigation system's unsalvageable; they did a number on it back at Dandis VII. Communications are down, but I think I can get it back up."

"First things first, huh?" His light settled on the ship's silenced FTL drive and regular engines—the systems still alive were running on stored energy. "She's hemorrhaging. All the work we did yesterday on the electrical system is failing. I still can't get any of the engines up. Habitation systems are threatening to collapse . . . We might be without gravity before long, so take your pick on what you want to fix first."

"The electrical system's tied to the others. It has to be the first."

Rein grunted his agreement, and they worked in concert to turn around the uphill battle. An hour passed before they brought the lights online, and Katya shifted to the habitation systems while Rein patched more of the electrical system. With luck, they wouldn't freeze to death. Not a horrible death—actually rather quick given the severe cold beyond their hull—but also not desirable.

Rein broke the silence that'd fallen in the room. He jerked his hand away as a spark leaped from the console. He did a sharp intake. "Not how I expected to go." He wiped his hands against the front of his shirt. "Largely expected a knife in the back on Reznic, just like . . ."

The thought went unfinished, his face grim as he reentered the console, fixing errant wires.

"We're not dead yet."

He snorted. "Not yet, but it's inevitable. What are we going to do?" He slammed the console cover shut.

"As long as we're still breathing, we fight and patch. Something will come along."

His lips twisted into a mockery of a smile. "We're a prick in an ever-expanding ocean. We have no idea where we are. For all we know, we could be parsecs from a space lane. Without navigations"—he inhaled deeply—"the odds of survival are abominable."

"Once we stabilize things down here, I'll get communications up."

"And if we're out of range?"

"I will keep broadcasting until someone comes into range."

He flexed his muscles as he swiveled toward the next console. He cursed under his breath. "We should've dumped that kid. You know that, don't you?"

"I couldn't."

"I get it. He reminded you of yourself as a kid: alone, abandoned. Or maybe he messed with your head. Just like he was born to. Can't fight nature, you know? I just wish I'd seen how deep his tenterhooks had sunken in."

She faltered. Had he? She ached remembering the all-too-real chill of the snow, the blo—Where did her will end and his begin? Had he found a mind similar enough to be compatible and latched onto it as Rein suggested? A mind he could mold and galvanize into protecting him, into keeping him alive? How deeply had he affected her decisions? She ran fingers through her hair. How had he changed her? A tingling sensation traveled down her back, her gut knotting.

An image of her father flickered in her mind's eye, his outstretched hand beckoning her to him. The room behind him was a pale yellow, with white trim and curtains—the nursery. She'd been terrified, a child bereft of any familiarity, yet there he'd stood, offering something universal to grab hold of, stability. She smiled. It didn't matter. In the end, her actions would not have changed. After all, she was her father's daughter.

"Think what you will." Katya slammed shut the cover to the habitation controls console, satisfied she had prevented future meltdowns for the time being. "He's not the problem."

Rein shook his head. "Unbelievable. You still can't—"

"If you need to blame someone, blame me. I'm the one who took us onto the *Aletheia*."

"And that's when your headaches started. You had one as we were boarding that ship." Rein sucked in his breath. "It began then—"

"No." Katya straightened to full height. "I stand by the choices *I've* made. My ignoring the warning beacons was what led us to this point, and that's why I promise you: I will dig us from this mess."

Rein cleared the space between them, invading her personal space, face mere inches as he examined every inch of hers. Every speck of orange in his hazel eyes stood out to her. His spit assaulted her face when he spoke. "And you don't even know how you're going to do that."

She swallowed hard. "The how is irrelevant. I don't give up." Katya rolled onto her toes, getting equally in his face. "We're patching this heap, and once we reach civilization, you're welcome to go your own way. It'd likely be for the best, because you've never liked me calling the shots, not since we've been space-bound."

Rein swung back to the console and retreated into his efforts. Despite her unease, Katya resumed working on the habitation systems. Every rattling sound caused her to tense as if expecting the true fallout to begin. He certainly banged around enough, dropping tools.

She closed her console and checked the generator. Finding nothing amiss, she faced the impulse engine, which tied in to the thrusters. If they could get a little control over their momentum, they'd increase their odds of survival; however, without the navigation system, it was a marginal improvement. She activated the engine's safety lockout, designed to prevent unfortunate electrocutions, before cutting into the frayed and burned wires, removing them. She rooted through the large toolbox for new wiring. With it in hand, she lay on the floor to get a better vantage point of the engine's inner workings.

Hours ticked by. At one point, Rein left the engine room, muttering something about checking the ship's other electrical components. The lights remained on throughout that time, a good sign that at least one problem had been solved.

Sweat trickled down her brow. Her short bangs plastered themselves to her face, and her muscles ached as she manipulated her body into awkward positions to reach some of the engine's other components. She lost herself in her efforts.

Rein cleared his throat behind her, or above her, she guessed, since she had slid into the small cranny between the engine and riveted floor. She almost hit her head against a metal bar tethering the engine to the wall.

"How's it going?" His tone had calmed, the heat from earlier having eroded.

So he was willing to work with her at least.

"The underside sustained minimal damage if even that." Katya wiped some of the grime from her face. "We'll be able to test it here momentarily." She shut one of the bottom panels, its wires proving to still be in good shape. "Let's give her a whirl. That's if the electrical systems can take it."

"I covered the majority of the ship, so we should be fine now."

"Define fine."

"There's a 98 percent chance we aren't pushed back to square one. I recommend having the extinguishers ready in case there's an electrical fire."

"Are the alarms up?" When she received a nod, she clapped her hands against her pant legs, clearing the sweat and grease from them. "Then, shall we?"

"No time like the present."

Katya launched the warming cycle from the engine's console after lifting the emergency lockout. Once the readings went green, she brought the engine fully on. It repeatedly clacked, a sound an engine this young shouldn't be making, but it revved to life. No alarms sounded — always a good sign. They stood for several minutes, listening.

Katya wiped more of the muck off, this time on her shirt. "Begin transferring systems off the generator and back onto the main system. I'm going to see about getting our pace slowed, and then I'll address our communications; maybe a ship will be in range and can give us a tow to someplace nearby."

"What's the plan if they're hostile?"

"If"—she put great emphasis on the word—"that happens, we'll deal with it." It was a situation she dreaded. The virus had fried both the navigation and weapons systems. Their best bet was to trick the hostiles into boarding, incapacitating them somehow and taking their ship. No easy task, particularly if outnumbered and likely outgunned.

He snorted, derision in the action. "On the fly, huh?"

"What do you want from me, Rein?" It rushed out of her mouth before she could stop it. "The scenarios are innumerable."

He twisted up his mouth. "Something. Anything!"

Katya glanced at the door, her hands balling into fists, the temptation to deck him strong—if anything, to end the conversation.

"Let's say we get picked up by some kind saps," Rein plowed on. "We can't keep doing that trick with the registry, not anymore."

"I wouldn't even try that now." She forced her fingers to flex. "We'll have to scrap her . . . if we can get to a planet without a relay. A relay and we're sunk. But better than starving or dying of dehydration."

When he bowed his head, Katya padded her way over to the door. As it opened, he cleared his throat.

"I've just always wanted what's best. You know that, right?" When met with silence, he faced her. "You're an idealist and need someone to ground you."

She revealed teeth as she released a full-throated laugh. "I'm not some animal that needs tamed."

His eyes lingered on her frame. "I never said that."

Katya's nostrils flared. "But you implied it."

"I've just wanted what's best for you." He raised his hands in contrition. "That's it."

But it wasn't. Her skin crawled as she passed through

the door. He'd wanted more. Behind her, he mumbled something under his breath, but she was already racing to the cockpit.

Mina and a now-quiet Sotiris, who had fallen back asleep, resided there. The prickling sensation in her head never followed. Some good luck at least. She didn't have time to sleep.

"Did the food help?" Katya asked while slowing them into a controlled speed with the thrusters. She did not bother putting the ship to impulse; without the navigation system, that would be a foolhardy endeavor. Let them creep for now and count their blessings that they hadn't hit anything.

"Not really." Mina shrugged. "Hard to say what's up with him, but he did go back to sleep."

Katya approached Mina's station. "Keep an eye on the viewscreen and be prepared to step in. I'm going to get communications up. Maybe get us a knight in shining armor."

Mina rolled her eyes at the last part before her features grew grim. "Isn't that a little risky?"

"More than a little." Katya popped off the panel hiding the communications console's wiring and then activated its safety controls. "We'll have to cross our fingers, won't we?" Katya slid the cockpit's toolbox over. "We're at the end of our leash, Mina. There's no other choice. If luck's on our side, our jump put us deep enough into the Fringe, where the Magistrate doesn't have a strong presence, that we might be fine. We ditch the *Minerva* and Rein sooner rather than later."

"Did something happen?"

"It's been brewing." She'd failed to fully understand, to appreciate the power of emotions, how they could evolve, mature, or fester. It'd been a point of contention between her and certain family members: She could be so removed, incapable of recognizing certain signals. "It'll be for the best."

As she eased herself into a sitting position on the floor, Katya groaned and massaged the area in her back where the muscles had tightened with the simple motion. The muscles quivered beneath her skin and required rest, more than the one-handed massage she currently did to quiet it. Despite it, she messed with the Gordian knot of wires in front of her, trimming the bad and replacing them.

Minutes, perhaps an hour, had passed when Mina yelped and jumped to her feet. The action caused Katya to clip her head against the console.

"There's a ship—it's on the viewscreen!"

"Damn it." Katya wiped her hands on her shirt. Sure enough, a rusty old freighter hovered beyond their viewscreen. Its markings were all but illegible; however, its design meant the freighter was Magistrate registered. "Mina, start blinking out a request for a tow. Say that our communications are down but should be up momentarily."

Katya dove back to the panel—this time to tinker with the actual communications chip. As she worked, Mina beat out their message three times.

"They're asking if we need help with repairs. Also, if there are pirates nearby."

She took a pen welder to the chip to repair one of the shorts. "Advise them against boarding and tell them there are no pirates."

On her feet again, Katya attempted to turn on the communications console while Mina sent the new message. Nothing. Biting her lip, she lashed out, kicking it. The screen blinked and wavered. Another kick and it shot to life. "Here we go." It loaded, and she opened a frequency. "My name is Katya; I am the captain of the *Minerva*."

Mina's face elongated. "That's your real name." The statement was pinched and barely a whisper—likely unnoticed by their potential saviors.

Still, she cut the microphone on their end. "There's no point in hiding; the Magistrate knows everything. In our situation, honesty might pay off."

"*Kaptain,*" a deep baritone voice, bearing a heavy accent, responded over the speakers. "Your"—he lingered on the r—"vessel took quite the pounding."

"We ran into a series of unfortunate events," Katya said. "We'd appreciate a tow to somewhere without a Magistrate relay . . . at your discretion since our navigation system is fried."

"Ah," the man said. "I see your predicament. You are in good fortune. We're headed to Barsaa. You shouldn't have problems there." There was a pause. "You're sure you don't need help over there?"

"To be frank, Captain?"

The man cackled. "How rude of me! I am Zakhar, kaptain of *Varyag.* I must say it is rare to find a fellow Mramorian out this way. If your name is indicator."

"I can't pay you. We—"

"No, no, this will be on me." Zakhar cut off Katya's further attempts of offering money. "Is your ship able to be towed at faster speeds?"

Katya slid by Mina and pored over the data being transferred to the pilot's console. "We'll hold together."

"Good," Zakhar's voice boomed over the speaker. "We will establish tow in few minutes. Communicate any difficulties once underway. Until Barsaa, I'll look forward to meeting you face-to-face, and maybe we can share a drink, no?"

"I look forward to it myself, Captain." Katya ended the connection and opened the long-dormant intercoms. "Rein, we've got a ride to Barsaa and will be underway shortly. Alert me if we run into any problems down there."

"Our ride, how do they strike you?"

"Like they don't mind flying under the radar themselves," Katya said. "But appearances are often deceiving. We should be prepared for Magistrate forces to be waiting for us." Leaning back into her chair, Katya swallowed. "I plan to go quietly if that's the case."

"A wise plan." Then the system went dead, Rein closing it. The word "finally" hung in the silence of the line.

Drumming her fingers against the console, Katya waited for the tow to begin. A wave of fatigue struck her, begging her to sleep. *Not a good time, little one.* She wondered if he would be able to decipher the thought. A beam emitted from the freighter, turning the portion of the viewscreen tuned to the outside a pinkish color. Then, Katya and Mina lurched forward when the *Minerva* jerked, falling in place behind the other freighter if they were that at all.

"Onward to that drink, my friends," Zakhar's voice rang from the communications console. "We'll arrive in two days' time."

"Thank you, Captain . . ." Katya hissed upon ending the transmission; her head pounded with renewed fervor. "Mina, keep an eye on things." She closed her eyes to shut out the pain, which now caused her muscles around her lids to spasm. "Check on me if I'm not up in eight hours."

Mina pinched her bottom lip between her teeth before releasing it. "Is that wise?"

Is anything she did ever wise? Katya snorted, her lips forming a small smirk. "It might not be, but I'm not an automaton. I can't exist without sleep. Keep an eye on things here. Don't be afraid to wake me . . . and keep Rein away."

Katya picked up Sotiris and headed to her quarters, never more grateful for the sensation of movement coursing through the metal floor, a controlled one at that.

CHAPTER FOURTEEN

The *Minerva* held together for the two-day journey, requiring only minor patchwork. Katya monitored the system from her seat in the cockpit, her head much clearer than the day they'd begun the tow. Though Sotiris had grown needy, and her sleep ceased to have any semblance of restfulness. At least he hadn't dragged her under again, letting her come and go from slumber. But the fear remained that one day he wouldn't. She jerked when Mina appeared over her shoulder.

"Is that Barsaa?" Mina's eyes fixated on the blue and green marble before them. In her free time, she'd dyed her hair black, though the fringe and undercoat were different shades of purple. Cosmic, Mina had said.

She, meanwhile, was ready to leave all things cosmic behind. The planet below, after all the dustballs and stations they'd been on in the past months, looked delightful.

"Get seated," Katya said. "We'll be on our own soon." Then over the com, she alerted Rein. "We're coming in. Let me know if any of the systems act up."

Their speed slowed as traffic—a random assortment of vessels, mostly beaters—swelled around the planet. Katya was unfamiliar with Barsaa beyond the fact that it was an outlying planet that was temperate with frigid north and south poles. The planet, despite its favorable conditions, had a small population. Or at least the cities didn't look large from space.

"We are about to release you," Zakhar said over the crackling speakers. "Follow us down. We'll be landing in the city of Zilar; it's located in main province. A warning: It can be a rough place, but I think you prefer rougher communities where people don't talk too much, no? Besides, there are no check-ins anywhere on Barsaa. Come and land as you please, and no one harasses you."

"Zilar will be fine." Katya prepped the helm. "I'm ready whenever."

Within seconds, the pinkish tone that encompassed the viewscreen vanished, and the *Minerva* dipped before Katya brought it level with Zakhar's freighter. As they entered the atmosphere, Katya clashed with the helm, its delayed reactions, and other misfiring systems. Grimacing, she compensated for the gravitational thrusters that were offline. Of all the things to fail . . . at least the shields held. She bit the lining of her mouth.

"Are we going to die?"

Katya growled in response and transferred more juice to the working thrusters. The ride got smoother by a slim margin. "Everything's under control."

She maneuvered their crippled ship downward, and the city's marble buildings became closer with each passing second. It was well manicured, and Katya couldn't comprehend why Zakhar called it rough.

She sent more power to the thrusters, curbing their descent as they neared the spaceport, which amounted to a cleared space several meters to the south of the city. No walls separated them, just green space. In fact, there were no structures near the port. A sinking feeling emerged in the pit of her stomach. They wouldn't find a ship here. Rough. His actual meaning made more sense now. Hovering over the port and the now-parked freighter, Katya eased her vessel down and cut the engine before turning off the other systems.

"Get ready to disembark." She patted Mina's shoulder and left to retrieve Sotiris. This time as she left her quarters with him, she made sure the blanket was secure over his face. The boy did not fuss, sleeping on. By the ladder, Mina waited for her.

"Let's get this over with," Katya said. "We owe a man a drink."

Rein entered the cargo hold at the same time they did. "I didn't see any Magistrate forces on our way down," Katya told him. "The world looks too peaceful for the Magistrate to have a large presence here."

"Looks can be deceiving."

She agreed even as she opened the ramp. At first, it didn't budge, but after repeated hits on the button, it jeeringly obeyed. Katya counted it a miracle that the ship had even been able to still gradually shift the interior's gravity to a close enough match of their destination's.

"Do you have to bring the boy?" Rein asked before they disembarked.

"With the extent of the damage, I'm not leaving him behind." She headed down the ramp.

Placing her free hand against her forehead, she blocked out Barsaa's bright sun. It'd been too long since she'd been under a real sun. Not since Ereago, come to think of it. She paused on the ramp to bask in the rays' warmth. Mina had the same idea.

"Is this a spa planet?" she asked.

"Probably parts of it."

In front of them, a tram came to idle. A humanoid stepped from it while his driver remained seated. He approached them but changed his direction when a man from the *Varyag* — recognizable by his voice as Zakhar — called him over. As Zakhar greeted the man, his rotund belly bobbed, seeming as excited as its owner. He clapped the Barsaa representative's back and spoke with his deep baritone voice. Then he waved over Katya.

"Ah, so this is the intrepid crew of the *Minerva*." Zakhar smiled, a peal of deep laughter bubbling in his chest. "It is good to meet you, my dear, face-to-face." His eyes roamed over Katya. "You are much younger than I had hoped. Much too young . . . too removed from home, huh?"

Her cheeks burned. "I don't remember the homeworld."

Zahkar bowed his head. "It is a story I hear too often. There are too many lost children across this universe." His tone changed as he switched the conversation. "My friend here" — he rested his arm around the representative's shoulders — "will see us to the city. Unfortunately, I will have to get rain check on that drink. He has reminded me of previous engagement — old age, it sneaks up on us all — but I'm certain we will meet again, and then we will get that drink. I will hold you to it. Mark my words! Now come, I will escort you to city with a few of my crew."

They filled all the cars attached to the tram, with Katya and her crew sticking together. Rein remained rigid throughout the ride, though Katya wasn't much better. She hadn't been looking forward to drinking with Zakhar, but his sudden remembered business disconcerted her. Zakhar exhibited no signs of stress or alternative motives; rather, he talked quite boisterously to his men and the Barsaa representative as they sped along. Occasionally, he would say something congenial to Katya and her crew — often little tidbits of Mramor, largely its food or to encourage Katya to visit. He'd been adamant about it.

And as they passed under arch after arch, Mina, who sat next to her, forgot any misgivings she held, leaning up against the tram's ledge, absorbed by her surroundings. Even Katya found herself pulled into the architecture of the white buildings, their green roofs, and the manicured trees and shrubbery. More and more "rough" reflected on the state of technology. Scenery-wise, in the "rough" category, Barsaa had nothing on Reznic.

The tram stopped in a heavily populated area of the city. "This is your stop, my dear," Zakhar said as they shuffled from the vehicle. "You should be able to find deals to help repair your vessel, if possible, or whatever you intend to do with it. Until next time . . . when we get that drink."

"Next time then," Katya said. "Thank you for your kindness toward strangers."

"Ah, some of the best people I've ever met have been strangers." A smile spread across Zakhar's face. "They have tendency to teach you more than you could ever imagine." He winked at her before tapping the driver's shoulder, and then he waved farewell as the tram hastened on.

"I don't trust him," Rein said.

"I don't know what to think of him." Katya watched the tram disappear in the distance. *"You should come home, da?"* Turning away, she circled to gather her bearings. "Either way, it's more reason to continue with our plan. Though"—she reflected on the small shops and the dated tech they'd passed while on the tram—"I don't think success will be in our future. Barsaa doesn't strike me as a planet that was on the leading edge of the space race."

"It does appear that the tech was imported." Rein placed his hands on his hips.

They shuffled along the street together, reading signs as they went. The natives were much smaller than most humanoids, their complexions an olive-green hue and their eyes completely black; if they had irises, they were indistinguishable from their pupils. Occasionally, one of the children would point at them, usually getting their hand batted down by an adult. The adults, on the other hand, ignored the off-worlders.

"Katya, there's a scrap metal dealer." Rein headed toward an isolated shop with a tall fence surrounding what appeared to be a salvage yard. Even it was nicely polished compared to similar establishments Katya had seen in her lifetime. They usually didn't bother with landscaping and fine architectural flourishes, let alone matching the architecture of nearby structures.

Katya followed him into the store. All things metal, from random parts to patches, lined the store, but given its small size, Katya doubted salvaging a ship would be in the proprietors' repertoire.

A couple of Barsaa natives greeted them, a man and a woman. Both wore oil-stained aprons and long, thick gloves.

"Can we help you?" the man asked.

"We're looking to sell our ship for scrap," Katya said, stepping past Rein. "It's a D-Class Garni freighter."

"Ah." The woman strode to a desk and browsed on a large, outdated console. "Gregey, this is the ship."

The man whistled. "We've never taken in a ship this big. And it's a relatively new model." He quirked one of his eyebrows.

"We ran into problems with pirates." Katya maintained an unaffected face, despite a sudden absurd thought: How many pirate attacks were just that and not a pilot's go-to excuse for the state of their ship? "Unfortunately, the damage is quite extensive. The repairs would cost more than getting a new ship."

"You won't find anything like this." The man, Gregey, tapped on the screen. "Not on Barsaa. Supply is small on our world. What's available isn't cheap, and it isn't located here in Zilar. You'd have to take the train to Zeetmor, our province's capital." The man stroked his smooth chin. "Still want to proceed with this transaction or move on to a more advanced planet?"

"Let's proceed." Without a navigation system or FTL drive, they weren't going anywhere. "Let's talk a price, but first, payment type. We need hard currency; no wired transfers."

The man and the woman exchanged glances before the man spoke. "Given the type of ship and the estimated worth, to get that large of an amount in hard currency will be impossible. Are you sure a partial wired transaction wouldn't be a possibility?"

If she held any confidence that her accounts hadn't been compromised or frozen, maybe. As far as a new account, she doubted she'd pass the application process. Outwardly, she shook her head. "I'm afraid our accounts were compromised during the pirate's attack. They realized we were without cargo and instead uploaded a virus into our computer systems; they managed to get away with some important information."

"So the computer chips will not be feasible for resale," the woman said. "Of course, we would need to examine the ship before agreeing to a price, but this information will lower what we're willing to pay."

"Understandably." Katya grinned, despite Sotiris adjusting his head against her shoulder. "Let us take you to it. We can decide on a price after you've inspected the ship, plus work out a payment plan if necessary."

"Lilian?" Gregey turned to the woman.

"I'll stay here."

Together with the proprietor, they caught a tram back to the *Minerva*, where Gregey examined every inch of it. Katya followed him through the process, rocking Sotiris. The boy stirred more, far too warm—he'd be acting out more before long. She adjusted the carrier when his little hand goosed her in an attempt to get the blankets off.

"Shh." Katya stroked his back before addressing Gregey. "What do you think?"

"It's definitely scrap at this point, but it's still better quality material than we normally get. There's no way I'll be able to pay the full amount in hard currency, not even with a digital transfer." Gregey stepped away from the panel he'd been surveying. "Our bank wouldn't have that kind of currency available. It'd also raise questions, requiring a stay while they made a decision."

Sotiris, now full-out rebelling against the blanket, kicked his feet into her hips while his hands flayed.

"Ah, the child looks ready to stretch his legs."

If he could stand. She dodged his statement. "Perhaps we can work out a deal. You give me all the currency you safely can, and we then set up an IOU contract. It can be a temporary investment on my part in your business because I won't be back for some time."

"I can give you a little over half up front," Gregey said, "and I'll give you a certain percentage of interest for your investment."

Sotiris sobbed, high in pitch and volume. She caught the blanket as it fell. Gregey didn't flinch or shirk as the toddler's face came into view. No, he remained amicable.

"A very lovely boy," he said, even coming closer to admire Sotiris, who turned away from the odd man and hid his face in Katya's shoulder. However, he still tried to kick away the rest of the blanket. "Is he all right? Does he have a fever?"

"No, just warm. He gets warm very easily."

"Ah, each kind to its own." He walked to the door. "Shall we make our way back to the shop?"

"We'll meet you there," Katya said. "We're going to collect what we need so we can catch one of those trains."

"We'll want to hurry then," Gregey said, heading toward the ramp. "It's already almost four, and the trains stop at seven when they take workers back and forth between the cities."

"They don't operate for long, do they?" Katya commented as she followed him.

"Why waste energy?" Gregey shrugged. "We don't need them to be running after dark, disturbing everyone's rest. Do you think it'll take you long to gather everything?"

"We travel light." Katya ignored Rein's pointed, flushed expression when he spotted Sotiris out in the open, uncovered. "We'll be at the shop in a half hour. Any personal effects we leave onboard, you are more than welcome to sell."

Gregey hopped on a tram, leaving Katya and her crew to stuff as much as they could into what bags they could carry on their own. There hadn't been much extra, besides articles of clothing, to argue about. Katya chuckled at the cropping of remorse that sprang forth when she left the salt lamp behind, especially since it'd been a pointless purchase to get information. But she had found herself drawing pleasure from it, as had Sotiris — when he was awake, that is. He would stare at it for prolonged periods in the days she'd had it, drawn to it even. Despite their fondness for it, she couldn't justify the oddly shaped and bulky object. Surely someone on Barsaa would cherish it like they had.

Having picked over their possessions, they met outside, burdened with duffle bags and backpacks, and caught a tram. The *Varyag* remained parked beside their old ship. It left her to wonder how Zakhar's business had gone. No activity occurred in or around the ship, suggesting he had yet to return. Perhaps she should have left a note, thanking him further, but now it was too late. They had to hurry. Constant movement offered their best chance of survival.

"Is it wise to have him uncovered?" Rein whispered into her ear.

"It fell, and he was screaming. That was going to draw attention, some of which might have gone beyond judgmental glares. We don't need local authorities involved. That man didn't recognize Sotiris for what he is. He may be a kid, but everyone who knows what an Oneiroi looks like reacts." Katya lifted her shoulder, causing Sotiris, who had been eyeing the scenery as they went, to glare at her. Chuckling, she pecked him on the forehead. "I don't think the Oneiroi have been on this planet."

"Still."

Indeed, spacers on the world could have had run-ins with Sotiris's people, but . . . "The planet's too warm for him, and the blanket's only going to make it worse. He'll fuss and draw attention to us."

Rein snorted and shifted his face toward the scenery. "I liked him better when he wasn't so vocal, and I didn't even like him then."

Katya didn't bother responding. It gained nothing to stoke the pot. They arrived at the salvage shop, and Katya filled out the paperwork and collected the hard currency, adding it to the sum she'd held onto from past jobs. As they had filled out the paperwork, the couple had not once asked for a ship registry; either they had suspected the *Minerva*'s legality or had never dealt in that many ships-for-scrap deals. With the paperwork and deal wrapped up, they raced to the train station, where they caught the last train to the capital.

By the time they arrived, the sun had long since vanished, and much of the city, except for the night district as a local had called it, had given in to slumber. The district paled in comparison to those on Reznic and the other worlds she'd been stationed on. Tame. Extremely tame with its legit late-night restaurants and bars, liquor stores, organized brothels, a few recreational hookah dens, and the spaceport, to which those still walking the street courteously directed them. Katya, at one point, pulled the blanket out of her bag and draped it over Sotiris, who, in the depth of slumber, failed to notice its dreaded return.

They trekked several blocks before their destination came into view: a small port that was more of a transit hub than a real spaceport. In it, they discovered exactly two merchants selling ships, all of which outstripped their budget.

Mina slumped against one of the port's walls and tugged off her shoes one at a time to massage her feet. "What's the new plan?"

"Take a transport somewhere that has more junk ships," Rein answered.

Katya grunted her assent from where she already stood in front of the lists of flights. Her finger stopped on one. "There's one headed to Jordah. It's a metro planet; it'll definitely have ships within our price range. Hmm. There's a layover at Station R-20." A layover presented a danger, but it meant a cheaper flight, and they needed to save what money they could.

Rein read through the other options for several seconds before he muttered a noncommittal utterance. Katya took it as an agreement and procured the tickets. They then lounged in a waiting area with Mina taking the time to nap; Katya would have, too, if she trusted Rein. Three hours passed before they boarded the medium-sized passenger vessel. Katya breathed a sigh of relief; with the small number of fellow passengers, they should be able to corral themselves away and receive privacy.

The passenger freighter's interior had open spaces with limited seating, a true Fringe transport. Katya ran the fingers of her free hand between her sweat-lined neck and her shirt's collar. As she walked around the clumps of fellow passengers that formed along the floor, her stomach churned, submerged in a sense of déjà vu.

Past the masses, Katya piled her bags in an isolated corner like pillows and sank into them, laying Sotiris to her side, where her body would obscure him. The vibration that, on another ship, would set her at ease made getting comfortable a challenge, even as Mina began to lightly talk in her sleep. Even Rein snored, comfortably settled on his bag a foot or so away.

She hated transports.

"Take him, please." Katya handed Sotiris to Mina. Her head pounded to the point she staggered as she walked, her body trying to take her into the corridor wall beside her. They'd arrived on R-20 at a late hour, according to the station's local time.

The corridors they passed through lay almost deserted except for a smattering of other travelers, many of whom had taken to the benches to catch some sleep. Their group proceeded alone, with Rein having stopped to use the men's restroom. Katya took in the sleeping travelers, tempted to join them. What sleep she'd been able to get on the transport would have to do, no matter how little. She couldn't recall her dreams, but they'd been unsettling.

When Katya spotted a cleared bench surrounded by beds of plants, she motioned for Mina to follow her. "Set up shop here for now and wait for Rein."

"Where are you going?"

"There's a bar up ahead, and I need something to dull my headache. I'll be back in a half hour. If I'm not, send Rein to get me." Katya reached over and patted Mina on the head, earning a glare. "Do you think you can handle him?"

"We'll be fine." Mina readjusted Sotiris so his head rested on her shoulder.

Satisfied, Katya strode to the bar. She didn't bother with its name or any of its blaring neon signs, which were written in an alien tongue. As long as they were well stocked, she didn't care. Her muddled vision welcomed the bar's ill-lit interior, a fitting touch for such an establishment.

Music played over a speaker system, more quietly than similar joints Katya had visited. She maneuvered around tables that filled its narrow space, opting for a raised one in a corner not far from the door. Situating herself into the chair, she covered her face with her hands as if she could will her pain away. A Tandelalay moon. That is what she wanted. On Reznic, the midnight blue drink had dulled many a headache and taken the edge off plenty of her days. Valens had laughed at the overly fruity drink, not that he had much room with his guilty pleasure: the sickeningly sweet, syrupy mess known as a Dergo sunset. They all carried their guilty pleasures, and the Tandelalay moon was one of the few that could make her an alcoholic.

Rubbing her face, Katya waited for the barkeep to come and take her order. Somewhere, a broadcast played, a local one with talks about the neighboring gas giant's conditions. Shortly after the report finished, it cycled to regional news with a segment covering overall Magistrate news. Esh . . . bombs, casualties, Plasovern—

Two drinks were slammed down onto the table, the one directly in front of her sloshing its amber liquid onto the table.

"Mind if I join you?" The woman in her forties drawled, her accent entrancing. She cocked a smile while resting her hand on her hip, which jaunted out, putting all her curves on display. Before Katya responded, the woman slid into the seat across from her and drank heavily from her own mug. "Don't worry; I didn't drug yours if that's what you're thinking. Coming from one woman to another, you looked like you needed one, love." Her breasts rested on the table when she leaned forward.

"I'm not interested in making a connection." Katya left the drink in front of her untouched.

"Oh my, all business, huh?" The woman lifted her drink, an ale of sorts; her other arm draped over her chair's back. "Let me guess—I love this game, by the way—you're a freighter captain. On the outs of it, I'd say, given you're without a ship. So, you've had troubles between jumping from one dustball to the next. Am I close?"

Katya narrowed her eyes at the wink the woman gave her. "Lovely," she muttered before swallowing some of her drink, a mixed concoction new to her. It hit her strong, burning her throat and warming her chest.

"It's your turn now, dearie." When Katya only took another sip, the woman laughed, throaty and melodic all at once. "You're just no fun, but I can't blame you given your situation. Let's try this again."

A tightening sensation formed in Katya's chest, either from the alcohol or the unwanted presence across from her. She'd place money on the latter. She almost asked the woman to leave but stopped when the other's stein hit the table with a solid thud.

"Yes, let's get honest. You're Magistrate, an officer. Or you were until you deserted." Her smile, resembling a predator, returned when Katya stiffened. "Now, that gets your attention. You're not hopping planets. You're running."

While her hand strayed to her firearm, Katya forced herself to center her breathing and present an air of neutrality. "Who are you?"

Around them, the bar's few patrons nursed their drinks, talked, or crowded around the bar's holoscreens, which displayed different sports and, in one case, news. A couple held flexiscreens, or scrolls, in front of themselves as they drank.

The woman gulped her ale. As she wiped the froth from her upper lip, she chuckled. "The resemblance in personality really is remarkable. Both of you *so*"—she put emphasis on the word—"serious. Though, she had a sense of fun to her. I actually met her in a place not too unlike this joint. Welcomed the atmosphere, she'd said. She was willing to play, but I think she was largely amused that a mouse dared to play with a cat. Only, in this situation, I'm afraid you're the mouse."

Katya gripped the butt of her pistol, tugging it slightly out of the holster. "Heh. Even mice can be deadly."

"I don't doubt it, but I'm not the cat you have to fear. The Magistrate, however . . ." The blonde shrugged.

She didn't release her grip. "Who are you?"

"Me?" The smile grew. "Some call me Storm, but really that's just a bastardization of my name. To be more specific, I'm Hedda Strom."

Katya cursed, her weapon all but forgotten as she rocked onto her feet. Her sudden reaction didn't even cause the other patrons to bat an eye. Ten total, plus the bartender. Did they all want to mind their own business, or were they in on it? Then there was Strom herself. She had to have come from somewhere, and she certainly hadn't entered the establishment behind Katya. A door in the back of the bar area was her only possible entry point.

"Please have a seat," Strom said. "I have information that you'll doubtlessly find . . . enlightening."

She hesitated to follow the suggestion. Sitting would make things worse, suggesting an affiliation with Plasovern, something already being propagated in the Magistrate. Her thoughts drifted to the newsfeeds about the organization. A sour taste filled her mouth, and she couldn't shake the thought that if she were still wearing Magistrate blue, she'd be dead. Yet if the patrons were actually there on Strom's behalf . . . She eased back into her seat.

"Information?" she said, to hint that her curiosity had been tickled. Not that she suspected more Plasovern agents in the room.

"With your similarities, I'm not surprised he latched onto you like a *vermond* piglet. Your mind's similar enough to his mother's to make him feel safe."

Katya's face burned. "What do you—"

"Know?" Strom finished and gestured to Katya's still quite full drink. "More than you."

Katya took a swig of her cocktail, welcoming the temporary erosion of her headache. Once the liquid went down, she cleared her throat. "You appear to have me at a great disadvantage. What's this information you're dangling about?" This time she sipped from her drink in a more measured fashion. She needed a clear head.

"It starts and ends with the *Aletheia*." Strom pushed aside her empty drink and gestured to the barkeep for another round. "We were rendezvousing with them that day; only, as you know, it never happened. The Breks interfered, eliminating the Oneiroi and taking a few prizes. When they caught our presence, we had to run."

"Why would they rendezvous with you?"

Strom brushed a strand of hair from her face. "We were going to escort them into Medzeci space."

Katya opened her mouth; however, she couldn't form words. Escort them? Why would they willingly enter the Medzeci Empire? The barkeep interrupted further thought when he brought over two new drinks. With a few words, the man sauntered back to the bar, leaving the two of them alone again. Strom lifted her ale, relishing its amber liquid as if she hadn't just dropped what amounted to a bomb. Strom waited for her to bite, to be reeled in. Katya ground her teeth together; she hated being played.

"What would entice an entire Magistrate warship to do that?"

"Truth."

She should have known the tango wouldn't end so easily, and with that, she downed more of her drink. It smothered the growing pain, similar to a nine-inch nail being driven into her skull. Katya thwacked her glass onto the table. Straightening, she lurched to the side, tempted to leave rather than further the conversation.

"The truth is," Strom said, fixing Katya in place, "the Magistrate has the defect down to a science."

Strom reached into a satchel that hung off her hip and removed a slate, which she activated. After several seconds of moving her finger across its screen, she arrived at whatever she sought and nudged the device across the tabletop. Katya frowned at it and, after a long moment, pulled it over the rest of the way. The screen presented sequences in two different charts. She glanced at Strom and then back at the screen.

"What am I looking at?"

"These took some effort to procure. To this day, I'm still amazed at our good fortune. I showed them to Kallistrate, Sotiris's mother." Strom pointed to the first graph. "No defect. And at a following Magistrate checkup, her son has the defect. They altered him during Kallistrate's prenatal appointments."

Katya blinked, imagining the sorrow at a future robbed; it'd be followed by a cold rage . . . enough of one to change allegiance. "What did you have to gain from sharing this information with her?"

"I have no love for the Magistrate, an understatement I assure you. But I do pity the Oneiroi, being leashed, altered further to an unknown conclusion." She sipped her ale. "Besides"—she set aside the mug—"we had something to gain: the Oneiroi off the front lines. It was important enough to take all manner of risks."

Silence lingered between them, Katya trying to digest all the information. Strom—she had no idea what the woman was thinking. Finishing her drink, Katya found herself thinking of her father's bottle of Vergian whiskey and how it would hit the spot right now. Despite that, she didn't touch the second drink in front of her.

"What were they hoping to find in Medzeci space?"

"I offered Kallistrate a chance to give her son normalcy, in addition to her people's other affected children."

"A cure—"

"No, normalcy. Sotiris can't be cured; his genes have been altered, and that just can't be reversed." Strom reclaimed her slate, powering it off and placing it into her satchel. "Kallistrate, her husband, and the rest were willing to try another avenue, and from there, determine what their masters had done to the rest, even if they had to tear the Magistrate apart to do that. First, however, they needed something viable to present to their council, an alternative to Magistrate fealty."

"This treatment, then, does it currently exist, or is it hypothetical?"

"We needed a patient with the defect, but even so, we are certain it is more than hypothetical." Strom leaned closer to her. "And that is why I'm extending the same offer that I gave Kallistrate to you."

"First, how did you find us? How did you know we had him?"

"Jia alerted us that Sotiris was still alive, to our relief; though, with the Magistrate's search for the *Aletheia*'s 'cargo,' we already had our suspicions, and our agents were vigilant. Then Zahkar—don't judge him too harshly— provided visual confirmation that you still had him. I joined you on the transport on Barsaa, and here we are now."

"And here we are." Without thought, Katya tapped her fingers against her leg. Normalcy . . . however, at what price? Her thoughts drifted to the *Aletheia*, the woman on the bridge. It'd been a risk she'd been willing to take for her son, but . . . "I can't forget the atrocities you and Plasovern have committed."

"And what about the Magistrate? It certainly doesn't have a lily-white record: annexing neighboring planets and subjugating those that wouldn't join the fold." Strom spat off to the side. "I have witnessed nothing as sickening as brave people being trampled and made to cower underneath the Magistrate's boots. They're an empire in all but name."

Retorts flew to Katya's tongue, but she controlled them. From Strom's posture, it'd be akin to arguing with a wall, potentially leading to a full-out verbal spar. The woman across from her was well stuck in her ways, shaped by life much like Katya had been. And there was no defending everything the Magistrate had done through its long existence, which had begun in blood. However, the collection of planets had matured, and Katya remained proud of her service. At least the Magistrate wasn't using bombs and shattering so many lives for a reckless cause.

"At one time, yes." Katya kept her tone low, neutral. "But I have no desire to debate the merits and shortcomings of the Magistrate." Katya rose to her feet. "I need to be getting back. We have a connecting ship to catch."

"You amaze me." Strom finished her drink and burped. "They've really done a number on you. Even after what you've seen, you still cling to them. I've read a file on you—a basic Magistrate file, so don't look as if I've violated your privacy—they remade you as they saw fit. They tore apart your world. Really, you are not much different from Sotiris, only your parents are probably ali—"

"Enough!" Katya swiped her hand down, hitting the table and skimming against her empty glass. It toppled off the surface and shattered on the floor. Katya struggled to stop herself from shaking. "I've had enough of this. Stay away from us because I'm not turning him over to you."

Strom caught her arm before she could pull away from the table. Her fingers pressed into her arm. "And what is your plan? He's losing muscle mass. Continuing as you are will be a death sentence for him. Kallistrate—she could have maintained a decent quality of life for him; you, you will be swallowed alive. The end you'll lead him to is the one she feared. Do—"

"I'll find a way that doesn't involve you or Plasovern." Katya broke the other woman's grip. "Thanks for the drink."

She met further resistance when Strom latched onto her again, this time by the hand. Before Katya could react, the other woman pressed a small rectangular device into the palm she held.

"Keep it," Strom said, all vehemence gone from her voice. "If you don't find that alternative way, call us . . . for Sotiris's sake."

Strom wrapped Katya's fingers around the communications device and then released her. Katya blinked. The device might as well have burned given her haste to deposit it in her pocket. Stumbling backward, she exited the bar, more than ready to be back with Mina and Sotiris, but she didn't make it far.

Red in the face, Rein dragged her to an empty side corridor, his fingers digging into her skin, bruising and scratching her. All her complaints and attempts to break free went ignored. His large hands kept her in tow. Isolated, he shoved her into a nearby wall; his hands squeezed her wrists, pinning her in place.

"What are you—"

"So we've thrown our chips in with Plasovern now?" His tone was uneven and pinched, similar to his face.

Katya strained against his grip, but it remained vice-like, and he had her at such an angle that freeing her hands was not an option. So she made one. Katya jammed her knee into his gut. The hold on her disappeared as Rein doubled over and gasped for air.

"Get a grip on yourself!" Katya freed her pistol and directed it at Rein. "She sought me out, not the other way around. And I told her I'm not interested."

Scarlet in the face, Rein struggled for breath. His body shuddered as he glared up at her, his eyes smoldering with hatred and bile.

"Yet you took it." He wiped away spit that had pooled over his lips.

"Without the intention of using it."

"Then why take it?!" The words echoed far past them.

Why hadn't she thrown the communications device back at Hedda, or let it fall to the ground? Instead, she'd secured it in her pocket, ready for use. She could easily toss it aside now to appease Rein, but she didn't open her pocket. He remained on the floor, not moving with the pistol trained on him. The same condemning expression lingered on his face.

Clearing her throat, she lowered her weapon but didn't return it to the holster. "I'm covering my bases." Her bangs hung in her eyes, but she refused to release her service pistol. "Beyond that, I really can't say; everything's been turned upside down. I-I don't know where to go anymore."

She swallowed, the lump in her throat painfully moving. "I don't trust Plasovern, and I don't trust Strom any farther than I could throw her. I've no idea if I'll keep this device or toss it in the trash. But that's my choice, not yours. You only get to make your own decisions. And you most certainly don't get to touch me in such a manner."

"If you would just listen—"

"Listen to what?! You're trapped in a past where we are Magistrate officers. Where we didn't have to worry about—about all this! We can't stay in Magistrate space, but we can't cross over either." Her mouth contorted. Her throat was so parched while she spoke for Rein, herself. "Because at least Magistrate space still has some semblance of a democracy, civility . . ." Home. They were both trapped. She blinked away moisture as she stood, shoulders shaking. A line needed to be crossed, but she was still just as confined.

Katya jerked to the side, lifting her firearm. "Stay back."

Rein was closer now—close enough his heavy breath brushed against her skin. His outreached hands remained suspended in the air despite the weapon pointed at him; however, it did hold him at bay.

"We're at an impasse, Rein. You have your wants, and they are not congruent with mine and Mina's. We need to go our separate ways before something regrettable happens." Part of her wanted to say it had already happened, had happened months ago after Rein had harmed Sotiris. But that would only serve as a flashpoint for the man.

His mouth formed a thin line, and the lump in his throat quivered. "I loved you! If you weren't still hung up on a dead man, you'd see—"

"You know nothing!" Her grip tightened on the firearm until her knuckles locked painfully. "Colonel Ulpius has nothing to do with any of this. I've never, in any manner, reciprocated any of your feelings." She licked her chapped lips. "We're two very different people, and I don't think you really see me as I am. And . . . I've never been one for those types of feelings. Ulpius was a fluke. He and I . . . we fell into step together." Her chest tightened. "After this flight, we need to go our separate ways. For both our sakes. I'll give you your share of the profits, but this is for the best."

He bowed his head. After several moments, she retreated, heading for Mina and Sotiris, internally counting down the minutes until they could board their transport to Jordah. And as she went, she cast backward glances, hand never straying far from the holstered pistol.

CHAPTER FIFTEEN

"A re you sure?" Rein asked, his tone flat and lacking any of the anger from the previous evening.

They'd been like vessels passing in the night on the transport—neither speaking, providing ample distance, lest the other fire shots. He'd brooded the whole time, his hunched back facing Mina and Katya. He'd only left that position to use the facilities. Now, his current void of emotion set her stomach on edge.

"It wouldn't be a bother for me to come and help you find your next transport or ship." He swapped his pack's strap to his other shoulder.

Katya inhaled the strong smell of industry in what amounted to an overbuilt city. The chemicals and dregs . . . she hadn't smelled a similar combination since Reznic. It was putrid but familiar, almost comforting. In the toddler carrier, Sotiris, even in his sleep, scrunched his nose as if affronted by the odor. She estimated after a half hour they wouldn't even notice it anymore.

Shaking her head, Katya pulled out a small portion from the proceeds of the *Minerva* and handed it to Rein. "It's not necessary. I think it's best we part ways here."

In front of them, Mina shifted her weight between her feet, her gaze shifting from Rein to Katya and back again. She'd known this moment was coming; however, she doubted the teen could grasp the reason for the sudden break. On board the transport, Mina had inquired about the visible shift but had accepted her insistence of "later."

Rein shifted his pack again before shrugging. The right corner of Katya's mouth dropped. There was a glint in his eyes, something she didn't trust.

"Your call." He grunted, striding off through the platform. Katya watched him leave, his back straight as a ramrod.

A chill passed through her body, similar to the time she had turned in a Freccian exam knowing she'd failed it. Language had never been her strong point—sometimes even the nonverbal.

"Come on." Together, she and Mina went in the opposite direction, mixing in with the throng of life-forms.

Not too long after leaving the platform clusters, they became lost among the masses. As they walked toward the crowded lower levels of the city, an uneasy sensation settled in her gut again. Around her, the scenery resembled a tetanus playground: cold, rusty metal everywhere. She swiveled on her feet to avoid a panhandler whose face was marked with oozing red dots. Katya had no idea what he had, but she was determined not to contract it. So determined, she almost stepped into a ball-jointed automaton that disjointedly moved forward, undeterred from its path.

"Almost like home." Mina wrinkled her nose and curled her lips as she said it. Her brown eyes, meanwhile, seemed to turn a shade darker before she tilted her head away from Katya.

"Yeah."

Facing forward, she sidestepped others in her path; the walkway had little rhyme or reason. Even the recreational lanes for hoverboards or bicycles had pedestrians on them. Despite the various distractions, her thoughts returned to Rein and the cold, calculating gleam in his eyes. He had been amiable enough during the parting, but there had been an undercurrent. He had been too calm and composed, especially after she had pulled a weapon on him. His offer to at least accompany them until they got a ship stood out to her.

"So, what's the plan?"

"We get a ship or quickly book another transport," Katya said. "Either way, we get off Jordah fast."

"Any particular reason why? Jordah's huge, and it'd be easy to get lost here, just like on Reznic."

"Rein's on-world." Katya slowed and directed Mina onto a side pedestrian street. A hover bicyclist zoomed by them. "And he doesn't know where his loyalties lie." People said a lot about women scorned, but men could be just as bad.

Mina rubbed the back of her neck, bringing her hand upward until her hair, now a shade of garnet with orange undertones, stuck out at odd angles. Katya wished she'd stuck with the more muted black and purple, but the teen had insisted, wanting to eliminate the dye from her pack. "What happened between you two?"

"He crossed a line." Katya rolled up one of her sleeves to reveal red marks, some more purplish "He saw me talking to Hedda Strom—"

"*The*"—Mina's eyes bulged—"Hedda Strom?"

"She approached me about Sotiris." Katya shrugged and concealed her arm. "She gave me some information and an offer, but that doesn't matter. Right now, we need to focus on getting a ride and new IDs." Katya frowned when she spotted a drone farther on the same road. She diverted paths onto an alternative route, Mina following. "Keep up. We're getting some headwear."

Katya and Mina found a store and purchased scarves. With the cooler temperatures and cornucopia of cultures living on Jordah, they would blend. Katya also bought two pairs of fashion sunglasses to hide aspects of their faces, at least enough that it would take drones and their operators a few extra seconds or minutes to make a positive ID. Feeling more concealed, they resumed their hunt for a method of travel.

Their feet took them to a shop on the same level that specialized in parts and smaller classes of ships. From its roster, the proprietor appeared to be a collector of rust buckets; some, from the photos and specs, were no longer spaceworthy, many belonging in museums. So their search continued until their stomachs complained.

"There's a sandwich shop over there," Mina said in a tone close to a whine. "It might be good to get off our feet, at least for a while.

Katya obliged the teen, and before long, they devoured their meals at a table isolated from the others. Katya removed Sotiris from the carrier and placed him on her lap. Smiling, she ran her finger against his cheek to see if he would wake to eat the now-cooled soup she'd gotten for him. Only after she ladled a small portion into his mouth did he sputter awake. Mina moved to block Sotiris from the view of the other patrons, though most of them—those not already immersed in their meals—watched a program running on a holoscreen.

Sotiris mumbled random sounds and reached for the spoon, showing more interest in the soup than the food they'd been forcing down his throat for months. A simple broth soup with rice and mystery meat had done the trick. Such a simple thing and he loved it. She forced down laughter as she spoon-fed Sotiris more of the concoction. Next to her, Mina elbowed her before nudging her head toward a table not far from them.

Two men sat talking, but she couldn't make out what they were saying, nor anything interesting about the two humanoids in general: just two spacers eating a meal and catching up. Katya shrugged and freed her hand from Sotiris, who'd latched on to keep the spoon in his mouth.

"They said Elites are on-world." Mina fidgeted in her seat.

"Fascinating," Katya replied as if they were simply discussing the weather. "Anything else?"

Mina fell quiet, her eyes closed while she strained to hear more of the conversation. Then she shook her head.

"Don't stress too much about it." Katya gathered some of their trash. "It's a large metro planet; it's bound to have Elites stationed on it. We'll just keep a lid on our little friend here."

"Reznic didn't have Elites."

Katya chuckled. "Trust me, Reznic had its share. They just weren't as flashy as the Oneiroi or as grotesque as the Breks." Though, some had passed through on special projects, but Mina didn't need to know that. She placed another spoonful of the soup into the toddler's mouth.

Sotiris finished the small container of soup, and Katya figured they, namely Mina, should be able to replicate it. She returned Sotiris to the carrier; he fussed and fought, rather pathetically, against his confinement. Gathering all the trash, she had Mina dispose of it before they set out again.

Several more shops peddling ships, with crafts that Katya had either questioned their functionality or were out of their budget, came and went. She suspected they would have to settle for a transport to another planet, one on the outskirts of space where they'd work and build up their funds. She didn't want to think of the years such an approach might dictate. It'd be a far cry from where she'd pictured herself all those years ago. She dreaded what it'd mean for Mina and Sotiris. They'd have to pick a cooler world, something tolerable for all of them. Still, Katya clung to the hope that it wouldn't come to that.

But even with their proceeds from the *Minerva*, they were outpriced, leading Katya to take them farther into Jordah's underbelly. And when the lift doors opened, it felt like they'd entered a new world. The sky was absent, obscured by the next level up's pedestrian ways. Graffiti sprawled across its metal walls, no doubt serving as calling cards to different gangs' turfs, and a certain level of grime hung on all their surroundings. More trash lined the fringes of the streets, which were limited to smaller crafts. The people themselves reminded her of Reznic—poor, hardened, armed, and eager for payouts. She and Mina didn't want to delve farther into the bowels of the city.

"More like home every minute," Mina muttered. "Next level would be even closer, I think."

"I'm afraid you might be right." Katya shifted a wiggling Sotiris while pointing to a malfunctioning neon sign that read "rax's hips & ars." Its burned-out letters suggested its wares were exactly what they wanted. "There's a shop this way."

By the time they arrived, the proprietor, a Borelle with long antennae, was throwing stuff under the counters. He had a plated head and an extremely angular facial structure. Differing from some of the Borelle Katya had seen, he had white dots as markings instead of the normal pale yellow, perhaps from lingering in the lower levels away from the sun. He glanced at them after they approached, his antennae shifting through the air before he resumed packing up his shop. Satisfied with the current appearance of the counter, he tossed what appeared to be weapons—very illegal ones—into a safe that had been concealed behind metal plating matching the rest of the store's interior.

Katya blinked. Obviously, they didn't frighten him. After ensuring Sotiris was concealed, she went to the counter, where he examined them again for a much longer span of time, his antennae slicing through the air. Then he grabbed another arm full of firearms and carted them to the safe.

"You appear to be in a hurry." Katya scanned the bins of odd parts and photos of ships on the walls, most in the form of floating holograms.

"Lizards," the Borelle said. "They've been tearing apart shops today. I'm just covering my bases, that's all. What are ya, meddling cops?"

"No," Katya said. One of the ships on the wall caught her eyes, a small D-Class ship that spacers had nicknamed "The Sparrow" due to its size and dull façade. It'd be worthless for moving cargo, but it would get them around and was also within their price range. "Lizards, you say?"

"Jar'rasks, Elites." The Borelle contorted his face as if he'd doused his tongue with lemon juice. "They're the Elites we got blessed with. Been here for months, a minor inconvenience. But this morning, they've decided to tear apart the city and stores. A friend on the next level up was busted for his exotic wares—"

"Illegal wares," Katya surmised.

"Honest compared to some of the stuff sold in the lower levels. Trust me." He slammed the safe's door shut, sliding the metal panel seamlessly over it. "I'm just hiding some of my exotics. Don't want to be lizard bait. The leather purses are psychotic—coldblooded, figuratively and quite literally now that I think about it. Some of the stories I've heard would curl your toes. They have a propensity to rip off limbs, ya know? No thanks, not for me."

"You might want to do a better job hiding your exotics."

"I'm actually thinking of closing shop and disappearing for a while. Can't be too safe, right?"

"Probably wise." Katya pointed to the small ship. "But before you do that, I'd like to purchase this passable vessel."

"Passable? Passable?! That vessel is spectacular, an amaz—" He retracted his current pitch after Katya headed toward the door. "It's passable! The man who sold it to me—er, gave it to me—he owed me a lot of money. It's spaceworthy and trusty but requires love. Can you give it love?" He leaned over the countertop, a smirk on his face. "Impulse speed, backup solar sails, and a newly replaced FTL drive, albeit pre-owned. The faults? It's not as fast as the newer models, though it has excellent maneuverability . . . some women really appreciate that."

"And some want to know more about the wiring," Katya said. Next to her, Mina rolled her eyes and went to check out the various racks of goods. "Is it a tinder case?"

"Wiring was redone shortly after I took over its ownership. There was no choice, or else it would have been the new owner's problem. I have all the paperwork." He opened a filing cabinet behind the counter and flipped through its contents until he removed a folder. He handed it to Katya. "Take a look."

Katya accepted the folder. "A little old school."

"When you have so many assets, you use every avenue to catalogue your ownership of them. Paper is very binding."

"And not as traceable."

The Borelle shrugged. "Some women like that too." He winked at her and shuffled a few more belongings out of sight.

Katya took the time to look at the ship's—the *Navar*'s—specs. On paper, it was decent. Not the greatest, but not the worst. They could probably get a couple of years out of it. It would be tight; they'd have to share quarters, meaning Mina would have to get used to sleeping in cooler temps. She wanted to actually see the ship, but . . .

"Do Elites come here often?" Katya flipped through the papers, not really reading them. "You said Jar'rasks had been here for months."

He tilted his head, his left antenna reaching forward. "From time to time, but normally there's warning before they arrive. The grapevine here is very active. This time nothing, then lizards." The antenna snapped back. "You're not a fan of Elites either. I thought not, and that's why you don't worry me."

Katya handed the folder back. "Where's the ship?" She ran her hand along Sotiris's back. His head rested against her shoulder, suggesting he'd fallen asleep.

"The Var'nada Docking Complex." He slipped her a map of the city and traced the route they would have to take with two fingers. "Just two blocks from here."

"Are you opposed to hard currency?"

"Are you opposed to a paper registry?" the Borelle asked, his mouth stretching to reveal pointed teeth. "I thought not. We sign it here. And if Magistrate ships give you a hard time, you tell them your ship falls under Code 23.5.20B: obsolete, chipless pleasure craft. You won't have to worry about installing a chip for three more years when that code expires, though I'd still avoid Core planets; they don't take kindly to the obsolete."

Katya handed the Borelle a wad of currency. He counted through it twice before sliding a quarter of it back to her. Katya raised an eyebrow, but he only shook his head. "I like you . . . you have spunk. Purchasing an unknown vessel without fully inspecting it beforehand. Either you're a fool or running from something. From the cortisol and epinephrine you're emitting, my money is on the latter."

"Seeing how you already have weapon trafficking on your plate, I suggest you don't dig any further."

He chuckled, the antennae bobbing with the action. "You're right. I don't want to know." He brought over an outdated registry and signed his name, Jearax, and passed it over to Katya. "Sign whatever name you so please. But try to remember it for when you decide to chip it."

Katya wrote down Kallistrate, on a whim or as an act of defiance, she wasn't even sure. The name popped into her head, still bouncing around along with the rest of Strom's words. Jearax took the paper and stamped it before sliding it back over to Katya, this time with a keycard, which was far more outdated than the *Maelstrom*'s passcode panel, and a set of codes.

"This is everything you will need. When you go off-world, you won't get too much hassle from the towers. There are lots of obsolete models in this sector, and most of the operators are on the dole of one gang or the other, or they just don't give a rat's ass if Magistrate procedures are followed. Too much effort, too time consuming."

Katya slid the paper with the codes into her satchel and slid the keycard into her pocket with the Plasovern communicator. "We'll be on our way. But trust me, if there's no ship or it's not spaceworthy, I will find you and take my money out of your hide."

"Then we have no worries." He handed her the full file, which also went into the satchel. "If you don't mind, I have more exotics to safeguard. It, however, was a pleasure doing business with you." He bowed and then disappeared into a back room.

"Mina." Katya nudged her head toward the door.

"That was risky," Mina said once the door shut behind them. "We could be trapped here."

"We won't be."

They walked one block when a drone buzzed past them. Due to its speed, Katya assumed it was on its way to a crime. She draped her arm over Mina, maintaining their pace forward, though the girl shook. After Dandis VII, Katya couldn't blame her. When they turned onto the next street, Katya stiffened. Another drone. Similar to the one before it, it also rushed to some final destination. At its speed, she doubted it'd gotten a decent read on their faces, but—

Mina shrieked and anchored herself to Katya, who found horripilation overtaking her. A tall reptilian life-form, a Jar'rask, loomed feet in front of them. Its series of massive teeth were lustrous even in the lower level's murky light. Katya's left hand drifted to her weapon, pulling Mina a step back with her other. The beast's tail whipped back and forth as it stepped forward, clawed feet scraping into metal, akin to nails on a chalkboard. Its Magistrate colors and emblems, plus a metal vocal emulator device embedded in its throat, jumped out to her.

"Stand down," the Jar'rask said in a deep, metallic voice that sounded masculine but that guaranteed nothing. "You'll be moved into our custody. There's no need to keep this charade going, Cassius."

Her eyes enlarged—heart dancing—at the mention of her last name. Katya grimaced when she caught the gleam of more eyes approaching them from a shadowy alley off to the side. More Jar'rasks. They now had them surrounded on two sides. Fast, extremely dexterous. The reptilians would overtake them in a straight-out race.

Katya yanked her AVI-13 from the holster, ready to fire—Mina beat her. The stun gun sent out a blast, hitting one of the Jar'rasks. The creature screamed, making Katya flinch, when the current passed through him. He happened to be standing too close to one of his comrades, and the current spread to him as well. The other Jar'rasks hesitated—more flabbergasted than anything. But already a growl rumbled deep in their throats.

"Run!" Katya prodded Mina back the way they'd come before pressing her free hand against Sotiris's back. "Don't stop running!" She followed, occasionally swiveling to get a few shots off.

They barreled into the main street, dodging around people before ducking into a side alley. Screams followed in their wake, likely earned by the Elites trailing them. Katya laid out a suppressive fire as they ran. Her throat tightened when two of the Jar'rasks climbed across the facades of buildings, racing toward them, their tails and massive claws maintaining their balance. Leveling her arm, she fired and struck one. It collided with the ground, creating a sizeable thud.

"Don't kill them!" one metallic voice shouted. "The boy can't be injured."

Hisses, grunts, guttural noises answered. The blood fled from Katya's face as the Jar'rask overtook them and descended from the buildings. Mina yelped and started to backpedal, a would-be fatal mistake at this point. Katya caught her arm with her free hand and pressed her forward. Their feet pounded against the pathway's metal surface, much like her heart did in its cage. An acidic flavor assaulted her taste buds. She should have capped him, pulled the trigger—damn it! Why hadn't she better heeded her father's warning? Duty. He was one of her men. And she was paying for it now. Mina hiccupped, her sobs growing more pronounced.

Flinching, Katya released the interior of her mouth, which she hadn't realized she'd been biting. She fired a few more volleys, preventing the Jar'rask from sinking into them, before turning her pistol on a door to blast its mechanism. Kicking it open, Katya dragged Mina in after her. Not the dead end she'd feared it would be, she guided Mina through what amounted to a derelict apartment building.

"Run! This way!" Katya waved toward one hallway.

They took off seeking an exit, with Katya swinging around from time to time to lay down fire. Hard to do when her targets were little more than specters. She tried to keep a low profile to protect Sotiris. Their pursuers didn't want to harm him, but accidental fire didn't discriminate.

She coughed. Her lungs burned unused to this level of exertion. She'd been on a ship for far too long.

She stepped over a long metal rod that'd been dumped in the hall. Litter was scattered across the floors. Mina almost tripped on a black plastic bag but caught her balance before she went down. A door off to the side of them opened but shut when Katya fired another round behind them. The Jar'rasks never fired back, but they didn't fall back either. Given another scenario, Katya would've marveled at their reflexes and ability to avoid her shots . . . if she hadn't been their prey.

Sotiris remained pliable and asleep. A small blessing.

"Mina, right!" They needed to get out before they were torn apart. Crowds in a busy street could disguise them and serve as roadblocks against their pursuers. The Jar'rasks would be unwilling to risk collateral damage. They ran through the hallway on the right, then zigzagged down another where Katya flipped a random cart behind them. She couldn't see them, but their clawed feet scraped against the metal. Out of breath, Katya and Mina found another door to the outside and took it. It opened to a crowded main street, though not the same one they'd been on. Katya brushed past a woman and her children. She held the blanket over Sotiris as they weaved through the crowd. Mina stayed close at her heels, her feet heavier, slowing.

"Keep running!" Katya shouted. Mina coughed and stuttered out something unintelligible.

At some point in their mad dash, the Jar'rasks had disappeared. Katya panted and swiveled around on the balls of her feet. Nowhere. At some point, they'd dropped from the chase.

"We lost them?" A wide-eyed expression filled Mina's face. Somewhere along the way, the teen had lost her scarf and garnet hair now stood up, disheveled.

The life-forms around them shuffled by undisturbed. Stands set up along the street continued business. A group of children kicked a can down the length of the street, their chortles and taunts blossoming as they went.

Katya's lips formed a narrow line. The Elites had given up their chase while they were still in the apartment complex. Removing the glasses from her face, Katya tossed them to the ground, where they joined the rest of the worthless trash. There was no way around the inevitable. She shut her eyes. They had a ship but were now lost. And even if they weren't, their new ship was a Sparrow. The Elites would have the best of the best, something that would outmaneuver them, much like the Jar'rasks themselves. Next to her, Mina panted and heaved as she sank to the ground and rested her head between her knees. They couldn't outrun them. Hiding had become their only option, if it was even viable.

"Get up." Katya slid her pistol into its holster. "Let's keep walking."

"B-but the ship's that way!" Mina pointed toward the way they had come. "I think."

"So are Jar'rasks." She extended her hand to Mina and helped her to her feet. "We need to keep going where they aren't. We might be able to double back around . . . find our bearings."

Katya led the way to some destination, one even she didn't know. Mina wheezed behind her, so she slowed her pace further. There was no urgency in her steps, not anymore. Sotiris grew heavier with each footfall. Her stomach tightened. Soon he'd discover the fate of the other Oneiroi children.

"Katya," Mina said, gripping her arm. " . . . I can't go any farther."

Mina's normal copper tone had gone pallid as if she were sick; the sweat lining her brow only enhanced that appearance. Katya spotted an alley and took Mina to it. Garbage filled it, leaving very little ground exposed. The overflowing bins hadn't been cleaned out for weeks by the smell of them. Mina kneeled down, trying not to touch anything, while Katya paced. Adrenaline still flowed quite readily through her veins, demanding action. Avenues passed through her mind, ways out . . . only her ideas proved no more solid than smoke, seeping through her fingers. Her training filtered through—not good enough. Her tongue clicked against her teeth.

"What's going to happen to us?" Mina's eyes pleaded for Katya to do something, anything to save them from this situation.

When you meet an obstacle, what then? The words, in Lieutenant Pinarius's harsh tone, filtered through her head, a holdover embedded in it from the academy. Katya turned away. *What do you do then?* Her training screamed at her—demanded action, demanded that she act like an officer. Only she couldn't bring herself to give Mina a curt order to stay alert and dismiss the question altogether.

"It doesn't look good," Katya settled on.

On the nearby street, a man on a bicycle careened by, pinging his bell to warn pedestrians.

Katya brushed aside her sweat-coated bangs. "Our best hope is to get lost on-world, maybe eventually work our way back to the ship, maybe after a month or two."

"But?"

Too clever. The girl had always been that.

Moistening her lips, Katya told the truth. "Jar'rasks are keen trackers. It'll be hard to get lost, especially with the presence of drones. To be honest, I'm surprised they aren't on top of us now. Given their reputation, I'd have thought they'd keep up the chase. That they haven't . . . I think that speaks to their confidence."

Mina stood, though her gaze remained on the ground. "If we give them Sotiris, maybe they'll let us get lost on-world. We'd be fine; we've survived Reznic . . ."

Katya blinked, the weight against her chest resembling a rock. "I doubt that. Strom explained our predicament quite thoroughly." Her hand touched the pocket where the communicator rested. There would be Plasovern agents on Jordah; they could extract them. "What we know about the *Aletheia* . . . they can't risk that getting out."

"How can you be certain—"

"I spoke with Hedda Strom, remember?" Katya scrunched her lips together before smiling without a trace of mirth. "She erased any doubt that the Magistrate destroyed the *Aletheia* and everyone on board it themselves."

Katya frowned when Sotiris jerked awake, yelping as if he'd been shocked. She freed him from the carrier and was met by his unfocused blue eyes. Then he blinked and shook, sweat crawling down his brow.

"What's—" Pain seared her mind. Similar . . . She buckled as Mina collapsed to the grime-covered ground. Wincing, Katya caught Sotiris's gaze, still wide, unseeing, sweat . . . or tears? She couldn't stave it off. Fighting the pull, Katya fumbled to get the keycard and communicator into a pocket on Sotiris's pants before she fell the rest of the way. Her remaining energy was dedicated to gathering enough control over her body so she wouldn't crush him. Similar, but not the same. Her mind repeated the phrase, tried to pull sense from it. Impossible. Her brain processes ended when she succumbed.

CHAPTER SIXTEEN

Akakios toweled himself off as he stepped from his shower, relieved to be free of sweat. He'd lost track of how many pushups he'd completed. They'd simply been an activity to disperse pent-up energy. To momentarily distract from the fact they were anchored in space with no destination. A waiting game. And they were playing it blind. He ruffled the towel against his head, drying his hair by a fraction. The mirror highlighted the dark rings that had formed under his eyes. Too much tossing and turning. He hung the towel on its hook. As he slid on his uniform, his limbs burned from his previous exertion. The muscles beneath, however, still bristled, demanding action.

Reentering his main room, which had long surrendered to the mess, Akakios further aired his damp hair using his fingers. He stepped on a useless dossier, its papers and photographs scattering and joining pieces of clothing he'd discarded. A few slates were also dispersed in odd places about the room: his bed, among the clothes, on his trunk . . . and who knew where else he'd set them. He'd once prided himself in keeping his quarters pristine, but now he let order molder.

Idle exercise. That was all he'd been able to accomplish in days. Charis, try as she might, had only scrounged up random bits of information about Strom and her potential whereabouts. Nothing concrete. And so their days of inactivity stretched on. Fastening his uniform's belt, Akakios returned to the bridge, ready for more of the same.

As he walked, Elpis greeted him with a salute. "Captain, I need a word with you." Her face was placid, though her chin jutted out.

"Walk with me."

They fell into step along the catwalk, a slow pace, drudgery really. Elpis's throat visibly tightened when she swallowed, not looking at him.

"We've been drifting for days now. Where are we going?"

"To be determined." Her nostrils flared at this answer. "But that's not what you have on your mind, is it?"

"I'm concerned about my commanding officer's well-being." Elpis cast a sideward glance at him. "We do seem to be approaching a definite conclusion. And—"

Akakios grunted and faced Elpis. "I'll be fine. I've made my peace on that matter since the day he was born."

"That was before you lost Amyntas and Kallistrate." Elpis pressed her lips together, her pale skin seeming to take an even lighter shade in the purple-hued light. "My parents were never the same after my older brother was . . . had passed. I don't remember him well; there was a sizeable gap between us—but that's beside the point. It changed them. They wallowed in their grief, let it gnaw on them, turn them down avenues they shouldn't—"

"I won't," he said more sharply than he'd intended. "If that's all, I need to see if there is any new information."

Her lips twitched. "We seldom see the signs to the avenues we turn onto until we're well down them, sir. Some never do . . . even when others hold mirrors." She swiveled back the way they'd come, heading toward the medbay. "We're here for you, sir. You needn't be alone."

Akakios blinked, moisture forming though never fully materializing. "The thought is appreciated."

Her steps continued on the metal catwalk after a brief pause, and Akakios carried on to the bridge.

Only Charis and Kyrillos worked at their consoles. The ship had been left to the autopilot to drift and wait for a more concrete destination. Charis rose to her feet upon his entrance. "More rumors have pinpointed Strom to this sector."

"Rumors . . . do you have anything better?"

"They are exceptionally good rumors, sir." Charis smiled. The blackish-purple skin under her eyes hinted toward another shortened sleep cycle. "The type that are spread by Plasovern sympathizers trying to procure meetings with her. A user, kkkLN34721, is responding to some; he might be a go-between. He's hinting that meetings in the Reello system are possible. It's coming from Intortus." She smirked, reading some cue on his face. "You told me you wanted me to dig, so I have . . . through waves of encryption and backrooms."

"What planets and posts are in that system?"

"Reello, Station R-20, Jordah, Station K-40, Magistrate Organizational Post 450, and Barsaa are the only ones comfortable for oxygen breathers." Charis launched the large star map and displayed the system.

"Have there been any hits on the *Minerva*?"

"None, but a lot of the planets in this system are considered partial primitives and don't have Magistrate relays, sir."

Akakios leaned in, taking mental notes of the system. The crew with Sotiris had perhaps more luck than he'd thought even possible, if they had survived the jump and made it to one of the planets. To arrive at a sector with planets that didn't have Magistrate relays . . . but it was also a double-edged victory. If their ship had been badly damaged—and after viewing footage from the peace officers' vessels, he believed it was—the odds of them finding a replacement were nil. The biggest planets population-wise were Reello and Jordah, both of which had Magistrate relays and thousands of Magistrate soldiers; however, if the *Minerva* had been dumped, none of that would matter: They could pass right under the Magistrate's nose without their marked ship. He exhaled. And back to square one.

"Are there cameras that we could check?"

"On Jordah, yes. But it'd take days to bypass the security without the keycode, and that is not even factoring in the time necessary to filter through past and current data." Charis rested her hands behind her back. "It's a huge planet, sir, heavily populated, probably with cameras well past the thousands."

"It's not practical."

"It's not." Charis gestured to the smaller planets on the map. "The other planets do not have such refined or widespread surveillance systems; most would be installed in stores or ports. They would be closed systems, not uploaded in any way to the Net, so they are out of the question. However, the stations . . . those might be the best option. It'll take time, but it's more realistic."

"Start it."

Akakios approached Kyrillos. "Anything interesting on the lines?"

"Nothing new, no inquiries from Command."

"What about on the other Elite stations?" The Magistrate, after all, would not leave them to hunt alone, even if they hadn't mentioned others were moving with the same purpose. But it would be a task only entrusted to Elites. "Anything interesting?"

"Like us, they all use their own languages, leaving Command's special translators to untangle the messages." Kryillos adjusted something on his console. "I can only understand what's in Magistrate or coded. Certain codes."

Akakios waved his hand dismissively. "But have there been more transmissions in this sector?"

"I'll monitor."

Akakios clapped him on the back before returning to the star map. "Where's Ambrosios?"

"Do you really have to ask what he's going to do with downtime?" Teeth peeked out between Kyrillos's lips.

"More monitoring," Charis barked at Kyrillos. "He's with Chrysanthos; I believe they are completing diagnosis on the engines."

"Diagnosis." Kyrillos chuckled.

"Sir, I've broken into Station R-20's cameras. I'm using the facial scanner to comb their records starting from the day after their escape from Dandis VII, to be safe."

<Will Command be able to see what we're doing if we use the facial scanner?>

She lifted a brow. <If they're monitoring the tech, yes.>

Akakios activated the intercom. "Ambrosios, senior officers meeting."

"We're within our operating parameters for our search." Charis now gave him her full attention, leaving the facial scanner as she rose to her feet. <Why are you concerned that they are watching?>

<In due time.>

Charis rested her hands on her hips. <I am your second.>

<I am not ready.> He bowed his head to her in contrition. <I don't want them swept away.>

Ambrosios arrived within a few minutes, suggesting that Charis's assertion had been the correct one. "Engines are running smoothly, and the new part is working well," he said. "So, what's happened?"

"We've hacked into R-20's cameras with the facial scanner," Akakios answered as Charis resumed monitoring the tech. "The facial scanner's use is probably being monitored. We'll need to move fast to secure them." His earlier thought voiced only to Charis went unspoken.

Ambrosios folded his arms across his chest and sank back into his seat. "Come on, Captain, what do you know? Yes, you want Sotiris out of harm's way . . . and you want to know what happened on the *Aletheia*, but I think you already suspect some sort of truth."

"I won't speculate." Akakios pinched the bridge of his nose, his mouth setting into a grim line. If it was true, if they had . . . he'd bury it. His jaw clenched. His brother would not be remembered as a traitor.

"Sir." Charis prevented Ambrosios from continuing his verbal prying. Her fingers glided across her console, and on the viewscreen, a video appeared. "I've got them."

In the video, the woman from Dandis VII walked with Sotiris and the girl. The male target said something before wandering off on his own. The man's image caused Akakios's throat to constrict. He'd injured his nephew. The thought of Sotiris being thrown brought his blood to a boil, narrowing his vision even. The woman and the girl walked out of the camera's range. The viewscreen went blank before Charis launched another camera. The woman handed Sotiris to the girl and then left. The feed of the girl and Sotiris advanced, consisting of her placing the bags in a manner that amounted to a temporary bed and taking a catnap. The woman did not return for quite some time; the man arrived at the makeshift camp before leaving again.

"This was taken two days ago," Charis said. "It appears they took a transport. I should be able to get into the system and find out what transport they boarded and where it was going."

"Where did the woman go?"

The feed disappeared as Charis rolled back the clock and jumped between cameras. Finally, they landed on a feed that showed the woman entering a bar. There was a long pause until his second officer tapped into the establishment's feed, a static mess. The proprietor had purchased a cheap surveillance system. The lines kept cropping up. Despite that, they could make out the woman sitting at a table, barely in the frame. Minutes passed, and she was joined by another woman who had come from the bar area. Her back was to the camera, conveniently hiding her identity. At times, the camera feed disintegrated, obscuring all images before returning to its poor quality.

"Are there any other angles?" Akakios asked.

"No."

During the filmed conversation, their target showed agitation. She stood, appeared to be shouting, and at one point knocked what appeared to be a glass onto the floor. Then the other woman handed her something, and they parted ways. Charis started to change cameras, but Akakios stopped her.

"Stay with the woman in the bar. I want to see if she shows her face." But the camera cut to static, and when the picture cleared, the woman was gone. "Can you clean it up?"

"No. The original quality is too poor."

"Retrace the cameras and follow our target back to Sotiris."

Returning to the station's cameras, their target ran into her male companion after leaving the bar. Akakios frowned as the man grabbed the woman and slammed her into a wall. She broke free at one point and pulled a firearm, some Preserver model, on him. The pair exchanged more heated words. She stalked off, and he followed. They both rejoined the girl and Sotiris, and a couple hours later, they boarded their transport.

"Do you have the transport?"

Charis nodded. "Transport 1A9934, bound for Jordah. They would have arrived earlier today."

"Sir," Kyrillos said. "I am picking up a lot of traffic from Jordah. Jar'rasks."

The muscles in Akakios's arms tensed while a burst of adrenaline hummed through his body. "Ambrosios, get us to that planet." They had to apprehend them before the Jar'rasks. A worse combination did not exist for Sotiris than a cold-blooded species that kept their vessels at a boil . . . and then there was their nature. Akakios tugged at his uniform's collar. They'd seen the Jar'rasks in action before, and it'd stuck with him. "Engage the FTL drive." He turned to Charis. "Go ahead and break into the planet's surveillance system."

"While we have the search area narrowed down, sir, it'll still take me days to break into the system without the proper clearance, as I've already told you," Charis bit out while rubbing her brow as if warding off a headache. "It'll trigger red flags."

Clenching his fists, Akakios shook his head. "Belay that order."

Through a portion of the viewscreen, which Ambrosios had programmed, the stars blurred together as the FTL drive sprang to life. They'd been at FTL for an hour when Kyrillos called to Akakios. "We have an incoming transmission, priority one."

"Ambrosios—"

"On it." He eased them from FTL, allowing the call's reception.

"It's for you, sir."

Akakios activated his personal communicator, to which Kyrillos transferred the call.

"This is Captain Sarris."

"Akakios." Kyros . . . why was he calling? "Where are you currently?"

"Near Jordah, we have a lead—"

"You're to stand down," Kyros said. "Sotiris has been retrieved and will be taken to Meracus Domus for immediate medical attention."

"Is he well?" Akakios paced, distancing himself from his officers, no matter how pointless the action.

"For now, he's fine, but they're concerned about his general health; he's malnourished and in need of fluids. They've determined that immediate introduction to the care facility is in order. They'll be leaving Jordah momentarily and will arrive in a few weeks, then Sotiris will get the care he needs."

A lie. A bald-faced lie. Sotiris had looked healthy enough in the surveillance videos, but Akakios bit back the retort and swallowed the boiling rage. "We're extremely close to Jordah." He pressed a hand to the com device in his ear. "Can they wait until we arrive? We can pick up Sotiris and complete the trip. He shouldn't be in the care of Jar'rasks. Our biology is too different. Their ship will put too much undue stress on him."

There was a pause over the line, and Akakios caught the rustle of fabric. "I had the same thoughts, but they're already underway, and you have new orders. You're to return to Sergrey as you'd planned. There, your crew will be debriefed and interviewed by Magistrate officials."

Akakios stumbled in his effort to say something. He blinked, not wanting the moisture to return. Sotiris whisked away while they'd be tied up for days with debriefing and interviews. Interviews. What would those entail? Reports were common, but this? "I want—need to see him, to actually see him . . . to hold him."

"I understand, my boy, I do"—even over the communications system, Akakios heard the catch in Kyros's voice—"but these orders, they come from Command. They expect you to change course immediately for Sergrey." Kyros cleared his throat over the line. "And that's not it."

His voice diminished, almost lost to the pounding in Akakios's mind: "You need to keep your head down, Akakios. I cannot stress this enough to you. I don't know what's happening, but whatever it is, it's occurring beneath the surface. Akakios, your family has been removed from the Etai's list."

Akakios's jaw slackened, the air leaving him as if he'd been punched. For a long moment, he stood, breathing shallowly, absorbing the information. There'd be no more contracts, no more children, no hope of their branch recovering. Grinding his teeth together, Akakios pictured Kallistrate's and Amyntas's smiling faces, his chest clenching. He cleared his throat—it'd grown tight enough he felt he might suffocate. "Why?"

"I couldn't say," Kyros said. "I was absent when my fellow Agoranomi members came to this decision, and the records are sealed. Even I can't access them. Has something happened?"

So few reasons merited removal—damn it, Amyntas! The thought ripped through his head. Why hadn't they told him? His muscles relaxed, leaving only soreness and emptiness.

"No. We'll do as ordered and be underway shortly." He moistened his lips. "Kyros, thank you for everything . . . that you did for Amyntas and me. I can never thank you enough."

Kyros remained quiet, perhaps afraid of the words and tone Akakios had used; he'd known him too long to easily dismiss it. "Keep yourself well, my boy."

"Always." Akakios clicked off his com. After straightening his uniform, he squared his posture. "We've been recalled to Sergrey for debriefing . . . and to undergo interviews."

Ambrosios blinked. "Interviews? What'll these interviews entail?"

"Kyros didn't say, and I doubt he's been told." All three exchanged glances. There was no way around this, at least not if Akakios wanted to achieve some modicum of truth.

"Ambrosios, set our course." Then Akakios employed his people's greatest advantage, no longer trusting their ship. <Belay that order.> The thought carried between all his senior officers. He then broadened out his call. <Everyone to the bridge.>

<So we finally come around to your hunch, huh?> Ambrosios leaned forward, eyes piercing Akakios, though not using the connection to rummage for information. <You have a crazy plan, don't you? You wouldn't have called everyone otherwise.>

Akakios shrugged, and they waited for the rest of the crew to file into the bridge. The majority, upon arrival, searched the room and their officers' faces in vain attempts to piece together what was transpiring. Elpis, however, wrung her hands and scrutinized Akakios with her cold eyes — one would have thought she'd been ordered to walk out the airlock. But then again, what he planned to propose wasn't all that much better or less insane. Chrysanthos arrived last, having had the greater distance to travel from the engine room. Akakios gestured for them to stand in front of him.

<We've been recalled. Debriefing and interviews.> Akakios placed his hands behind his back, legs spread at ease. Like Ambrosios had, they balked at the mention of interviews — more than likely, a few conversations were being carried privately. <What the interviews will entail remains a mystery. However, they'll undoubtedly be linked to our mission. I suspect they want to make sure we didn't uncover too much.>

His lips tightened, along with his throat. <My — my family has been revoked from the Etai's list.>

Pelagius gawked, his mouth quite wide, almost as if he had meant to say something. He only regained himself when his twin elbowed him.

<My family has only had two born with the defect, not enough for removal. Councilor Kyros stated that the records had been sealed even from him, a member of the Agoranomi.> Akakios choked out a laugh. <There are few reasons to dictate such a course of action without the requisite amount of children born with the defect, and once I stopped allowing grief to cloud my mind . . .> His fingernails dug into his hands, still concealed behind his back, leaving vibrant red marks undoubtedly. <What transpires here will not leave this room.> Akakios swallowed hard against the acidic taste in his mouth. In front of him, his crew bore somber expressions. <I believe Kallistrate and Amyntas intended to enter Medzeci territory. Willingly.>

<That's quite the leap, Captain.> Charis clenched her armrest as she rose.

<Kallistrate believed she could control the defect. The ship was off course, and I'm starting to believe the reported location of the attack was even farther out.>

<Or the attack occurred exactly where the report says it did, and they were only slightly off course, investigating an anomaly, which turned out to be Plasovern,> Charis pressed. <A whole crew wouldn't cave to the whims of their commander, not a crew of our people, not when it meant treason, not when it endangered the whole. You're heaping trespasses on the dead without proof.>

<But that's just it.> Akakios waved his hands about. <Really look at the information we have! I loved my brother and sister-in-law—I still do—but with an objective eye, I can't ignore facts that have been brushed under the rug by the Magistrate. Plasovern couldn't have destroyed the *Aletheia* in a manner that would leave only a few metal plates as debris. They don't have that firepower. Who has that firepower? There are only two options: Medzeci or the Magistrate.>

<What about the spies on the inside?> Pelagius asked. <They might have been able to rig the *Aletheia* to explode. They've done it before—not to military vessels, but it's possible.>

<I believe what the 'good' doctor said. Our targets aren't Plasovern, but whether they were on the ship before or after the attack remains to be seen, and the answer is on the Jar'rask ship.> Akakios faced Charis. <You're right: We don't move individually. The crew wouldn't have followed Kallistrate's whim, nor would she have led them blindly.>

Akakios paced, his hands aching as they clasped each other. <What would make a crew follow their commanding officer, despite it being an act of treason? Let's be honest. The Medzeci Empire has not been the ones obstructing and withholding information from us.>

No one offered a hypothesis. Akakios launched several of the compiled files from the destruction of the *Aletheia* on the viewscreen: reports, figures, and images of the destruction. It'd been a minor component to their mission; they'd never studied the files, not as a unit. As he started to flip to another, Ambrosios stopped him.

<Stay on that one.> His first lieutenant approached the viewscreen and launched the star map. He selected a section on the star map that was nearer to Medzeci space and zoomed in. <The attack occurred out here.> His index and middle finger etched the area he was highlighting. <You see this? They tried to cut it out and blur it in the official photos, but it's still plainly the Nag's Head Nebula. They were way off course . . . enough so that the crew would've been aware.>

<Why? Why would they have gone to Medzeci after everything?> Pelagia asked. After the hefty price their people had paid during the Fringe Campaigns. That hung in the air.

Akakios examined the star map, at the last stars his family had seen. <Ambrosios, can we intercept the Jar'rask ship?>

<Yes.>

A certain gravity settled across the bridge, the potential order sinking in along with all its connotations and fallouts. Elpis's face, in particular, was pinched and blanched; her clasped hands quivered against her abdomen. Next to her, Chrysanthos focused only on Ambrosios, and Akakios didn't doubt that a private conversation was occurring between the pair; it was only to be expected. Charis, Pelagia, and Pelagius remained at attention, their training as soldiers falling into default, while Kyrillos monitored transmissions, detached from the crazy scheme his commanding officer was hatching.

What makes a crew go rogue? The question lingered in Akakios's mind, no longer in regards to the *Aletheia*. Here they stood at the precipice. And what did they hope to achieve by crossing it? They had more to lose than gain, all for his own selfish reasons. Because he had to know why. What had caused them to . . . His mind flickered to the last transmission between him and Amyntas, a few weeks before the end. His brother had to have known then what they had planned to do. Why hadn't he said anything, hinted even? Akakios swallowed hard, his hands clenched harder behind his back.

<I won't force you to come with me on this excursion,> he sent through their connections, breaking the silence that hung over the bridge like a black crepe. <What I purpose to do will only have one outcome: treason. There'll be no return. And I can't promise justification. However, I cannot see them taking the actions they did without reason. Not when it went so against our nature.>

<What do we do after?> Elpis's thought ricocheted through their bonds, shrill and loud. <We won't be able to return home!>

<Maybe. But if the *Aletheia* crew knew something, and I think they did, it should be uncovered. The best way of doing that is to speak with that woman. It's instinct—no, it's because I believe in my brother and sister-in-law . . . > He brushed his sleeve against his eyes.

<I can't fault you, Captain,> Ambrosios sent, allowing Akakios time to compose himself. <Having a little brother myself, I'd need to know too. I'd also want to lash out at the right party.> He shifted his gaze to Chrysanthos, who inclined his head. <We'll stay with you.>

<We're in.> Pelagius draped his arm around Pelagia in half a bear hug, earning himself another jab from her elbow.

<Don't be so brash, you idiot.> Pelagia rounded on him, poking him again in the side with her fingers. <This is a solemn moment, and it should be treated as such.> She returned her hands to her hips. <This>—she gestured around the bridge—<doesn't just affect us but also our family members. There'll be repercussions for them, and like the captain, they won't understand why.>

<But—>

<It's a calculated risk,> Charis interrupted Pelagius, <that banks on the enormity of secret the Magistrate is keeping.>

<I'm betting it's big, given Commands' level of tampering.> Ambrosios hovered over the navigation console. <Captain, we need to make this decision fast. The gap between us and the Jar'rasks is growing. A few more minutes, and I don't know if we'll be able to catch them.>

<We're in!> Pelagius pumped his fist in the air.

Akakios ignored him and eyed the rest of his crew, one at a time. <Are there any objectors?> His gaze lingered on Elpis, who shook her head before crossing over to the door.

<Someone has to patch everyone up.> She palmed open the door. <Because I have a strong feeling you're going to need a doctor.>

Without another word, Elpis left, the door closing behind her.

<Since we're proceeding>—Charis flexed her fingers over her console—<I'd like to have more of a plan.>

<It's a good thing we'll have a few hours to make one.> Akakios eased into his seat. <Ambrosios.>

The FTL shot to life, accelerating them through space. And as it did, they laid the groundwork for their next steps.

Antiseptics assaulted Katya's nose, stinging. It, in addition to the sweat that crawled down her face and the tightness around her wrists and ankles, heightened her discomfort. Hisses and other guttural, animalistic sounds emitted somewhere beyond her. Awareness seeped into her. Jar'rasks. The angry-sounding noises drove figurative spikes into her head. Elevated. She was definitely elevated. The tightness that cut into her wrists and ankles was brought on by metal, which secured her to a flat examination table of sorts. The room was sweltering. Cracking open her eyes, she witnessed one Jar'rask bite at another. More grating hisses. Her head spun, and she found it hard to focus. Drugs? Now they flashed their teeth at each other, grunts rattling deep in their throats. Neither bore the embedded communicator device.

A third came into her limited view. This one had a communicator implanted into its throat; it gleamed against the black scales. Despite having the device, it hissed up a storm, along with its brethren. The officer, or at least Katya assumed he was one since he had the implant, swiped at the two bickering Jar'rasks with his tail, hitting them with it. They balked but bowed and slinked away from each other.

"Our guest is waking," he said, allowing the implant to takeover.

Katya winced and jerked her head away as the Jar'rask ran a clawed finger against her face. Unperturbed, he followed through with the motion, digging in his claw's tip upon reaching her chin, cutting into her skin. "Ah, my sweets, don't bother resisting."

Katya swallowed. "Where are my companions?"

"The boy's fine, wide awake and no longer a danger." He wheeled something over but kept it out of her line of sight. "The girl? Well, she won't be so fine. Neither will you, really."

Katya flayed against the metal table when an electric current coursed through her body. It stopped after a while but almost instantly resumed. Unable to stop herself, Katya screamed, every fiber of her body echoing agony, except for her feet, which were numb. No questions were asked. The only constant was a barrage of pain. Drool escaped the corners of her mouth, mingling and pooling with the sweat.

The current ceased, leaving her to pant and swallow the excess spit. Moments passed, and nothing. The Jar'rask moved from the controls.

"What do you want?" Katya choked out between breaths.

"Want?" He swiped his long tongue against her face; it left a mild tingling sensation that disappeared shortly after. Did their saliva have something in it? "We want nothing; we're merely passing time in an enjoyable fashion. No different than humanoid adolescents removing the limbs and wings from lesser life-forms. No different at all. You've outlived any other form of usefulness than to appease us." His tongue flickered against his snout. "We have needs . . . knowing this, the Magistrate throws us a bone every now and again."

Wincing, Katya relaxed her hand, which she couldn't recall having tightened into a fist. "I'd" — she winced — "be careful trusting the Magistrate. Elites can be just as expendable."

"Baash!" The noise rumbling through the implant resembled humanoid laughter, only off-kilter. "Why should I care?" He — or so Katya assumed — lapped at his own snout. "A well-earned end is a well-earned end; nothing is more fitting for traitors. As far as if it happened to us" — he tilted his head toward his two companions, hissing and flashing their teeth at each other — "we'd move on."

He chuckled his odd mechanical sound as one snapped at the other with its jagged, razor-like teeth; his slanted eyes followed each motion the pair made with a cold interest that bordered on predatory. "The Magistrate has forced this cooperative effort on us. And who knows, maybe one day we'll be forced to evolve into a species that can actually stand being in each other's company without wanting to kill each other."

The Jar'rask bared his teeth, the action resembling a grin. Something rattled on the cart.

"But that still belongs to the future." He lifted a device, his clawed hand holding it up against the bright light. Katya's breath caught in her throat. A laser cutter, powerful enough to cut through certain thicknesses of metal. It would cauterize as it cut, so at least she wouldn't bleed out. But it'd do nothing to dull the pain. "But don't worry. There's still more time to play, and we have a certain reputation as hosts." His claw tapped against the implant, his pointed teeth grinding together. "I enjoy this type of talking. I've found it serves to heighten my subjects' fear . . . they give off the most delectable scents."

Katya howled when the current returned, ripping through her body. She pounded her head against the table out of compulsion. By the time the current stopped, she could not feel her limbs. She swallowed hard, tears flowing down her face. Was Mina undergoing the same amount of torment or worse? Had she pulled the girl off Reznic for this end? Her eyelids opened and closed rapidly against the tears. And Sotiris . . . what fate awaited him in the loving embrace of the Magistrate? Locked to the table, Katya's muscles convulsed. All her best intentions . . . she'd failed them.

"Are you almost at your limit?" The click of a button followed and then a different hissing upon the laser cutter's activation. "Pity."

She bit her lip, trying to prevent herself from whimpering.

"Don't worry. You'll survive this, unless you go into shock. If you do that, I'm afraid we don't have the technology to bring a humanoid out. We know this by experience . . . sad story, I assure you."

The other two Jar'rasks drew closer, tongues swiping through the air and flicking across their snouts. Katya flinched and squeezed her eyes shut, though she couldn't stop herself from envisioning the two eating her newly discarded limb. A jolt went through her body, sending her into another spasm. When it stopped, the cutting device inched forward. Katya steeled herself, preparing for the eventual cut.

"Gagh — gagh, gagh!"

Her eyes shot open. A trail of red trickled from her torturer's nose, dropping onto her arm. He gasped out hisses and let out some gargled noises before hitting the Jar'rask next to him, pointing toward the door like a man on fire. The other merely dropped, blood dripping from its nose. Seeing this, the third Jar'rask bolted for the door. By the time he reached it, her torturer had slumped to the floor, sputtering and twitching. Katya, eyes wide, watched his chest go motionless. The image of a Brek superimposed itself over the face of the Jar'rask.

Katya gaped at the scene, light-headed and breathless. Blood pooled around them. A sick fascination crept over her — or perhaps disbelief — as the bright scarlet liquid trickled across the ship's metal floor. Shuddering, she broke from the trance.

He'd killed them. Sotiris had killed them: the Jar'rasks, the Breks. Tears swelled again despite her eyelids flickering to block them. On the *Aletheia*, he'd felt his mother's brain waves break apart, and he'd lashed out at the ones who'd robbed him of them, of her. Just as he'd felt her pain and reacted to prevent the same sensation, the same loss from occurring again. She wondered if the third had made it to where Sotiris was being kept or not.

Clicking her tongue against her teeth, Katya lifted her head, pressing forward against pain. Focus. Mina and Sotiris. She needed to get to them, and there was only one way. Steadying herself, Katya contorted her right hand.

One, two, three! She yanked downward, the metal cutting into her skin. Hissing, she ceased the action to gather herself. Then she tugged again, willing her bones to give way so she could pull that hand free. She growled and strained against the restraint. *Pop*! Katya screamed, hissing as her limbs shook. Batting away tears, she groped the tray that the Jar'rask had rolled over. Her hand found a sharp instrument, which she struggled to grip with her damaged hand.

"Heh!" She stuttered, air escaping her lungs when the instrument clinked back onto the tray. Flexing her fingers, forcing them to work, she tried again. Mina and Sotiris dominated her mind. Failure was not an option. Her grip tightened around it.

The tool in hand, Katya pried its sharp metal tip into the restraint's seam. Sharp needle-like pain traveled throughout her arm into her shoulder while working it. Whenever her grip threatened to give, she forced herself to tighten up as she rattled it about. It connected with the restraint's inner mechanism, and gravity sent her toppling headfirst to the floor, her legs remaining confined at the ankles to the table. Screaming, Katya caught herself with her hands, including her much-abused right one. Her vision dulled as she stammered and cursed, screaming at times.

Blindly, Katya stretched to get the laser cutter, the one her torturer had dropped. Like a madwoman, she chuckled when her fingers wrapped around it. Using her left hand and the cutter, she disconnected herself from the table.

She tried to stand, only to topple to the floor. Need to get the blood circulating. She flexed her legs and toes, massaging them as well with her left hand. One of the Jar'rasks had a firearm. Prying it from his belt, she held it. Heavy and oddly balanced. Vitellius had probably been commissioned to custom build it by the Magistrate. While Avitus designs carried a certain elegance, Vitellius's bespoke of might and ruggedness: the backbone of the

Magistrate, the maker had been dubbed. A poor fit for her as it'd been designed for Elites like the Jar'rasks and Breks; however, it would have to suit her purposes.

Lurching forward, she returned to her feet and headed out the door, her gait unsteady. Along the way, she found herself somewhat dependent on the walls for balance. Even so, she stumbled along the hallway, bringing more feeling back to her legs with each step.

CHAPTER SEVENTEEN

As Katya snaked through the hallway of what seemed to be an A-Class Boita warship, she drifted away from the wall, no longer so reliant on it. Above, the lights produced heat and brought out the obsidian-like metal's gleam. A faint scent of methane hung in the corridors, probably produced by its inhabitants. Doors were evenly placed throughout, and the ship appeared to be similar in build to the *Aletheia*. Katya wiped her forehead with her throbbing hand, now a lovely shade of purple with hints of red, blue, and black. Beyond the lights, the ship's environmental controls had to have been set to produce a large amount of heat. Perhaps if that was sabotaged, the Jar'rasks would . . .

She paused. A body lay in the corridor in front of her. Evidently, the third Jar'rask—the reddish-tan one—hadn't made it far. His prone figure sent shivers down her spine.

Only a toddler, yet he was capable of . . . no, he didn't understand. He'd lashed out to stop the pain that was overwhelming her without thought to what his actions meant. The Jar'rasks, similar to the Breks before them, had simply been bad in his mind. Still—she stood over the corpse—such powers, especially in the hands of a child, were unnerving.

Gritting her teeth, she clutched the Jar'rask firearm in her left hand. Mina would be nearby in one of the other interrogation rooms. She would find her, her and Sotiris. Her grip on the gun ached.

An eerie silence swathed the corridors. No screams, no loud Jar'rasks, not even footfalls beyond her own. A faint hum from the ship was all. As she went to open the first room's door, Katya raised her gun. Empty. She moved on to the next and met the same results. When she opened the fourth door, movement met her, and she pulled the trigger. Shit! Her jaw slackened when the trigger stuck. The Jar'rask surged forward, teeth snapping at her. The trigger required more pressure. Dodging the creature, she pressed two fingers against the trigger, which gave way. The Jar'rask collapsed to the floor with a thud, a hole in its head. Katya scanned the room. Its table was empty and pristine; however, given the antiseptic stench, that didn't mean it hadn't been used recently.

Warm breath pawed at her neck. Katya swung around, but she found herself colliding with the floor after something hard—a scaly tail—struck her legs. In a blur, she rolled, gripping onto her firearm, her lifeline. The Jar'rask's tail whacked against the floor multiple times, following Katya as she went. Cleared of its radius, she lurched to her feet and tried to get a good bead. The Jar'rask rushed her, staying almost on top of her, whipping its tail akin to a club.

Stay ahead, stay ahead. She fumbled for the trigger and strained to pull it. A graze. A damn graze. Katya almost laughed, knowing she'd only succeeded in pissing him off further. She darted onto her feet and fired another shot; this time it hit the Jar'rask dead-on. Rasping, Katya straightened as the Jar'rask collapsed to the floor. Both Jar'rasks in the room carried a larger model of firearm than the one she had; she imagined the trigger would be even harder to pull. Still, she removed one from the brown Jar'rask nearest the door and fixed it on her belt, which cut into her skin because of the weapon's weight. She checked its other possessions, pausing when she found a flash grenade. She pocketed it before stepping out of the room.

In the hallway, a door that had been shut lay open. Tightening her grip on the smaller firearm, she slinked into the room. No Jar'rasks—

"Mina . . ." Katya darted to the teen's side, setting her weapon on the floor by the table.

Sweat glistened on the teenager's brow from exertion or—Katya hissed, sucking in air upon finding a stump, cauterized, where there should have been a forearm and hand. Katya fingered the table's controls and caught Mina as it released her. The girl sputtered but didn't regain consciousness. Katya fought to stay collected while she eased Mina onto the floor. She rubbed the teen's cheek and offered the same soothing coos she would use with Sotiris.

"Mina, I need you to wake up; I need you to focus on my voice. Can you do that?" Katya patted her cheek, applying more pressure now. "There we go. Keep your eyes open. I need you to do that, you understand?"

Mina sobbed when she grew more aware of her surroundings. She mumbled a string of sounds, none of which made sense.

"You're free now, but we aren't out of this yet." Katya tried to stand, but Mina grabbed her with her left hand, whimpering. "Shh . . . I'm not going anywhere. I'm going to see if I can get you some water and something for the pain. And then, we'll get you somewhere safe so I can find Sotiris."

Katya dug through the room's cabinets, sorting through glass pharmaceutical bottles for ones with Magistrate labeling; finally, she recognized a mild pain reliever. It would at least take some of the edge off. After grabbing a syringe, she returned to Mina. "I'm going prick you, but this will help." Katya reached for Mina's injured arm, only for the girl to recoil. "I need to inject it there, at the site of the injury."

"Injury—" Mina choked out. "Th-they cut off my arm!"

"And this will help with the pain." Katya grabbed Mina's arm and drove the needle in, injecting the drug, a little more than the normal dosage. "We'll get out of here. I promise you. And when we're out, we'll get you a prosthetic—it won't be the same. No," she continued when the girl sobbed again. "It'll never be the same, but we'll pull you through this."

Tears cascaded down Mina's face. Probably her own, too, since she found her vision blurred. She squeezed Mina's shoulder and stood, this time to retrieve water with a metal bowl she'd found. Jar'rasks were just as dependent on the liquid as humanoids were and had a small sink in the space, though its purpose here was likely to clean up after sessions. She brought Mina into a seated position and eased the water into her mouth, all while minding the door. The hallways were too empty, especially for an A-Class warship. They hadn't fully staffed the ship. She recalled the fighting pair, her torturer's words. Jar'rasks required plenty of space to avoid each other, or there would be a bloodbath.

"Feeling better?" Katya asked.

"No."

"I didn't expect you to." Katya wiped the sweat from Mina's face with her own shirt before helping the girl to her feet. She draped the girl's arm over her shoulders, running her free arm under Mina's armpit. "Let's move. We're going to get you close to a hangar bay and hide you while I get Sotiris. We owe our escape to him."

Mina goggled at her.

"If Rein"—venom seeped into her voice when she said that name—"had seen what our boy is capable of, he wouldn't have been so quick to throw him. He was able to target a few of the Jar'rasks on this deck with his special ability."

Katya retrieved her firearm on their way out of the room.

"How are we getting off this ship?" Mina leaned into Katya, her legs threatening to buckle.

"There'll be ships in the bay, fast ones that the Elites use for missions." The heat of the ship and her effort to support Mina . . . sweat slid into Katya's eyes; her mouth tasted of salt. "I imagine we were brought here on one since they aren't about to land an A-Class warship over such a trivial matter. With luck, we'll be able to sneak onto one of those fast ships and outfly anyone they send to get us."

"What . . . aren't you saying?" Mina's voice wavered as she spoke.

Katya chuckled; it lacked any levity. "First, I have to hunt down Sotiris and then knock our captors out of FTL. If we launched a ship from the bay at this speed, we'd be torn apart." Katya glanced at the ceiling. "And there are probably cameras, so we have to move fast. The good news is I don't think I've triggered too much attention yet."

They would have been met by more Jar'rasks at this point if she had, yet here they remained unfettered. They limped through the corridor until they reached a lift. Katya guided Mina in and entered level thirty, where the hangar bays were located on ships of this size. Placing Mina against the back of the lift, Katya faced the door, her firearm raised and ready. The door slid open within a few seconds. On the other side, nothing. Katya stepped out and checked the corridor, meeting the same results. At some point, Mina had wobbled out after her.

"Come on." She returned her arm to support the girl. "Let's find you a hiding spot."

That spot took the form of a storage room, which Katya assumed had to be near one of the main hangar bays. Different parts lined its many shelves, along with specialized suits for the Jar'rasks. Katya positioned Mina at the back of the room and made sure she was well out of sight, adjusting a few pieces of equipment to fully obscure her. Satisfied, she crouched beside the girl.

"Stay quiet. No matter what, not a sound." She handed the smaller of the two firearms to Mina, leaving the safety on for now. "Test the trigger; it's a hard push, and I want to make sure you can manage it."

Mina did as told. She had to use two fingers, but she managed it.

"Leave the safety on," Katya continued. "If the door opens, take the safety off. But stay quiet, don't move, and don't fire unless seen. Aim for the head. I'll be back as soon as I can. I promise I'll get you and Sotiris to a ship and find some way to slow our hosts down."

Mina swallowed, sweat dripping from her chin. The girl had to be edging the line between dehydration and exhaustion. "How are you going to find Sotiris?"

Katya towered over Mina after straightening. "I have a feeling he can help me. I'll be right back. Stay awake. Stay alert."

She thumbed the door open again and retraced her steps to the lift, moving like a mother fox to put distance between her and her kit's location. The lift doors closed. Where are you? Sotiris's little tendrils didn't greet her. Had he woken? The lift hurtled toward the ship's upper levels. Come on. Katya continued to think as loudly—if that was possible—as she could, hoping to draw out the boy. He had tried communicating with her before, but unfortunately for the Oneiroi child, their brains weren't exactly compatible, hence his attempts drudging up long-buried, forgotten memories.

The lift slowed. Katya's lips formed a thin line, and she hoisted up the larger firearm. It stopped. *Swoosh!* She compressed the trigger with three fingers and hit one of two Jar'rasks square in the chest. He fell backward with the force, as did Katya. She cursed while sharp, jagged pain radiated throughout her shoulder and arms. The recoil was beyond anything she'd experienced before. She had to ditch the firearm and find another smaller one. Gritting her teeth, she braced herself and fired again. Only there was a delay with the gun, and the second Jar'rask took full advantage, dodging the shot while also drawing closer.

As Katya fumbled with the gun, she hit something, a button, a latch—something. "Ehhh—" She almost dropped the firearm when it sent out bolts in rapid succession. She couldn't control it; the shots went every which way, but one—maybe three—hit her assailant.

Katya discarded the overheated gun, which burned her hands, and unfastened one of the downed Jar'rask's smaller handguns, one she could at least manage. She also sequestered a slate, larger than most standard Magistrate-issued devices, from a pocket in its leather uniform. The device featured sizeable buttons at its bottom in addition to thicker glass, which the Jar'rask had apparently been licking to navigate the menus. Despite all that and the foreign language it was defaulted to, it was basic, and she knew the way to the language selection menu like the back of her hand. She had to press harder but still could navigate its menus. She smirked as familiar letters and words replaced the unfamiliar ones.

Ducking into a dip in the ship's corridor, Katya launched the ship's specs, scanning through them. Basic rooms. None of them, except for the medical wing, struck Katya as places where they would stow Sotiris. She surveyed the next level's rooms where she would be getting close to crew quarters. Already on that level, there were meeting rooms and several guest quarters. Would they put

Sotiris there? Seeing room. She paused on that room, drawn to it. It was on the same level as the guest rooms but separated from them, more isolated.

Katya reentered the lift and pushed the Jar'rasks' corpses from its doorway before hitting the button for the next level up. She prepped her new weapon. A round black spot stuck out against the silver ceiling, a camera. If their monitoring was decent, this might be the shortest escape attempt ever. Additionally, the possibility that Sotiris wasn't even on this level loomed over her. But it felt right. Perhaps their minds were not so incompatible; either that, or he was crafting hers into one that met his needs.

The door opened to a vacant corridor. Disembarking, Katya slinked toward the seeing room. As she cleared a corner, she eliminated a Jar'rask before her presence even registered. Silence hung afterward. No alarms. No rushing enemy. Pressing her lips together, she ran along the corridor, never straying far from the wall to obscure her passage. None of the Jar'rasks had even attempted to summon their brethren via com, unable to move beyond their natural instinct to act on their own and not trust their own kind. A major flaw, one that should have sent red flags to the Magistrate's ruling council.

She could exploit that weakness. Maybe she'd even get out of this. Of course, if there was a known threat—especially a sizeable one—the reptile creatures might band together in a temporary alliance. But that might be where a sudden freeze could make a difference. They were reptiles, so the sudden drop could potentially slow them. It might be her only option when it came time to knock out the FTL drive. Katya brushed salty moisture away from her eyes. The key, however, would lie in how quickly the temperature change would affect them.

Katya crept nearer to the corridor with the seeing room, stopping short of it. Hisses and grunts of more than one Jar'rask emitted from the hall. Keeping close to the metal wall, she peeked down both ends of the hallway. Four Jar'rasks. They hovered near the vicinity of her destination. Katya fingered the flash grenade in her pocket. She'd hoped to save it, but—

A commotion broke out, one of the Jar'rasks biting at another. Katya retreated away from the corner, resting her head against the wall and forcing her limbs to stop shaking. With their senses, she couldn't linger here. She removed the grenade and activated it.

Clutching the firearm in her left hand, she tossed the grenade with the other, wincing with the effort. A bright burst of light blossomed in the corridor. Now. She pivoted around the corner, bathing the hall in a hailstorm of blasts. One down. Two—the other two sprung toward her, tongues lapping at the air to find her. Katya shot again, but with her arm giving, the shot went low. One of the Jar'rasks stumbled when struck in the knee. Its comrade, meanwhile, had crossed half the distance between them before Katya landed a solid hit to its chest.

Krezk! Katya backpedaled as the Elite soldier descended on her. Damn it! Katya swung out her leg. Her kick threw off the Jar'rask's balance, but he'd already compensated, jaw loosening with sharpened teeth ready. Too close. Katya squeezed the trigger and dodged its falling corpse. The remaining Jar'rask tried to make a hasty retreat, crawling along the floor, but Katya stopped it. Silence followed. Nearby doors remained shut; still, her fingers rested against the trigger as she approached the room.

"Eck—" Katya flinched, pain emerging behind her right eye. With her free hand, she activated the door, only for it to blink red. Passcode. It required a passcode. Or card—there was a card reader. She searched the Jar'rasks' possessions even as her vision grew spotty. There! She grabbed a card from one of the Jar'rasks. Grimacing, she straightened. Sotiris's excitement seemed to rise as her vision dimmed.

Stumbling to the door, Katya used the card. A green light flashed, and the door opened. Tears streaked her face upon entering, the liquid freezing to her face. Sotiris. Visible puffs exited her mouth with each breath as she lumbered across the room to where the toddler lay on a makeshift bed. Sweat drenched his brow even in the frigid room. His eyelids moved faster than she'd ever seen in his sleep before.

With chattering teeth, she took another step before crumpling to her knees, her vision blurring, eroding. She crawled forward, then froze. To the side, a preteen lay suspended on a bizarre gurney. Black hair, far too lean, pale—Oneiroi . . . what Sotiris, with his defect, would grow to resemble. A variety of machines—controlling and maintaining bodily functions—hung from his body; their lines suspended by metal stands.

Something warm trickled from her nose. It traveled across her philtrum to her upper lip, a coppery taste reaching her tongue. She wiped the substance away; her eyes widened when she saw red. Sputtering, Katya scrubbed the remaining blood from her face. She banished the Breks and Jar'rasks from her mind. Her gaze settled on the older Oneiroi, her thoughts flickering back to Jordah and their capture. They had used an Oneiroi, one with the defect. He'd yanked Sotiris out of his dream world, ousting their unknown defender. This is what the Magistrate had done to them, turned them into unseen weapons.

Clawing her way forward, Katya reached Sotiris, more blood—its warmth contrasting with the room—dripping from her nose.

"W-we need . . . go." Katya rested her head next to him. Consciousness rapidly fled from her as surely as her blood did. Her head pounded, eliminating rational thought. Her brain could be turning to mush, being pulverized from the inside. She touched Sotiris's small hand, squeezed it. The ship needed to stop spinning. Then maybe she could put distance . . . a portion of her brain chimed in that there'd been a distance between them when they had been on Jordah. A sinking sensation took root.

She lost track of how long she sat there, her head next to Sotiris. But gradually, the pain lessened, allowing her to sit and wipe away the blood. Across the way, the other Oneiroi stared at the ceiling with unfocused icy blue eyes. A squeak from Sotiris drew her attention. He stretched his hands toward her.

"Yeah." Katya lifted him after her vision settled.

She glanced at the other boy, taking in all the machines, some of which exited from his back. Sotiris nestled his face into her shoulder, and her thoughts reminded her of Mina waiting in a storage room. She gave the boy one last look before proceeding out the door, first picking up the handgun she couldn't recall dropping. There was nothing she could do, at least not at the moment, not when he had presumably been hooked to those machines for the majority of his life. Technology, Katya could understand. Medicine, particularly pertaining to other life-forms, was not among her talents.

Her kids had to come first; she could try to do more for the other Oneiroi once they were safe. Their parents deserved to know what had become of their children, the *Aletheia*. What weapons the Magistrate had made: unseen, no capability of defending against them . . . No wonder Plasovern strove to create a cure. The Oneiroi on their own were fearsome, but this defect . . . She wiped her nose again, subconsciously. Strom's words rang in her head as she ran with Sotiris, her promises. Katya checked Sotiris's outfit; the communicator device and the keycard remained tucked within his pocket.

Jar'rask footsteps reached her, and Katya retreated the way she'd come before darting into another corridor, one that curved. If the Jar'rasks continued down the corridor she'd just abandoned, they would stumble upon their comrades and then realize Sotiris had been taken. She sped up, time slipping away for a stealthy getaway. She hoped there'd be a lift along this stretch of hallway. But perhaps an alternate route would be wiser. If they stopped the lifts, she'd be trapped. Passing several evenly spaced doors, the end of the corridor came into view a few feet ahead, opening to another one. No lifts.

Swoosh!

As a door to her left opened, Katya swung around. A pounding consumed her hearing, her pulse skyrocketing.

"You bastard!" Katya's cheeks burned. Her firearm trained on the man who faced her. "Nice cushy quarters, aye, Rein?"

Rein lifted his hands, a muscle in his neck pulsating. "I gave you a chance, Katya. You spat in my face. Now put the gun down. You're just making things harder on yourself."

"I'm the armed one here, not you." Katya ran her finger along the trigger. "Do you even realize what they did to us—what they did to Mina? You turned us in! You—"

"I tried to put a good word in for her," Rein said, arms still suspended in front of him. "I really did, but—"

"In the end, you didn't press. You had to look out for yourself. You are—you are beyond words!"

Farther down, Jar'rasks spoke in their reptilian tongue, distant for now, but that could change. Only one sound. The blighters were fast.

Beads of sweat formed on Rein's face, his hands wavering. Katya jerked her attention back to him, the manic energy blossoming in his limbs, which resembled coils ready to spring. The hisses and shrieks echoed. Fire or run. A tremor passed through her arm, the barrel shaking—a smile played on Rein's face. She caught it out of the corner of her eye. If she turned her back to him to escape, he'd take advantage of it, anything to curry more favor, and with Sotiris, she'd be off-balanced, too distracted. He might even wrestle the firearm from her, especially with her bum hand.

His weight shifted, and Katya pulled the trigger, maintaining a steady hand just long enough. The firearm emitted its recognizable sound, and a dull thud followed. Katya didn't give Rein a second look. Biting back nausea, she let her feet carry her at a record pace in the other direction.

The emergency alerts would be sounding before long. Lifts would be locked—a hatch.

Katya bent down and pried it open, tears flooding her eyes as prickles coursed up her right arm. This enterprise would kill her, but there was no choice. "How about we end this like we began it, aye?" Sotiris merely batted his owl-like eyes at her.

She did not have anything resembling a carrier, leaving her to settle him into a more seated position against her hip after she'd strung the gun onto her belt. Then wrapping his hands around her neck, she put pressure on them, hoping he'd understand to hold on.

"Tightly," she said, still unsure if the word held any meaning to him. "No sleeping."

Satisfied with his grip, Katya swung both of them into the lit maintenance tube and closed the hatch behind them so as not to leave a red flag. As they descended, she was forced to loop her right arm through each rung; her hand couldn't be trusted to support her and Sotiris's weight. It made for slow going.

"Only a couple of floors to go."

With each rung, she talked to Sotiris; the majority amounted to nonsense, being little more than noises and randomly slung together words designed to keep him from sleeping and her mind from screaming in pain. He blinked at her, a dazed expression on his face.

"Just a few more rungs," she told him—herself. An orange glow alerted her to the next level's hatch.

"Shi—" Katya grappled at the rungs when the ship shook violently. Sotiris screamed, his little fingernails digging into her skin. His eyes went quite wide—until he closed them tightly as if he were willing himself into his sleep state. Her grip wavering, Katya ran both her arms around the rung while the ship shuddered. Her left arm and elbow braced Sotiris in case he succeeded in his mission. The motion slowed to a mere tremor several minutes later, and then to nothing. They were dead in space, Katya realized, noting the absence of the small vibrations that the engines and FTL drive would send into the metal walls of the maintenance tube.

Katya jerked her shoulder up and smiled when blue eyes glared back at her. "Rest of the way now."

Her heart pounded. There had to be an external factor for why the ship had stopped, and it would either be a boon or bane for them. No matter what, she'd capitalize on it. Grab Mina and then a ship. It became almost a mantra to her as she descended the rest of the way.

Now low enough, Katya pressed the mechanism holding the next level's hatch in place. It opened with a whoosh, and she pushed Sotiris through before excavating herself from the tube. Overhead, the warning lights blinked manically. A Jar'rask could be heard over a speaker, hissing out something. She readied her weapon, then picked up Sotiris. They reached the storage room without anyone impeding them, though Sotiris's weight wore heavily on her hip.

"Mina, it's me," Katya said after closing the door behind her.

Mina, in return, staggered onto her feet, using the wall she had been resting against for support. "W-what happened?"

"This"—Katya gestured to the warning lights with the firearm—"has to do with something else. The ship was pulled from FTL, and not by me." She eyed Mina's pale face;

beads of sweat still clung to it, and her eyes were dull. Tremors also passed through her limbs. Was it shock? "We're going to the hangar bay. Be prepared for more resistance," Katya said. "Depending on what stopped the Jar'rasks, there may be a lot in that area."

Mina nodded. Katya frowned when more visible tremors overtook the girl. But there was no choice.

"Here." Katya handed her Sotiris while taking the firearm away.

The girl sagged with the toddler's weight on her hip; however, she managed to remain standing. It'd be rough going, and Katya wasn't certain if Mina would make the distance with Sotiris. Gnawing on the interior of her mouth, she prepared herself to take back the toddler if needed.

"I'll cover you both. You just get to the ship I point out and get it started. Understood?"

The girl nodded again.

"Can you do that?" Katya pressed. She wanted more than a nod at this point, especially when she was anticipating a heavy presence of Jar'rask Elite fighters. They were on full alert now, resembling hornets whose nest had been kicked repeatedly. "Can you?"

"I got him," Mina said rather snappishly, bringing a grin to Katya's mouth. There was still fire there.

Katya turned off the safety on the handgun she had taken from Mina and led the way to the door. Outside, the hallway was empty except for the emergency lights. Gesturing with her hand, she directed Mina to follow her. They continued together, slowing as they neared another corridor. Clawed feet clacked against the metal ground, and there was the telltale hissing that belonged to Jar'rasks. A group of three raced in front of them in the other hallway, never glancing their way. They were headed to the hangar bay. Her grip tightened on her firearms.

"Wait here," she whispered before darting into the next corridor.

Sure enough, farther down synth glass revealed the hangar bay and some of its varied vessels. Gritting her teeth, Katya fired shots at the Jar'rasks' backs, tearing as she struggled with the handgun in her right hand. They toppled, unprepared for the attack.

"Katya!" Mina screamed.

Katya swung around. Successive blasts exited her weapons, sending more Jar'rasks to the ground. "Mina, keep going!"

The teen stumbled past her toward the bay; Katya followed close behind, catching up after taking out a couple of Jar'rasks coming at them. Yanking out the card she'd picked off the one Jar'rask earlier, Katya opened the synth glass door to an observation deck overlooking the hangar bay. Attached to it on the other side of a wall of synth glass was a grated catwalk—several like it crisscrossed throughout the bay, creating different levels. On either side of the bay were two open lifts that connected all the levels. Katya closed the sliding door behind them and shot its control panel, effectively sealing it.

"W-which s-ship?" Mina asked. She leaned into one of the observation deck's walls. She was probably minutes away from passing out.

Coming to stand beside the girl, Katya squeezed her shoulder. "We're almost there. I promise."

Around Mina, Katya examined the ships. Several of them were personal fighters designed for hunting down and stopping enemy ships. They would need something larger but equally fast. A siren blared, and Sotiris wailed. More hissing and grunted words, or at least she assumed they were words, followed over the intercom. They sounded more frantic.

Farther below in the tiered bay, some of the small fighters exited. The ship was under attack. She checked the Plasovern communicator. No, it hadn't been accidentally activated. Had Strom had them tailed? Were they now mounting a rescue effort? Or had there been an incursion? Pirates were out of the question; they weren't stupid enough to attack an A-Class warship. Likewise, Medzeci wouldn't encroach this deep into Magistrate space.

Flashes appeared on the other side of the shielding, and remnants of fighters struck it and the exterior of the warship. What had—

A larger B-Class Boita interceptor glided in through the shields. Katya's eyes widened: It was Magistrate. Their credentials had allowed them entrance, despite any defense the Jar'rask on the bridge might concoct. A major weakness. It left Katya to wonder why the Magistrate hadn't weeded it out long ago. Perhaps the easiest answer was it'd never been exploited before.

"Mina," Katya said, pointing to a C-Class interceptor one level above the bottom floor. It was fast and large enough for all of them. "That's our ticket."

"What about them?" She nudged her head toward the B-Class Boita.

"The Jar'rasks should keep them occupied long enough for us to get out of here. They'll make a great diversion."

Together, they hurried through the door, feet banging on the grated catwalk. They climbed onto the nearest lift, with Katya lowering them; however, the lift traveled no faster than sap. Below them, five Magistrate officers—specials ops from their uniforms—exited the interceptor and engaged the Jar'rasks. Their ship, meanwhile, fired bursts of its own, targeting the hangar bay's defenses. After the bay's gun turrets were dismantled, it turned on the live fighters that had angled themselves to take out the intruders.

Amidst the fray, the team of Oneiroi—their telltale pale skin and black hair clearer—moved unperturbed. Their movements were meticulous, eerie in their silence. No directions were barked; they simply moved, knowing precisely where their fellows were. In some cases, the Oneiroi didn't even hit their targets, yet the Jar'rasks crumpled to the deck, writhing.

As Katya and Mina's lift descended, more details came into focus. Three males, two females, though the one with her shaved head was only distinguishable as such by her slighter frame. A captain, commander, a lieutenant, and two ensigns. Katya's pulse thrummed. They would overpower them in a second if given a chance.

Mina faltered, but Katya prodded her forward. From the tremors passing down the girl's back, her mind was considering similar possibilities.

The one bearing the rank of captain was the same Oneiroi Katya had seen on Dandis VII; she was certain of it, despite how homogeneous the species appeared on the surface. The lift halted on the designated level, and she pressed her hand against Mina's back, guiding her toward their intended ride. Words would have only been coated by the sirens and weapons discharge. Despite it, Sotiris shrieked, his hands covering his ears.

Mina obeyed her and took off ahead. Katya trailed behind, minding the action below them. The Oneiroi were a formidable team, working in perfect harmony to cut down their enemies.

The Oneiroi almost had the Jar'rask contingent contained. Katya paled when one of them—the commander, her hair in a braided bun—shouted and pointed at her. The lieutenant whirled, firing a blast a foot in front of Mina. The girl screamed and dropped, her remaining arm shielding her head. Katya joined her to present less of a target. Sotiris became more hysterical, wailing, gasping for air.

"Mina," Katya called. "Get her going."

Below, a deep male voice belonging to the captain roared at them. "Give him back!"

Mina looked over her shoulder at Katya, tears spilling over her eyelashes. "I can't crawl with him."

"Leave him," Katya said. "I'll get him."

"He doesn't belong to you," the captain bellowed in perfect Magistrate, only a trace of an accent. "He belongs with his family. You may have had good intentions when you picked him up—I don't know what they were, but I've come to suspect they were good. But you've done enough. I'll take my nephew where he can get the help he needs."

Mina crawled past Sotiris to their mark. The boy laid flat, his hands balled into fists while his face scrunched with tears. Her own throat tightened. The boy deserved to be reunited with his family. Tears prickled in her eyes as she watched Sotiris twist on the catwalk, unable to crawl or even rock onto his stomach. This man was his uncle, or so he'd said—but who else would've attacked fellow Elites for the boy?

Distrust warred in her, stories of the Oneiroi surfacing. Perhaps they'd take Sotiris and leave her and Mina behind as husks. Katya pressed her forehead into the grated catwalk. What would they do with him? Would they find a way to place him into the Magistrate's care? Would they pursue an alternative? Sweat crept along the back of her neck. Could she even do better than them, his own people?

Letting go of her handguns, Katya reached into her shirt and removed the Jar'rask slate from where she'd stashed it. The C-Class interceptor breathed to life, causing three of the Oneiroi—the lieutenant and ensigns—to run toward the lift. She stood, both hands above her head, hoping no one would shoot.

Clearing her throat, Katya shouted, "I took him from a tomb." She paused to let her wording sink in. "He was the only living thing among corpses." She wiggled the hand with the slate before tossing it to the captain, who leaped forward to catch it. The lift was now at the Oneiroi's level. They would be up soon. "Go to the seeing room—"

The female commander's hand shot up. "Cap—"

Katya swiveled. *Boom!* Pain seared through her shoulder and chest, dropping her to the walkway. Bursts of weapons fire followed, from the floor and above. Pressing her hand inches above her left breast, she met dampness. Tremors overtook her, but she kept her hand pressed against the exit wound. Above, another contingent of Jar'rasks had set up and now traded shots with the Oneiroi. One blast scuttled near her, ringing off the walk's metal.

Lurching forward, Katya scooped up Sotiris and raced toward the ship. She didn't care to guess how much blood was leaving her. Her heart rattled an unsteady cadence. Below, heavier armaments entered the fray. The Jar'rasks had launched a two-prong assault. A blast ricocheted off the ship when she reached its hatch and stumbled in, just behind the cockpit.

"Detach and disembark!" she barked.

Mina did as told. Bracing herself, Katya pressed her right hand against her wound. Her extremities had a creeping chill; potentially, shock was setting in. She staggered around the metal screen that separated the small cockpit, with its two closely placed chairs, from the rest of the ship. She set Sotiris in the secondary chair and stood beside Mina's seat. The girl whipped them through the shield and into space. A welcome sight. Tapping the teen's shoulder, Katya nudged her head to the side, and Mina slid out of the seat.

"You're wounded!"

Taking the helm, Katya said, "Get something to stem the bleeding, a chest seal."

The warship fired blasts at them, aware that their interceptor had been hijacked. Katya dodged them, the ship proving to be exceedingly responsive to her commands. The systems were also more advanced, even to the point of nullifying the need for RMP pills. She'd never flown something so . . . peppy.

In another situation, she would have enjoyed it. She gritted her teeth through the pain, each movement jarring her wound and her aching hand. Get clear, get clear. Pulling out ahead of the blasts and stray fighters, she launched the navigation charts while staying out of reach. She picked a random destination—one in the middle of nowhere—for a jump. Satisfied, she activated the interceptor's FTL drive and punched it.

CHAPTER EIGHTEEN

Akakios clutched the slate as he navigated the corridors of the Jar'rask warship—the *Gershna*—with his team. Ambrosios and Charis flanked him with Elpis in between. The twins guarded the rear. They met marginal resistance, though the majority of the ship's inhabitants saw fit to hide from them, either waiting for them to leave or planning to launch a sneak attack. Taking in the corpses they found along the way, it appeared the Jar'rasks had already been dealt some black eyes.

The majority of the Jar'rasks' resistance came from above, where their officers had the lifts locked down. Fortunately for them and their brethren Elites, Charis had been able to override their commands. His main concern with their "fellows" was that they'd be able to get their ship back online, effectively trapping his team; however, Akakios was confident that their strategic shots and the virus they'd uploaded into the A-Class warship through a Magistrate backdoor would keep the *Gershna* dead in space. But the longer they tarried, the more likely it was that they would have to take the bridge. A prospect Akakios didn't relish. A jump into the heart of Magistrate space or even near a military post would be disastrous. Their careers were already sacrificed . . . he wouldn't let them so easily throw their lives away.

"The lizards are running scared," Ambrosios commented, breaking the eerie silence. "Good thing your gut about something being fishy was right, aye? After our entrance, we could be tried for treason and summarily executed. I still think you should've left one of the twins behind with the ship."

"Kyrillos can manage the *Boreas*'s armaments. And I think Chrysanthos's skills in combat have improved." Akakios cast a sideways glance at Ambrosios, who snorted.

Their methods constituted treason. There were no alternative words to describe them. But they'd been able to uncover something of a truth, unconfirmed as it may be — an outsider's word could never be trusted. *"I removed him from a tomb."* Those words ran endlessly through his head, and he had to fight the sickening image of Sotiris with his parents' bodies nearby. But the image was stuck. And no matter how hard he tried to dislodge it, push it to the back of his mind, it remained, leaving him cold.

They passed more corpses near the seeing room. Whatever was in there had better be good. Good enough to warrant their venturing farther into this boiling vessel. He'd thought to disregard it and pursue Sotiris immediately, but curiosity won out. Curiosity to know more about the people Sotiris traveled with. There'd been an edge in her voice, one he couldn't shake. No matter what, he would track that woman. His nephew needed —

Akakios grimaced, inhaling sharply when another mind touched his with the finesse of a badger. Frantic, confused . . . the mind could only belong to an Oneiroi. Similar to

Sotiris, the being behind the door spewed images and emotions in the manner of a child who had forgotten how to communicate. But this child delivered to the Magistrate had a completely different method of communication, or language, than Sotiris. It wasn't the Magistrate tongue. Akakios frowned and mentally responded in an attempt to settle the other Oneiroi. Unlike his nephew, this one had been around another very different species for far too long.

Next to him, Ambrosios stopped, his hands going to his head. His face scrunched and went an even more ghostly white as he stumbled, bracing himself against the wall. Across the communicative bond between them, he felt their wayward friend thoroughly examining his third in command's mind. Elpis approached Ambrosios, only to be waved away. Akakios heard Ambrosios mutter something about being fine.

Going to the door, Akakios found it locked.

"I'll get it open," Charis said. She brushed past him and got to work. A fine layer of sweat clung to her forehead, the heat wearing on her. "Whatever would this team do without me?" She smirked when the door popped open. "Not get through doors."

Pelagia clapped her twin's shoulder. "We'd just use Pelagius's head." She chuckled at her brother's expense.

Akakios inhaled when welcomed cold air struck his face. Their suits had made their passage through the Jar'rask vessel bearable, but this room, well, it was a relief. Even the lights were dimmed, perfect for their eyes. Removing his sunglasses, Akakios stepped in and froze. Clenching his fists, Akakios swallowed his revulsion while the muscles along his jawline twitched. What he'd expected—whatever it'd been, it hadn't been this. All the machinery, the slight frame . . .

"Elpis," he managed to say.

She approached the boy, an adolescent, one of the children they'd sent away, and launched her examination. In the doorway, Pelagius swore, and his sister clenched her AAR, spoiling for a fight. Akakios rubbed his jaw and turned away, blocking out all the tubes and mutilations to the boy's body. Had Kallistrate and Amyntas found out about this? That this was the fate waiting for Sotiris?

"Both of you outside," Charis ordered the twins. "Sir, we'll keep out unwanted intrusions."

The trio exited, the twins griping about returning to the heat.

Ambrosios moved closer to the boy. "I think this is a cousin on my line," he said. His eyes were mere slits, no doubt due to the preteen's continued intrusion into his mind. "Never met him in person; there was no ceremony with him . . . Zinon. I think that was his name. Probably around fourteen or fifteen. He was the second mark on the family and was delivered into the *care* of the Magistrate." Ambrosios frowned. "Poor Chrys . . . Little Zin has found that connection and is fascinated with it."

Akakios tapped Elpis on the shoulder. "Can we get him off these machines?"

Elpis squeezed her lips together as she examined each tube and machine. "Some of the machines, not all of them. They've been keeping his bodily functions running in a manner that counteracts the degradation resultant of the defect; he's probably been on them since he was three." Her hand skimmed against one of the machines attached to the boy's forehead, carefully avoiding its buttons. "The defect has been encouraged. These are neural devices, and they've been used to induce sleep. The gurney is designed to lessen bedsores, and these" — she peeled a little round metal device from the boy's legs — "are stimulating the muscles to prevent complete deterioration and blood clots. They're probably placed all over his body. What did they hope to achieve?"

"They wanted to harness the defect and use it as a weapon . . . like they've already been wielding us. However, these children are soldiers groomed to do whatever their handlers ask them to." Akakios ran his hands through his hair. "Elpis, get him prepared to leave."

"Then what?" Elpis asked, her tone rather sharp. "Some of these machines, I have no idea what they do . . . it'll take time to grasp everything these have done to him. How am I expected to maintain his health on the *Boreas*?"

"I know you, Elpis. You'll think of something."

Swallowing, she shook her head and then said more quietly while gesturing to Ambrosios, who was resting his head against one of the metal walls, "And what if he drags us under?"

"If Jar'rasks can keep one of our kind in this manner and not be drawn under, then we can—without these machines, without using these children like this." Akakios's voice cracked, images of Kallistrate cradling Sotiris bringing tears. "These are our children."

Elpis ran a hand over her pinched face. Her hands were shaking, but all the same, she inspected the machinery, more intent on removing them. She murmured something under her breath as she tracked each tube's path, peeking under the gurney too. She touched a smaller machine under it, formulating some plan, or at least Akakios hoped she was. She had to.

She stood from her stoop and clasped her hands in front of herself, stilling them. "I'll do what I can. Some of these might be portable." She bit her lip and faced the gurney, her hand seizing its edge. "This may be beyond me."

"Do what you can. We aren't leaving him."

Then facing away, Akakios came face-to-face with a metal table with a variety of items scattered on it: women's clothing, a few clothes belonging to a toddler, diapers, general toiletries, a few slates, blankets—Akakios touched a familiar toy in the shape of a Polikós yak. Its fuzzy surface still as soft as the day he had bought it. And there was the light cube, used to stimulate the mind. Akakios's lips quivered while he banished a memory of trying to dissuade Amyntas from purchasing the device, one a child with the defect couldn't possibly use.

His hand faltered on Kallistrate's journal. He couldn't bring himself to crack it open. She may be gone, but it still felt like a breach of privacy. Prickling curiosity stirred to know what had been on her mind during those last days. But cunning as she was, Akakios doubted he'd find that answer among its pages.

He almost choked on his spit, catching the silver glint of a holophoto frame. His hands clasped it. There they were, all three—two smiling back at him, the third asleep. He hadn't seen this photo before. Without a doubt, it was probably the most recent—the last—taken.

His thumb passed over the image of his brother's face, causing it to flicker. The woman didn't have to take these objects; in fact, they would have hindered her. "Ambrosios, if you're able, go ahead and pack these. We'll return them to their owners."

"Captain," Charis said from the door. "We've got guests."

"Elpis, get to work. We'll handle them."

Akakios joined Charis, Pelagia, and Pelagius. The air in the corridor had shifted, growing cooler, though it had a long way to go before it became comfortable. Slowly, their virus was tipping the scale in their favor now that it'd embedded itself into the habitation system.

<We're taking the bridge,> he sent along the channel between them.

Elpis would need all the time she could get. And even then, it might not be enough if the Jar'rasks had managed to work past other elements of the virus and had called for help. But they would worry about that possibility later, he decided.

Akakios fired off a blast, eliminating one of their attackers. They ran farther down the hall until they came across a group of six Jar'rasks, all wearing full armor. Their foe had created a makeshift barricade out of ration crates from the nearby mess hall and only lifted their heads above it to fire at the Oneiroi, who were forced to shelter behind the thin ribs in the metal wall.

For now, they had to survive. Survive and find a way home—expose what had become of their children. He faltered and had to throw out his elbows to rebalance himself, ducking behind an outcropping along the wall in the process. A blast buzzed by and dinged off the wall a ways behind him.

Did the Agoranomi know? Had Kyros . . . A grim line formed across his mouth. No, the man would have never approved of such a thing. None of them would have; it broke everything their people held dear. He moved into the open, lining up his AVI M-10.

Charis collided with him as a blast screamed by. <Get with it, sir!> she shouted in his mind.

Gritting his teeth, he nodded. Focus. Clear this, take the bridge. He brought up his AVI M-10, breaking up bits of the crates with its rapid fire. *Clang, clang, clang!* It beat against armor. Between his and his teams' fire, the Jar'rasks lay battered.

Stepping over them, a rush of adrenaline spiked through Akakios.

Sotiris, he thought, I won't keep you waiting long.

Stars and empty space, void of any civilization. Katya found it comforting. Bending over, she retrieved the cold compress, which had fallen off her battered hand, and returned it to its place even though it was no longer as cold as it should be. Her shoulder burned with the movement. She'd taken painkillers . . . She couldn't remember how long ago she'd taken them. There'd also been antibiotics with the bandages and chest seal. She hadn't bothered with the zerna ointment, given the severity of the wound.

Resting her head against the back of the pilot's chair, she rubbed her sleep-encrusted eyes. Mina and Sotiris were back in the crew area—a cramped section that served as sleeping quarters, a galley, and a general location for R and R—where they slept on. She stared at the stars, not really focusing on them. Her mind still felt clouded. The ship would be easily tracked. She needed to move.

Tears escaped her eyes as she grew immersed in the glowing orbs, nebulas, and distant planets. She'd forgotten how beautiful they could be. She wiped the moistness away and removed the IV that'd been keeping her hydrated. There'd been no blood packs for humans, and she was certain she needed a blood transfusion. She rose and swayed, grabbing onto the metal mesh wall. When her world steadied, she went to check on Mina and Sotiris.

Mina still looked like death warmed over, but her face was more relaxed as she slept in the top bunk. Of course, the strong painkillers they'd found on board were undoubtedly responsible for that. Katya touched the IV attached to Mina. She'd have to detach it soon. Below, Sotiris blinked at her. He'd rolled onto his stomach at some point.

"It's ironic that you're the only one who can't sleep." She held him close; he, in turn, nestled his face into her good shoulder. His somewhat vacant gaze suggested he'd reached a point where he was too tired to sleep. Whatever had passed between him and the older Oneiroi child had taken its toll.

Katya returned to the cockpit and sat with Sotiris. The gleam of the communicator on the console caught her eyes. It rested on top of the Sparrow's keycard.

The keycard offered an alternative. They could double back to Jordah. She bowed her head. Not viable, not in a stolen interceptor. Not . . . not with her current condition.

Hers or Mina's. What other options were available? She'd tried to formulate other paths, only to find zero that were feasible. No money. Stolen, traceable vessel. *"If you don't find that alternative way, call us . . . for Sotiris's sake."* She leaned over the chair's armrest, facing the crew area. Mina remained asleep, so she grabbed the communicator.

Clearing her throat, she activated it. Static. Katya almost set it aside when a voice cut through the white noise.

"Strom."

Just one word, spoken knowingly and with confidence. She'd been expecting this call, for them to run out of rope.

Katya sat straighter. "I'm taking your offer. On two conditions: I remain Sotiris's guardian. I have a say in his medical care. The second . . . I need medical care for the girl who's been in my care."

"Agreed on both counts."

Exhaling, Katya steadied her breaths. "We have a hot ship; we'll need to ditch it, or we could end up like the *Aletheia*."

"Don't worry," Strom responded, her voice steadier than Katya felt. "We already have a ship en route; it's following the signal from the communicator. It started transmitting the moment you activated it. We'll get you out."

Katya closed her eyes, blindly setting the still-active communicator onto the console. She needed a stiff drink, something to dull the growing sense of dread. Except she needed to remain alert, wary. She needed to protect her own as she had always tried to do. She found some measure of comfort from Sotiris's weight against her chest, though when he shifted, she gritted her teeth, killing a moan.

Her stomach coiled, even as the pain ebbed. What had she done? Her hold on Sotiris tightened. An old Magistrate saying sprang to mind: "Let no ill come from this."

Minutes stretched together, then a ship broke out of FTL. It brought with it a path from which there'd be no return. After the other vessel had aligned with them, a connector tube stretched from it to their hatch. Standing, Katya approached the would-be opening, Sotiris in her arms. Mechanical sounds vibrated through the metal hull when the connector fixed itself to their ship. A pause.

Katya eyed the weapons locker but then jerked her attention back to the hatch at a knock. Edging her way to it, she opened it, stepping backward after two heavily armed men lumbered in. Her body went rigid, but they bypassed her, heading to the cockpit. The damage Plasovern could do with an interceptor . . .

"What are you—" The question went unfinished after a chuckle diverted her attention to the open hatch.

Strom sauntered toward them, her red lips quirked. "Just look at you." The other woman eyed her bloody shirt, shaking her head like a disapproving schoolmarm. When she reached the opening, Strom stretched out her hand, the connector tube behind her endless. The same cocky smile from the bar formed on her lips when Katya took it.

"Welcome to the other side."

CAST OF CHARACTERS

Akakios Sarris: The Oneiroi captain of the *Boreas*, he will stop at nothing to rescue his nephew, Sotiris, for his deceased brother, Aymntas, and sister-in-law, Kallistrate.

Ambrosios Carras: The Oneiroi first lieutenant of the *Boreas*, he serves as its pilot and lead interrogator. He is the spouse of Chrysanthos.

Charis Velis: The Oneiroi commander of the *Boreas*, she is the second command after Akakios, prized for her levelheaded nature.

Chrysanthos Carras: The mechanic of the Oneiroi vessel *Boreas*, he holds the rank of master chief petty officer. He is Ambrosios's spouse.

Elpis Moros: The medical officer on the Oneiroi vessel *Boreas*, she holds the rank of lieutenant commander.

Faustus Cassius: Katya's adoptive father, who works as an archaeologist. He descends from a prominent Magistrate family, with his brother Pontius having a mysterious position within its government.

Hedda Strom: A woman of legend and myth, she is one of the several heads of Plasovern, known for her brutality in the struggle for planet sovereignty.

Jia: A doctor working on the mining station S4-G3.

Katya Cassius: The captain of *The Maelstrom*, she has had several Magistrate ground postings and is only a year into her first space-faring post.

Kyrillos Rallis: The second lieutenant on the *Boreas*, he oversees communications.

Kyros Anagnos: A member of the Oneiroi's ruling body, the *Agoranomi*, he has long been a supporter of the Sarris family, particularly Akakios's branch.

Mina: A sixteen-year-old Reznic girl, she is learning to be a pilot under Katya's tutelage.

Pelagia and Pelagius Tocci: Fraternal Oneiroi twins, they serve as ensigns on the *Boreas*.

Rein: A Reznic native, he pursues Magistrate citizenship through a military career.

Sotiris Sarris: A three-year-old Oneiroi child, he was born with a genetic mutation. Also goes by Aquila.

Usha: A Filitre, she is known for her drug empire, with there being speculation of Plasovern ties.

Valens Ulpius: A colonel, now deceased, who'd overseen day-to-day operations in a sector on Reznic. He and Katya were romantically involved.

Zahkar Kozlov: A freighter captain from Katya's homeworld, Mramor, he might have an interest in planet sovereignty.

Coming in 2021
DESCENT
"I can't help but wonder, Cassius. Do you still bleed blue?"
THE PROMISE
S.M. WRIGHT
kindle
HERITAGE LOST
S.M. WRIGHT
Start at the beginning

ABOUT THE AUTHOR

 A lifelong resident of northern Indiana, S.M. Wright is an author of speculative fiction with the occasional jaunt into historical fiction. She has been writing since grade school and harbors fond memories of her mother taking her to Young Authors Conferences, which further encouraged her to pursue writing. She has published two works of short fiction—*Acceptance* and *A Long Way Down*—before launching her ongoing *Heritage Lost Series*.

Wright is a staff writer for a local newspaper/magazine company, where she is also an editor for two of its publications. When not working or writing, she enjoys spending time with her clowder, geocaching, knitting, and reading.

Connect with her on . . .

Website: smwrightauthor.com
Newsletter: http://eepurl.com/hvAsX1
Facebook: www.facebook.com/smwrightauthor/
Twitter: @smwright04
Instagram: @smwrightauthor

www.ingramcontent.com/pod-product-compliance
Lightning Source LLC
Chambersburg PA
CBHW071150100726
47908CB00002B/313